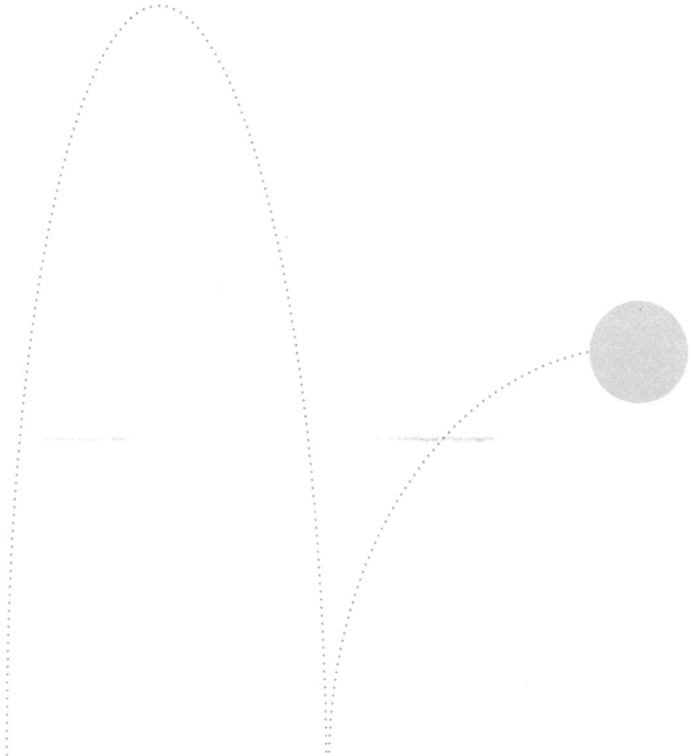

Superball

Superball

NC Weil

Fool Court Press, LLC

Cover Design by NZ Graphics
Book design by Nita Congress
Printed by Lightning Source

ISBN: 978-0-9834893-3-7
LCCN 2016910600
First Edition
Published in the USA
Fool Court Press, LLC

http://FoolCourtPress.net

Acknowledgments

I'D LIKE TO thank early readers Lorine Kritzer Pergament; members of my Evergreen critique group: Jan Gurney, Aaron Ritchey, Diane Dodge, Andrea Stein, and Jen Herfurt; the Mercury Café's monthly Stories Stories night, brainchild of Edwin Forrest Ward and Marcia Ward, where I've found a place to share my fiction and nurture my inspirations. Friends and family have encouraged my efforts: Page, Jess, Louis, Sandra Haber, Ruth Schilling, and particularly Tim, my partner in crime all these years, striving against the odds to keep the written word vital. And where would I be without the understanding and skills of my cover designer Nick Zellinger of NZ Graphics, and the layout artistry of Nita Congress?

Superball is a work of fiction. Boulder is a real place, and some of the locations referred to are (were) real, but characters and events are entirely my own creations; other than historical figures, any resemblance to actual persons is purely unintentional.

Dedication

To Boulder, where the abstract meets the concrete,

and

to Norman Stingley, inventor of Zectron and Super Balls,
those astoundingly bouncy balls that have brought fun to millions
since 1965.

book one

Fall 1981

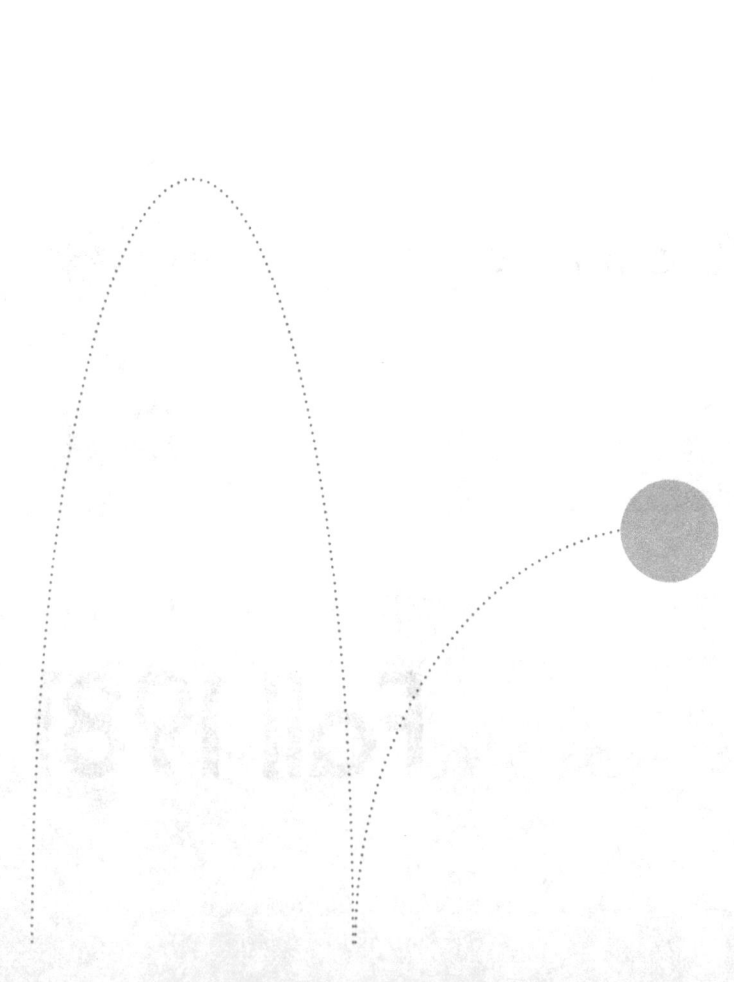

chapter 1

Erase, Erase, Erase

THEY'D DODGED DEATH together in a snowed-in car and made love in past lives—as ancient Greeks, as dragons—and saw those connections through time as a promise of enduring union. How then could Laura cross him off, not even face-to-face but in a letter? Was Walt supposed to write back: *Ms. Reiner, regret to learn this heart didn't fit. Return it in the original packaging for a full refund*—?

She'd said it all: she loved Cob. She was sorry. She closed her letter with just her name, no *truly yours* or even *sincerely*—certainly not *love*. But the Walt and Laura Show should've run for years. They were mates. He still puzzled that their cosmic insights—meant for each other, *made* for each other—amounted to nothing.

Walt had been a nomad since, but passing through Boulder where he'd lived with her before their Karmafornia misadventure, he realized the endless loop of life on the road was getting him nowhere but tired. Here perhaps he could pick up the skein of his pre-Laura life and take it a new direction. At twenty-six, he should be settled. He knew how to get by. Wasn't it time to reach higher?

He'd been back in town maybe a month when he was accosted by Eddie, Laura's old friend from Carling, the small eastern Colorado town where she'd grown up. The guy must have been on the lookout for him—Walt hadn't shaved or cut his hair since the day he'd left California. Eddie recognized his voice and cornered him for questioning.

Over coffee, Walt was surprised to learn that while he'd sat in Santa Cruz reading her rejection letter, Laura up in Berkeley had clobbered his rival in the temple with a wine bottle. And killed him.

"The jury wouldn't buy that it was an accident," Eddie said, "so she got three-to-five. She's due out next year on parole, and from what she's told me, thinking about you is what's kept her going."

Just like that, he was plunged back into the labyrinth of their past. Thinking he'd come so far, here he was staring at the same featureless walls and deceptive turnings he'd taken so long to extricate himself from. During his struggles with Cob, he'd come to understand her chosen man—now he envied him for being freed from the karmic trap that apparently still held their lives captive.

Laura's letter, cutting every tie he'd made to California, had demolished any curiosity about her, Cob, whatever that love did for them. Hadn't even dreamed about her for probably a year. Why had her unfinished business showed up here, in Boulder of all places, where he and Laura had met, fallen in love, lived together, before she decided on grad school in Berkeley? And here sat Eddie, looking at him, expecting—a rush of joy? Some outpouring of gratitude? A tip?

"She asked me for your address—"

"Nope, not interested. I'm so done I'm burnt." And with that, he pushed back from the table and sped out. His feet took him uphill, toward the mountains where he could focus instead on a rocky trail, hike this out, get enough distance to see what this news looked like for the man he was now.

• • •

SOON THE FLAWLESS SEPTEMBER day had swept him into its spell. His legs wouldn't stop, uphill and down on the Mesa Trail, dodging roots, skidding on the steep parts, loping on the balls of his feet, lungs reminding him he hadn't been at this altitude long but his legs wanting motion, and gradually his breathing caught up. After a few miles he turned around and loped back, sweating but feeling good, savoring the pungence of dust and pines, scuffing up history in small doses maybe he could handle.

Reaching Tomato Rock, he scrambled up to sit—in contrast to

the roseate sandstone slabs of the Flatirons, it was a squashed orb about twelve feet high and twice that across, dark red with acne pockmarks. He'd discovered this rock as a teenager: during a summer visit with his dad's sister and her husband in Santa Fe, they'd spent a week in Boulder at a Chautauqua cabin. Every day he'd hiked and explored: Green Mountain, Royal Arch, the length of the Mesa Trail. Tomato Rock became his private spot—to think, to watch birds and deer and clouds—he belonged here.

That fall, he applied to the University of Maryland, two miles from home, only to appease his parents—if CU didn't accept him, he planned to move to Boulder anyway. Fortunately for peace in the Sanders household, he'd been admitted. The bonus of moving West turned out to be Colorado women, hardy and independent and down-to-earth, more inclined to hiking boots than to hose and heels.

Sun slanting in through the pines warmed the rock, locusts shrilled and buzzed in the grass. It felt good to be back here—why should he let a ghost drive him off? If Laura was coming, if she found him, so be it. Boulder would shield him.

• • •

FOR STARTERS, HE SCROUNGED work cleaning the Atheneum seven days a week. In his student days he'd been the projectionist here, but the best the manager could offer now was this janitorial gig. Jobs were scarce, so Walt took it, glad at least for the flexible hours; as long as the place was clean when they opened, the manager didn't care when the work got done. He got to see movies free—all the Burt Reynolds he could stomach—and it met the basic requirement: paying the rent for a bedroom in a group house off downtown. With utilities and phone split six ways, it was pretty cheap. The other five residents were past college, hanging out:

Romo, Stu, and Pick were Deadheads. Romo, who'd signed the lease, was a stocky muscular redhead with a long braid. He'd drive his Blues Bus Oldsmobile to any Grateful Dead concert within seven hundred fifty miles: Kansas City, Missoula, Austin. He'd taped more than a hundred shows, the labels of his favorites smudged beyond deciphering, and stayed solvent as a low-profile pot peddler: never seen to handle more than an ounce, good stuff. Stu was his tall stooping sidekick, terribly shy; he used his Spanish degree translating at a day-labor agency. Pick was a skinny New Yorker as shaggy as Walt, always barefoot regardless of winter and broken glass, his feet so grimy that even No Shoes No Shirt No Service places didn't realize. He lived on a spartan monthly stipend from his big-shot lawyer dad, who found that paying him to stay out West was the easiest way to deal with him.

Lucy'd studied modern dance at the university but couldn't break into the local scene: her style, her shape, her technique were never quite what they wanted. As hostess at a Mexican restaurant with a gay clientele, she made pretty good money. Walt accompanied her to one dance performance, but her resentment at not getting a part even though she could "dance rings around that cow" turned him off.

Barbara was a Palo Alto palomino: graceful and well built, perfect tan and long blonde hair, friendly in that California costs-nothing-to-be-nice way. She worked at the Free Clinic doing paperwork and taking blood. Some poor donor would be looking like a bulletin board, the doctor jabbing around for a vein, and she'd come to the rescue. One afternoon she and Walt were getting friendly in the living room, listening to her Leonard Cohen album *New Skin for the Old Ceremony*. At a critical moment, Walt saw a black widow walking up her jeans.

"Ah, 'scuse me," he said. "Two's company but three's definitely a crowd." He trapped the spider in a mason jar, taking that interruption as a cosmic stop sign. Barbara's knowing smile agreed: the kinship they felt didn't need sexual confirmation.

He took their imprisoned intruder into the kitchen to set on the table, where it might live six weeks, with air without food. "We have a truce," Romo had explained. "We don't use bug-killer chemicals, and the black widows stay out of sight. Show themselves, go to jail." Often a visitor would fool with the jar, then suddenly realizing what was inside, set it down in a hurry.

Upstairs, across from Lucy's bedroom and beside the tall narrow dormer Stu occupied, was Walt's room. His main window looked north over a busy street, and he hoped the smaller west-looking one would provide a view of mountains once the spindly maple out front dropped its leaves.

On the main floor, Romo lived in the largest bedroom, which looked onto the house's gravel parking area. Barbara's room, across the hall from his and directly beneath Walt's, had French doors opening to the living room and a blind wall to the traffic. Pick lived in the twelve-by-ten cellar whose stone walls had a multitude of crevices: widows but no windows.

Because it was a shabby house on a busy corner, street people wandered in sometimes. Lucy hung a small brass bell on the front doorknob so the household would hear that door open, but when they forgot to lock up, money and camping gear disappeared. Deciding the bell wasn't enough, Romo locked the front door and said to leave it that way, and use the kitchen entry.

• • •

IN HIS TRAVELS, WALT had often taken classes to broaden his skill set and meet people. Job? Check. House? Check. Time for his next round of instruction. He checked the Free School catalog and signed up for "See and Draw" Tuesday afternoons and, since he'd missed the first session, wrote on his registration form for the instructor to call him.

That evening, fresh from his "Laura wants you back" scare, he heard Romo say her name when he answered the phone.

His heart stopped. "Who?" he said faintly.

"Luna," Romo repeated.

She was the drawing teacher, and told Walt to bring pencils, a pad of thick paper, and a gum eraser. They'd meet at the public library downtown and from there walk to a good vantage.

He arrived early and stood near the main entrance people-watching. Soon he spotted the group, all carrying drawing pads: a fortyish woman in overalls, surrounded by a pair of teenagers, a bearlike shaggy guy, and a slim gypsy-looking woman in an embroidered vest. Coming over he introduced himself, and Luna and her students did likewise. After he'd met them all, another voice said,

"I'm Anna."

She'd been behind Luna, but she was the kind of person you might not notice anyway. There was something blurry about her, as though part of her were in the process of leaving or arriving. She had limp shoulder-length brown hair and bluish-gray eyes—a shade you couldn't pin down to a color—and her clothes, heavy for this fair breezy day, revealed nothing about her body: hiking boots, jeans with dirt on one knee, an oversized dark suede cowboy coat worn shiny on the sleeves and pockets.

Luna led the way toward the foothills, following the creek path. "Here's a good place," she said, stopping. "Today I want you to work at least an hour on one thing. Remember, draw only what you see. And erase. Erase. Erase."

Walt considered his options: some big rocks in the creek, beyond those the road, and a house. Upstream: more rocks, a group of trees; downstream, too many bushes. He chose the rocks in the creek, and got to work. But he couldn't get his sketching to convey their roundness. Luna squatted behind him watching.

"You're trying too hard," she said. "Don't think, see. Just make lines where you see lines, and if your eye can't see any, don't draw them." She put an index finger on the part he'd been laboring over. "Do you see this on that rock?"

"No," he admitted.

"Erase it. If you want to imagine rocks some other time, go ahead, but in this class you're going to see them."

"OK." So he erased, and saw, and drew. When he finally looked around, his gaze collided with Anna's, watching him. In a brief intense moment their eyes exchanged a "who are you?" before she looked at her pad, a flush pinking her cheek. As though she were his next subject, he noted her profile: an arc, forehead curving toward her slightly hooked nose, then narrow lips and receding chin circling back. But her averted eyes had the "I know you're looking at me" intensity of someone acutely self-conscious; he gave his attention back to pencil and paper.

At the end of class as they all headed to the library, he fell into step with Anna, asking to see her drawing. She'd rendered a cluster of bushes across the creek, her work much more realistic than those damn rocks he'd struggled with. No matter how much he erased, either he wasn't rubbing out the lines that had to go, or he'd never put in the right ones to begin with. Maybe there wasn't a good line on the whole page: his lumpy balloons piled in the air had no rock qualities that he could see.

"I'm hopeless," he told her.

"Your first class—giving up already?" Her voice was alto and husky—he felt a zing in his chest.

"Next time I'll try something less three-dimensional."

She laughed. "Like what?"

He laughed too—what a stupid thing to say. "Something with a shape made of lines."

"You can get some practice in before our next class, you know."

"I don't want to get too far ahead of my guide—I'm blind."

"Really?" she said. "You wear contacts?"

"That's not what I mean." He glanced at her. "No. Do you?"

"Since I was fourteen. Glasses at seven, when the teacher had my desk shoved against the blackboard and I still couldn't read it. Anything more than two feet away's a mystery."

"You like contacts?" he asked. "I heard they're uncomfortable."

"No worse than glasses. At least with these I can see."

Back at the parking lot, Luna said, "Let's meet at Chautauqua next week, in front of the dining hall." She had to give directions to the teenage girls, but everyone else knew where it was. As the group separated, Walt looked around—Anna had vanished. On his walk home he thought about her—hiding in that big old coat, her gaze darting away. Contact lenses, on eyes that shunned contact—that was funny.

He dreamed *they were sitting by the creek—the whole class— then swimming in warm green water. He was fully clothed, pulling his drawing pad along. Anna swam past naked: legs fluttering, her arms white against the water, hair waving. Her breasts were shallow, with nipples like the jujubes he found on the theater floor, and he won- dered what they tasted like.* He woke dizzy. His libido, AWOL since Laura's dismissal, was back—not just the recurrent itch, but desire.

• • •

AT CHAUTAUQUA, LUNA LED them up past the sixty-foot-high faded-green auditorium built in the 1890s. Sun delineated every shrunken warped board of this cavernous firetrap, a beloved venue for summer concerts and movies.

"Pick your view," she instructed. "Plenty to choose from. You could sit in the shelter here, or try down by the dining hall."

Walt paced, studying the building. The shelter would put him too near—how would he ever fit something so big on a piece of paper?

"You don't have to draw the whole thing," Luna said. "Pick a section that interests you, put that in the middle of your page and see where it takes you."

He chose the cupola. Since it was on the roof, he put it near the top of his sheet, trying to keep things proportional. This was much easier than those rocks, and Luna praised his effort.

"You could do a larger version of just that element if you want to get in every line, but part of drawing is learning what to leave out."

He wasn't sure how that jibed with drawing what he could see, but his paper had way too many lines, merging and obliterating each other. He flipped to a clean sheet and let the cupola fill the page, just enough roof to land it somewhere. That was better. Maybe he should be drawing tiny things—a dozen blades of grass, a patch of lichen—the world had so much detail. Having studied that cupola closely, he felt as though he'd replicated not only the image but the structure itself. He liked that.

At the end of class, Luna offered a ride down to the library. The teenagers went with her; the bearlike guy had his car, and the gypsy-looking woman lived nearby. Walt caught up with Anna to walk downhill with her.

"You disappeared last week," he said. "I was gonna invite you to dinner. Ever have soufflé?"

"No, I don't think so."

"It's my specialty: fun to make, and wonderful—like eating the richest air you can imagine."

"Well, I don't know—"

"I have five housemates, and none of 'em bite." He turned to grin at her. "Where you from, Anna?"

"Here."

"Me too."

"No you're not." She let that sink in, then said, "I was born here."

"Oh… No, I'm from Maryland. But this is home."

"There's no natives around anymore," she muttered. "They all left."

"I was glad to get out of my hometown—a chance to start fresh." They walked in silence another block. Since it seemed unlikely a CU student would be taking a Free School class, he asked, "You work?"

"I'm a window washer, about thirty hours a week. Sometimes we get really busy but it's calm at the moment."

"I clean a movie theater—Saturdays and Sundays are the worst. So are you coming over for soufflé?"

"I guess." She shrank into that coat as though it were a cloak of invisibility.

"We'll hit the market for a baguette. And Liquor World for white wine."

"Where's your house?"

"Near there—you'll see. Like the Grateful Dead?"

"I saw them in Denver once, and I have *Terrapin Station*."

"Three of my housemates are Deadheads."

"Druggies?" she said warily.

"Nah, they're OK." Though Pick was certainly a stoner, Stu rarely got high, and Romo was judicious about consuming his merchandise. Walt's consumption was occasional, a fact he decided to hold in reserve. Anna. He wondered if she'd get sweaty walking all the way downtown—a good mile—but she only undid buttons, and the coat's weight kept it from flapping open. Her bearing and stride seemed androgynous, as though a sculptor put her together without deciding whether she'd be male or female, then never got around to those finishing touches.

Arriving at his house, she stopped short at the sight of his '65 Dodge Dart hippie-mobile. "Wow, some car."

"This is Plug," he said, patting the hood affectionately. "A bunch of us painted him a few years ago. Some of that hasn't held up too well: these used to be dragons on the hood, and bison on the trunk. But the doors still look good." He showed her the driver-side yellow octopus against ribbons of indigo and turquoise water and ropes of dark-green kelp, then the passenger-side jungle with spider monkeys, parrots, and vines. Last, she admired the chipped remains of full red lips surrounding the grill.

She shook her head. "You said you couldn't draw."

"I can't. Just as well the dragons faded—that's the part I painted."

chapter 2
Intimition

PICK AND BARBARA were discussing movie options
when he introduced Anna. "How about soufflé?"

"Sure. I have some spinach," Pick offered.

"Walnuts," Barbara suggested.

"What's usually in it?" Anna asked.

"Sharp cheddar," Walt said, "but we can jazz it up. What's your
preference?"

"Walnuts, I guess. Spinach makes my teeth feel weird."

Barbara got a call and carried the phone to the next room for a
long chat, and Pick went outside. Today, Anna was his only student.
Walt got out ingredients—eggs, mustard, milk, butter, cheese, flour,
walnuts, cream of tartar—and utensils—whisk and whip, measuring
cups and spoons, spatula, saucepan and lid, a casserole and a cake
pan it could sit in to bake, big bowl to beat the whites, smaller bowl
to put the yolks in, and a teacup to separate each egg. By the time
he'd completed his assemblage, the tabletop was covered.

"You really need all that?" Anna asked.

"If you haven't used everything in the kitchen, it's not French
cooking." He started the roux in the saucepan on low heat, instructing
as he whisked flour into an equal amount of melted butter: "Keep
the heat down, and time it one minute to cook out the starchy taste.

After that, start adding milk a little at a time, whisking so it doesn't glump. Smooth it out and add mustard, salt, and pepper. While that heats, grate the cheese."

"Why grate it, if you're just going to put it in the sauce?"

"It melts quicker. Once the sauce starts bubbling, turn it down. Add the cheese and walnuts, broken small—big stuff sinks to the bottom—then turn off the heat and cover the pan. Preheat the oven to 375° at this altitude. A straight-sided casserole works best," tapping the dish. "This'll hold a seven-egg soufflé."

He demonstrated separating an egg. "Gotta be careful—if any yolk sneaks in, the whites won't hold air." He dumped the white into the big bowl, the yolk in the smaller.

"Let me," she said, separating the others one by one, then regarded skeptically the puddle of albumen in the bottom of the big mixing bowl. He began to beat; when the whites frothed up, he tapped in a little cream of tartar and handed off the whip to her. As the mass expanded to nearly fill the bowl, he took over, scooping with the whip to see how peaks were forming.

"Don't overbeat—they reach optimum fluff then lose it again." He lifted the whip and the peaks sank slowly. He beat further—glossy and stiff, the whites retained whatever shape the whip made.

"Now you've achieved lightness—time to blend. Add the yolks to the sauce, then," twisting the whip in one hand, "lift in some whites and fold very gently, rolling the light with the heavy. When that's sort of mixed—easy does it—cascade the sauce slowly over the whip wires into the whites, bringing up whites, bringing down sauce. Every step's an opportunity for disaster: flat soufflé's like rubber. Now, into the ungreased casserole it goes, lightly." He carefully tilted the bowl so the mixture rolled over the whip like a stream turning a waterwheel.

"Scrape the bowl, ease in the rest, now run the scraper around the edge of the casserole to free the batter from the walls, spiral it into the center, then lift it out." He ran some hot water into the cake pan, set the casserole in it, and slid his creation into the hot oven. "It bakes almost an hour, and nobody's allowed to stomp or slam doors or play music with a heavy bass."

"So what do we do in the meantime?"

"Make a salad."

She opened the fridge, where a wall of jars and bottles and pitchers defeated the interior light.

"How do you find anything in here?"

"We each have a territory." Walt extracted a metal bin, from which he chose lettuce, a cucumber, half a purple cabbage, a carrot. He set out a big enameled bowl.

Pick wandered back in and went straight for salad detail.

As they washed lettuce and spread the leaves on a white muslin towel then rolled it up, patting to dry, Anna asked him, "Are you a Deadhead?"

"That's me," beaming beatifically as though no finer claim could be made.

"Anna's in my drawing class," Walt explained.

"Cool," Pick said. "Show me your stuff."

"Once we're done here," Anna said, tearing up the last of the romaine. Walt sliced layers off the cabbage while Pick grated the carrot. "This would be easier to paint than draw."

"Maybe just a piece of the cabbage," Walt said, "or the bowl—a side view so you wouldn't have to deal with all these salad textures."

Walt and Anna got out their pads. Barbara returned from her phone call and she and Pick critiqued their efforts.

"This would look so much better in color," Pick said.

"Black-and-white is basic," Barbara said. "Without the crutch of color, the lines say more."

"If they look decent," Walt said. "This bowl is sad. Maybe I should stick to straight lines."

"Like what you drew today at Chautauqua," Anna told Walt, flipping to the cupola in his drawing pad. "This is a lot better than those rocks."

"Yours is good," Walt praised. She'd drawn three steps of the dining hall—every nail was there, every knot, ridges of grain, warp, splinters… "Any special reason you're taking this class?"

"I told you I'm a window washer. I spend all day looking at something that, if I'm doing a good job, I can't see. It's weird. After a while my eyes need to soak up something visible."

"But you like the job?"

"Instead of staring at haze and water spots, people see sky

and trees." She grinned. "You could see the world if you washed the windows here."

"What would it cost to have you clean them?" Barbara asked.

"Really?" Anna said. "You'd hire somebody?"

"I didn't say that," Barbara said. "We're not Harry Homeowner with disposable income here. But I'm curious."

"I have to see how hard they are to get at, whether you have storms, if there's mullions or big panes—"

"I'll show you around," Walt said, "and you can give us an estimate." Seeing her hesitate, he added, "We won't hold you to it—we just need to know what to backcharge the landlord." He and Pick and Barbara laughed: as far as the owner was concerned, they could carpet, landscape, the whole nine yards—they still owed the full rent.

Walt walked Anna through the middle room, a space that seemed wasted—nothing in it but a weathered cable spool table piled deep in clutter. They crossed into the living room. In there she counted windows, then at the far end, gestured at the French doors, curtained on the bedroom side. "What about these?"

"Sure—any glass." Through Barbara's room they went, into the hall, and across to Romo's big room. She counted his windows, glanced into the bathroom—one frosted pane and a long bright-white tub with no shower—then came upstairs. She noted a tall window in Stu's front dormer, then two windows in Lucy's room overlooking the gravel parking patch.

Walt opened his door. He had a mattress on the floor, a two-by-four supporting a dowel for hanging clothes, a peg rack on the wall hung with jeans and t-shirts, and a small unpainted dresser. By the door, his short unpainted pine bookshelf was half full of paperbacks.

"My pad," he bowed, hoping he wasn't scaring her off. His heart was soaring, for the first time since Laura— "What's your estimate?"

"I have to check ladder placements. Are there storm windows?"

He raised his small west window—just the screen.

"That takes down the price," she said, "but you must lose a lot of heat."

"Romo warned he's stingy—we won't use the heater much. I don't care. I'll just pile on more clothes."

Next she went outside, where daylight and temperature had dropped together; rubbing her hands, she stepped back into the kitchen warmth. Walt caught the screen door before it whacked, then gently closed the inside door.

"No banging around," he said. "Soufflé's more sensitive than a sleeping child."

"I babysat for years," Anna said. "Most children sleep very deeply. You could drop them and they'd never notice."

"Is that what you did?"

"No." Her face turned bright red. "That's just how knocked out they were."

"Well," smiling to show he was teasing, "this is a fussy baby— have to tiptoe around." How long would it take to earn her kiss— tonight? The last session of class, six weeks from now? Longer? Never? Flow, he reminded this desire so sharp and ready, as though the last few years spanned the interval between one dream and the next. Hurrying things would put him out of sync.

"Got some paper?" she asked. "I need to write this out."

He furnished the back of an envelope and a pen. She put down numbers, then other numbers, doodling as much as calculating and sitting back announced, "A hundred bucks is my guess. Ladder setup by the street's tricky—the traffic's right there. If you want a firm bid, ask my boss—want his card?"

"Sure." To get in touch with her once their class ended.

PERFECTLY CLEAN

A bold statement. Hardly anything in this world qualified, but it listed:

Windows • Carpets • Floors • Janitorial Service
Stefan Shapiro, Proprietor

"Thanks." He tucked the card in his wallet. "Whose windows do you wash?"

"Doctors, professors, downtown stores—and construction cleanup."

"Been at it long?"

"About a year. Stefan's very fair, and these doctors' wives trust him—they don't want just anybody tromping through their houses, you know. They refer him to their friends. You said you're a janitor. You should call him—he's always hiring."

"Cleaning's not really my thing," Walt said. "I used to be a projectionist."

"Wow, that sounds like a great job—why'd you quit?"

"Well, I wouldn't say I quit—there just aren't that many screens around here. I don't want to commute to Denver, and the new theaters are putting in automated systems—they pay some usher to turn the thing on, maybe fiddle with the focus, but if the machine screws up, they just give people a chit for another show. I used to stay in the booth so if a reel was out of focus or not framed, I'd be right there to fix it before the illusion was lost."

"Illusion?"

"Of being where the images take you, not sitting in the dark looking at pictures."

"Oh, right." She considered him. "Is that what you like about it—controlling people's illusion?"

He'd never settled on an answer to that question. Seeing movies made him happy, but so did his closer engagement with the process—he felt privy to another level of knowledge when he ran a film from the booth, alert to the reel cues, looking out sometimes over the heads of the audience, watching the shifting beams of light on their way to the screen. "Maybe."

"Do you fall under the spell too?"

"No, I have to pay attention so the reel changes are seamless, and rewind, splice, do projector maintenance. I love movies—films, I should say—but I can't really watch when I'm working."

"Ever think of making one?"

"Nah," he said. "Even a low-budget movie runs tens of thousands—gotta be a hustler to raise that much bread."

"You're kind of a hustler," Anna told him. "I only met you a week ago and in our second conversation, you invited me to dinner."

Interesting that he felt abashed: she was the one embarrassed. He intook breath to press down that internal flurry, then said, "Hope I haven't offended you."

"I don't trust easily. Don't rush me."

"OK."

She was really shy: if he asked the questions bubbling through his mind, she might not stick around. So he cooled it, inviting her to the living room to choose dinner music. She flipped through a stack of albums and pulled out *Workingman's Dead.*

"We also have quite a few concert tapes," he said.

"I like this record," she waved it, "except the cocaine song."

"Ever do any?"

"Once. It was over so quick, I don't get why people blow all that money."

"Same reason as betting on a three-minute horse race, I guess. Part of the high is all that money disappearing fast."

"Some rush," she said in disgust.

"Never worked for me," he said. "I prefer pot, and psychedelics. Dropping acid Fourth of July at the Rainbow Gathering: that's the best."

• • •

THE ORIGINAL RAINBOW GATHERING was at Strawberry Lake, Colorado, in 1972, the summer Anna was almost thirteen. She remembered masses of street people and hitchhikers in Boulder—her oldest brother Roger made scathing comments about dirty hippies and their crappy gear—cheap ponchos, backpacks held together with rope. She wasn't allowed to go on the Hill by herself, and when she went with her other brother Harold, they had to weave their way through the odd-smelling multitude, deflecting spare-changers at every step.

Hippies seemed another species: long unkempt hair, ragged bell-bottoms, homemade leather shoes or filthy bare feet. Tanned as though they'd never spent a day indoors, males and females alike wore bells and beads and patchouli oil, and floated to music playing in their minds. Anna's changing body felt pudgy and damp, and those slim bra-less women in diaphanous calf-length skirts and embroidered peasant blouses open to their cleavage depressed her. She couldn't imagine just lighting out like that, shedding caution and convention. She felt like an unhatched egg, the world on the other side of a shell she hadn't dared crack open.

She'd seen ragtags in haloes of flies, so stoned they couldn't tie their own shoes; Rainbow Family free spirits embraced the ethos of dirt. Still, they fascinated her. She was tempted to dab on patchouli oil just to try it. But Roger was so critical, she didn't dare.

Those scruffy hordes had been gone for years—seemed odd to be meeting a hippie now. Walt's bushy hair looked clean, but his car—hadn't anyone told him that era was over? "Really, you've been to a Rainbow Gathering?"

"Yeah," he smiled wide. "Amazing cosmic energy. And mass telepathy. Tripping with hundreds of people in one mind—"

Telepathy was imaginary—the worst thing about being human, she reflected, was being trapped in one's own mind and language: all efforts to communicate fell short. One person's thoughts couldn't just show up in somebody else's head. But Walt's eyes were glowing as though he could still hear all those people.

"*Sounds* great." Her eyes asked for confirmation.

"It is," and his smile buzzed her like an electric current. "What's your psychedelic of choice?"

"Um, mushrooms, I guess?" That's what her brother Harold preferred. She'd never tried them. She'd been tipsy once but never drunk, and only smoked pot when someone else offered it. All her life, it seemed, she'd dawdled in some eddy while the stream of experience flowed swiftly on, leaving her behind. Whenever she thought she really knew something, understood some fragment, she'd get slapped down with its insignificance.

In school she'd been proud of her ability to organize her thoughts, write cogent papers, contribute to discussions—but the larger world didn't value such things. She'd loved academics, but pursuing a higher degree seemed absurd—study what, and why? She wasn't using her BA in Comparative Lit—what would be the point of digging further into that safe cubbyhole where learning was uncoupled from life? Manual labor was supposed to be an antidote to that insubstantial existence, yet here she was, shown up again as the naïf she remained.

Walt said, "Let me know if you want to trip sometime."

His interest in her drawings and this dinner invite were all right, but obviously he wanted more. One part of her mind was up on its toes ready to dance; another part warned that he'd seen the world while she'd done nothing, and as soon as he figured that out he'd be gone. She couldn't deal with that again.

"I told you I'm slow," she warned. "I mean it." She went back to the kitchen to fidget with the place settings, one eye on the clock.

Barbara was putting out plates, and Pick was at the table rolling a joint; he stood up as he twisted the ends closed.

"Appetizer?" he offered.

Looking at Barbara, Anna shook her head slightly.

"You're on your own, Pick," Barbara said, and while he went outside, she applied the corkscrew to the chill-misted wine bottle.

As Walt returned from the living room, Anna reached for the oven door handle. "Can we peek?"

"Absolutely not. Tall or flat, we won't know till the clock says— just be patient."

"Three minutes," she said, stepping back: an age.

"How's the wine?" he asked.

Barbara splashed some into a jelly glass, swirled it, held it under her nose, then delicately sipped. "Try this, Anna. As the snobs would say, it's fruity, with enough body to stand up to a rich dish like soufflé, but nothing low-rent about it."

Anna sipped from the opposite rim, tasted again, then gave it back, nodding. How would she know? She hadn't ventured beyond jug wine with spaghetti.

Walt tasted it. "Yeah, this'll be good. Time to saw up the baguette." He lined a bowl with a frayed kitchen towel and piled thick slices into it.

"I think it's time," Anna ventured.

"Everyone has to be at the table when it comes out." He opened the back door, retrieving the salad he'd set out there to chill—there was no room in the fridge for that big bowl. "Hey man, c'mon in."

Pick stepped in exhaling a cloud, and everyone sat.

Walt placed the soufflé in the middle of the table. It was beautiful—golden brown, spiraling like the road to a castle, three inches above the casserole's rim at its summit. With a wide serving spoon, he cut carefully through the delicate crust and set a soft yellow mound on each plate. What remained in the dish sagged, its fragrance filling the room. When everyone had salad and bread, Barbara raised her glass.

"Here's to eggs—who'd ever guess they could be so clever?"

Walt watched their faces with proprietary pride. "What do you think, Anna? Worth the wait?"

"It's a triumph," she said. This was real cooking: air made savory. "Where'd you learn?"

"My aunt taught me. I spent the summer with her and my uncle when I was seventeen—'72, I guess. She made a soufflé, and once I tasted it I asked her to teach me. It's been my signature dish ever since."

After another bite, he said, "Shoot, I forgot," hurrying from the room. "Uncle John's Band" came on, and he was back.

Pick, keeping time with his head, said, "Hey, I have a great jam version of this from a Boston concert—want me to play it?"

"No, this is fine," Walt said.

"Car's coming over later," Barbara remarked.

"He should've come for dinner," Walt said. "There's enough."

"Car?" Anna repeated.

"My ummer," Barbara said and at Anna's puzzled look elaborated, "A friend of my mom's could never figure out what to call the guy her daughter went with: she was too squeamish to say 'lover,' but her daughter said he wasn't her boyfriend, so she'd introduce them to people as, 'This is my daughter and her um, er...' So she started saying 'ummer,' and everybody knew what she meant."

"That's good," Anna said. "I invent words."

"Such as—?" Walt said.

"Well, my favorite's 'intimition.'"

"What's that mean?"

"Intuition about time—not clock watching—sensing when to do something or go somewhere, and arriving at just the right moment."

"Do you have that?"

"Yeah. Last Sunday afternoon all the Perfectly Clean crews had to meet to trade equipment and vehicles, and we converged simultaneously from four different jobs. You can't plan that—or if you do, it doesn't work. It was perfect timing."

"Timing's everything," Barbara agreed. "That's a great word, intimition."

• • •

ANNA HELPED WITH THE dishes, then Walt offered her a ride home. Though it wasn't cold, she buttoned her heavy coat. He started for the passenger door to open it for her, but she was already getting in. He drove as she navigated, toward the foothills, then north. Her house was narrow, two stories, with a bare porch across half of the front. If this were his place, he'd get an old couch so he could sit out where the fresh air came off the ridge, and add a railing to prop his feet on.

"Hey Anna—"

Her hand was already on her door latch.

"Thanks for coming over," he said. "Hope I wasn't too pushy."

"I'm not ready—"

"For what?"

"For anything," she said. "I'm recovering."

"I am too. Let's go see a movie sometime."

"Maybe." She got out of the car, walked alongside the house—and vanished.

On his way home, he ruminated: who was behind those dodges? He'd never dealt with such a shy female before. When he got home, he asked Barbara.

She smiled. "You like her, don't you?"

He sang the opening lines from "Here Comes the Sun," then shook his head. "I'm so lonesome, all of a sudden."

"Intimition," Barbara said. "Take it at her pace."

chapter 3

Sinsemillian Window

AS WEEKS PASSED, Anna kept to herself, but when their second-to-last drawing class ended in mid-November, she agreed to join Walt to see *Cat People*. Before the movie started, she said she'd liked Malcolm McDowell ever since *if...* Then the screen lit, and she fell silent. Walt appreciated her interest in film. Laura'd always wanted to fool around during movies, and even when he'd convinced her to keep her hands to herself, her restlessness spoiled the experience for him.

As the closing credits scrolled, he asked, "What'd you think of it?"

"New Orleans was a perfect setting," she said. "Mystical, creepy—dark spirits live there."

"Ever been?"

"A friend of mine moved to the French Quarter, so I visited her in September thinking summer was over—I almost drowned from the heat and humidity. But I loved the voices. Their accent's beautiful. Most Southern accents sound horrible, but the Delta drawl's like music." She mimicked it for him, and he had to admit it was appealing, but maybe it was the timbre of her voice that did it for him.

"You like Nastassja Kinski?" he asked.

"Yeah, but better than her, I've seen every Werner Herzog," giving it the German pronunciation, "film I can—her father Klaus Kinski was his star. That guy's insane. Ever see *Aguirre, the Wrath of God*?"

"One of my favorites." He invited her out for coffee, and they talked about movies they liked and others they couldn't stand, till at eleven the waitress announced they were closing.

"Oh wow," she said, "I have to—No wait. That job for tomorrow's postponed. It's construction cleanup, and they're not done making their mess yet."

"Come over."

"For a little while, I guess." They walked to his house—he only drove to keep the battery charged. Anna claimed Boulder was a walking town, although once he got some money ahead, Walt planned to buy a bike.

While she chose tea, he put on Van Morrison's *Astral Weeks*, turning off the living room speakers, closing the music into the kitchen. They talked awhile, drinking peppermint tea, then he pulled his antler pipe from his shirt pocket.

"I have some outstanding sinsemilla," he said. "Ever smoke sinse?"

"I might've."

"It's all buds—doesn't attack your brain, just makes you aware."

"Umm, I'll try a little, but then you have to walk me home."

"Sure." Then, because she looked like a cornered coyote, he smiled gently. "I won't hurt you."

"You don't know that—nobody knows that." She stood up. "Let's just go."

"Smoke first." They did a bowl; he tapped out the ashes and reloaded. She hesitated, but joined him till that was gone.

"Once more for luck?" refilling round three.

"I feel like you're setting me up."

"We're just traveling through the flow together," he said. "You can leave whenever you want—no strings."

Her look said she doubted that, but she lifted the pipe to her lips and drew as he lit another match. He knocked out his pipe and stowed it, and put on his peacoat. She shrugged into her cowboy coat, slipped on a knit earband, and stuck her hands into a pair of men's fuzz-lined suede work gloves.

"Aren't you done growing?" he asked as they headed across town. "Your coat's primed for expansion."

"It's a hand-me-down from a friend—I like it: it's windproof and I can wear plenty of shirts underneath—won't need another coat for years."

They took the walkway that ran along the east wall of her house, descending half a dozen concrete steps to her door, and as she got out her key he rubbed her shoulder through the layers, encouraged when she leaned into his hand. They stepped into her large chilly basement apartment. The switch flicked on two bare lightbulbs showing pale walls and a dark tile floor. The room, the full length and half the width of the house, was fringed with dresser and bed, bookshelves, kitchen setup by the dirt-level front window, and a closetlike bathroom against the inside wall. Only a wicker rocking chair sat out in the middle. Her narrow wood bunk, neatly made with an army blanket, had no pillow; a print of Marcel Duchamp's *Nude Descending a Staircase* was tacked up behind it.

"My humble abode."

Only the one poster, a candle stub stuck to a jar lid, a cracked wooden dish of pocket junk—no sign of anything decorative or feminine. "Kind of austere," he said.

"It suits me." Anna turned on the heater by the door. The *whoosh* as gas lit then the soft hiss as it fed the burner were the only sounds. He picked up paperbacks stacked by her rocker—*The King Must Die* by Mary Renault, *Labyrinths* by Jorge Luis Borges, *Five Red Herrings* by Dorothy L. Sayers. Thought-provoking range of taste—on her shelves he saw Russian novels, James Joyce, Dante, plays by Tom Stoppard and Euripides, tattered paperbacks of *The Hobbit* and *The Lord of the Rings*.

"Were you at CU?" he asked.

"Yeah—got my degree a year ago spring."

He opened *Labyrinths*. Most of the pieces were only a page or two, but in his recollection, dense; profound imaginary worlds. "Which of these is your favorite?"

"'The Zahir'—something you can't get out of your mind—eventually it crowds out everything else. Could be anything—a tiger, a song—"

"Like the Bee Gees' 'How Deep Is Your Love'?"

"Aargh," she groaned. "You had to say that. Exactly: once a *zahir* is in your head, it sticks. According to Borges, the stickiest ones eventually drive you mad."

"If all I could think of was the Kool-Aid jingle, they'd have to put me away."

To drive out the tune now knocking on their brains like a salesman who wouldn't take no, she turned on her radio. Bob Marley and the Wailers saved them with "Exodus"—they danced while the room warmed, Walt swaying over to her shelf to park her loose books. He tossed his coat onto her rocker; she only unbuttoned hers.

When the song ended, he moved close. "I've waited what seems like a long time—may I kiss you, please?"

She ducked her head; to intercept her gaze, he squatted.

She half smiled. "Jeez, don't beg."

Her lips were dry and tight—must've been ages since she'd kissed anyone. She made a little umming sound into his mouth—pleasure? uncertainty?—then her lips were kneading, tongue touching his. No blush in her kiss, her energy welcoming; her flavor under the mint and smoke evoked the scent of cottonwood trees. Heat surged through her palms on his shoulders; he hugged her, and longing hit his chest like a crowd at a concert rushing the gates.

"Oh god," he gasped, "I forgot. Thank you."

She pulled back to see his face, their eyes meeting now completely through this open sinsemillian window. "Forgot what?"

"How it feels, to care."

His hands moved over her coat, finding her pulse even through the layers. It was here in his mouth, her blood thumping the surface of her tongue. He touched her hair—smooth, dry, full of static from the earband she'd pulled off. She twitched her shoulders and her coat dropped to the floor, he put one hand over her breast, her nipple pushing through her shirts. His hard-on stood at full attention.

"Anna, d'you have birth control?"

"No."

"I do. Can we—?"

She m-hmmed, kissing him again.

He'd bought Trojans after his dream about her, and carried them everywhere figuring you never know. Might need the whole pack tonight.

David Bowie was singing "Golden Years." Turning up the radio, she said, "The good thing about basements is sound doesn't travel upwards very well." They stepped apart to shed clothes.

Her breasts were big and loose—jelly, not melons. She had a farmer tan—t-shirt line just above her elbows and a V at her neck, the rest of her body white and pink and buff-colored, almost a gold haze to it. A lump on her left collarbone attracted his fingers.

"What happened here?"

"Broke it falling out of a tree. The doctor said it'd heal stronger if the ends overlapped, but it sure doesn't feel stronger to me."

"If my doc had done that, I'd be a gimp—my thigh bone broke in two places."

"I knew he was wrong—too late now." Her shrug moved her breasts; when he kissed one, she shivered.

• • •

SHE TRACED HIS RIB cage and the sparse curls above his solar plexus—a featherweight—Cory's body had been dense. Well, good—maybe her memory'd stay out of the way so she could enjoy this. Since coming back, she'd kept to herself, but when Walt asked her to the movie she found she'd been thinking about him, hoping he hadn't given up since their soufflé dinner.

His mouth was friendly and eager, and the more she kissed him the more she wanted to. The flip-flops she kept under the bed so she'd never have to take a step barefoot on this cold damn floor, lay forgotten.

It wasn't the sinsemilla so much as having his heart engaged after such a long dry spell—he thought he'd never stop. On her small bunk, she laughed and threw herself against him, gripping his thigh, butt, back, an arm for leverage while he played with her breasts. Her lips softened to his kisses, tongue dry from fast breathing, her soft "whoo, whoo, whoo" matched with his barnyard baaing and mooing, punctuated by giggles till they finally toppled apart, gasping, one of his legs draped off the bed, hers vertical against the wall. His whole body happy from ankles to ears, he let his eyes fall shut, swimming through a deep nap till her fingers fished him out, inviting another hard-on.

Who was this Anna, where'd she come from? His heart was in glory.

• • •

COULD IT STILL BE night? He'd been inside her as long as he could remember, flying, her mattress Steppenwolf's Magic Carpet Ride. The bed frame creak was keeping time, he was pretty sure he was falling, but her gravity outdid Earth's. Once, on acid, he'd gone very slowly from sitting upright to lying flat on his back, nothing pulling him floorward but his fascination with the textured ceiling. He was practically tripping now—a whole new view from Anna Road was opening up.

Her kiss tasted of salt—she must be thirsty. Wobbling across her cold floor, he ventured to the sink, peering out the dirt-splattered window—the street lay quiet under a soft cloud aglow from city light. Back beside her, he shared a glass of water, then, lips revived, they resumed placing them on each other, every oval a new disclosure, and pretty soon he was putting on his next rubber. Once she'd taken him completely apart would she reassemble him, or just leave his heap of quivering nerves wrapped around a bundle of bones and flesh?

They huddled into her wool blankets—the heater had defanged the chill, but wintry air seeped under the door, making them grateful for each other's warmth. She turned off her radio and they snoozed, the narrow bunk more than sufficient.

A familiar silence woke him: snow. He saw white against the front window, though the room was too full of its own scents—sex and basement mustiness, the phantoms of coffee and toast—to admit its damp freshness. Her temple rested on his arm, her face wearing a wide smile he congratulated himself for putting there. He hadn't felt so fine in years—not since Laura. *Don't*, he scolded himself. *Let Anna be who she is. Love her because she's shared herself, not because Laura stopped.*

Anna's eyelids flickered, opening into his full gaze. "Hi Walt."

"Hello Anna. Good to meet you."

"Meet me again," and as her shins crossed behind his thighs, holding him, she laughed, "You're really turned on, mister."

"You're the switch."

When he came to again, light was struggling through the front window where she stood making toast. He rolled onto his side, facing her. "Mmm."

"Want coffee?" she asked.

"Do I have to wake up?"

She grinned. "Or I could knock you out again."

"Yeah," he smiled. But she was dressed. "Going somewhere?"

"Out to walk in the snow—there's about four inches on the ground. It's pretty coming down—big fat flakes."

"Just gonna leave me here?"

"I figured you wouldn't move till you had to," coming to stand by her dresser.

"If you're not in it, this bed is no longer my favorite place." He tugged her hand, she bent to his kiss. "You wouldn't believe how happy you've made me."

No. No no no. Just sex, just some fun. She said, "Don't think—"

"Think?" he laughed. "I can't."

"Good," she said firmly. "Don't."

"Something sad must've happened," seeking her eyes.

Her gaze fixed on her hand rubbing her sleeve. "There's no point talking about it."

"Let's make a deal, Anna—let's just share this," palm on her thigh. "I won't burden you with my misery if you won't tell me yours."

"Like Marlon Brando and Maria Schneider in *Last Tango*? No identities, no history?"

"Identities maybe," he said. "People who try to draw, and love movies?"

"Y-yeah..."

"Don't go yet." He reached up under her shirt, working her bra open with blind fingers.

"No, I—"

"OK then, let's go out for breakfast."

"I already—"

"While we're out, I'll get more Trojans and we'll see how many I can fill."

She flinched, eyes seeking some neutral corner, away from his questing look, his mouth ready with a kiss. For a year now, she'd battled for equilibrium. Days would go by without that lacerating regret and shame, but here she was crumbling, a flood-gouged riverbank. *What am I in for?* she asked herself. *And how do I get back out?*

"Sorry I stayed?" he murmured.

"I will be soon."

He let his hands drop. She adjusted her clothes, mouth tight. "I need to be alone now." Her stare reached far beyond this room.

He dressed, then gave her a brief kiss. Her lips, so much softer and fuller now, gave only a ghost of an answer.

He left.

His cheeks, hot enough to melt snow, matched his burned heart—why'd she shut him out? Somebody hurt her. The details surrounded him like snowflakes, indecipherable but numerous enough to bury him. Alone, breakfast in a café would be a waste. He stopped by a bakery for day-old bagels and munched one on his way to the theater, to clean it before going home, to crank up the radio and sing loudly and suppress this ache before Barbara read him. He couldn't tell her; couldn't tell anyone.

The smelly theater repelled him. Besides the usual clash of soft-drink syrups and rancid butter, this morning he found vomit in the men's room sink. In the auditorium, the screaming blower chased loose cups and wrappers across the floor while he walked rows, flipping seats up, kicking Milk Duds loose from the painted concrete. Down by the screen, he swept the debris into giant empty popcorn bags. Did customers realize the stuff came pre-popped and dyed yellow, warmed under the concession stand heat lamp? He opened the alley door to chuck two trash-filled bags into the dumpster.

At the closet by the men's room, he inhaled deeply, then moved fast: open the heavy glass jug of ammonia, dribble some into the mop water, recap and put the bottle back, then hurry across the lobby for his next breath. By the time he'd spot-mopped the auditorium floor, the fumes had completely zapped his olfactories. He cleaned the bathroom, swabbed out that sink, polished the front glass with Windex and newspaper, vacuumed the carpet, and put the cleaning stuff away. At the panel, he hit off the lights, then let himself out the front. In the alcove beneath the marquee, snow curled toward him, melting on the concrete. Out by the curb it was seven or eight inches deep by now.

This job taunted: *What are you willing to put up with to live here?* Janitor? He'd come down pretty far from his projectionist days. Anna and Boulder resonated the same frequency—last night he was in, today he felt marginal.

After sex, animals are sad. Was his urge to howl nothing more than that? The four-part clock chime on campus followed by the bell tone of hours marked eleven. He didn't even know her—how could he be hurting like this? With all his joy absorbed into her dismissal like water spilled in sand, if he didn't have two condoms instead of yesterday's half dozen, he could convince himself he'd imagined the whole night.

His heart had been so alive, but today he was as dead again as if Anna'd sent him home without a kiss. That would've been merciful... He hummed Joni Mitchell as he walked, and when he got home he put on *For the Roses*, singing along with "Cold Blue Steel and Sweet Fire," the talons of need, planted in him now.

Maybe she'd accept Joni's message. Finding a blank cassette, he taped the whole album. These songs spoke to her shyness, certainty that had fled so quickly, the ache. He taped "You're Gonna Make Me Lonesome When You Go" from Dylan's *Blood on the Tracks*, then the Dead's "Cassady," a song for someone on the run.

On the flip side, he recorded a few numbers off *Abbey Road*, then all of Neil Young and Crazy Horse's *Rust Never Sleeps*: for his money the best rock'n'roll album of all time. He ended with "Dreams of Barbarella" from Commander Cody's solo album *Flying Dreams*. Walt hadn't made a tape for anyone since he broke his leg. Well, his heart was shattered then too; same experience. He wondered if Anna had a word for a recurring moment in the cycle—not déjà vu, but the same situation in a different setting, a milestone to gauge your progress. Or stuckness.

"Should get there tomorrow or the next day," the clerk at the post office said, stamping the padded mailer. By class next Tuesday, she'd have a chance to listen to it—if she didn't just drop it in the trash. Hoping she'd open it, he left off his return address.

After depositing maybe twelve inches, the storm gave up and the sky cleared. As he trudged toward Chautauqua, he reflected on the chaos this much snow would cause in Maryland. Everything would come to a halt for days. Here, people just drove slower and saved the less urgent errands for later. After school, kids raced around and had snowball fights, teenagers trekked door to door with snow shovels, and everyone smiled.

From the mesa, he looked out north and east over the city, sunset splashing the snow orange then crimson then magenta, threads of cloud stitching colors to the air. He slogged home with cold feet, arriving just as Romo and Stu sat down to rice and veggies.

"Pull up a bowl," Romo said, then added as Walt served himself, "Thought I heard you in the kitchen last night, but you weren't around this morning."

"I was here with a friend—spent the night there." He clammed up. Anna was so shy she could probably sense people talking about her.

chapter 4

Möbius Strip

ANNA SPENT THE day walking, cowboy hat tilted to keep snow out of her face. She'd got hit in the eye once and lost a contact. Instead of sympathy, her brother Harold had teased her about "that rogue snowflake." With everything glittering and no distinctive tiny sound of the lens hitting the street to alert her, there'd been no hope of finding it. Once was plenty for that sort of mishap. Tugging her hat lower, she leaned forward, the spinning flakes screening her from the world. Usually she loved snowfall—powdery clumps decorating every twig and rail, clinging even to the faces of bricks and stone walls—but today the beauty was a blur as her focus shrank inward.

Oblivious, she bashed into the end of a bus stop bench. Her kneecap seared and stung. To test for damage, she braced against the seatback, planting the ball of her foot and turning her leg in and out—*doing the Twist*, she thought, and laughed, just for a second. *Why'd I let him stay? That was stupid.* But once they started kissing, nobody could've stopped them. *Why'd I smoke with him? Now he'll feel entitled.* He was probably discussing her with his housemates right now; she cringed. Too bad she'd have to miss the last drawing class. *Guess I'd better lay low. Is it time to move?*

Stopping by the natural foods store, she considered a housing ad on the board: to pay that much rent she'd have to work full time. *Damn it anyway.* At a table near the registers, she scanned listings in the paper, marking a couple that might be OK. *Only got that apartment six months ago, and paid to put in a phone. What a waste.* Living alone hadn't insulated her after all.

Back home, she pried off her wet boots and called the office. No work tomorrow or Friday, but all weekend. Too cold to read, she took a steamy shower—then the second she shut off the water, the chill closed in. Drying fast, she got in bed, the smell of his hair on the sheet bringing tears to her eyes. As she warmed up, she drifted to sleep and dreamed.

He was with her again, so turned on, softening her up with kisses, hands enjoying her breasts and legs while she crouched over him playing him like a violinist, drawing music from their motion. Then in midkiss, he was Cory. Betrayed expectation burned its way out, the bitter flood waking her; she couldn't shut it off.

• • •

WHEN SHE'D ARRIVED IN London to live with Cory, they were out of sync. Work obligations kept him away for weeks at a stretch, while isolated in his small flat, she went insane, trapped by a culture she didn't fit into—all that time and nowhere to spend it. Walking had been her only relief. She'd take a bus to the busiest shopping district and move at top speed down the broad crowded sidewalk, dodging her way among people who emerged from taxis and stores, stopped to converse, or hurried for a bus. Her fast pace took her to the split second of *now* Neal Cassady had pursued so religiously. Not thinking or planning, she just sensed openings in space as people stepped apart, never colliding though she was almost running, nobody even aware of her. She was in the moment and they were behind it; before they could detect her presence, she was gone.

She walked holes in her shoes before inertia overcame her, then spent two days? three? staring at Cory's blank apartment wall, catatonic. Something broke through—the clunk of the mail slot downstairs, or the guy across the hall opening his door. Once she got out of that chair, she realized that if she didn't leave she'd never move again. Buying a one-way ticket, she dragged home her skinful of shards and began, one fragment at a time, to reassemble. Window washing gave her purpose and restored her sense of competence. Stefan and his customers praised her, and physical concentration engaged just enough of her mind to keep those memories submerged. But work couldn't drive out the pain.

Cory, older, jaded, wrote off their failure like a business expense. But he'd been her first real love. She didn't deserve him, but that didn't make his demands fair. She did whatever he wanted, despising herself but not sure how to refuse, relieved each time he left—except then she was alone again. Finally, her misery had so twisted her, she didn't wait for him to ask but laid out her body for him to paw over like the irregulars bin at a discount store. By the end, his pleasure was so small no amount of abasement could coax a fond word from him, and she crept inside herself where not only he but her own feelings couldn't trespass.

She had pride, didn't she? What happened to the independent woman he'd met the summer before? Three seasons of love letters had created a vast illusion. She knew Cory's words; she didn't know him. In a jitter of anticipation, she'd arrived at his flat. But when he opened his door, he'd said, "Oh." She spent two months trying to erase that disappointment from his eyes, and finally the only thought her brain would support was *Go home*. Whatever mirage that might be.

Back in Boulder she found her parents' nurture debilitating, eroding the autonomy she'd paid so much for. To escape their effusiveness, she got a job and rented a room in a ratty house.

One spring day, she was clear-headed enough to detect the house's cobweb of bad vibes and went to find new digs. Moving into this apartment, she'd sidled cautiously into normal life—till contact with Walt proved the plaster on her reconstruction was still soft. The recovery she needed was better made on her own. Since junior high she'd mimicked the handwriting of teachers, the gestures of friends; gradually she recognized her sponge nature. If she drew Walt into her personal disaster, she'd never be sure how much of New Anna was her own evolution, how much absorbed from him.

But after last night, could she convince him to just forget it? *I have to.* With vacillating urges and bad dreams, she had nothing to share except this body that fit so well with his. The scene was too familiar: Cory all over again. But this time she knew to protect herself. *Knowing's only part,* her mind scolded. *Are you strong enough?*

• • •

THE NEXT DAY, WHEN she got back from walking in the snow, a package was in her mailbox. During her weeks at Cory's flat, the postman's visit had been the nadir—or occasional height—of her day. Even now, a surprise piece of mail gave her a surge of joy. She turned over the padded envelope—from the unfamiliar handwriting and Boulder postmark, she guessed Walt had sent it, but why no return address? Prying open the staples, she pulled out a bandana-wrapped cassette. The tape had no labels beyond Side A, Side B. The index card folded into the box listed song titles, but after a glance she just put on the cassette, sinking into her rocker to listen.

How'd Walt know *For the Roses* was one of four albums she'd taken to Cory's? When the tape reached the end and shut off, she sat rocking, nudging the floor with a toe to keep moving, her thoughts roaming with "Cassady." When she finally flipped the cassette over, she got a thrill. *Rust Never Sleeps* was new to her, but she recognized Neil Young's nasal voice, and what guitars! Walt actually understood.

Inspired, she phoned his house; a woman reported he was out. She realized it was Barbara, and thinking about how lovely and poised she was, Anna hung up, her funk settling back around her like cold, wet clothes. She was reading Wallace Stegner's *Angle of Repose* when the phone rang.

"Anna, it's Walt. I was out flat tracking—it was great. Ever cross-country ski?"

"Since junior high—I'm pretty good. Know how to telemark?"

"No. Show me sometime?"

"I might." Why'd he have to be so friendly, making her want to be with him? "You sent this tape, right?"

"Like it?" His hopeful smile beamed straight through the phone line.

"It's really—appropriate. You can't imagine. Thank you."

"When you stop focusing on your own pain, you realize it's the human condition. I think that was Buddha's revelation—sort of de-fangs it."

"Oh, you think so?"

"No," he laughed. "But didn't that sound good?"

"You sound good," she admitted.

"Want to come over?"

"I'm cold and my boots are wet."

"Want a hot bath?"

She remembered their long, very clean, tub. "You don't mind?"

"I want to see you. I'll come get—give me time to dig out my car."

Forget it, was on her tongue, but she really wanted a hot soak. And maybe—

In solidarity her friends had badmouthed Cory, but they didn't even know him. Blaming time and miles offered neither remedy nor satisfaction. The person who'd helped most before Walt showed up was her Grandma Francis, who never asked questions, just loved her as though she were the most wonderful person who'd ever been born. They'd laugh over old photographs while Grandma told stories of getting lost with Grandpa on their rock-hound adventures.

But that love was a hug when she needed a kiss. Walt's insight was uncanny, knowing which songs to tape. Above the dirge of memory, she heard the music afresh. Where'd he come from? First he'd drawn her out of solitude, then into her neglected skin—and now he was Puck, tripping through her head, playing her history like panpipes. On impulse, she got out a sheet of paper, cut a strip an inch wide off the long edge, turned one end over to put a half-twist in it, then taped the ends together to form a loop.

As he'd warned, he was slow getting there. She finally saw his car creeping along the ruts. Maybe tomorrow a plow would reach this street.

"Hi Anna," he smiled as she got in; she thought he'd kiss her but he swayed toward her, then back upright, his lips compressing into uncertainty.

"Thanks Walt—this is really nice of you. How are the roads?"

"No problem till I turned off Ninth. It's deep here." He drove slowly.

"I made you something," she said. "A paradox. A little bit of math magic. A Möbius strip."

"Which is—?"

"A piece of paper with only one side." She grinned at his doubting look. "When we get to your house, you're going to prove it."

• • •

HE WARNED HIS HOUSEMATES the bathroom would be occupied awhile and gathered a towel, washcloth, his robe for Anna, and at her instruction, a pen. She adjusted the water to very hot, and as it roared into the tub, pried off her boots.

"Walt," she said, noting the absence of a shower curtain, "would you not look at me while I'm in the bath?"

"All right."

"Or watch me get in either?"

He turned away, but he hadn't figured she'd take so long, easing her way slowly into hot water, dipping then removing each hand and foot, working them deeper and leaving them in longer. While she acclimated, he stared at his bathrobe hanging on the door, thinking of Laura wearing it when they'd lived together. A surge of pain unbalanced him. He leaned on the wall and closed his eyes.

"I'm in now," she said. "You OK?"

"I pretend I am—isn't that what you do?"

"Yeah," echoing the loneliness in his voice. Then she said briskly, "Time for the Möbius strip."

Sitting on the floor with his back against the tub, all he could see was the top of her head. Pen ready, he held the paper loop. "What do I do?"

"Trace a line down the middle, all the way around."

He fed the strip beneath the pen. "OK, I'm back where I started."

"Look at it."

The line was on both sides. He saw the half twist and understood why it worked, but— "That's amazing."

"Isn't it? I think you and I are like a Möbius strip—the different sides we think we're on are actually the same place."

The clouds around his heart shifted to allow light through. Clear love. Not that tangle of need and karma with Laura, just love, by itself.

Silence soothed the room.

Knees comfortably bent, he looked toward the ceiling. "Anna?"

"Hm?" She sounded groggy—that hot water must be knocking her out.

"Can I draw you sometime—not your clothes, you?"

"Draw me?" in a small voice.

"I've discovered I see things better that way. I want to see you."

"What if we drew each other?"

"Sure. You pick when and where."

Silence again.

"Oh I know," she said. "I'm house-sitting for my parents over Thanksgiving—you could come by."

"That works," adding, "I was afraid I'd never see you again."

"Well, I think we should cool it."

"Is that why you're in a scalding bath?" he teased. "To cool off?"

She didn't answer.

After a while she ventured, "Walt?"

"Hm?"

"When we're out in public, don't touch me—no intimacy, all right?"

"You have a lotta rules—my instinct's to break 'em—"

"But this is private," she insisted. "No one needs to know what we do."

He was past caring what anyone thought of his lifestyle, but she was younger, and this was her hometown, after all. "OK, but if you shut me out, I'm back in darkness—"

"Are you afraid of the dark?"

"Tired of it. And I bet you are too. We're on the same wavelength, y'know."

"The same side," she said, "of the same piece of paper, no matter what it looks like." She set her dripping hand, bright red from the hot water, on the rim of the tub, and he leaned his cheekbone against it.

chapter 5

Soup

DONE WITH WORK Saturday, Walt took in a silent film matinee at the library. He was leaving when someone hailed him—Eddie again.

"Walt, my man, can I offer you a beer?"

"No." He turned away, but Eddie was on him like a tick.

"A cup of coffee then? I'm prepared to foot the bill."

Walt shrugged and came along. What could the guy want now?

At Bookhead they waited for coffee, then sat by the low wall that partitioned the seating area. After recounting his futile job hunt, Eddie leaned back in his chair and announced, "Laura sent you something."

"Whatever she says, I don't want—"

"It's a picture. Incarceration's done her no harm, one might think."

"Don't," closing his eyes. What was Eddie up to? But when he looked again there was the snapshot—couldn't get his eyelids down fast enough to shut her out.

"Quite something, isn't she? One could make the argument that beauty is a manifestation of an awakened state. In her case perhaps the catalyst was the School of Hard Knocks. On the back she's written—" but Walt was in motion, grabbing his pack, knocking over the chair in his haste. As fast as the slush of yesterday's snow would permit, he tromped north through town, not stopping till he'd ascended the last hill. Winded, he bought a pint of Jack Daniels and caught a bus back home.

Slumped on his mattress, he propped his head up high enough to slug back the whiskey, while Dylan's *Blood on the Tracks* played its litany of relationships gone south—perfect songs, to the point. No comfort at all. Beyond his window, the energy of Saturday night increased. Out there, people were partying, seeing friends, fishing for sex.

Could Laura possibly think he still loved her? Did she expect to pick him up again—*I changed my mind, I want this shirt after all*—then once she'd used him up, make her final discard? His thoughts spun in a small circular rut until he fell asleep.

He dreamed he was sitting on a snowbank with Anna, holding hands, not cold, though they were naked. The world was glittering around them till the wind started blowing, then as they tried to protect each other from the blizzard, Laura appeared and threw a blanket around Walt. He hugged himself inside it, from the corner of his eye seeing Anna plunge off into the whiteout, her face stiff with pain. Laura's vigilance held him captive, till the storm dropped its last and dissipated. Alone again, he followed the furrows of Anna's tracks, picturing her dragging her feet, despondent, exhausted. He found her, frozen, the world all shades of blue and white around the bloody snow where her hands couldn't tear a hollow log wide enough to crawl inside. As he stared, Laura found him. "You can't do anything now," she said, leading him away.

He woke parched and hung over, wishing he could shut out the day. Instead, he had to hurry—the first matinee started in two hours and this weekend's midnight movie was *Rocky Horror Picture Show*. The Atheneum would be a disaster. Stu was idling in the kitchen, so Walt drafted him in exchange for breakfast. Walt cleaned the bathrooms and lobby, then vacuumed, joining Stu to finish the auditorium. Popcorn flung like confetti was easy to blow to the front, but glitter stuck where it landed. The mop was going to sparkle forever, which would've seemed funny if the manager hadn't appeared while they were finishing, pressing a finger across the stiff velour of an aisle seat, making glitter squares jump like fleas.

"Hnh!" he snorted. "That the best you could do?"

Walt's weekly pittance didn't include vacuuming seats and he wasn't about to apologize, so he turned away, mopping a nonexistent spill while Stu busied himself wiping armrests with a rag. The retreating jingle of the manager's keys signaled the coast was clear; they put away the cleaning stuff and left.

At a nearby café, Stu dug into an omelet with hash browns and toast while Walt nursed a cup of black coffee, his head being split with a wedge and sledge. Every time he thought there was nothing left to shatter, pain stabbed from a new angle. Stu drove them home, and Walt went to bed shivering and sneezing.

The next day he had a sore throat and full sinuses. He dragged himself to the bathroom.

Barbara was coming out. "Walt, you look awful—can I get you something?"

"Soup."

He shut the door on her next question. Back upstairs he tuned in public radio, surprised to catch a program on the Jonestown mass suicide three years earlier.

He'd been at Laura's in Berkeley that day. She'd already left for class, but he and her housemates heard the news, sharing their shock, revulsion, and disbelief. Reverend Jim Jones's reputation as a force for good among poor, mostly black, Bay Area residents had been tarnished by his increasing paranoia. When he retreated from San Francisco to the South American jungle to found Jonestown, family members of his followers persuaded Congressman Leo Ryan to investigate. They'd heard that anyone straying from his groupthink was being ostracized, even beaten. But Ryan and several of his staff were murdered at the Guyana airstrip. It was impossible not to wonder: Had the Jonestown residents really died willingly?

The earnest young woman recounting the tragedy was drawing parallels to Reverend Sun Myung Moon and his brainwashed tribe, but her view was simplified by hindsight. No one could honestly make sense out of nine hundred people drinking cyanide-laced Kool-Aid, let alone claim any other act was comparable. What insanity had been in the air? Ten days later, Dan White assassinated Mayor Moscone and Harvey Milk in San Francisco City Hall, and got off with a slap on the wrist thanks to the Twinkie Defense. Junk food made him a murderer?

A whole community was ushered out of life by a kids' drink? Was the sourness behind all that death the equal-and-opposite reaction to an oversugared existence?

He switched off the radio, sorry to have been reminded.

Twenty minutes later, Barbara came in with a bowl of miso soup. She sat by his mattress while he slurped the rich broth then set down the empty dish.

"Thank you," he rasped.

"Speak," she said. "Why so depressed all of a sudden?"

"The past is collapsing on me like a mine cave-in."

"Confession might get you out from under—tell me."

He described running into Eddie and hearing things he didn't want to. "Barbara, I'm trying to start fresh here, but Laura's breathing down my neck." He rubbed his eyes. "That was bad, seeing her picture."

She shook her head, her judgment demolishing the free man fantasy he'd been propping up. Though she was too kind to say it, she plainly thought he still cared—otherwise, why was Laura so threatening?

• • •

LUNA AND HER STUDENTS stood around in the library entry to escape the cold wind—everyone but Anna. At ten after, Walt called her number. He hung up after a dozen rings, but he'd bet anything she was home. Driving over, he knocked on her door.

No response.

He knocked again, calling, "I know you're here."

She opened the door a few inches. "What do you want?" her eyes hard and dark.

"You're missing the last class," he said.

"I know."

"What's wrong?" When he'd dropped her off after her hot bath Friday night, she hadn't kissed him but she didn't seem hostile.

"You still love her," she said flatly.

"What?" Out of left field. "Who?"

"Whoever she is. I was at Bookhead having coffee with my boss Saturday, and overheard you. The other guy said she wants to see you. He said she's beautiful."

"Anna—" His sinuses throbbed. He massaged his forehead. *What did she think she knew?* "Yeah she's beautiful: Like a really sharp knife, like a coral snake right before it bites. Like a blizzard before you freeze to death." He hadn't meant to say that, and now he couldn't meet her eyes. She'd see that dream self: hunched, exposed, defeated.

"But she's not done with you," she said.

"No history, remember?" Not that the characters in *Last Tango* managed to keep it buried. Wasn't there some middle ground between amnesia and memory so vivid it crowded out the present? "My feelings for her are dead."

She blinked, her expression softening.

"At least come to class," he urged. "Don't miss that because of me."

"I guess," getting her things.

• • •

"**DRAWING'S A WONDERFUL WAY** to stop time," Luna was saying. "I always take my pad and pencils when I travel. If I'm stranded in an airport, or waiting for a store to open, or I just want to be outside, I find a spot to draw. Sometimes I use colored pencils, other times just a number two pencil: it's always worthwhile. You don't have to draw anything spectacular—a pot of geraniums will do, a chair, a doorway. A piece of bread on a plate. Whatever it is, I guarantee you'll see details you didn't know were there."

"Do you teach colored pencil?" Walt asked.

"In the spring. I don't teach winter quarter."

They looked around this second-floor conference room. Below, through the glass, they could see shelves and the circulation desk. Having learned his limitations, Walt sat on the floor to draw the underside of the table. He focused on where the leg mounted to the top, noticing lumps of gum, a label, a glob of what looked like caulk—he'd do better if he didn't feel so crappy. Luna glanced at his page, crouching so she could see what he was looking at, and pretty soon put her finger on a line.

"Erase."

He grinned. "How do you know I can't see this?"

"It isn't there." Absolute. He wasn't that sure about anything. "Trust your eyes."

As class ended, he glimpsed Anna slipping out. When he accosted her, she halted, stiff. "Wait up." Gathering pad and pencils, he joined her. "Talk to me?" averting his face to blow his nose.

"We could go for coffee—" she said.

"I'm too germy to be in public. Let's just sit in my car."

"No," she reacted with a grimace. "Come over for tea."

• • •

"I SHOULDN'T BE INVADING—" but she aimed him at her rocker.

"I refuse to talk in a car," she said, turning on her hotplate and filling the kettle. "My mom likes gossip, and the car's her confessional, so I'm trapped. For years, she'd be driving me someplace, and start in: 'Did you know—' One time she said their best friends' son had been stealing from his folks and doing drugs in high school. By the time she told me, that was ancient history. She even admitted Ron wasn't having trouble anymore—so why say anything? It's like she needed me to be in on the dirt. Now when I see Ron, I picture him going through his dad's wallet." She paced the room, shaking herself as if to repel the memory.

She made rose hip tea; he slurped his down with a handful of vitamin C tablets.

"I was wrong," she said, her back to him, addressing her hands. "I wanted us to be in the same place, but we're not. Cory— That's over. But yours isn't."

"It has to be. I'd kill myself before I'd go through that again." He rose and moved near her. "Anna," he said softly. "Why's she get to stamp out my little spark of happiness? Why should you have to know about all that?"

"I was so surprised when I recognized your voice in Bookhead. I think Stefan and I were at the only table where I could've heard you." She turned to face him, eyes sharp. "Guess the past didn't want to stay buried, huh?"

He stepped away, gesturing to the room in general. "How much do you want to know?" Pandora's box was open now, and Greed, Jealousy, Manipulation, and Selfishness were swarming. In the myth, Hope stayed behind, but his hope had been invested in keeping that lid shut.

"What did you do for her?" she persisted.

"Everything. She told me to come, I came, told me to wait, I waited. Told me to help her other man, I pulled him back from the brink. Told me to get lost," he slumped back into her rocking chair, "and I've been lost ever since."

As though his defeat freed her, she said, "Maybe we can help each other. Everyone assumed that if I let Cory push me around, it must be OK. But I didn't accept it—I was just stuck with it."

"All I wanted was her love," he said. "Thought that was noble, and no price was too much to pay. Man, was I wrong."

"That wasn't really love then."

"Sure felt like it."

"Love can only happen," she said, "when there's no weights and chains."

He held his hand in the air a few inches from her waist, raising his eyebrows. He couldn't drag her onto his lap, she had to choose. By watching her use her will, he might resuscitate his own.

Anna sat across his thighs. "You're a good person. I wasn't sure such people existed."

"I'm spineless," he said. "When she was going to Berkeley I tried to stop her, but she not only went, she pulled me along—"

"Are you—" she hesitated, "gonna leave town?"

He shook his head.

"So when's she coming?"

"Next year, Eddie said—don't know if that means January or December."

She looked away and murmured, "Is she really beautiful?"

He wished she wouldn't ask that. "I'll prove how beautiful you are, when we draw each other."

"Maybe we shouldn't," she said.

"Why not? It's you I want a closer look at."

"You'll go back to her."

"I can't. We were so brave and sure, we were gonna wrestle karma to the ground and walk away free. All I've learned since is when to jump out of the way, before the wheel crushes and cripples me again."

She hugged him, her lips to his cheekbone.

"Don't kiss me," he said. "You'll catch my cold."

"I'll make you chicken soup."

His heart hiccupped. His mom had always made chicken soup for him when he was sick—fixing it himself didn't offer the same comfort. "You will?"

"When I was dying inside no one took care of me. I can do that."

He pressed his face to the pillow of her breasts. She kissed his hair, then stood up.

"I'm going to the store to buy a chicken, and celery, and more garlic."

"Let me give you a couple bucks." He pulled a five from his wallet.

"No, that's too much."

"It's either this, or a ten."

"I'll bring you change then."

"Change," he mused. "You're the change I need."

Just like that, her eyes were bright. "What did the Zen master say to the hot dog vendor?"

"I don't know," he said. "What?"

"'Make me one with everything.'"

He laughed.

"And he did," she continued, "so the Zen master paid him a five, but the vendor didn't give him his three-fifty. So he said 'Where's my change?' and the vendor said, 'Zen master, change comes from within.'"

• • •

SMELLS OF GARLIC AND chicken fat woke him—he'd conked out on her bed, where she'd tossed a blanket over him. She was in her rocker reading, and outside her window the streetlight was on. He checked her clock radio—almost 9:15.

"Hey Anna."

She turned toward him.

"I've got an idea—*Heaven's Gate* is at the Atheneum. The second show starts at 9:30. Let's see it, then I'll give you a tour of the projection booth."

"I can't. I have an early job." She looked away. "I made you soup because it's the least I could do, but don't ask me to fix what's broken. I don't know how."

"Broken is right," he said. "That was destructive, being an also-ran in her life—after grad school, after Mr. Brass Balls. I just picked up after their party, again and again, even when they invited me. Cob said triangles are strong; all I know is they have the sharpest points in geometry."

Her face saddened, and she sank back in her chair like she was there for the long haul.

"Don't pity me," he said. "I went along with that whole scene."

Anna folded her glasses into her shirt pocket.

If she didn't want to see, who could blame her? He dressed, pulled on his boots, and went past her to lift the lid on the soup. "I better go," filling a bowl, groping through her drawer for a spoon.

Her nod set the chair to rocking slightly.

Standing over the sink, he ate quickly, then grabbed his pack. "'Fare you well,'" he sang from the chorus of "Cassady"—and went out.

chapter 6

Slammed

HEAVEN'S GATE WAS too many movies. Flush with the success of *The Deer Hunter*, Michael Cimino unleashed his ego. Unfortunately, the range wars of the 1880s weren't as compelling as Vietnam, for the audience or perhaps for him—he wandered, having fun with roller skating and frontier life, taking his time setting up the final confrontation. Using Roman military strategy to defeat bad guys in the Wild West must have seemed brilliant on paper, but on screen it was contrived. Was no one on the project capable of saying no? Cimino borrowed the premise from *Shane*, gunmen in dusters from Sergio Leone or *Butch Cassidy*, the mud-and-lumber boomtown from *McCabe and Mrs. Miller*—but those films had proportion. Shooting for an epic, he killed any good movie lurking in its subplots.

Too bad Anna hadn't come—Walt had missed only the opening credits, but no way would he sit through this again—yet it would've been fun to talk about. Instead he loitered in the auditorium till the audience was gone, then started cleaning. A lot of abandoned drinks tonight, so he brought out the mop bucket and nudged it ahead of him down the rows, emptying cups into it before bagging them. He found a wine bottle, a used rubber. A two-by-three-inch ziplock bag of white powder. He held that up, considering. Could be anything.

Romo knew a chemist. Why not find out what it was? So he stuck it in his back pocket and went on working.

In different circumstances, he'd have screened a cartoon for Anna. As it was, he spent just long enough in the projection booth to dump the peanut shells and vacuum—sure missed running movies. When he was done, he turned off everything but the lobby nightlight—at which point he noticed the police car idling in front of Plug. He let himself out, locked up, and turned. One cop was now standing by their car.

"Evening," the guy said.

"Good evening, officer. Just finishing up—I'm the janitor."

Looking at his buddy, the cop nodded, then drilled Walt with a look. "We'd like to talk to you at the station."

"What about?" He was flipping through to his ignition key when the cop flung open the cruiser's back door.

"Get in."

"Huh? What about my car?"

"What about it?" voice hardening. "Let's go," so before anyone put hands on him, Walt climbed in. With him caged in the backseat, the squad car squealed a U-turn and headed for the station, no siren but fast anyway.

Boulder was the last place he'd expect to be hassled. Did they assume, based on his long hair and beard and Plug's paint job, that he had drugs on him? He flashed on the little plastic bag. Would it be enough to draw time? Several beat officers had recently been caught peddling confiscated coke. The chief was countering that image with a "Clean Up the Streets" campaign: arresting panhandlers, charging transients and drunks with vagrancy. Would anyone believe Walt had just found what was in his pocket? Why hadn't he dropped it in the trash?

At the front desk he unloaded change, keys, a crumpled grocery receipt, a book of matches, and from his other back pocket his handkerchief. His peacoat yielded a pen, a wadded napkin, his wallet, two condoms. With all that in a large manila envelope, they had him sign a big book—like a movie character registering at a hotel.

"Frisk him," the desk sergeant said.

The cop detected the ziplock ridge. "Finish emptying your pockets."

Shit. He put the bag on the counter; they all eyed it.

His cold had been waning as he cleaned the theater—motion seemed to help—but now his head felt stuffy again. "I want to talk to a lawyer."

"Oh sure, make your call," the desk cop sneered, setting a heavy phone on the counter. Walt dialed the house; after seven or eight rings, Barbara picked up.

"It's Walt. Um, listen, doesn't Romo have a friend who's a lawyer? I need him at the police station—"

"Now?"

"Soon as he can get here."

He sat in a cold little room hugging his shirt, and looked up when he heard his name. He'd met Lloyd once. He and Romo had run into him downtown and had a beer. He was tall and slim with a neat moustache, a strong square chin, black hair combed straight back from a high forehead—he'd fit right in a William Powell–Myrna Loy *Thin Man* flick.

"What's your story?" Lloyd asked, dragging over a chair so they sat knee to knee.

"Still don't know why they brought me in, but when I was emptying my pockets they found a teeny bag I picked up cleaning."

"What was it?"

"White powder. I didn't open it. There's not very much."

"A gram, you think?"

"Probably." A twenty-eighth of an ounce—so little, but that was the threshold.

"But that's not why they brought you in?"

"I don't see how—it's just something off the theater floor."

Lloyd sat back. "You're in the clear. They might watch you, but they'll have to let this go. Tell 'em you're ready for questions, then I'll take you home."

They were brought to another little room, this one overheated. A detective motioned them to the Formica-topped table and sat opposite looking tired, his limp greasy hair shedding dandruff onto his dark polyester suit coat. He scratched his scalp—Walt wanted to tell him to go wash—his own hair might be undisciplined, but he kept it clean. The guy gestured left; Walt realized the gray blank wall was one-way glass.

"Officer Braden said your car has Maryland plates," the detective began. "Been in town long?"

"I live here."

"Residents are required to register a vehicle within thirty days, and get a Colorado driver's license."

"I didn't get around to it yet." As many out-of-state cars as Boulder had, why was that a big deal?

"Remember this woman?" The guy set down a three-by-five photograph: midthirties, fluffed blonde hair, blue eye-shadow, bright lipstick, slightly puffy cheeks, gray eyes. Dark eyebrows—must dye her hair. Not anyone he'd strike up an acquaintance with.

"I don't think so."

"Ever go to a bar called Joan's Joint?"

"Never heard of it—in Boulder?"

"Lower level on the downtown mall. She met a man there this evening, he bought her a drink, they left together. We think he slipped her something—she came to in an alley—she'd been sexually assaulted."

Hazy, tired, feeling thick headed, Walt couldn't quite grasp why they thought he'd know anything about this unfortunate woman. He looked at Lloyd, who shrugged. So he said, "I was at a friend's house this evening, then I went to the theater to clean it."

The detective shook his head. "You'll have to prove that."

A preposterous notion was seeping through Walt's confusion: *They think I assaulted her.* While he tried to comprehend this, the guy continued,

"Under the circumstances, Mr. Sanders, we plan to keep you in custody." His blue eyes were frigid. "We consider you a flight risk."

Walt blinked at Lloyd, who cleared his throat.

"My client's concerned about being searched when he was brought in. He hasn't been placed under arrest. Will charges be brought for items in his possession?"

He and the detective locked eyes.

"Our concern at the moment is finding this woman's assailant."

"How long do you expect to hold my client?"

"We'll do a lineup tomorrow around noon. If that's a negative, we'll release him."

They all stood. Walt shook Lloyd's hand. This was some bizarre mistake, and he'd be out of here soon, but he sure appreciated Romo's connection. Without a lawyer, he'd feel even more helpless. "Hey, listen—my car's parked in front of the theater—it'll get towed in the morning—could you please ask one of my housemates to bring it home?"

Lloyd turned to the detective. "Will the department release his keys to me?"

The guy nodded. "He can sign 'em over to you."

Lloyd clapped Walt on the shoulder. "Don't worry, man—I'll stop by for the lineup. You'll be all right."

• • •

HE'D NEVER SPENT A night in jail. A cop led him back to a big, fairly crowded cell, pushed a button that rolled the heavy barred door open, and gave him a push. He crossed the threshold, and the door rumbled shut. In one corner, half a dozen Mexicans stood and leaned and crouched, all looking at him. Judging by their clothes, they did painting and construction work. Two were obviously drunk— they might all be—but after sizing him up, they turned back to each other. Beside them, claiming the lone bench, sat a pair of very large men, gone to fat but with huge shoulders and meaty hands, the thickness of their necks making their heads look shrunken. One had blood on his cheek where a cut had opened, the other had a split lip. They looked like twins, and if they hadn't been fighting each other, he felt sorry for whoever'd met those fists. One looked at him dully, the other stared at the floor. In the corner near the door were two street people—he'd seen them on the west fringe of downtown, panhandling—here courtesy of Clean Up the Streets, no doubt.

He felt exposed out in the middle, but the wall was occupied all the way around; he sat on the concrete floor to one side of the door, away from three drunk college boys. A thin mean-looking guy hissed in a furious whisper about his wife and that other guy, "Shoulda killed the bastard and that bitch too, damn 'em"—he seemed two degrees below boiling, heating himself to some outburst. In the last corner two punks slouched, their scruffy mohawks and safety-pinned clothes chosen for shock value.

They reminded Walt of his brother Grant who'd gone punk after seeing Dead Kennedys in San Francisco. He lived in Baltimore now in a crowded rowhouse; they hadn't seen each other for years. Walt had sent the occasional postcard, but moving so much he'd lost touch. One of his intentions in staying put was to reconstruct some bridges—writing and calling family and old friends—but he hadn't. Flight risk. Yeah.

As hours passed, the Mexicans propped against each other to sleep, the punks nodded then jerked awake, on guard. The college kids' conversation grew louder and stupider, and the big guys cast annoyed glances at them. Walt scooted closer to the door, so if they decided to shut them up he'd be out of the way. The street people were fast asleep, content to be someplace warm; the angry guy ran out of huff and put his back to the wall, snoring with his mouth open.

Walt sat watching, and worry invaded his thoughts like the cold soaking into him from the concrete floor. Given the gulf between who he was and the guy they were looking for, he hadn't really taken the detective seriously, but sexual assault was a felony, and only in the pages of civics textbooks did innocence guarantee freedom. Under pressure to find the violator, the cops had picked him. A mistake, but here he was. Right now, Lloyd's certainty about that white powder seemed naïve.

In the morning, a cop came for him, stood him in front of a ruler backdrop with a numbered slate in his hand and took two pictures, front and profile, then fingerprinted him and stuck him back in the cell. A while later, another cop took him to a stagelike room. The lights glared in his eyes where he lined up with four other guys; all had longish hair and jeans. Squinting past the spotlights, he could make out a woman talking to the detective beside her as they studied the lineup.

"See anyone you recognize, ma'am?"

"Not him, I'm pretty sure not him. Could that one turn around?" The cop barked at Walt. He startled, and as commanded, stepped forward and shuffled slowly in a circle. "Maybe?" the woman said. "My head still hurts." She looked over all five suspects, then she and the detective left.

Walt was brought to a room where Lloyd paced, chomping on gum. "Is it time to go?"

"Their lab got an ID on that white powder. It's a knockout drug—starting to show up in what they call 'date rapes.'"

"Oh man, that's really weird."

"Tellin' me," Lloyd said. "Now they want to book you for sexual assault."

"That's—that's impossible. I don't—" The bottom dropped out of his stomach, and he just stared.

"They want another statement, and they want to interview your alibi."

His mind was writhing; this was crazy, but what about Anna? Dragging her into this could be the death blow to the newly hatched Walt and Anna Experience. You'd have to trust someone to weather an accusation like this, and she doubted even her own body.

Whenever his circumstances defied sense, he found himself weighing his life against cosmic purpose, looking for meaning or at least a pattern. But all he saw here was chaos. "So do I have to call her, or give 'em her name, or what?"

"You tell them her name, they contact her."

And she wanted to keep their relationship under wraps—this might even show up in the paper. "How long am I stuck here?"

"A few days, a week maybe, while they round up evidence. If they can't come up with more, they'll let you go. If they charge you, could be a long haul."

"Charge— What about my job?"

Lloyd shook his head. "No concern of theirs. I'll call your employer."

"Let him know right away so he can find a replacement—the theater keys are in the bunch I gave you, on a separate ring."

"Want me to notify anybody else? Your family?"

"No, I don't want to get 'em all stirred up." Who would take it worse? Mom would be upset, but she'd know he wouldn't assault anyone. But in Dad's world, you either walked the straight and narrow, or you were capable of anything. For him, a guy who would smoke pot would rape someone. The small blessing in all this was he wouldn't find out unless Walt told him. "Only call them if I'm charged—but I can't imagine—"

"The department's just trying to put a case together. You're their strongest suspect, with the victim picking you from the lineup."

Walt closed his eyes a moment, hoping he'd open them onto a different scene. No such luck. "Anyone move my car?"

"I think Barbara did." Lloyd looked at him enviously. "She's *something.*"

"Barbara's my friend and confessor." He reached into his empty pocket. "What do I owe you?"

"So far, I'm doing Romo a favor—he thinks you're being hassled because of how you look."

Walt shook his head. "I think I've incurred the wrath of the cosmos. Assaulting a woman? That's so far off-base, it's a joke."

"I'd wait to laugh, if I were you."

chapter 7

Anna Karenina

ANNA'D NEVER HAD this much trouble with ladders. Stefan coached her when she started, concerned she might not be strong enough but wanting her to succeed. That alone had made this job worthwhile—his confidence in her was the spark for her own. He was maybe five years older, brotherly not paternalistic. After that London debacle, she felt she'd landed in a safe spot He'd showed her how to move a ladder so the weight was manageable, and she understood the physics of it, but today six inches of snow complicated things. She snagged her boot on a garden hose while carrying the extended ladder, which swung quickly from vertical, coming down on her shoulder with a stinging blow. She hadn't dropped a ladder for months—made her feel like a rank beginner. She'd hurt tomorrow, but right now she had a job to get done. Gritting her teeth, she levered the ladder back upright and crossed the patio to position it for the next set of windows.

She'd climbed halfway up when its feet slid, the upper ends whacking down the siding as she dropped her bucket, clinging to the rungs in panic. The feet hit some obstacle beneath the snow and halted, and finally her fingers agreed to loosen so she could climb down. "I should be getting hazardous duty pay," she muttered as she examined where the feet had stopped. The ladder had slid off the icy concrete and was now planted firmly in the dirt—she extended it two more notches so she could reach the windows. At least the padded tops of the uprights hadn't marred the siding. She took tiny comfort in realizing the only damage was to herself—bruises to her shoulder and now, to her dignity. Back inside the house she refilled her bucket with warm water and soap, then steeled herself to finish those second-story outsides.

This job would've been tough even after a decent night's sleep—which she didn't get. Toward morning she'd nodded out in her rocker—didn't even want to lie down in the bed Walt had vacated. She was relieved he'd left, but it felt like he'd ditched her. Not "See you later," but "Farewell"? Finishing the outsides exhausted her, but by noon thirty, with storms stacked against walls throughout the house, three-fourths of the job remained. After a bite of lunch, she called the office, but Stefan wasn't there. He never was; Karen expected him to check in soon.

She began upstairs, storms then insides, putting each window back together as she finished, plodding—the first bedroom, the second. In the bathroom, a triangular wicker shelf unit with a million things on it—hairpins and barrettes and makeup and nail polish and a dish of potpourri—snagged on her shirttail and fell, dumping across the floor. The flimsy thing had a cracked leg and didn't want to stand back up. She piled everything including the broken dish on the bathmat to deal with later. The doorbell chimed. Stefan stood there, grinning, full of energy. Pleasing people and selling his services were his favorite things.

He picked up on her low mood instantly. "What's wrong, Anna?"

"I don't know if I can finish here today—I had trouble with the outsides."

His brow knotted. "How far'd you get?"

"I still have half the upstairs, all the downstairs, and the French doors."

"You're taking too long—this is an easy job."

"Stefan, I'm having a terrible day," squinching her eyes to keep from crying.

Immediately sympathetic, he gave her a hug, patting her back. "You've been hurting all week. Sit down, talk a minute."

So she told him about overhearing Walt at Bookhead. Stefan didn't remember; had no reason to. But as she explained about Walt's old lover, he got the picture.

"He stuck around just long enough to make me care, and now he's gone."

He stood up. "That's a shame, Anna. But sympathy won't get these windows washed. Now, realistically, will you be done by five?"

He always said he'd rather know the bad news right off than hear some rosy report followed by a call from an irate customer. "Maybe by seven," she said.

He sighed. "It'll be dark before that, and you know you have to see windows to get them clean. I don't have time, but I'll do storms while you do insides."

"Thank you, Stefan," she said, thinking she'd rather be yelled at than coddled.

He filled another bucket so he could work downstairs while she finished the bedrooms. His skill was a wonder. He could squeegee a window in one quick graceful pass, catching drips as he went, ending at the opposite corner with the whole pane clean and dry. If she worked that fast, there'd be streaks everywhere. With the storms done, he took over the dining room table to telephone customers about bids and schedule estimates. After calling the office, he informed Anna the police wanted to talk to her—at the station.

That was strange. "What for?"

"Karen didn't know," he said, "but finish up here first. Keep the truck tonight—you have to meet me in Hunt Ridge at 8:30 tomorrow—construction cleanup. I'll leave your job sheet in the truck. Want me to load the ladder?"

"Would you please? I'm not pulling my weight here today, I'm really sorry."

"Everyone has bad days," he smiled. "Just don't have 'em all the time."

"I won't."

Collecting his dog-eared schedule book, pager, and estimate binder, he turned to her. "If it's a problem, with the police? Call me at home."

He headed out. As she put the storms in the last window upstairs, she heard the ladder rattling, the truck door closing, his car zooming away. Stefan did everything fast—drive, work, eat, talk—and better than most people; he belonged in the dictionary under "whiz."

With time pressure relieved, she got into a rhythm that had her done by four. She propped the shelf unit back up and put things on it as best she could recall, leaving the broken dish with a note beside the invoice on the kitchen counter.

Driving downtown she tried to imagine what the police could want—was Harold in trouble, and called her rather than have the folks find out? He got fired once for being hot-headed—argued with a supervisor and told him off. He'd never had a boss he respected. Did he pick a fight? Or get busted? Dad wouldn't bail him out if it was a drug charge. Did Harold think she had money socked away? By the time she stood at the counter inside the station, she was convinced the call was about her brother. The cop buzzed the intercom, and shortly a man in a suit came out.

"I'm Detective Finerty. I need to ask you some questions about yesterday, specifically last night."

She hadn't seen Harold for weeks. "What's the problem?"

"We were given your name by a Mr. Sanders."

"Who?" A mistake…

"Come with me, please." As she followed, he said, "He didn't know your last name, so maybe you don't know his—Walter?"

"Oh. Walt? What's going on?" That car of his had to be a police magnet.

"Sit in here." They entered a small room; he shut the door, pulled out a chair for her on one side of a table, and seated himself opposite. The chair, pink molded hard plastic seat and a strip for back support, with splayed tubular steel legs, evoked its own set of memories. Junior high chemistry lab. Breaking the test tube halfway through the week of experiments. While she shook off thoughts of failure, the man explained they'd picked up Walt at the Atheneum. "He said he was with you last night."

The detective had a neutral manner, not sneering or aggressive—it was easy to explain about their drawing class, and making soup. "I guess it was 9:30 or 10 when he left."

"Where was he going?"

"The theater—he was going to watch the movie, then clean."

"He's been implicated in an assault. The victim identified him in a lineup today."

"Assault? That doesn't sound—"

"Drugged and raped. He had the stuff in his pocket when we brought him in."

His words were so unexpected she couldn't process them at all. "What drug?" When they'd been stoned, she could see all the way inside him. "When?" she asked faintly.

"The victim met her assailant in a bar shortly after ten p.m. She was found unconscious in an alley about eleven."

As though she were back on that ladder, sliding suddenly on ice she couldn't see, her whole system clenched—muscles, lungs, heart, nerves—and her brain froze up—was he saying—? This detective had to be wrong but—"Did you say 'identified'?"

"Out of five in a lineup—yes ma'am."

She thought she'd vomit but just stomach acid came up, burning her esophagus. "That can't be right," she whispered, throat raw.

"How well do you know him?"

"He's my, um," then thought of Barbara's word *ummer*—but that wouldn't mean anything to the detective. "Um, friend." But was he? If she'd been that wrong about him, she couldn't ever trust anyone again; it would mean all her perceptions were some fantasy. All her instincts, wrong? All her life lessons learned at such cost, worthless? Logic elbowed its way through her shock, protesting. Why would he pick up some stranger? And unconscious? Like screwing a corpse? That was crazy. "No," she said firmly. "Couldn't have been him."

"He's in custody—would you like to speak to him?"

In a stupor, she nodded.

He conducted her through a maze of fluorescent-lit bare halls into a clear-walled room divided in half by heavy Plexiglas. He closed the door on her side and she looked at the high ceiling with the sprinkler head directly above her, thinking this was like some trap in a movie where the enclosure collapses or floods or fills with smoke and the hero barely gets out, snagging his clothes to make the escape more hair-raising. She moved to the partition, watching angled and reflected kaleidoscopic facets of Walt approach—kind of like *Nude Descending a Staircase*, she thought. She'd always figured the painting represented movement through time. Was it a view through a prism instead? But as he arrived, the facets resolved into just Walt. He put his hands on the dividing wall—he sure looked ragged and tired.

"Thanks for coming," he said, his voice muted by the slats of the metal speaker.

She put up her palms to match his, an inch of Plexiglas between them. Now that she was meeting his eyes, that detective's words seemed nonsense. "Walt, I couldn't sleep last night—did you mean 'farewell'?"

"You wanted me gone, didn't you?"

"I—guess I'm not used to the idea of, of someone—"

He nodded. "You can stop worrying about Thanksgiving. Looks like the cops have solved that one for me."

"Really? You're going to be here that long?" End of next week?

"Either they'll catch whoever assaulted that woman, or find something that lets me off—or keep me. I'll be the last to know."

"Can I get you anything?"

"Looks like I'm gonna have time for a long novel—been planning to read *Gravity's Rainbow*."

"What about *Anna Karenina*?"

"Tolstoy? I've never—"

She couldn't suppress a little smile, which his lips mirrored. "My full name's Anna Karenina Brubaker."

He tossed his head, exactly like a horse just out of its bridle. "Really? Mine's Walter Foster Sanders—WFS, which I've concluded stands for What Fucking Stupidity."

"No," she laughed, "it's We're Fools Silly." Abruptly she was warm all over.

He looked directly into her eyes. "*Anna Karenina*, huh? All I know is she threw herself under a train."

"Then you better find out why."

• • •

WALT SANK INTO DEJECTED boredom in his cell. This was better than the tank. He had this little bunker all to himself, with a slab to lie on—not comfortable, but he wouldn't expect that. Funny the way he and Anna kept turning in this dance, away then back together. When he got out of here, he should stay far away from her, but they'd given each other a lift—she must've had a crappy day too. Last night, her nurture had suggested she was coming around, accepting his affection—until she retreated into herself as though she'd been chased there by some inner cop. Maybe he was like nicotine: a little would give her a high, later she'd want more. But too much all at once was poison.

"Hey hairboy," said the guard, his shoes loud on the tile floor, echoing off dozens of hard surfaces. Jail architecture must be a master class in human discomfort—buzzing fluorescent lights that made even the healthiest people look dead, right angles everywhere, no distinction between day and night, gray-palette-reject colors: gray-green, gray-pink, gray-brown. No privacy, nothing soft or warm. The guard extended a thick hardback through the bars.

"Thank you." Walt opened the cover. Inside was inscribed, *You've always been Anna Karenina—time to meet her. Love, Mom and Dad. September 6th, 1974.* Closing the book, he held it against his chest as though it had a heartbeat. Aware of the guard staring, he nodded. The guy walked away. Walt settled his spine against the cold painted cinder blocks and began to read.

• • •

ANNA LEFT HER APARTMENT only for work, then came straight home, dejection folding around her. Why would they keep Walt in jail if their accusations were baseless? Sure, police made mistakes like anybody, but what if she'd been wrong about him? After all their joy, raping a stranger made no sense, but didn't people always say they had no idea, when confronted with ugly secrets about someone they thought they knew? Psychopaths were supposedly very persuasive, with more energy than normal people. That certainly fit; having sex with him had been so intense. If he was still there Saturday, she decided she'd visit for another look.

She dreamed. *His eyes were red suns flickering with menace. "It's not what you know about someone, it's what you don't know,"* he said smugly. *"Ever wonder why I've been on the road so long? Only an idiot would take at face value what I've told you."* Then he said it was her fault he raped that woman—she wanted him to leave, didn't she? What was wrong with her, couldn't she make up her mind? Every word pushed her further—down an alley, around a corner, into

a courtyard stinking of garbage, a light in a third-story window drawing her attention. A plate flew out, falling in an arc, shouts exploding
with its shatter as though the plate were cursing, jagged pieces flying
at her. She woke trembling with her teeth clenched.

Despite the dream, she kept hearing his voice small and sad, saying if she didn't trust him she didn't trust herself either. That felt true.

Arriving Saturday at the detention center five minutes before
the posted visiting hours, she signed in, then waited, watching the
second hand move on the wall clock, pulling the minute hand one
tick each time it passed twelve. But it was fifteen minutes before a
guard finally came for her.

Walt stood close to the divider. Today he was more present-
able—someone had lent him a comb—but worn and blue and
lonesome—exactly the way she felt. She wanted to slap herself for
doubting; his gaze welcomed her scrutiny.

"How's the book coming?" she said finally.

"I finished it last night. Wow—must be scary, being named
after her."

"My parents liked her independence. They met in a lit class, and
my dad's admiration for Anna when the other guys thought she was
just melodramatic convinced Mom to marry him."

"There's a line I copied down—when everything's falling apart
for her and she's afraid she's lost Vronsky, Anna says to him *Respect
was invented to fill the empty place where love ought to be!*"

"Is that what respect is?" she asked. "Second best?"

"She makes a good case." He leaned his forehead against the
partition.

"But the book doesn't end there." She took refuge in talking
about it. "It ends with Levin's struggle with faith and purpose."

"Tolstoy was right," he said. "Inventing meaning without believing it is just an exercise—as if faith has no power. To me, God isn't
abstract, God is everything—matter, energy, the vibrations we call
thoughts that spill out as words, the behavior of individuals and
cultures, the charged space between our atoms."

"Sounds pretty abstract to me."

"People and animals, soup, rocks, air—everything. Not abstract
at all."

"Then what's the purpose?" she asked.

"God's evolving through us. Every time we act with what Tolstoy called goodness, that's evolution. There's only one rule in my religion—Treat everyone the way you want to be treated."

"So how do you treat someone who's abused you?" She needed to know what he was going to do when his old girlfriend made an appearance.

"You want them to leave you alone, so you leave them alone."

"Does that work?" Sounded unlikely.

He puffed out a breath abruptly, giving her a hunted look. "Not always."

She shook her head, under her breath said, "I wish—"

"Me too." He shrugged.

She felt like a visitor at the zoo, which made her want to leave. "Are they letting you out soon?"

"How would I know? I gave 'em a sperm sample yesterday. My lawyer says once they test it, they'll either charge me or let me go."

"When's that? It's already Saturday."

"Monday maybe? The lab's probably closed weekends."

"Want something else to read?"

"I want to draw—my pack's in my car." As she backed toward the door, he said, "Hey, thanks for the book, and for coming."

"Sure, see you later." She pushed the buzzer, and the guard let her out. At the front desk, she asked, "Can I give an inmate pencils and a drawing pad?"

The cop frowned. "No pencils longer than three inches, no wire in the pad."

At Walt's house she knocked on the kitchen door—no response. She waited, then tested the doorknob: unlocked. She opened it, calling, "Anybody home?"

"Hold on," a female voice called, then Barbara stepped into the room in a t-shirt and undies, blonde hair damp from washing. Seeing her, Anna felt grungy. "Hi, c'mon in—what's up?"

"I just saw Walt. He wants his drawing stuff from his car."

"Be right back." She whisked out of the room, Anna glimpsing painted toenails. Was Laura like her—beautiful, poised? Competing was impossible—how'd she get tangled up with him anyway? Anna's misery was flourishing now, a rosebush with dozens of blooms, spent or full or still buds—inadequacy, naïveté, failure. It should've clicked with Cory. Meeting him was great, their letters enthusiastic; in her heart, it was a done deal. Then she got there, only to find out the ground had shifted. Cory couldn't understand it either. What should've worked, didn't. But he had work, a busy life. She had nothing except him.

Since his job took him to another city, he only showed up at his London flat on weekends. She thought that would allow her to get to know him gradually, as if they were dating, but it turned out she was just living in someone else's space, tiptoeing around his stuff, leaving no trace of her presence. Being human furniture made her easier to disregard, though she only realized that later. After a week in some hotel, he wanted to be home, but feeling trapped there she wanted to go out. They couldn't stop clashing—the kinship they'd constructed on paper was imaginary.

Every detail was a struggle. If she called him from the pay phone downstairs, she had to have her handful of coins ready to press into the slot, its fast insistent beeping making her frantically clumsy, the connection lost before she could buy another two minutes. Stores didn't sell peanut butter—considered pig food—and the strong bitter coffee was nothing like the American brew; what they called orange juice was a neon blend of chemicals. The cinema that showed films she wanted to see was far away and she was afraid to venture out alone after dark, sitting instead behind heavy curtains listening to the nightly ritual of drunks smashing bottles in the street. She hated broken glass, but it was more plentiful than dirt.

Where was the natural world anyway? In the park at the end of the street with its tumor-warted trees, the weedy ground winking with shards? In the well-groomed large parks with artificial waterways, where if she sat on a bench more than five minutes some guy tried to pick her up? Nature was domesticated, the air used so many times it had no energy left to nourish lungs and brain. When a flash flood in the Rockies made the *London Times*, she longed to be in the vicinity of such a storm, not stuck in Blandsville where it rained or else didn't, every day neither hot nor cold, the sky somewhere between white and gray, nights empty of moon or stars.

Barbara, now wearing form-fitting green painter pants, bounced back into the kitchen, a set of car keys in hand. She brought in Walt's pack, and while Anna applied the point of a kitchen knife to remove blank pages from the pad, said matter-of-factly, "No need to be shy—he doesn't have anything going with me."

"Oh, I—" Blushing, she focused on chopping one of his pencils into thirds, sharpening the stubs, then bundling them with his eraser in a plastic bag. "He's out of reading material—what's a good book?"

"*Hitchhiker's Guide to the Galaxy* by Douglas Adams: Monty Python in outer space. Even if he's read those, he'll enjoy them again."

"A little humor'd be good," Anna agreed.

"Let me grab a couple." She was back in a moment with two paperbacks, and said, "Walk with me."

On their way to the Justice Center, Barbara quizzed her about Perfectly Clean, a business she knew was part of Boulder's Tibetan Buddhist community—she had definite opinions. "They're all compensating," she declared. "About three-quarters are Bu-ish."

"What's that?"

"Buddhist-Jewish."

Like Stefan. "Why?"

"They crave hierarchy and structure, just not the one they inherited."

Anna pondered that. "I did a meditation weekend in trade for some work—I liked it, although somebody said I should have a red and yellow cushion not a black one. Like anybody's butt could tell the difference." They laughed together, and she felt better.

At the prefab concrete building, Barbara opened the door. Anna, who'd sort of planned on coming in, didn't want to be there with her. She felt too confused and exposed to stand next to Walt's gorgeous housemate, wondering what he thought.

Seeing her hesitate, Barbara flashed the patient smile a mother gives her kid for doing something harmlessly dumb. "Don't worry so much," she admonished, and went in.

On her way home, Anna thought about that. Worrying was a reflex: anticipating disappointment. Should she be laughing instead? Walt said silliness was his salvation. Maybe she could enjoy their relationship by ignoring whether it made sense. Or was that just the blurred logic of being nearsighted?

chapter 8

Mouth of a Criminal

MONDAY AFTERNOON WALT was rereading *Hitchhiker's Guide* when the guard opened his cage; books and drawing materials under one arm, he followed him out to the front. Lloyd stood by as the detective handed Walt his envelope.

While he reloaded his pockets, Lloyd said, "They're not giving that white powder back."

"Wasn't mine anyhow, just hitched a ride."

"C'mon, I'll take you home." They went out to Lloyd's high-mileage '64 BMW as he explained, "They picked up a better suspect Saturday. His sperm was a match."

"Lucky for me."

"Damn straight—otherwise they weren't gonna let you go."

"Now I really owe you."

"You're unemployed. The theater manager said he was hiring somebody else."

"Oh, right." Money was gonna be tight till he could hustle up work, but it was a chance to do something different. He'd been more broke than this: had enough traveler's checks to cover December rent, could even sell Plug as a last resort—not panic time yet. "But give me a bill—I'll come up with it, five bucks at a time if I have to."

"Forget it; it was a favor to Romo. If he wants something out of you, it's his to collect. I don't need it."

"You sure?"

Lloyd pulled onto the gravel beside the house. "You could put in a good word for me with Barbara."

"I'll tell her you're a decent guy, but I can't—"

"Just help me with some visibility. I'll take it from there."

Walt's room was chillier than the cell, but it had that human touch—he lay back on his mattress enjoying the give. When Lucy tapped on his door, he sat up, inviting her in.

"So is everything cool?" she asked. "Did they drop charges?"

"There never were any."

"Does that go on your record then? Y'know—when you apply for a job and it says were you ever arrested?"

He pondered: he'd been detained for questioning, and finally released. Innocent until proven guilty, right? "I don't think so." He stood up. "I do need work, though. Any ideas?"

"Stu bought the Sunday paper—it should still be in the living room."

Help Wanted had the usual listings—security guard, journeyman carpenter, paralegal, nurse's aide, school bus driver. Hm. He'd never driven a bus, but people learned. The pay wasn't bad, though he knew the hours were chopped up—stints morning, noon, and afternoon, with the occasional field trip to liven it up—but at least it wouldn't be seven days a week. Ah, here was an immediate money-maker—phone book delivery. He called: Yes they still had lots of routes open, he could work as much as he liked. Pay was by the route, he'd need his own car.

He put in his bus driver application first; they said if he qualified they'd call in a week to start him on the license process. From there, he drove to the directory distribution site, a warehouse north of town where they made him watch a training film featuring a guy who was fined ten bucks a pop for leaving directories in mailboxes—those were property of the Postal Service—the poor guy had to do three more routes just to break even. And beware of dogs: the company assumed no liability if some territorial mutt bit him. He chose two routes, and the warehouse man helped him load plastic-wrapped bundles filling Plug's trunk, backseat, even the passenger seat and floor. Another hour before sundown; might as well get started. His first route included Anna's house. As daylight was failing, he put a book on the porch upstairs, then knocked on her door.

She opened it a little way.

"Your phone directory, ma'am," he said in a flat nasal voice.

"Oh, thank you," her eyes crinkling as she pretended not to know him; she stepped back, opening the door wide. "Would you put it over there, please?"

Lifting her phone, he slid the book underneath.

"Want some dinner?" she offered.

"Ah, dinner. Is it Starch Medley in Hamburger Grease like they serve at the local House of Bars?"

"No," she laughed, "it's Piled Toast."

Leaning against the sink, he watched her monitor two slabs of brown bread in her toaster oven. When they were done, she spread them with peanut butter, then slices of sharp cheddar and apple, heaped on cottage cheese, and topped that with clumps of alfalfa sprouts. She handed Walt his plate, and they sat side by side on her bed to eat.

Seemed like an efficient way to get all the components of a meal, he thought, *and if you were neat about it, not much to clean up.*

When the phone rang, she told whoever it was she'd call back.

"Who was that?" He realized too late he was butting in.

"My friend Burke. You have to meet him."

"You said I wasn't second fiddle," giving her a crestfallen look.

"Burke's my buddy." She sat back down, talking between bites. "We argue about art and music. He was my Friday night date when I was strung out writing to Cory. We invented a game called bounce-ket-ball—basketball played with a superball."

"I love superballs," he said, heart rebounding off her cheer.

"You have superballs." She ducked to hide her face.

He waited for her blush to subside but color was still climbing her neck, up to her ears. Clearing his throat, he went to the sink. "Thanks, that was good," putting dish soap on her sponge to wash his plate. There were mugs in the sink so he washed those too, rinsing them, giving her time. "Want me to go?" casually, as though he were asking where she stored dishes. No answer, so he looked over—she was still sitting on the bed, one knee up, forehead against it, arms around her shin. He came over. "Should I go?"

She nodded.

"Thanks for dinner—first decent meal this week." Then in his nasal tone, "Take care of that phone directory, ma'am—won't get another for a year." He kissed where her hair began its whorl at the back of her head, then went out, closing her door gently.

● ● ●

WHICH DIRECTION WAS SHE supposed to jump? He was like a superball, bouncing at her from every which way, surprising her so she couldn't follow through her plan to shun him. Sex had unhinged her—she'd be on a ladder and the rush of heat from her groin would make her dizzy; she'd have to hold on till the wave passed. Or she'd be driving across town and suddenly have no idea where she was or how she got there—after growing up here?

She put on her boots, buttoned her cowboy coat, and went walking. Her feet took her downtown, and finding a pay phone she called Burke. He wasn't really doing anything, just thinking about music; they agreed to meet at the record store. While watching for him, she leafed through Joni Mitchell albums, then the Grateful Dead. When her short rotund friend showed up, he had a baby-faced smile for her. They cruised the jazz section together, and after some debate he bought a Keith Jarrett solo piano album. From there they walked to Bookhead and browsed the bargain table. She picked up *Paris Was Yesterday* by Janet Flanner, a memoir of Gertrude Stein's circle of artists and writers. After paying thirty cents for it, she joined Burke in the coffee worship café.

When the owner first put in tables and started selling coffee, Bookhead was an ordinary place. Then he hired a guy with guru pretensions who figured out how to make the grinding of coffee beans, the measuring into a filter, and especially the slow and delicate introduction of boiling water to the nest of grounds, into a ceremony. A certain sector of Boulder society loved ritual, so pretty soon his self-absorbed performance had a steady audience. That became a nuisance for people who only wanted something to sip while they talked, because you could seldom just walk up and buy coffee—the devotees were in line, jockeying for that first cup from a fresh pot, and by the time they'd all been served there wasn't any left and the guy had to clean everything with meditative care before he'd start over. You had to really want coffee; it could take half an hour. Anna thought that was ridiculous but Bookhead was a good hangout, and only customers could sit in the café. So she and Burke waited, and finally took their cups to a window table where they could see up and down the street.

"What've you been up to, Anna? I haven't seen you."

"Burke, you gotta help me," hanging her head. "I'm in love."

"You should change your name—it makes you do tragic foolish things."

"Change it to what?"

"Annie Oakley."

"Think I should be shootin' 'em instead of fallin' for 'em?" She mimicked aiming a rifle, squinting down the barrel.

"Yeah. It's gotta be simpler."

"Anyway, he, um, we—"

"Um?" he teased.

She nodded.

He laughed, then she did. "Good um?"

"So good. Ummm."

"You silly girl. You're not happy if you're not in love, but being in love makes you so miserable. How miserable are you?"

"Almost fell off a ladder."

"Don't do that—he can't be worth breaking your leg."

But that reminded her Walt had broken his leg, though he hadn't said how it happened. They'd told each other just enough to prove to the demons of history they weren't forgotten, then tiptoed away from the inferno.

"You should meet him," she said. "What are you doing for Thanksgiving?"

"My parents are having me over. What about you?"

"I'm house-sitting—my folks'll be out of town."

"Join us," he said. "I'll tell my mom—then after dinner we'll escape and do something fun. I got a new keyboard, and you can play pedal steel."

His offer was tempting—she loved the wails even a novice could coax from the strings with that smooth heavy slide. "I haven't decided."

"Today's Monday—you don't have that long to make up your mind."

"Sure I do. I can change my plans fifty times between now and Thursday."

"But you won't have time to grocery shop. When are your parents leaving?"

"Thursday morning early."

"So I'll come to your house, and we'll bake. Pumpkin—what else? You could make pecan pie." Burke loved high-calorie desserts.

"I can't stand that, or mince pie." She frowned at her coffee. "Anyway, I might be busy."

"Too bad," but now he was gazing at her longingly. "I want a piece of mocha swirl cheesecake at the deli. Would you split one with me?"

"I can't have cheesecake without coffee, and this is my quota."

She watched him purse his lips, disappointed. He loved doing things he shouldn't, and she was his partner in crime. That way he could say it was her fault, he had no intention of eating all that heavy stuff but she made him… But she didn't want to play tonight. She sighed.

"Change your name," he said. "I'll bring a rifle and help you drive him off."

"No!" The word bursting out so quick and hard startled them both.

He sat back with a mocking grin. "Well all righty. Does he know your name?"

"He just finished the book."

"And didn't run screaming?"

"He couldn't—he was in jail."

He shook his head in disapproval. "What are you doing with a jailbird?"

"He's not—it was a horrible mistake. He's out now."

"Jails are filled with innocent people," he said sarcastically. "The criminals are all at large."

"You should meet him, Burke. He's a nice guy."

"I think I better. Cory was perfect, and where's he?"

"Don't talk about that."

"That's what you'll be saying six months from now about what's-his-name."

"Walt."

"Walt. You'll ask why I didn't stop you, and I'll have to say I didn't even know till it was too late." He gave her a calculating look. "You're already in over your head."

She nodded. "I drowned."

"I see. So you're hedging about Thursday because maybe he'll ask you to join him, or you'll have him over. My only question is, does he have to wait till the last minute when you finally make up your mind, or are you gonna invite then uninvite him twenty times?"

"Sounds awful when you say it like that."

"It *is*." He slapped the table. "Don't jerk him around," putting her on notice she was mistreating Walt, wanting him so much then chasing him off. She was floundering—how'd Walt get away with declaring himself spineless, leaving it all up to her? "So when do I meet him?"

"Wednesday? We can have cheesecake at the deli, all three of us."

"Finally, a decision. What time?"

"Umm... Eight?"

"Eight's good," he agreed. "Want a ride home?"

"Walk with me."

"But my truck's here."

"Then walk back and get it. You need the exercise."

"That's true." Burke stood, putting on his down vest. "If we're walking, let's go."

At her apartment, she showed him her drawings—he complimented the one of stairs at the Chautauqua dining hall, another of the locomotive in the park. She made ginger tea, offering him the rocker while she sat on her army bunk.

"Get another chair, Anna, so he can sit someplace besides your bed."

"I never thought of that."

"You don't think of things that are right in front of you—how can I trust your judgment? How do I know you didn't fall for the mouth of a criminal?"

"He's not a criminal."

"Says you. Where's he from?"

"Maryland, and California, and all over."

He grimaced. "Why's he here?"

"He was a student, came back to live."

"What'd he study?"

"I don't know."

"I'm gonna ask him five hundred questions, because you didn't. You should be a nun, Anna Karenina," wagging a finger at her. "Save a lot of people a lot of grief."

"Be nice about it."

"Sure—I'll ask you questions too."

"No, don't embarrass me—"

"But you blush so extravagantly; it's my favorite thing you do."

As though it heard him, blood ran to her face like excited children to the window—what? what?

"I need to know more about him, Anna. You never knew a guy in jail before."

"He's harmless."

"Not to you."

"Besides that," dismissing her own well-being with a wave of her hand.

But he'd run out of reassurances. "So do I have to walk back to my truck alone? I'll get cold with no one to talk to."

"I'll come with."

"Then how will you get home?"

"You can drive me." Laughing, they headed downtown.

chapter 9
Shouldn't Isn't Can't

"**AS OF THIS** moment there can be no illegal substances or activities in this house, or discussion of them over this phone line," Romo announced at their house meeting the Tuesday before Thanksgiving.

"What's up?" Pick said.

"The boys in blue are looking this way—wouldn't be surprised if they show up with a search warrant. They must find *nothing*." His glare was enough to raise blisters as he looked at each housemate in turn. "No pot." He looked particularly hard at Pick. "Can you comply?"

Pick consulted his fingernails. "Uh, I dunno. What if I bring someone over, and they have some?"

"Nope. Nobody here with even a roach, a used pipe—"

"Aw, man, I don't think so."

"Then you better move. I'm going to a Dead concert in Houston, Thanksgiving morning till Sunday. When I get back you gotta be gone."

"Shit," Pick muttered.

"Lucy?" Romo turned his hawk stare on her.

"I'll keep my stash someplace else." She liked coke.

"Walt?"

"It's about gone—I'll find someone to hold it for me." His friend Tom, he thought.

"Sorry guys."

"For how long?" Barbara asked.

"I don't know. They might wait a couple months, then pull a surprise raid figuring we'll have something around. So we better not."

Later, Walt stopped by Romo's room. "Going out of business?"

"I have to—gotta lay low."

"Did I put 'em onto you?" Couldn't help feeling that way.

"It's an occupational hazard. Like they say about motorcycles—if you ride long enough, you *will* have an accident."

"Lloyd wouldn't take any money for the legal help, said he owed you a favor—so I guess I do. Want me to move out?"

"No, this is not a good time to start looking for housemates." Romo reflected. "You could paint your car."

"Paint it how?"

"Red, or green, or blue. One color." He was serious.

"OK."

"And get Colorado plates. You lost your job, right?"

Walt told him about his prospects.

"Maybe I'll drive a school bus too. I need a legit income." Romo stretched till his shoulders popped. "It's hard to know when to quit. Gamblers don't—they get up a little, can't stop playing till it's gone. I have to walk away clean. I don't care about the money, I don't even care about the dope. Right now, I'm thinking about my freedom. How was life in the can, Walt?"

"Bad. You're absolutely right, Romo." Walt thought about what he had to do. "Hope the weather warms up so I can paint Plug myself. I can't even afford Earl Scheib."

"Stu knows a guy at a body shop—maybe you can finagle some indoor time over the holiday."

"Good idea."

"Sooner's better." Romo pulled his heavy red-gold braid over his shoulder and examined the end. "I feel like I'm sittin' on a live wire. Either I move or my ass is fried." He frowned. "Pick's gotta go—can you make sure he leaves?"

"Thought you made it clear."

"He's such a stoner, I'll get back from Houston and have to plant his sorry ass in a snowbank and pile his shit on top of him—no thanks. See, I think they'll be waiting when I drive up—I really do."

"Why not stay in Houston then?"

"Texas? Are you kidding? No, they can play their little game, but they ain't catchin' me." Romo sighed. "Paint your car and get Pick gone, and I'll consider Lloyd paid off."

"It's a deal."

• • •

WALT DROVE OUT TO Devero Auto Body. Chet Devero was a wiry tightly wound guy in his midthirties with stained hands and a pompadour, who said his wife had invited her mother and sister to help cook all day Thanksgiving, so he planned to be at the shop, catching up on paperwork. He even had some paint he'd sell cheap— a custom color the client rejected—supposed to look gold but it came out babyshit-brown.

He had a laugh when he saw Walt's car. "Sure you wanna paint over all this?"

"It's time."

"What about a haircut?"

"Hadn't planned on it." They circled Plug together, Devero scuffing the paint with a penknife here and there.

"Don't have to scrape. Minimal trim—not a big masking job. Put grease in the keyholes before you mask 'em—if paint gets in you gotta replace your locks. I'd say—" he rubbed the back of his neck and circled the car again, "five or six hours. Dunno how this'll take paint."

"Who'll be here?"

"You'll do the prep, everything I tell ya, and when it's ready I'll run the sprayer. Once it's dry you get to unmask and clean up. Got plans for Thanksgiving?"

"No."

"Well, I'm leaving at three. If you're not done, you'll have to finish outside."

"Will it be dry?"

"Dries quick—should be. See ya at eight Thursday." They shook hands. "Oh, and cash for the paint."

"Traveler's check OK?"

Devero squinted at him. "Only one kinda cash I know of."

• • •

WALT RESUMED PHONE BOOK deliveries, feeling odd: he'd started a landslide and now everything was shifting around him, going down. He'd knocked Anna loose from whatever was anchoring her, then his encounter with the law had started a second maybe bigger slide—Romo shifting gears, the prospect of getting busted, and now he was ready to paint over his past. Maybe Devero was right about his hair. If he looked clean-cut and had a serious job, Anna might— But by the time he finished his route, the barbershop was closed.

He was thinking about dinner when Anna called. She said, "My friend Burke wants to meet you. Join us tonight for cheesecake at eight downtown."

So he asked Barbara if she'd ever cut hair.

"No, but my friend Rita does. She might be around this weekend."

"I mean now."

"What's going on, Walt?"

"Can't you feel the earthquake?"

"Romo's really freaked out—in two years I've never seen him like this."

"He's smart to quit now. Houston'll be his last hurrah."

She grinned. "Wish you were going?"

"Nope. I have business here: paint my car, get Pick on his way—" He almost said "propose." What a ridiculous idea, but that's what he wanted to do: kiss Anna's fingers and ask her *please please*—

Barbara was watching his face change, amused. "That girl's really under your skin."

• • •

AN HOUR LATER, WALT sat on a stool in Rita's kitchen, shaving mirror in hand. She was from the Bay Area too—had the same luminous palomino skin as Barbara, though with auburn not blonde hair.

"How do you want it cut?" she asked, working her comb through his tangles.

"Short."

"With all this beard?"

When he left Santa Cruz he'd just let it grow—told people shaving was a hassle on the road, but the truth was, the vigor of his hair kept him from noticing how everything inside had stunted and died.

"Hell, why not?" he said finally.

"Then do that first, so I can cut your hair based on your face—there's stuff in the bathroom."

It felt very strange to be using someone else's bathroom, sink, shaving cream, razor—but he felt like a traveler, hitchhiking through, heading for new territory. The attention people gave his car had provided him a nomad's niche, helping him hustle work. Plug was still broadcasting that message, which his shagginess reinforced. Time to present himself as a man with purpose. He turned his left cheek toward the mirror and scraped. He didn't crave the mainstream but he wasn't going to avoid it anymore, if it went where he wanted to go. His moustache went last. Once he was comfortable exposed, he'd decide whether to let any of it grow back.

Rita and Barbara nodded, the shine of their eyes all the approval he needed. He broke up grinning. "Let 'er rip."

Rita pinned a sheet around his neck then experimented, combing his hair back. "You have a good forehead—let's show it. Pretty short?"

"I trust you. Do what looks right."

He shut his eyes as she scissored. His scalp tingled; as weight disappeared, the world leaned in closer. Eventually, Rita announced he should look. His forehead, nose, and cheekbones were tan and everything below them irritated red, but here was his high school graduation picture—only now he was leaner, older, seen some miles. Again he had that avalanche sensation—as long as he kept moving he'd be OK, but if he stopped, it'd bury him. *Silliness*, he reminded himself. *Lightness*. Rita brushed loose hair off, then unfurled the sheet. Standing amid the gold and brown twists, he coiled one on his finger.

"Got a little bag?"

"I just bought new guitar strings—one of those envelopes should work." She gave him a transparent one he tucked the lock of hair into.

"Gonna sell this?" he gestured to the clumps on the floor.

"Hm—I might. If anyone thinks it's worth money; you want some?"

"I got the cut I want," he grinned. "What kind of music you like, Rita? I'll buy you a record."

"The Go-Go's—*Beauty and the Beat.*"

On the walk home, Barbara chattered while his head got cold; he decided to buy a hat. Forgoing dinner, he drove downtown and parked by the army surplus store. With fifteen minutes till the place closed, he tried on berets, Union Army hats, driving caps, thought long about the brown felt cowboy hat with feathers on the band— nice, but he'd only been on a horse once. Then he saw the fedoras and liked the look, as though he'd just stepped out of *The Maltese Falcon.* He chose a charcoal gray one—the most he'd ever paid for a hat, but he was due a check Monday for the routes he'd done so far. The distribution center was open Friday; he could stock up and work all weekend.

• • •

ONCE THE CHEESECAKE PLAN was set, Anna got restless. Burke was bound to say something, intentionally or not, that would make her squirm. But thinking about it wasn't going to help, so she went walking, and pretty soon she was downtown pacing the length of the brick mall. Too cold to sit, too soon to go into the deli, so she window-shopped—this town never stopped changing. In college, she'd joked that if you got tired of Boulder you could hang out in a different neighborhood for six months, then when you went back, half the businesses would be new.

Potter's had been a drugstore; now it was a bar, a busy pickup scene stocked with cokeheads in flashy clothes. Noise spilled out as she went by. In the next block, a guy in a fedora tipped his hat as he passed her, then she heard "Hi, Anna" in a gruff voice. She turned, wondering if she'd imagined that—the man was standing a few paces away, looking at her, arms crossed over his chest, a sideways grin on his face.

As though he knew her. She stepped closer, examining him; he stood like a piece of statuary. When she was circling behind him, Walt's voice said, "Hi, Anna."

"No!" She shot around in front of him, grabbing his arms. "No—it can't be."

"Why not?" he laughed.

"But where's your hair?"

"Saved you some," handing over the envelope.

"But—"

He put his hands on her shoulders and leaned in to kiss her. She started to fight him off before her lips told her, *Wait, I know him.* His brim was bumping her forehead; he plucked off the hat, then put his arms all the way around her.

"Come with me?" he said into the back of her hair. "I'd like to do something I never did before."

"Such as?"

"Take you to a hotel room and love you till it's time to meet your friend."

She pulled back—*Who the hell.* "You've really changed."

"Not very much. It's just hair—it grows, you cut it. Or else you don't. I realized this evening it was the history of a lost man. I don't feel lost anymore."

"Well I do—you knocked my feet out from under me."

"So I can catch you and lay you down. Please?"

"You said I was in charge," eyeing him askance.

"You can say no." He watched her face. "Ever say no?"

"No."

"Then say it now."

"No."

"No you won't say it, or 'no'?"

She shook her head. "This is silly."

"Yeah," he grinned, and without his beard, his amusement seemed twice as wide.

"You really want me to say no."

"I want you to say what you mean, whatever that is." He set his fedora on her head—too big—it sat on her ears. "Can I buy you a hat?" he offered.

She looked at the envelope in her hand. "Buy me a drink, mister."

"Where?"

"The Catacombs."

Walt offered his arm, she curled her hand against it, and they walked around the corner and downstairs. Choosing a spot near the door, he pulled out her chair, pushed it in as she sat, then plopped his hat on the table.

"I really feel like Anna Karenina now," she said. Vronsky was a military man—in his peacoat Walt looked like a sailor on leave.

"Then shall we drink champagne?"

"Yes." She checked him out: the familiar—eyes, nose, and forehead—and the new—flat cheeks and rounded chin—the whole of his face. It dawned on her that he was good-looking. The waitress arrived with bottle, glasses, and an ice bucket on legs. She popped the cork, poured, and iced the bottle with a napkin on its neck, then left.

"Cheers!"

Glasses in hand, they looked at each other. Anna felt seasick.

"No wait," Walt said, raising his fedora to hide his face up to his eyes. "Recognize me now?"

Her vertigo subsided. "If someone showed me pictures of clean-shaven men and told me one was you, I'd never pick you out. I don't believe it now."

"So pretend we just met."

She was counting on Burke to throw cold water on this impulsive attraction, but Walt all clean-cut might make a good impression. What if Burke encouraged him? "I just don't get it—what do you want?"

He closed his eyes and sank back, smile expanding. "I want something so silly I'm not even sure—"

No, she wasn't ready to hear that. "So what triggered this transformation?"

"Well, jail time had something to do with it. And finding out your name and meeting your namesake. And changes at home."

"What changes?" The less he talked about her, the better.

He leaned forward, she turned her ear to catch his murmur about a house meeting, a deal with Romo to relocate Pick. "And, I'm looking into real jobs."

"Like what?"

"Teaching."

Her dad had been in the Boulder school system for decades, and complained about idealistic young teachers who lasted only a year or two before red tape and disrespect sent them packing. Did Walt have any idea what he was in for? "Seriously?"

"Yeah. That's partly why I cleaned up."

"Gonna start wearing a suit?" Yesterday she couldn't have imagined that; now any sellout seemed possible.

"If I have to. I don't mind. My identity's not tied up in how I look."

"But the face you offer the world *is* your identity. You've abandoned the guy I—" Unable to finish, she ducked behind her hand—she hated blushing when she was trying to make a point—some imp playing with her thermostat, upstaging her words.

"I can grow it all back—I just wanted you to see me. If you meet a clean-shaven guy," he said, "and he lets his beard and hair grow out, you still know him, but if he's shaggy from the start, you've never seen him—so you don't really."

I sure don't, she thought, while he continued enthusiastically, "You're the first person I've wanted to meet since I left Santa Cruz. Congratulations."

"Hope you don't mind if I close my eyes." With them open, gravity was on the job, but when her lids dropped she felt the Earth turning, the magnetic field tugging her head North, moon pulling her tide. She swayed. A touch on her shoulder steadied her. These champagne bubbles were making her lightheaded—should've ordered a shot of vodka.

"You're not spineless," she informed him. "You know what you want," which only reinforced her own reticence.

"I'm working on it—we'll see where it takes me." He lifted his glass again. "Here's to you—" They clinked rims and drank. He emptied the bottle into their glasses, then stood, putting money on the table. "Time to go."

"We have to finish this first."

"While we walk—c'mon," he said.

"We *can't* leave a bar with drinks in our hands." Didn't he know anything?

"Sure we can—let's go." He shrugged into his coat, put on his hat, and, cupping a glass against each palm with stems hanging between his fingers, led the way upstairs and out. On their way down the street, he handed over her glass.

• • •

BURKE WAS PACING IN front of the deli. Spotting them, he said, "That's illegal, you know."

"Right," Walt said. "Better help us get rid of the evidence," offering his glass. After Burke took a sip, he extended his hand. "I'm Walt," and they shook. "You know this woman?" nodding toward Anna.

"I'm never sure," Burke grinned, Walt grinning back. "Let's go in—my feet are cold."

They waited for a table, Walt still holding the glasses natural as you please, nobody showing a flicker of concern. When they got their booth, he took one bench, Burke the other. Anna hesitated at the end of the table. Finally she decided she'd rather sit next to Walt than look at him—every glimpse of his exposed face startled her afresh. They opened their menus, as though they couldn't get cheesecake and coffee without reading about them first. When the waitress came, Anna agreed to split her piece with Walt, Burke ordered his own, and they all asked for coffee.

After she left, Walt tapped the rim of his champagne flute. "Don't abuse words," he told Anna. "You said we can't leave a bar with drinks in our hands. But we did. Shouldn't isn't can't."

"Actually," Burke said, raising an admonitory finger, "in Russian they *are* the same word: *nel'zya* means *it is forbidden* and also *it is impossible*. The cohort in power had to keep the lid on tight—Russians have never respected authority." He laughed. "But you've proven there is a distinction. Here you are, enjoying your bubbly in an establishment where you not only didn't buy it, they don't even sell it."

"Seemed a shame to waste it," Walt said, taking another sip and setting the glass in the middle of the table.

Burke drank some, then glanced around the busy room. "Nobody here seems to care."

"Except Anna."

"But Anna keeps track of all the rules, didn't you know?" Burke said. "She's given me severe lectures about the proper order in which to wash dishes—"

"That's because," she said, "people don't think about how they're doing it, they just haphazardly scrub this and that, waste a lot of water, and don't really get things clean." She drank off the rest of her champagne and set her glass in front of Walt.

"I'm afraid to ask how it's supposed to be done," Walt said.

"When I write Anna's biography," Burke said, "I plan to call it *The Right Way.*"

The waitress arrived with a tray and arranged their desserts, mugs of coffee, water, napkins, forks and spoons, and a small metal pitcher of cream. After they'd sampled their cheesecake, Anna said, "Walt, tell him about your week in jail."

Burke raised his eyebrows.

"A cascade of errors," Walt said. "The cops didn't like my out-of-state plates or my out-of-control hair so they kept me—"

"What hair?" Burke said.

Walt laughed. "I think Anna's feeling a little off-center because a few hours ago I had a full beard and long bushy hair."

"Really."

"Show him your souvenir, Anna."

She pulled the clear envelope from her jacket and handed it across the table. Burke fished out the twist of hair, letting it uncoil.

"Hm," he said. "I see what you mean." He curled it around his index finger. "But the cops didn't cut it for you?"

"No—I just decided this evening. Anna didn't know."

"Well, that would explain her sulk." Burke slurped down the rest of Walt's champagne.

Forking another tiny bite off the cheesecake, she glared at them both. "Burke, you were—"

"I was worried about you seeing a criminal. But now that I've met him, I think he'll do."

"Do what?" Walt said.

"Make her smile from time to time—between agonies, you know."

"Agonies?" Walt nudged her gently. "Really?"

"Other people are the source of all my misery," she said. "On my own, I am a serene and happy person."

"I dispute that," Burke said, picking up his mug. "The Dalai Lama is serene—a man who's lost his country, who still smiles and blesses people wherever he goes."

"I never claimed—" she bridled.

"And right now, with almost no provocation, you are again proving that 'serenity' is not a suitable word to describe your state of mind."

"In her defense," Walt cut in, "I have seen her very happy and carefree."

"Thank you," she said.

Walt was pacing his bites of dessert to match hers, though he'd barely touched his coffee, drinking water instead. "It's time to molt," he said. "I'm painting my car too."

Anna turned to him, eyes wide. "No, no, you don't mean that."

"Yes I do. That's how I'm spending Thanksgiving."

"Thought you were the only game in town," Burke teased her. She bristled. "You should see it, Burke, before he ruins it."

"Now that I'm on the cops' radar," Walt said, "I think it's time."

In troubled silence, Anna studied the coffee precipitate flecking the bottom of her cup. The Walt she'd fallen for was an illusion. Subtract the hair, subtract the car—what was left to trust? It appeared his hippie ethos of peace, love, and going with the flow was gone—leaving what?

Burke asked, "So is that janitor gig your only job?"

"Actually, that's over—but pretty soon I expect to be driving a school bus."

"Buy some earplugs," Burke advised.

"A raincoat, I was thinking," Walt said, and they both laughed. Then he talked about odd jobs he'd done—fixing cars, installing signs, facing walls with rock or stucco, home repairs… "I've been on the move awhile, making money any way I could, but next spring I'll be twenty-seven—time's starting to slide away. I'm ready for some traction."

They walked back to Plug, Walt bringing the champagne flutes. Burke admired the decorated car, while Walt commented that streetlight didn't do justice to colors. They stood around while feet then hands then noses got cold, Anna studying the army store's window display as though she were planning to review it, while the guys talked about the slant six: Detroit's most durable engine. Walt offered to drop Anna at home, Burke said he was going to the jazz club if anybody felt like joining him. Walt convinced Burke to take one glass but when he offered the other to Anna, she wouldn't even look at him.

He simplified her choices by tipping his hat and getting in Plug with the second glass, driving away while she stood looking after him.

Every time she fell in love, her heart went into Anna Karenina mode: an ungovernable state of desire flooded her rationality, washing away memory and restraint. But Walt's abrupt change had stranded her, forcing her to reconsider whether she loved the person he turned out to be. Maybe she ought to just walk away.

I can't, she thought. *Or do I mean I shouldn't?* Was rejecting him wrong, or was it simply impossible?

chapter 10

Search and Destroy

THE SNOW THAT hadn't fallen Friday was starting, so Walt put on his fedora, borrowed Stu's army greatcoat that hung past his knees, and spent the day distributing phone books. At a thrift store he'd bought a fold-up grocery cart, which made it easier to deliver a block's worth at a time—at first, anyhow. But as the snow deepened in late afternoon, its wheels jammed; with his boots getting wet, he finally called it a day. He was making good money. He'd cleared January's rent by now, and a cushion seemed a welcome possibility.

At the house, his last paycheck from the theater was in the mail on the kitchen counter, along with a Thanksgiving card from his parents. He should've phoned them—usually did on holidays. He'd been too depressed and worn out Thursday to even think about it. After painting Plug, he came home and ate plain rice—everybody was gone except Pick. Walt had offered him a beer, then they went through the alternative weekly's housing ads together, circling the good prospects. Pick, warming to the exercise, called a few. One turned out to be a Deadhead, so Pick went to check out the place. Walt relaxed in the empty house, playing records and wondering why trimming his hedge made him untrustworthy.

Sunday afternoon Romo got back from Houston, smile dropping from his face the minute he walked in. Walt sat at the kitchen table drawing the mismatched cupboards as Romo looked him over.

"Guess you went all out," he said. "I'm pretty sure I didn't ask you to cut your hair."

"It left with the car. Somewhere out there, hippie-mobile and shaggy mane are hanging out together, laughing at me."

"Turn your head," Romo said, then nodded. "You clean up nice."

"Thanks."

"Pick gone?"

"This morning. Didn't exactly tidy up, but there's no telltales."

"Thank you," collapsing into a chair. "All the way back we were singing, it was great, then soon's I got here I remembered. It's like I died."

"I know what you mean," Walt sighed. "Anna's really upset about my new look, and the car. How was I supposed to know she was in love with my hair?"

Romo snorted and went back out to help Stu unload.

The narc squad showed up half an hour later with a warrant. They took their time, going through the kitchen drawer by drawer, emptying the freezer and opening every frost-caked tub and leaving the ice cream to melt, in the living room slashing the couch and armchair to pull out stuffing, dismantling the stereo system, ripping the covers off the speakers. Following them around seemed to goad them to greater destruction, so Romo and Stu and Walt retreated to the kitchen table, wincing at every crash. Romo called Lloyd, and by the time the smashing began to subside, he'd arrived.

"Your car too," the lead man said to Romo.

"I'm their lawyer," Lloyd said—standing up, he had several inches on the narc. "May I see the warrant, please?" He read it, then said, "There's no reference to vehicles on here. You need another one for that." He handed it back, and the two looked at each other a long minute. "Shall I call the station to clarify?"

Going back to the dining room, the narc yelled, "Let's go!" The trio got into their squad car, revved it, and kicking up a spray of gravel from under the snow, roared off.

Romo heaved himself to his feet. "Cleanup time." Lloyd left, and they got to work. Barbara came home from her weekend with

Car in Aspen, and as soon as she walked in began shrieking curses. When Lucy showed up at 10:30, Romo called another house meeting.

"They didn't find anything, so they're not done. Stay clean. And look for wires."

• • •

ANNA, PASSING WALT'S HOUSE in the afternoon en route to a job, noticed the cop car. On her way home at midnight the place was still lit up, so she asked Stefan to drop her off.

"First job's at 7:30," he reminded her. "Want me to pick you up?"

"Yeah, I'll be at home."

No one was in the kitchen to answer her knock, so she opened the door far enough to call, "Hello—Walt?" Romo came in with a roll of duct tape, startling when he saw her standing between door and jamb, neither in nor out.

"Oh, Anna. Come on in. Walt's in the bathroom."

"I'll wait here," looking open-mouthed at the heaps of silverware on counters, food dumped on the table, broken dishes on the floor. In one corner she could see broom tracks in a fan of flour.

Romo explained, "He's doing repairs."

She went to see. The lid of the toilet tank lay in three pieces by the tub, and splintered lath and plaster were strewn across the floor. Walt stood with one foot in the sink, the medicine cabinet resting on his knee, trying to hold a shim in place while he slid the cabinet's top corners into the wall cavity. He was talking to it as though it were a horse reluctant to go into a trailer, pivoting his foot closer and lifting his knee higher, feeding the cabinet edge with a screwdriver.

"Need another pair of hands?"

He turned, the cabinet slid, he caught it. "That'd be helpful, yes. Watch your fingers—the edge is sharp."

She took the weight off his knee. "Got it?"

After driving screws into the studs, he put the mirrored door up to the unit and tapped in the hinge pins. When he was done, he wiped his hands on his filthy jeans and smiled at her. "Thanks—that was taking too long."

"Couldn't anyone help you?"

"We're all busy—the narcs really laid waste—they didn't like that the dining room floor's higher than the kitchen so they ripped up half a dozen boards—the landlord's gonna be pissed."

"Can they do that?"

"Sure, they had their magic piece of paper. It doesn't actually say 'Search *and destroy*,' but they did. And found nothing."

"Thank god for that."

"No, thank Romo. If Pick had been here, we'd all be in jail right now."

"Then they should thank you. Didn't you help him move?"

"It's my fault the cops noticed us. I'm surprised Romo hasn't punched me out."

"It's not like they went easy on you."

He took a long breath and let it out slowly. "Well, here you are speaking to me. I feel honored."

She flinched at his sarcasm. "I can leave."

"Yeah I know. You're pretty good at that."

What an accusing look. "I told you I'm shy."

"Is it shyness that makes you like me with hair and shun me without it? What difference does it make?"

"You *are* different—you're so—hard now. I thought you were hurting too."

"I am hurting, Laura."

"What did you call me?"

"Did I say—Luh—"

She nodded. "Why?"

He sank to the floor amid the entrails of the bathroom wall. She squatted beside him, afraid if she touched him he'd say something worse.

"I can't play this game anymore," he said thickly, forearms draped over his knees. "'Now she loves me, now scram.' It's much too familiar."

"Burke really chewed me out for the way I treated you."

"What's it to him?"

"It's important to have a friend who'll tell you when you're making a mistake."

He looked at her doubtfully. "What mistake?"

"Acting like I don't care—but you scared me. You know how before you unwrap a present, it could be anything, but once you tear off the paper, it's only what it is?"

"Yep."

"Getting rid of all that hair unwrapped you. When the detective told me why they put you in jail, I couldn't believe it—all that loving wasn't a lie. But when you cut your hair and painted your car, you took away that person—now I don't know who you are...or what you're capable of."

"Wow, that backfired one hundred percent," shaking his head. "Hair's a costume. I didn't think we could get any closer till I showed you my face. But if you don't like what you see, that's a different problem."

"No no, I—"

"Forget it," he said. "We were stoned and lonesome—only fools should expect anything." Then, very straight, without hope or accusation, "What is it you want?"

"To know who you really are—not your hair or the paint on your car, not even your sad stories—just you."

"So how's that supposed to happen?"

"I want to be around you, do things together, get acquainted."

"Is sex in the equation?"

She blushed. "It's knocked me off balance..." She put her hand on his shin, he let his palm slide over her knuckles, his cheek resting on his knee while he watched her. She looked at their hands, thinking she'd pushed him too far. If you hurt somebody and you can't apologize—

"What if it—was—part of the equation?" she said.

"Then you got me," closing his eyes looking trapped.

"Want to come over? Stefan's picking me up early."

"Lemme check."

He stopped off in Romo's room, a moment later leading her upstairs. "Come see what they did to my space."

Lucy was struggling with a dresser drawer that wouldn't go back in; Anna stopped to help her, then came on into Walt's room. Her first impression was dirty snow—brown and white drifts of feathers on trampled clothes, sleeping bag, and bedding, his gutted pillow thrown to one side. His peg rack was on the floor, holes gaping in the plaster where it had been mounted. His mattress was propped against a wall; several bands of duct tape ran diagonally across it edge to edge. The narcs had shattered the base off his ceramic lamp, dumped out a coffee can of pennies, ripped down a poster whose corners were still tacked to the wall. Below the street window, they'd gouged a big hole, dropping plaster on top of his clothes.

"Oh Walt, oh my god."

"I feel exactly like this room—you want to know who I am, get an eyeful."

"Is this really legal?"

"Everybody knows people are clever about hiding drugs—could be anywhere—inside walls, inside mattresses. They tore the lining out of Stu's heavy coat."

"That's so wrong."

"The best part is, they can come back and do it again."

"You're kidding."

"Romo's pretty sure they will—he found a wire in his room, and they could be tapping the phone. Assume every word you say is being recorded."

"Yeuuch, I don't like that."

"Welcome to Police State 101. Take notes—failure and they jail yer." He lifted one edge of his sheet, shaking gently so the feathers would slide off without taking flight.

"So is it OK to come over?" she said.

He half smiled. "Romo doesn't mind."

"And you?"

"Convince me."

His arms were strong holding her, his kiss had authority—was taking charge male nature after all? But he'd called her Laura—if he'd risk exposing those old wounds, why was she being cowardly? Downstairs, he checked his peacoat, lifting two rubbers halfway out of the pocket and arching his eyebrows at her.

She nodded. "Let's go."

• • •

IN THE MORNING SHE sat on the bed dressed, eating her toast while he drowsed naked, head in her lap. She brushed crumbs off his cheek, snagging on stubble.

"Are you going to shave anymore?"

"Gotta get back in the habit—sorry."

His hair was woolly—if she didn't think about that mane he'd cut off, she kind of liked this. When Stefan honked, she slipped off the bed, squatting to kiss him. "Just lock the knob and pull the door shut when you go."

"How late will you be?"

"I think it's a big job—I'll work till dark. Shall I come over?"

"No, I have to deal with the mess. Call me when you've been to Planned Parenthood." She'd told him last night she'd go on the Pill, then their discussion took an odd turn—at Laura's insistence, Walt had learned a lot about birth control; when he suggested a diaphragm instead, Anna was equal parts daunted and offended—why should he know more than she did? But Walt stood his ground. The last thing either of them needed was something that made her moodier. She'd read about blood clot incidence in women using the Pill, so she appreciated that he wanted that option off the table, but it felt like capitulation to agree with him. Cory had never given a thought to the whole issue: whatever she used was her business, as long as she was careful. *Guys don't want to know*, she'd been told—then here was one who did, and it bothered her. Why? And why should she have to force herself to do what was sensible? If she was such an ignoramus, should she be having sex at all? But his palm cupping her neck was the warmest touch on Earth. Regardless of what her brain said, her body had already decided.

She kissed him again. At impatient honking, she scrambled out.

In the van, Stefan demanded, "What took so long? Thought you'd be ready."

"Walt's here," buckling her seatbelt.

"Things better?"

Satisfaction gave her face an unaccustomed glow. "Right now they are."

"Good. Ready to scrape paint?"

"As ready as I ever am." But recently he'd drafted her as helper on a carpet and upholstery job, and he'd been impressed with her thoroughness cleaning a corduroy armchair. His approach to work was to take on anything he had the skills to cover. Upholstery cleaning paid well, so he'd decided to branch out, investing in an upholstery cleaning machine. "When am I shifting jobs?" she asked.

"I have to find another window washer, and hustle upholstery work. Takes time." He asked about all the lights on at Walt's, so she told him about the narc raid.

"They were so destructive," she said. "I can't believe they can do that."

"Little by little we let our rights slip away," he nodded, "and one day we'll look up and they're gone. At that point our best hope is not to be a target."

"Right—throw someone else to the wolves, to keep ourselves safe?"

"We have to resist being governed by fear," he said. "Fear and desire are faces of the same coin. We have to get past that to understand who we truly are, and to live fully human lives."

"That's Buddhist philosophy, right?"

"The deepest understanding of every religion teaches that we have to free ourselves from illusions of duality, and from grasping after them—I just think the Buddhists are more direct about it. This world that keeps us busy, well, it's not imaginary exactly, but it's not reality either. Jewish, Christian, Zoroastrian, Taoist mysticism all arrive at the same conclusion, by different paths."

"So why all these Buddhist Jews? Why not embrace your own heritage and be a Jewish mystic? Is there something wrong with that?"

Stefan made a face. "Jewish mothers. They know too much, they're too intent on control. It's less of a struggle to find our own way."

It was on her tongue to argue with such a bald generalization, but she reflected on how her discussion with Walt had made her feel. It wasn't easy to have someone you love tell you what to do—should love have such a hard grip? Yes, she'd ask for a diaphragm when she saw the gynecologist—but when would she have her own ground to stand on? She'd read enough about Zen to know they cultivated "doubt-mass"—yet here she was, with more doubts than anyone she knew, and far from feeling grounded or accomplished, the more she doubted the more she felt like a naïf, awestruck by everything, continually needing instruction.

chapter 11

Bounce-ket-ball

LUCY MOVED OUT —the raid was too much for her. The four remaining housemates screened prospects carefully; they didn't want to end up with someone who'd get them all busted. By the end of the week, they had a tenant for Lucy's room: the new window washer for Perfectly Clean. Terry fancied himself a poet and took classes at Naropa Institute. On the scale of a Harvard MBA opening the doors to high finance, a Naropa diploma was going to be useful for patching a broken window—but Terry didn't mind, saying the place "put the 'cool' in 'school.'"

As December slid by, Walt and Romo started driving school buses, and Walt signed up for pedagogy and classroom management starting in January at the university. Life was taking on a new shape: defined, steady. How ironic—wandering, he'd been in stasis; now that he was planted, he was getting somewhere.

One Saturday he was out walking, enjoying the sun, and on his way past a park, noticed Burke on the basketball court, diving suddenly then crying "Aha!" Approaching, he saw Anna too. A neon-orange superball zoomed off the backboard, coming Walt's direction. He chased it down, then threw it at the hoop.

"No no," Burke said. "You have to *bounce* it in—this is bounce-ket-ball." He then hurled his ball at the blacktop, and it rebounded far over the backboard.

"Finesse," Anna teased. "Don't kill it." She threw down a purple ball, which bounced up through the rim from underneath. "Extra points," she crowed.

"That's no points at all," Burke said, and Walt had to agree going through the hoop that way wasn't much of a challenge.

"The curious thing about a superball," Burke explained on his next attempt, "is the phenomenon of the *second* bounce."

"The longer one, you mean," Walt said.

"Exactly. Why? A tennis ball bounces consistently, and so does a basketball, a soccer ball, a Ping-pong ball. But a superball, after an almost vertical first bounce, jumps out on the second."

"Right," Walt said. "Then the third bounce is like the first—something about the material?"

"It's space age," Anna said, her ball striking the rim and coming back at her. "What do you expect?"

"It stores energy," Burke said, "maybe because it's solid."

"But golf balls are solid," Walt said. "How do they bounce?"

"Badly," Burke said. "If they hit something hard, they get dented."

They played till one ball was lost down a storm drain and another AWOL in the grass, then strolled to the nearby supermarket to restock at the vending machine.

"Come on over," Burke said. "My dad shot a deer and gave me a roast."

"I had venison once," Walt said. "How are you gonna cook it?"

"Dad marinates it first, then puts the roast on a grill above a pan of water with hot coals underneath—he covers the meat with a bucket to trap the heat, and the steam cooks it—it's pretty good that way."

"What's a good marinade?"

"Actually, I use Caesar dressing."

"That's weird," Walt said.

"Think about it: marinade is a blend of oil, vinegar, and spices." He gestured "Voilà," then said, "salad dressing, see? Let's get a move on."

Burke's housemate spent most of his time at his girlfriend's, an arrangement that suited Burke: he had more space than he could afford solo, and his tendency to play piano at two in the morning didn't disturb anyone. Walt prowled his record collection. Jazz, classical, and singer-songwriters: Randy Newman, John Prine—and Patti Smith and Elvis Costello too.

That made him wonder how Grant was doing. Whenever his name came up in conversation with his folks, Dad changed the subject; Mom would hint that his brother needed someone to talk to: Walt must have influence. He knew he didn't. Grant had set himself apart since high school, scorning Walt's taste in music and his friends, as closed as if his older brother were just one more parent. Anyway, who was Walt to decide someone else's life didn't work? He put on Elvis Costello, then started for the kitchen.

Anna and Burke were chopping vegetables, arguing in a spirit of fun. She was so sure of herself, so relaxed and open—only in the glow of sex was she like that around Walt, the rest of the time second guessing herself, changing her mind, hesitant. Someone had made her cease to trust herself. With Burke she reverted to some earlier persona before that had happened. Walt felt like an intruder—if he made her self-conscious about this simple-hearted play, she'd have no refuge. He went back to reading liner notes, choosing the next record.

He felt he knew more about Thelonius Monk than Monk himself would ever have allowed in print, when fingers walked through his hair. Anna squatted in front of him.

"Everything all right?" Her eyes puckered. "Almost forgot about you."

"Just giving you two some space. If I horn in, he'll feel demoted."

"No, no, Burke likes you." She glanced toward the kitchen. "He's my best friend." Picking up a Billie Holiday album, she shook her head, looking at the song list. "Maybe lovers can't be friends. I wanted that with Cory, but this other dynamic just took over. When we first met we talked a long time, but thinking back, that whole conversation was just a mating dance. We were in Scotland and people were really prudish—we got kicked out of his hotel, and by then my hostel was locked up for the night—we wandered all over town trying to find a private spot, and ended up in a graveyard."

She laughed. "When the sun came up and we finally made the big score in the wet grass between headstones, I crossed over from being somebody's child or sister or student—I was just myself. I felt like *Winged Victory*. Two days later he had to leave for France. I only saw him once more before I came home but we traded addresses—" The light left her eyes. "Now that was a mistake. Without that pile of love letters, we would've realized we didn't know each other."

"Why'd that—"

"In letters you show your best side: your dreams, all the nice stuff that people can see for themselves in five minutes anyway, with no ugliness to balance it out. A friend could tell me about growing pot on her dorm windowsill, but I already knew her, so that was just something she did—it didn't define her. But when Cory wrote that *Midnight Cowboy* was the best movie of the sixties, it was this huge fact—I bought a copy of the shooting script and read it twice—then when I was with him I mentioned some detail from the movie. He was blank on it, and when I reminded him what he'd written, he said he liked *Butch Cassidy* better. I felt like such an idiot, the way he looked at me."

"How'd he—"

"'How could you get so hung up on something I wrote in an idle moment?'" She drooped. "Nobody says brilliant things every time the phone rings, but at least the words aren't there to go over a hundred times—you say 'em and they're gone. Letters would've been fine if we'd kept the Atlantic between us. It was the difference between what we wrote and who we were that didn't work." She sat all the way down, massaging her knees. "So if I left town tomorrow and sent you a letter, would you write back?"

"I'd make you a postcard," he said. "Ever do that?"

She shook her head. "Make? How?"

"Get four-by-six index cards. Take an image you like—a newspaper photo, a cartoon, your own drawing—put that on one side, and your message on the other."

She smiled. "Sounds like fun."

"Limits your verbiage too."

"Jeez—that's what Cory and I should've done. All that mooning about his fingertips and his eyes—should've kept that to myself."

"Hey, you didn't know. Nothing wrong with sincerity."

"There was though—I said things I meant metaphorically that he took literally—not good. Or, as the monster said in *Bride of*

Frankenstein, 'No good! No good!'" in a perfect imitation of terrified Boris Karloff warding off the blind hermit's cigar.

"'Soup—good!'" Walt said, and they laughed. "Is that a great movie or what?"

"It's in my top ten," she agreed. "It has everything—a misunderstood monster, a blind saint, a naïve scientist, an evil doctor, mobs of pitchfork- and torch-waving peasants, those giant arcing electrodes, and Elsa Lanchester's zigzag hairdo."

"All it lacked was Charles Bronson as Igor," he said.

"Charles Bronson?"

"*House of Wax*—he's the assistant who dips Vincent Price's enemies in wax."

"Vincent Price gives me nightmares," she said. "I can't watch his movies."

"Oh no, he's great—an educated man warped by trauma—he's frightening because he's suave and cunning."

She mused, "Grandma Francis says people go to horror movies 'to be safe and feel scared.'"

"So do you hate feeling scared because you don't think you're safe?"

"Hmm. Maybe."

"Safety's in your head," he said. "You can have deadbolts, alarms, guards—but that stuff won't keep out fear."

"So how safe do you feel, knowing the cops are watching?"

"Gives me the creeps. But I'm not paranoid." He laughed sharply. "They really are out to get me."

"Very funny." She looked toward the kitchen. "Let's see if Burke has everything he needs for the cooking."

He was on the patio stacking chunks of sandstone to support the edges of a small grill. He'd put a cake pan underneath, but hadn't found anything to cover the roast. Not only was a five-gallon bucket too deep, the plastic would melt against the grill.

"We need a tin pail," Anna said.

She made a phone call, then announced that her Grandpa Francis had a small zinc washtub they could borrow. They piled in Burke's truck, Walt feeling nervous—he hadn't even met her parents—wasn't that supposed to come first?

She breezed over his hesitation. "Don't worry—they're really sweet."

"They are," Burke agreed. "Down-to-earth folks." He drove west and parked in front of a small ranch-style house with varnished wood siding. Anna led the way, and as they approached the door it swept inward. A silver-haired gentleman in gray slacks and green dress shirt welcomed them. His smile-creased face had large features—wavy hair, broad chin, oversized ears—with his voice a deeper version of Anna's husky alto. Out of the kitchen came Anna's grandma, a short, barrel-bodied woman with wispy silver hair and shining eyes. She hugged her granddaughter, then held her hand while Anna made introductions.

"You remember my friend Burke, and this is my sweetie Walt."

"Oh very good," Grandma Francis said, taking Walt's hand. "She said you're roasting venison, is that right?"

Burke told her how he planned to do it. She looked at her husband.

"Never tried that," he said, "Let me check Herter's." From a shelf near the wide front window, he removed a book titled *The Professional Guide's Handbook*, trailing a thick index finger down the table of contents. "Plenty of good advice in here: How to dress and skin a deer, how to transport a carcass, how to hang it to keep off scavengers—lots of things hunters need to know. Do you hunt, Walt?"

"No, I never have."

"I used to hunt elk—every year I'd keep going out till I bagged one, then have it butchered, and we'd eat off it all winter. Now, an elk's a lot of work to bring in—purt' near the size of a horse. The trick is to spook him the direction of the road so you don't have to pack him so far—otherwise you have to take him out a haunch at a time, and hope you get 'em all before the coyotes find out."

"Really?" Walt said. "Coyotes would attack you?"

"No no, they want the meat—they're smart too. If your elk's in quarters and you can only carry one, they figure out pretty quick which pieces don't have you attached. Never heard of coyotes attacking humans, unless they have rabies."

"Who, the coyotes or the humans?" Walt realized too late that sounded flippant.

But Grandpa Francis laughed. "Well, there's probably more rabid people than coyotes, if you read the papers." He led Burke out back to see if their washtub would do.

"You should come for dinner sometime, Anna," her grandma said. "And bring this young man. Do you like pot roast, Will?"

"Walt, Mrs. Francis," he corrected.

"I won't put you on the spot—Anna and I'll talk."

• • •

WHEN BURKE DECLARED THE venison done, it was well past dinnertime. They carved off slices on the bias, each piece more succulent than the one before. With a green salad, wheat rolls, and a bottle of wine, it made a feast. This wasn't some factory-produced animal—Walt had driven by the immense feedlots east of Carling where thirty thousand head of cattle spent their short lives putting it in one end and crapping it out the other; no comparison.

"Didn't know you were such a carnivore," Anna said, watching him devour chunk after chunk of roast.

"My household is vegetarian, and I respect that—I wouldn't bring this home—but I'm an omnivore. Far as I'm concerned, we're all in line for the cosmic stomach."

Burke laughed. "Leonard Cohen once asked a vegetarian, 'What have you got against plants, that you eat them exclusively?'"

"Right," Walt said. "Who says wheat isn't sentient? And every breath takes in organisms our immune systems kill off, but if we stop breathing to spare them, we destroy ourselves. We're steeped in death because we're alive—I accept that."

"Is that original sin?" Anna asked.

"Maybe—my answer isn't guilt though, it's to live consciously, treading lightly."

Anna looked melancholy, as though that were a test she'd failed, another of many, and for a moment she seemed young. Not the child playing with Burke, but a girl-woman who'd opened her door to the larger world, then stood hesitating on the threshold. Dragging her from shelter wouldn't equip her to handle exposure, anymore than tugging on newly sprouted plants made them grow faster. But how long would it take her to step out of her own accord? Once more Walt was waiting, the woman he wanted not ready for him.

book two

Christmas 1981

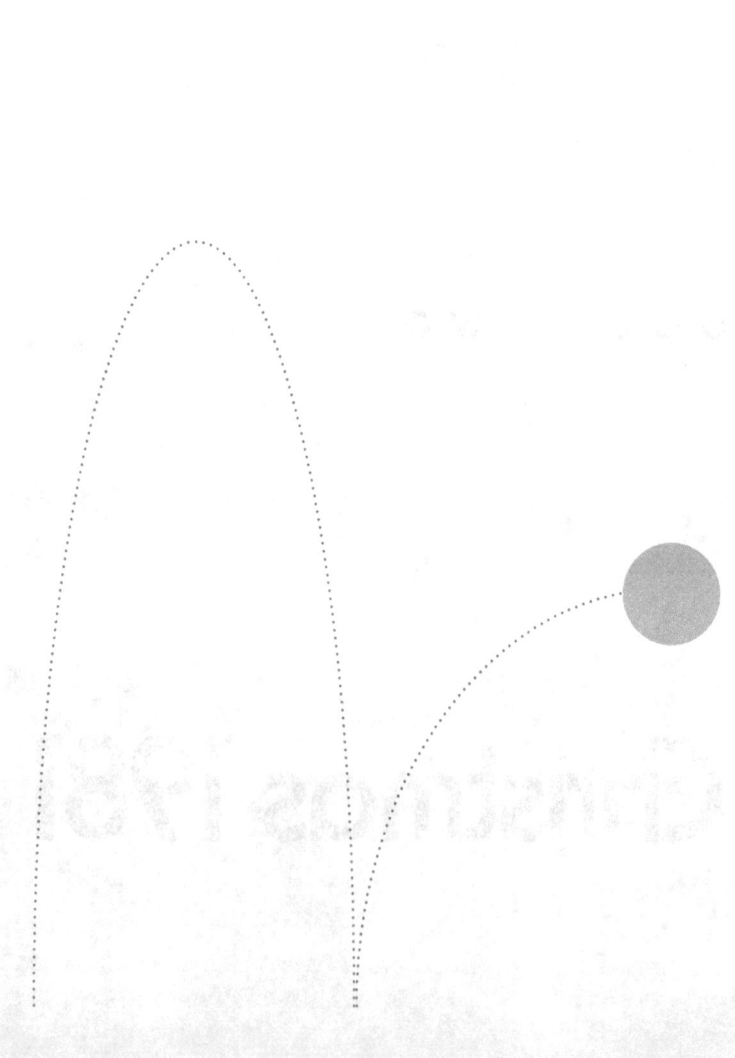

chapter 12

Egg on Your Face

THE CLEAVER BIT, its *thonk* transporting Walt half-way across his life, back to playing executioner with Wen and JP, sentencing zucchini to death, then dispatching them with JP's dad's bayonet. Halloween, fourteen—those Dark Ages when the urge to master everything helpless, to destroy lest you be destroyed, was in full flood. He'd consigned that time to some nether corner of memory: some other bloodthirsty mercenary did those things, not Walt, champion of the weak and meek. The decade rolling over to 1970 turned the trio from commandos to Peace and Love; this flash of satisfaction at splitting a pumpkin shocked him. But Anna only saw him pause, as though suddenly in doubt.

She was house-sitting at this farmhouse east of town over Christmas, looking after her friend Jill's dog, cats, and chickens. She'd invited Walt, telling him it was a chance to draw each other. Her mom had asked her to bring him to Christmas Eve dinner—just she and Dad, Harold, and Roger with his girlfriend would be there. Walt readily accepted, teasing her for keeping him "her dirty secret." His parents had offered him plane fare to Maryland, but he'd rather be with her.

"Scrape the goo then cut it smaller," she said. Midday Christmas Eve, she was giving him a pie-baking lesson. As instructed, he stacked pumpkin chunks rind side up in a big pot, added half an inch of water, and set it, covered, on the stove; while that steamed, he helped peel, core, and slice apples into a bowl. She sprinkled them with cinnamon, flour, water, and a drizzle of honey, then let the filling sit while the oven preheated. Her tools were assembled: a small bowl, a pair of table knives, a wooden spoon, a rolling pin, two glass pie plates. She wiped down the counter and put on an apron, tying another on Walt.

"I'm not a total baking novice—I used to make bread," he said, "but I got out of the habit, traveling."

"Pie isn't like bread." She scooped flour into the bowl, pared thin slices off equal chunks of butter and margarine, and with a table knife in each hand, scissored through the flour to cut the fat small. Blending in more flour, she made a hollow, poured in cold water all at once, and stirred quickly. The flour mix and water turned to a dough ball, which she rubbed against the sides of the bowl, collecting the loose flour. She set that aside.

They prepped the steamed pumpkin: scraping off the rind, squeezing out excess water, and heaping the pulp in a bowl. She measured into a mixing bowl enough pumpkin for one pie then beat in eggs, molasses, and honey, added allspice, mace, cloves, and a pinch of nutmeg, poured in a can of evaporated milk, and after whipping the mixture, tasted. The unused pumpkin went into the freezer in a yogurt tub.

They needed two bottom and one top crusts, so she cut off a fat third of the dough, patted it into a ball and rolled it out, curling it over the rolling pin a few times so she could reflour the counter. When the circle was fourteen or fifteen inches across, she draped then fit it into a pie plate. Folding and crimping edges, she raised a rim and pricked all over the walls and bottom with a fork—to prevent bubbles, she said. Pouring in the pumpkin mixture, she set the pie to bake an hour.

Walt began rolling the other bottom crust. The dough was elastic, nowhere near as fragile as it looked. But it was making a fan, not a circle. Anna had turned hers a lot—maybe that was his problem. The rolling pin stuck to the dough, tearing a hole. He rolled the other way, and it tore worse. She inhaled to speak.

"No, let me screw up—I'll figure it out." Her posture was judgmental, but how bad was it to mess up a pie crust? It tore again; more was on the rolling pin than on the counter now. He wadded it up, scraping blobs and packing it in his hands—better start over. He floured everything and applied the rolling pin to the ball of dough—where it hardly made a dent. His critic was nodding.

He bore down on the uncooperative mass. "Is this wrecked?"

"It's getting there—don't fold it anymore—just roll it to size and stop."

Sounded simple—*easy as pie*. When at last the fracturing crust looked big enough, he patched half a dozen pieces into the glass pie plate, mashing edges together, then pricked the insides with the fork. Anna sprinkled flour into the bottom, stirred the apple mix again, and dumped it in. She handed him the last chunk of dough for the top crust.

He held it a moment—*this time, do it right*—then gingerly shaped a ball, set it on the floury counter, floured the rolling pin, and rolled cautiously, stopping after every pass to redust the work surface. His pains were rewarded. It didn't stick or tear, just spread. When it was big enough to cover the pie, he beamed, triumphant.

She approved. "Now it needs steam vents. I always draw something—a piece of fruit, a fancy letter..." She handed him a paring knife.

"I'll do you—hold still." He cut her profile in dashed lines, then added ear, mouth, eye and eyebrow, cheekbone, vertical slashes of hair. It would have been a better effort if the knife hadn't dragged on the crust, every cut pulling it out of shape. He turned the dough over the rolling pin and laid it on the pie, adjusting, liking how the lumpy filling compensated for the drawing's flaws. The bottom crust was stiff, but the top pliable enough to bond. He pinched a ridge all the way around, and this pie went in to bake, twenty minutes after the pumpkin.

With the counter cleaned up, he pulled off her apron. "Time to draw."

"Where?"

"Right here in this warm kitchen."

"We have to—we don't—"

"We have hours—when the pies are done we just take 'em out, and go back to what we're doing."

So they got pads, pencils, and erasers, put chairs near the stove, and undressed. He arranged her legs and the angle of her torso, then moved his chair as instructed to offer a good view—he hoped drawing him at the same time would keep her self-consciousness under control. He started with one breast, then her side down to her hip, her butt spread on the chair, her thigh, bent knee, calf, ankle, foot—one continuous line. Working upward from her breast, he immediately ran into difficulty with the angle of her arm, then had trouble putting her shoulder where it belonged, and her neck and head. The lower part was easier so he went back to that, shading the curve of her breast, a scribble of hair for her bush, the line of her other thigh.

It'd be a new year soon. When would Laura show up and what was he going to do about it? The strongest refutation would be marriage, but when would Anna be ready for that? He was as sure as she was doubtful—how was that supposed to balance out? She'd get this spooked look: wishing he'd never showed up. Still, an invite to meet her family felt like progress.

"Could you put your leg back?" She'd crossed them.

"Oh, sorry—like this?"

"Your foot was more to the left," he said. "People are so hard to draw."

"Even if I was holding still?" She must enjoy blaming herself.

"Yeah. Humans don't have nice crisp edges—what I see keeps fading and changing. There's hardly any good lines here."

"I can't do it," she said flatly.

"Mine's nothing great—the idea's to try."

"No, I just can't—concentrate." Abruptly she stood, and grabbing her clothes, left the room.

He sat uncomprehending, hands lifeless over his pad and pencil. Music came on—Joni Mitchell's *Hejira*. Well, being exposed wasn't easy for Anna. And maybe she was picking up on his nervousness. Her parents would probably realize she was sleeping with him; would that bother them? His face still startled her, as though she kept hoping his beard would reappear.

He went back to sketching, trying to add enough of the chair that her pose made sense, but without her, the proportions were lost. The chair legs were too long, then too short, then he couldn't remember how much of the seat had been visible. He drew and erased until he gave up and obliterated the chair, then looked at what was left: her leg and right side, her other leg but not the rest of her trunk—blocked by her pad—and no shoulders or head. This partial image seemed emblematic of their relationship: a few lines he was filling in with his own desires. Did he know Anna at all even now? How much of their sparking was indulgence, how much resonated deeper?

He gave up and got dressed. The record had finished so he turned off the stereo, looking around. Her coat was missing from the rack by the big front door, and outside he saw tracks marking the steps in snow that had been falling lightly since early morning—about three inches by now.

Here he was again, hanging out in a stranger's house. He should go home—but what, or where, was that? His group house, where after the raid things were still weird? Go back to Maryland, pretend he belonged there? California again? He didn't know anymore.

In her waffling way Anna was as coercive as Laura, but hadn't he encouraged that? If he wanted her to treat him otherwise, didn't he have to say something? But asserting himself right after his haircut had scared her. The struggle wasn't worth it if she wouldn't let him into her head. He wanted to trip with her. Romo used to have mushrooms sometimes but they couldn't speak of it now—that was how Thought Police worked—made you change even your conversation so the ideas they punished were never expressed. They didn't have to lock up your body if they could imprison your mind.

He needed a willing ear—and he thought of his friend Tom, who'd introduced him to the projectionist's booth when they were college sophomores. They shared a love for movies and their man-behind-the-curtain role. Tom was home, surprised to get his call.

"Hey, Merry Christmas almost," Walt said.

"What's up man?"

"I'm with Anna, making pie."

"How's that going?"

"Oughta be better. Know where I can get any psychedelics?"

"Got some blotter—speedy but it's the real deal."

"No mushrooms?"

"My supplier left town. Want some of this?"

"I guess. You home later?"

"My shift starts at 6:30."

"People go to movies Christmas Eve?"

"Christmas too." Tom sang the opening lines of *Eleanor Rigby*. "You sound lonely, Walt."

"Not exactly—adrift in uncertainty."

"Hey, wanna go skiing tomorrow?" Tom said.

"Yeah, good idea. I'll call you later, or stop by—when are you done?"

"11:15, around then."

Deciding he better go look for Anna, Walt put on his boots. Jill's huge black lab bounded up, so Walt let him come as he followed her footprints, blurring with snow, out the driveway, turning north on the far shoulder. Hearing a snowplow he called Doc to him, clipping on the leash; the truck rumbled by, obliterating Anna's tracks. Walt trudged with the dog another half hour to the four-way stop where he circled the intersection. Plows had been up and down both roads leaving no sign of her.

"Well Doc, guess she'll come back when she's ready—let's go home." At the house he turned the dog loose and removed his boots on the porch. When he went in, the burning smell was a slap of reproach—the pies! He ran for the kitchen and grabbing a hot pad, yanked open the oven, which finally woke the smoke alarm. He waved the acrid cloud apart. The pumpkin filling was shriveled and black. He set the dark brown apple pie on the stove, not sure if it was too far gone; everything smelled liked burnt pumpkin. Carrying the ruined pie out the kitchen door, he set it on the back stoop and heard a crack—stupid, the glass pie plate had broken in half contacting the snow.

"Not doing too well here," he scolded himself, leaving it there— just stink up the house if he brought it back in. He opened kitchen windows and turned on the exhaust fan, left the back door open and flapped the hand towel to disperse the smoke. About to turn off the oven, he realized they'd need another pie, so he left it on and got the ingredients back out. Here was her recipe for filling, but she'd made the crust from memory—all he could do was guess.

His dough was brittle but he overlapped the pieces in the pie plate and pressed them together, and set that aside while he mixed pumpkin stuff. There was too much for this smaller pie plate, so he poured the rest into custard cups. He finished cleaning up and she still wasn't back, so he started heating water for tea.

The wind was rising—hoped she knew what she was doing. While things baked he read some Rip Off Comix he found in the living room, made chicory tea, pulled out the custard and reset the timer, and went back to reading *The Adventures of the Fabulous Furry Freak Brothers*. Half an hour after the pie was done, the phone rang.

"Carson residence," he said.

"Walt?"

"Anna, where are you?"

"Hunt Ridge Shopping Center." Five miles away. "My boots are wet and I don't want to walk back—can you pick me up?"

"Sure—everything OK?"

"Fine." Through the fade of the phone connection he couldn't gauge her mood. Before he put on his boots he considered, then left the apple pie on the counter but hid the new pumpkin pie and custard in the dish cabinet.

Hunt Ridge was the acreage northeast of Boulder where rich people built sprawling houses near the golf course, beyond city zoning laws and taxes. Anna was pacing under the eaves of the supermarket; she said nothing the whole ride back.

As they came in the house, she caught the burn smell. "Ew—did you take out the pies?"

"Got a little overdone actually—maybe they're OK."

She examined the apple pie on the counter. "It smells all right, don't you think?"

"Yeah," then said casually, "check out the pumpkin pie," waving toward the back door.

Her face contorted as she saw how burnt it was. Starting to pick it up, she realized the pie plate was in pieces. "What happened here?" an accusatory ring in her voice.

"When I set it in the snow it broke."

"One pie's not enough, and there isn't time to make another one." She turned on him angrily. "Why didn't you say something? I could've bought one at the store."

"There's a solution, but first you have to admit you abdicated responsibility."

"What?" she flared. "This is my fault?"

"You cut out without saying anything. I was concerned and went to look for you, and while we were gone it burned."

She sat, discouraged but still smoldering. "You didn't take them out?"

"I *did* take 'em out."

"I mean, when it was time."

"No," he said. "Did you?"

She was clenching her teeth by now, so with a sigh he set the new pie on the counter; she blinked as he got out the custard cups.

"Where'd those come from?"

"Same place the first one did," and while she sorted that out, he left the kitchen. In the living room he looked around—not where he wanted to be—put on his coat and kept going, out to the chicken shed. It was nearly dark inside, the small window opaque with grime, the musty smell of droppings and old straw making it seem warm. Once his eyes adjusted, he displaced a hen so he could sit on her straw-mounded crate, checking first for eggs—she hadn't laid any since morning collection. She clucked and fussed but as he sat still, she settled on his lap. He stroked her feathers, and after one peck she left him alone. Anna's emotional riptide was exhausting—where'd the lightness gone? He vowed if they couldn't have a good laugh over this stupid pie business before the day was over, he was through. He already knew about pain.

He sat awhile, humming "Home on the Range," which the chickens seemed to like, and finally decided it was time to go in—they'd have to head to her parents' soon. He'd take her there anyhow. At this point, hanging out with Tom at Big Screen was more appealing. Moving the hen back into the straw, he checked the others for eggs and found one. Holding it carefully, he went indoors.

Anna was lying on the couch with her back to the room, possibly asleep. He stepped quietly over and laid the warm egg against her cheek. She reached up to brush it away. It rolled. He clutched and found himself with a liquid handful of egg which dripped and ran on her jaw and down her neck. She yanked herself upright in disgust.

"Yecch, what's that?"

"It was a very fresh egg," he said. "Now it's just a mess."

She knotted her brow. "What's with you?"

Indignation plus egg equals ridiculous. He started to laugh, smearing her hair for good measure. She grabbed his wrist as she stood up, deflecting his hand to his own face, laughing now too—that was well-traveled egg by the time it stiffened on their skins, but by then they were too busy to notice.

"Let's take a shower," she said finally.

"How soon do we have to go?"

"Now."

"Not yet—got your diaphragm in?"

They cleaned each other then heated up, first in the bathroom then moving to Jill's high wide bed where they bounced till he cashed in. As they snuggled afterwards, she pulled the alarm clock to her nose.

"It's five—that's when we're supposed to show up—the drive'll take half an hour plus."

"Call your mom, tell her we'll be there in an hour, hour and a quarter. That way I can bask a little longer before you stop speaking to me again."

Her cheer dimmed. "Walt, am I like that?"

Maybe she expected a chivalrous answer but he wasn't up to it. "Yep."

"I'm sorry."

"Don't be sorry, be different. I bet you apologized to Cory all the time."

"I sure did."

"And what good was that? Instead of chowing down on guilt afterwards, quit before you get there—when you mean it, there's nothing to be sorry about." He walked his fingers across her belly, watching her face. Her sex-induced serenity was already fraying into nervousness.

"Do you really want to meet my parents?"

"Mm hmm." His kisses traveled up her arm, he blew a raspberry into the fold of her elbow.

"How do you expect me to take you seriously when you break eggs on me?"

He grinned. "I expect you not to—I told you before. My god is silliness and if I can't laugh, I'm outta here."

Her face crinkled into an answering smile. "Don't go yet."

chapter 13

Run Like Ink

IT WAS ALMOST 6:30 when Walt parked in front of the house where Anna'd grown up: ranch style, with a huge front window. The quiet street ran west toward open land, those mesas and Flatirons hidden behind low-lying clouds.

Walt and Anna each carried a pie up to the porch. The young guy who opened the door was about his height but heavier, deep-chested with narrow hips, his straight brown hair pulled back into a two-inch ponytail. He wore jeans and an untucked dress shirt. Taking Walt's pie in one paw, he grasped his hand with his other.

"I'm Harold, good to meet you." His voice could fill a gym.

"Walt." He usually avoided handshake contests, but he wanted Harold's respect. With palms in full contact they pumped hands, Walt gripping first to meet the bite of Harold's grasp. Their eyes raked each other in brief assessment, then both let go and Harold stepped back to usher Walt inside.

Anna slipped past, whisking both pies to the kitchen. Her mom came out smiling, cheeks ruddy, her hair streaked silver. Two inches taller than her daughter, she wore a red and green plaid skirt and green blouse that emphasized her hourglass figure. Anna had on old jeans threadbare along the thighs and a faded blue turtleneck with a small hole at the neck seam. She removed her hiking boots, then padded around in wool socks. Walt, though he'd said nothing about how she was dressing, wore his newest pair of jeans and his best flannel shirt, tucked in.

"Introduce me," her mom said. Her father emerged from a back room. He must've started with Harold's top-heavy build, but age had thickened his hips and abdomen. He was wearing khakis and a cardigan over a polo shirt. His salt-and-pepper hair was an inch-long burr; metal-and-horn glasses magnified his observant quality.

"Mom, Dad, Harold—" Anna began, then looked around. "Where's Roger?"

"Late," Dad said.

"*We're* late—I figured he'd be here by now."

"Not yet."

"Well, this is my friend Walt Sanders." They how-do-you-do'd all around, and Walt bussed her mom's cheeks, both his hands clasping one of hers. Then he shook her dad's hand—grip strong as Harold's but without that challenge. The older man nodded as their eyes met.

Walt said, "Nice to meet you, Mr. and Mrs. Brubaker."

"Heaven sakes, don't call me that—I'm Carolyn."

"Frank," her dad said.

"Well," Carolyn said, "The turkey's been done an hour—it'll be dried out if we don't eat soon."

"Then let's start," Frank said. "Roger knows what time he was supposed to be here: it's his loss."

"He's circling the block waiting for us to sit down," Anna said. Everyone laughed, but no sooner had they taken their seats than they heard footsteps on the porch, and in came Roger and his girlfriend.

"You're late," Frank announced, but Roger looked at the array of empty plates.

"Nope, right on time." He introduced his girlfriend Leslie, everyone greeting while he dropped coats on the nearest chair and guided her to sit to his right. At thirty he was the oldest sibling, short brown hair receding from his broad forehead. He wasn't as bulky as Harold but an inch taller, cigarette reek clinging to his khakis and tucked-in button-down shirt. Leslie was slim with a tight skirt and hose and heels, a snug three-quarter-sleeve sweater, streaked blonde hair, full makeup—not just eye-shadow and lipstick like Carolyn—and she wore a dozen clinking brass bangles.

They passed dishes and the platter of turkey, Walt pleased to share the feast he'd missed at Thanksgiving.

"So, Dad," Roger said, "I brought the papers for you to look over—I'm ready to pay off Rich."

"He co-owns a construction company," Frank explained to Walt. "He's planning to buy out his partner."

"What do you build?"

"Retail, light industrial. Right now we have five jobs going—a gas station, a hamburger joint, a drugstore, a carpet warehouse, and an add-on to an auto dealership."

"Where?"

"Northglenn—too many regs in Boulder—permits take forever and there's all these rules about setbacks and footprint—not worth the bother unless it's big. If they approve the new shopping mall, we'll bid on that."

"He contributes to urban sprawl," Anna said acidly.

"It'll happen anyway," Roger retorted. "Why shouldn't I make money off it?"

"That's such a mindless attitude."

"What do you make washing windows? Enough for child support and house payments? Talk to me when you're worth something."

"Enough," Carolyn scolded. "It's Christmas Eve—I don't have to listen to this."

"Sorry," Anna apologized, her face crimson. They all bent to their meal.

Harold cleared his throat. "Tell us the story of the week, Dad."

"Dad's the vice principal at the consolidated high school," Anna told Walt. "The principal's the diplomat, deals with the public. Dad's the disciplinarian."

"Well," Frank said, "this week it was the knife that wasn't actually a switchblade."

"Anyone get hurt?" Harold asked.

"Not yet. Yesterday was the last day of class before vacation, so I was out in the hall wishing students a pleasant break, and saw two young men pushing each other. Those two—I've talked to both more times than I care to recall. But I saw metal. I boomed at them—"

"Dad has this incredibly loud voice," Anna murmured to Walt.

"They stopped, and I removed a knife from one young man's

pocket. He said it wasn't his, I asked was that his pocket, and we all took a little trip to my office. He said he was giving it back to the other young man, I told him possession of a switchblade is grounds for expulsion. He said it wasn't a switchblade, I demonstrated I could lock the blade open—it was a buck knife actually—and told him he was in violation. I asked what would happen when he was expelled, and he said he'd have to find another place to live—his father beats him black and blue. He's already working afternoons and weekends at a service station, not making much—less than you do, Anna—didn't seem likely to cover rent. I told him to leave the building, but I gave him my card. I've dealt with him for two and a half years now. He thinks the entire world is against him—and does his best to keep it that way—but we have an understanding. He knew I'd expel him for the knife, but he flashed it fifty feet from my office; that tells me something."

"You must have a jaundiced view of young people," Walt said.

"Hmm? No, not at all—if I did I'd hate my job. I feel I can take credit for those who actually graduate, and go on to leave these difficult years behind them. I haven't given up on this young man, and he knows it. I wouldn't be surprised if he earns his GED in a year or two. He's made some poor choices but he's not stupid."

"I'm taking teacher certification courses starting spring semester," Walt said.

"Really? What age?"

"My BA's in geography, so I don't think I can teach at the high school level. Grade school, I guess."

Frank shook his head. "If you want a job not just the credential, I suggest junior high—those are the kids no one wants to deal with. They're half-crazy from hormones, awkward and hostile. I was principal at a junior high for two years, and it was always an adventure. On the day that took the prize, I met with a quiet girl who'd shocked the hall monitor by decorating the bathroom with indelible marker. While I was deciding what to do with her, a group of fast girls were sent over—they'd started an all-girl band and wrote some very pungent stuff about certain boys, and of course the songs got into the wrong hands. And their parents were even worse: 'My little Susie doesn't even know those words.' The kids flip-flop on almost a daily basis—no assumption is safe. And do they ever need dedicated teachers. I recommend it."

"Sounds thankless."

"No, the thanks may be scattered, and you won't get them when you deserve to, but they'll be that much more welcome when they surprise you. Everyone loves the little kids—their mischief's on such a small scale it's hard not to laugh when you're scolding them. And high school students are young adults, inclined to discuss things. But in junior high they're not cute or mature. The boys are still children, telling potty jokes and roughhousing, but the girls are young women who rip each other apart verbally on Monday, Tuesday they're best friends, and in tears again Wednesday, obsessed with the way they look but oblivious to how the world sees them."

"I have to do general coursework first," Walt said. "I haven't committed to a particular age group."

"Student teaching's the clincher—you should find out right away whether you like being in charge of five classes' worth of fidgety kids, knowing that what you're trying to teach is the least interesting part of their day."

"Have you taught, or only done administration?"

"I taught math at the junior high and high school levels for many years. In a way I'm still teaching, only now they're life lessons—I prefer this."

"Where you from, Walt?" Harold asked.

"Originally Maryland, then I was a student here, and I've lived in California, and traveled quite a bit."

"He's an invader, Anna," Roger sneered. "She says Boulder's going straight to hell because of the invaders—first they were from Texas—well, who can stand Texans?—then in the sixties and seventies Californians brought their drug culture. Last few years they've been mostly from New York and New Jersey: big-city jerks and litterbugs. Anna hates 'em all—didn't she tell you?"

"This town's had a positive influence on me," Walt said mildly. "I don't litter, and I'm generally polite."

"Which is more than I can say for some people," Anna glared at Roger, who looked smug as he forked up a chunk of mashed potato–smeared turkey.

"I won't ask again," Carolyn said. "Anyone who can't be civil at my table will have to leave."

"All right," Roger said, but he didn't apologize, and Anna couldn't look at him without reddening.

When they finished dinner Walt suggested a walk—he'd eaten too much. Anna was quick to agree. Roger wanted to show Frank his contract, and Leslie volunteered to help Carolyn clean up—she wasn't walking in snow in that outfit. Harold stretched and said he'd come along if they didn't mind, so the three went up the street and west across government property, a pale cloud hovering thirty feet above the white field. Harold lit a joint, passing it to Anna who hit and handed it to Walt. They finished it as they walked, the tightness leaving their midsections.

The cloud began to lift and they stopped to watch. Like a curtain hoisted skyward, it revealed the Flatirons, lines and patches of snow limning every irregularity, every tree branch—every pine needle if their eyes were keen enough. The dark areas weren't black but a deep frozen blue. And in the midst of that two-tone mountain land-scape, the dots forming a large star shone yellow. The sight jarred Walt: couldn't humans enjoy a place without putting their mark on it?

"Why's that star there?" he demanded.

"Always has been, long's I can remember," Harold said, "from Thanksgiving to New Year's—they used to put up a cross at Easter, but they stopped that."

"Doesn't belong there—it's like graffiti on Half Dome."

"Well, what are you gonna do about it?"

"Tell my council member it looks tacky."

Harold guffawed. "That'll get 'em—they'd rather die than be lowbrow."

"How can they ban billboards and tall signs and allow that? What do you think, Anna?"

"To me it's part of the landscape."

"Hnh," Walt said. "A friend of mine said 'an ounce of history's worth a pound of logic,' and he's right—it's like you don't even see how ugly it is. If someone painted the word 'Boulder' on a Flatiron, I bet you'd hate it."

"Well yeah," Harold agreed.

"So how's that star any different?"

"It's familiar, that's all."

"It represents continuity," Anna said. "We can use some of that—I read recently that less than five percent of city residents have been here longer than twenty-five years."

"You don't qualify," Harold teased. "You're only twenty-two."

• • •

ON THE DRIVE DOWNTOWN, she asked Walt to park at the library—she wanted to talk. *Only twenty-two.* Harold might as well have said, "Only twelve."

Walt drove across the unbroken snow of the public lot, parking halfway between library and municipal building, and cut the engine. She led the way toward the creek, then as they reached the snowy cottonwoods, settled to a slow pace. Glancing at the path, she kept her eyes mostly on him.

"Walt, be honest. I'm really just a way to avoid Laura, aren't I?"

He didn't answer right away, his eyes remote, looking at some memory. "I think there's some truth in that—or there was. She wants me and she's selfish enough, what I want's secondary—I couldn't defend myself before and I don't know if I can now. I hoped being involved with someone else would inoculate me."

"Right—so I'm just—"

"Wait—" raising a hand. "That's where I started, but you've changed that—changed me. The way I feel about you has nothing to do with her, whether she shows up or doesn't." He stopped, facing her. "I love you. Luna taught us to see what we're drawing—when I looked, there you were—my heart's been drawing and erasing ever since, trying to get you right."

Her gaze skated sideways, avoiding his. "Your picture of me today with no head or anything made me feel like a stripper."

"No no—it was just so difficult—I went for the easy lines first, that's all."

"You just wanted to look at me."

"To see you, yeah. Anna, some people can see beauty in someone cruel or selfish by separating body from mind from heart, but for me it's all one. My body loves yours, my heart too, my brain, my spirit—I want to look at you because I love you."

She studied the snow-capped boulders in the creek.

"As long as we're on the subject of honesty," he said, "what are you so afraid of?"

"You think shyness is fear?" Heat washed into her neck and cheeks; maybe in the semidark he wouldn't notice.

"Isn't it?"

"It's my nature—hiding works for me."

"But you're not; I can see you."

"Not according to that drawing."

"I drew your head for the pie crust, don't forget."

True. And not a bad job, either. Was it his former girlfriend who scared her so much, or that he said he loved her but might change his mind? In a decade their age difference wouldn't matter, but right now five years was a chasm, one whose depths she'd already stood on the brink of, Cory on the opposite side. She'd told herself they'd been separated too much, giving reality no opportunity to intervene while they piled hopes on a flimsy foundation—but all her friends had seized on their seven-year age difference. Cory'd been overseas awhile; she was his way back in. If that had gone according to plan, they'd have returned married, by now could have a child.

If all that was appalling—and it was—why'd she fall for another older guy? All those jobs he'd done, places he'd been. Other than her London summer, she'd hardly been anywhere except with her family. She felt like a lousy hand of cards Walt was using to bluff his way out of a predicament. Wasn't going to work—both men saw in her their means, not an end. Walt did love her; she believed him. But Cory had too. At first anyway.

Walt's laugh startled her. "Know what I want to do right now?"

"What?"

"Drive up Flagstaff and put out those damn lights. That star's a desecration."

"Interesting—that's the opposite of what they had in mind, putting it up."

"Would you paint a giant American flag on the Grand—"

"Fine, enough, your point's been made."

• • •

THE STEEP NARROW ROAD was sanded till they approached Flagstaff House halfway up. No parking valets were in sight, but the restaurant was spilling light across the hillside—must be a private party. Plows hadn't dropped their blades beyond the driveway, so Walt drove just far enough not to block it and parked. From here they could see most of the star, strung across the slope above the road.

"I don't think you can just unplug it," she said.

"We'll unscrew the bulbs then."

"There's dozens—it'll take too long—somebody'll call the police—"

"There must be a line we can cut."

"I bet it's in metal casing. One year someone turned it into a peace sign, then the city made it harder to mess with."

But Walt was studying the layout. "Gets power from the restaurant."

"Forget it Walt—look, somebody's coming." A car pulled in beside them, a couple with two young kids got out then scrambled up the snowy bank, climbing the slope to stand inside the star. The dad set first the small child then the larger one on his shoulders, to see better.

Walt grumbled, "We'll come up some foggy night and unscrew 'em all."

"Yeah, let's do that. You're right—it doesn't belong here. Should be on a building, not a mountain."

On the drive down he said, "Damn it, I really wanted—" then let the words die. "Hey listen, I'm gonna meet Tom pretty soon, have a beer and talk—you could come with, or I could drop you at your apartment till we're done, or—" He pulled over. "Or you could drive out to Jill's, and pick me up tomorrow to go skiing."

"Really, you don't want to—"

"I know what coercion's like—you gotta tell me if that's how you feel."

Maybe for him mind, sex, and heart were one, but inside her they were not only separate, they better stay that way. Otherwise, her body would be running the show, making the same bad choices that had devastated her with Cory. "If I take the car, how do you get home?"

"Tom'll give me a ride," he said. "Don't worry about it." He glanced at her. "Be bold, make mistakes—you'll like yourself better."

Cory was a mistake, but not a bold one; she'd been doing what everyone expected. "I like myself."

"Good. Take the car." He drove to Big Screen, put Plug in park, and they got out, meeting between the headlights. When they finished kissing, her glasses were fogged; she took them off and stood on tiptoe, face six inches from his. Her gaze took him in thirstily, anticipating a drought.

"See you," she breathed, a last quick kiss before slipping out of reach, around the door into the driver's seat.

• • •

HE ENTERED THE THEATER lobby as moviegoers straggled out. Up in the booth Tom was packing cans while the last reel rewound.

"Hey buddy."

"Oh hey Walt. Where you wanna go?"

"The Fox?"

"That's fine—should be calm tonight."

"Much of a turnout here?"

"Eighteen for the 7:10 screening, eleven for the 9:15. Fewer tomorrow, I'm guessing."

At The Fox they found a booth in a corner, away from the TV screen and the sparse pickup scene at the bar. Walt ordered a half pitcher of beer.

"Had a surprise the other day," Tom said. "You must be in tune—"

"Don't tell me Eddie found you…"

"Who's Eddie? I got a letter from Laura."

Walt grimaced. "I told you before—that's over."

"Look, I know you're hot for Anna, but don't you remember when we were all tripping that New Year's? Didn't that mean anything?"

Walt had been in Maryland, and Tom with his lover Opal and Laura in Santa Cruz, and through the link of acid they'd joined that night, Walt witnessing Tom's long-term connection to Opal and feeling Laura's with him. But nothing had come of those pledges— Laura got more deeply involved with Cob, stringing Walt along till she finally saw no point in pretending, and Tom was here and Opal in California.

Walt said, "Then why aren't you with Opal?"

"It's happening—I'm going out next summer and we're getting a place. She thinks we should marry, but I advised living together first so she knows she can stand me."

"You're really doing that?" Walt beamed. "Congratulations."

"That whole California cycle's coming around again, then right in sync Laura's letter shows up. She wants to apologize."

There was a subtext to Tom's interest. He'd fallen for Laura before she and Walt left Boulder, and when they were in Santa Cruz had sex at least once. In contrast to Walt's open relationship with Opal, neither Tom nor Laura saw fit to inform him, but Opal knew, and seeing no reason for secrecy, mentioned it to Walt. Was Tom getting back at him for laying Opal, or just overwhelmed by Laura's new vibe, or possibly both? All Walt knew was that Tom had his own motives for beating the drum for Laura. Maybe he just wanted her back in hustling range, or hoped to catch the fallout when Walt rejected her, figuring she'd be vulnerable after a couple years in prison. What a fool, if that was his rationale. Berkeley'd already proved a tough environment wouldn't soften her.

He said, "There's damage not mended by 'I'm sorry,' and she should know that. Do me a favor—don't tell her where I am."

"She knows you're in Boulder. She said her parole hearing's May first."

"I'm not leaving town to avoid her. Tell her I want Never. To. See. Her. Again. If she sends anything I don't want it."

"Then what should I do with this?" Tom produced a letter with no stamp, *Walt Sanders* in that precise compact script he hadn't seen since Santa Cruz.

"Send it back."

"Really? She's had a bad time."

"The guy who loved her died, Tom. And this guy—" poking a finger at his own chest, at his heart, "doesn't love her, and her sad stories mean nothing. This guy knows what he wants, and she's not on the list."

Tom put the letter on the table, Walt turned it face down so he wouldn't see the lines her hand had formed, shaping his name—like voodoo. They talked about car problems and work. Gesturing, Walt knocked over his beer, the envelope floating in the amber puddle. The waitress brought a towel to sop up the spill.

Tom patted the letter sort of dry, then dropped it between them. "You're hiding behind Anna," he said.

"Untrue. I'm doing things for her I've never done for anyone, Laura included."

"Such as?"

"Training for a real job." He told him about the classes he'd signed up for, his hopes. "I'm a man now—I cut my hair and painted my car. I'm swimming in the flow, not just floating anymore. I met her family tonight. I love her, Tom."

"How do you do it? You thrive where there's nothing but barrens clear to the horizon." Tom shook his head and drank more beer. "So what's the plan for skiing?"

"I'll call you in the morning." Anna might come, and Harold had expressed interest—he'd just play it by ear. They put on coats. As Tom pulled the envelope off the table, the flap stuck and tore, showing blue smears inside where the ink had run. He offered it but Walt put his hands in his pockets.

"At least read it," Tom said.

"I don't want a dialog with her."

"When she shows up it won't be that simple."

"Sure it will," Walt said. "I'll spill beer on her and she'll run, just like that ink."

Whatever he thought, Tom was good enough to laugh at his joke.

chapter 14

Christmas Presence

ANNA COULDN'T GET warm. She felt guilty taking off in Walt's car. He said he didn't mind, but if she didn't want him, why lean on him for favors? Bundling up in blankets, she sat on the big couch hoping a pot of camomile tea would make her sleepy. Oblivion stayed away. Jill's taste in literature was atrocious—all these awful comic books lying around—but she picked up Richard Brautigan's *The Hawkline Monster*, and his short chapters and odd sentences kept her reading. It was a brief peculiar novel—"Gothic Western" indeed—she kept laughing. When she'd finished, an image persisted: One of the twin daughters of the scientist had been Magic Child before she became Miss Hawkline, and the chapter "Death of Magic Child" was about one identity making way for another in the same body. Death without the leftover meat. Somehow that made it both more pervasive and less drastic than she'd ever thought. The girl who'd gone overseas naïve and hopeful had died in Cory's apartment; being with Walt had restored spirit to that numb body. A new spirit? Another identity?

If their value to each other was to purge failures, they weren't done. His old girlfriend still haunted him and Cory, though their lives were severed, continued to ramble through her mind. She recalled the joke about the devout man stranded in a flood—when the water was up to his windows, two guys came by in a rowboat and urged him to come with them. "The Lord will provide," he said, declining. When the water had reached the second story, a crew in a power launch told him to hop on board; again he refused: "The Lord will provide." When the water had chased him onto the roof, a helicopter hovered, a man climbed down the ladder; still he said, "No, the Lord will provide." He drowned, and showed up indignant at the pearly gates. "I had faith—why didn't you rescue me?" he demanded, and God said, "I sent you a rowboat, a power launch, I even sent you a helicopter—what were you waiting for?" *So why am I spurning Walt's help*?

By 2:30 in the morning, the house was an icebox, all that tea and a pair of cats asleep on the blankets leaving her wakefulness untouched. Getting up to boil more water, she reached into her jeans pocket—Walt's car keys. She should be with him. Roger always said she was wishy-washy, and suddenly she recognized that and didn't like it. Flinging on boots, heavy coat, cowboy gloves and earband, she drove to Boulder. The streets were deserted—not even a cop. She parked at Walt's, but the kitchen door was locked. She tested the front door; locked too. She aimed a piece of gravel at his small window over the front porch. Nothing. She threw another, which rattled on the porch roof. A light came on and the front door squealed open, a small bell tinging.

"Who's there?" Romo said.

"Anna—can I come in?"

He stepped aside, wordless; she went past him, upstairs. If she knocked on Walt's door she'd wake Stu and Terry, so she slipped into his room, stumbling over his boots just inside.

"Huh?" His eyes flashed open.

"Walt—" She crouched by his mattress.

He sat up, their reaching hands collided. "You're an ice cube—what's wrong?"

"Nothing, I just—" She half fell on him to hug, and shaking off a layer of sleep he pulled her alongside, throwing his blankets over them both. Still in her coat, beside him naked, they rested heads on his pillow.

"What's goin' on?" he drowsed.

"I keep treating you wrong—we should be helping each other."

"Feeling guilty for borrowing my car?"

"No," well, mostly not. "God sent you to—"

A puff of breath—he must be laughing. "God sent everybody on every fool's errand in the world."

"It's Christmas—time to share."

"So you're my Christmas presence, huh?" His tone became playful. "Should I open you? Maybe I better wait." Then somberly, "Tell me something."

Tensing, "What?"

"Is the rest of you as cold as your hands?"

"Yeah."

"Come take a hot bath."

"Won't that wake people up?"

"We don't have to make a racket."

"But what if somebody—"

"You are the queen of all worriers, lady." He kissed her, his free hand undoing her coat buttons, reaching in, up under her shirts—his warm fingers proved even her breast was cold. "Take this stuff off, OK? Everything." They sat up, she shed glasses, coat, shirts, and bra, pressing her cold spine into his warmth to unlace her boots while he kissed her neck, his hands rubbing across her breasts and belly. Boots off, she lay on her back and lifted her hips to slither out of her jeans; change clinked as her pockets emptied onto his sheet.

"If I wasn't crazy about you," he said, "think I'd put up with all this?" After another long kiss, he asked, "Got your diaphragm in?"

"Oh shoot! I have to change the goo, but I left the tube at Jill's."

"You're somethin' else," he said in resigned amusement.

"I'm just a beanbrain—you shouldn't waste your time with me." Clawing the rest of those coins off the sheet, she curled away from him.

"Oh no you don't—you can't come in here, wake me up, turn me on, then say 'sorry, catch you later.'" As she inhaled to object—he really was turning into Cory—he said, "Over on my dresser there's a nice new pack of rubbers. You're already cold—you get 'em."

She hurried to grab the narrow box; this house was way colder than Jill's. Under the covers again, she huddled, shivering. He stroked her back but didn't acknowledge the condoms, just petting her like a big cat. She was about to ask if there was a problem when he murmured, "Put one on me, if you want any."

Now he was giving orders?

As if he could read her mind he said, "We're ridin' the same bus babe—get on board." She was never going to get warm otherwise, so while her mind sifted through rhetoric about sexual politics, her fingers opened a foil pack and rolled the rubber over his erection, then since he was still just lying there, pushed him flat and came down on him, the monologue in her brain reaching a crescendo and becoming babble. Abandoning her head she sank into her desire, breasts squished in his hands while his train rumbling through her tunnel heated her all over, Walt laughing between her legs till he began to gasp and pulled her against him, giving her a dry-mouthed kiss before their fast breaths climbed the scale toward a *sotto voce* shriek.

His racing pulse was inside her and under her fingers spread on his chest. Was this what he meant, saying heart and sex were the same? Her entire body was pounding—she could feel every vein and artery, not a cell of her cold anymore. When she kissed him, the surge in their tongues matched. His hands climbed through her hair from the back of her neck, rousing every nerve, his kisses crossing beneath her jaw, onto her throat. Pulling out he rolled her onto her back, mouth visiting breasts then sternum then navel, finally her vagina which felt lonesome being empty, his tongue sliding over her knob, giving her a big smacking kiss then working her hot spot. She cried and flapped wings, back arching, every level she ascended taking him higher. Flutter-kicking the covers she screeched, flopping her head side to side, pounding the mattress—he caught one hand to twine fingers.

Hand still laced with hers, he cleared stray hairs off her cheek, then planted a small kiss there. He could almost hear her nerves popping like champagne corks even now, his own pinging joyously—what was Tom so skeptical about anyway? Did loving once disqualify you from ever feeling that way about anybody else? All he ever needed was here, breathing into his shoulder and humidifying his sheets, that fast trip from arctic to jungle still roaring in his ears. His heart was so wide open, if not for these blankets the glow would light the room. Instead it was filling her—he could see it in her eyes, feel it rebounding like a superball in a tight space, that second bounce the big one.

• • •

"**WILL YOU TRIP WITH** me today?" he asked. "Harold's bringing mushrooms."

"I shouldn't."

"We both should. I need to know you in that dimension, now that I love you."

"Stop saying that."

"You can't stop me feeling it. Are you slipping?" pulling her on top of him. "Tumbling? Fall on me, flatten me: Let me be your pancake."

"You're so ridic—"

"I'm so happy."

Well, he was, and she couldn't help shining it back.

"Coming skiing today?" he asked.

"First we have to feed the animals at Jill's."

He groaned—that was the opposite direction. "You didn't last night?"

"I ran out the door without my brain last night—I need my dia-phragm gel too, and my new ski socks and parka."

"Right. Where are your skis?"

"At my apartment."

"You're kinda scattered."

"Like the scarecrow in *Wizard of Oz*—'that's me all over.'"

"So tell me," he teased, "what would you have done if I was outta rubbers?"

"Driven around looking for an all-night pharmacy I guess."

"On Christmas Eve? Good luck." The light was early and spar-kling, frost climbing the corners of his windows. "Let's get it over with then." He nudged her, pulling the blankets back, and though she pressed into him, he kept tugging till she was exposed and his heat couldn't compensate for his room's frigidity. She dressed quickly then snatched the covers. Clutching too late, he lay bare to the cold, then grabbed the nearest garments and flung them on.

Plug growled when he hit the ignition, but after a few objections the engine turned over, valves rattling while the oil slowly warmed enough to circulate. Once the temperature gauge had crept off the C, Walt put him in gear and aimed eastward.

On their way out of town he stopped so they could admire the frost-tinged mountains without those lights marring the spectacle.

After a few hours of sun this image would be gone, the silver retreating and blue warming while other colors emerged—dark green conifers, sandstone between the white lines that might persist another day—still beautiful, but tamed by light.

She filled dishes for Doc and the cats while he visited the chickens, gathering eggs and putting down cracked corn. He thought it might be too cold for them outside but they wanted to find out, so he let them into their fenced yard to peck through the snow. Leaving the coop door open a few inches, he went back in the house where she had coffee started and was serving up pie. Carolyn had given them what was left, saying she and Frank couldn't possibly eat all that. Anna dribbled a little runny whipped cream on the pumpkin and set out forks. Tasting hers, she smiled. "Good pie."

"Thank you. Y' know, we're both very fortunate I found that egg yesterday."

"Why?"

"The pie was already burnt—what difference did being pissed off make?"

"I was mostly mad at myself—having you draw me was really awful but I couldn't ask you not to, then once I started walking I didn't want to come back."

"Shoulda said something. How can we trust each other if you won't tell me how you feel?"

"See? I can't do anything right."

"No, I don't buy that." As her face unclenched to wonder what he meant, he said, "Guilt's more addictive than heroin—you should cut back."

"You think I enjoy—"

"You think blaming yourself doesn't hurt anyone but you. That isn't true—every time you cut yourself I bleed."

"That's a worse guilt trip than anything I dreamed up," she exclaimed, and they both laughed.

"What I mean is," he said, "why be a rag cleaning up everybody else's mess?"

"What makes you think I'm doing that?"

"Because I did—and I'm here to assure you there's no satisfaction in it." How was he supposed to respect himself when to Laura he was a convenience? Being as available as air devalued him—she sought the resistance she thrived on, in Cob. "Martyrdom's selfish. In exchange for trashing your situation you get moral superiority, but where does that leave people who care about you?"

She drooped. "I flunked Human Relations before, and I still can't get a passing grade."

"Life lessons aren't like school—they come along whether you want 'em or not, as many times as it takes till you learn. Dropping out's not an option."

"Wish it was," she said under her breath, then pierced him with a look. "So did you learn yours?"

"Some—but there's no end to 'em, far's I can tell. When I got tired of slogging, I discovered embracing the struggle works better. Eventually you'll realize some good came from your relationship with Cory—maybe not what happened, but what you've learned since."

"I keep looking for that, wanting it," she said plaintively.

"Physicists say energy's conserved. On the atomic scale, everything's accounted for. Whatever you do fits somewhere—there's no loss."

"So what did you learn from heartbreak?"

"To seek balance," he said. "To believe the Flow would keep me going, out of pain into the next joy. Absurdity's my salvation. Without it I'd be a goner."

• • •

WHEN THEY'D FINISHED BREAKFAST she said, "It's only 8:15."

"Too early to call people—let's draw some more." With the boiler going and the oven on, the kitchen had warmed pleasantly.

"You can only do my head," she said.

"If only—will you draw me?"

"I'll try." Walt tilted his chair onto its back legs, socks planted against the edge of the table, his pad on his legs while she leaned her chair against the bifold pantry door, beginning to sketch. They worked in silence till he put down his eraser yet again.

"I surrender. This is impossible."

She let her pad fall to her lap. "You're done?"

"Done for. How about you? Keep working—I'll sit here."

"I gave up before you did."

Side by side on the table, the drawings looked as odd as police composite sketches. She laughed, "We're pretty bad."

"Your legs were so much simpler."

"Could I—" she blushed intensely, turning away.

"Yes," leaning over her bent head. "Tell me what to do."

"Sit there—with—with—" she gestured, her hands at her waist folding open forward.

Guessing, he took off his jeans and boxers. "Right?"

She nodded, still scarlet. Back in his chair he pulled his shirttails apart and waffle shirt up, letting his arms fall back, closing his eyes. He could feel her looking at his penis, it came erect at the thought and stayed that way, pulses of embarrassment and desire flowing off her while he daydreamed from skiing to how fine last night had turned out to be, to wondering if he could make his hard-on wave at her.

Finally she closed her pad. "Thank you, I'm done."

He opened his eyes, moving nothing else. "Show me?"

"No, never. It's my secret."

"One more thing," he said, index finger pointing upward, summoning the sky to witness. "I want one more Christmas presence from you."

"What?"

"Let's go out and roll in the snow naked."

She looked at him in bafflement.

"Would you?" he said. "Please?"

"But that's—you're—"

"Silly," grinning now, "I know. Will you?" He was already pulling off the rest of his clothes on his way through the living room; as she followed hesitantly, he ran down the steps into the yard, yelling, "Come on out, the snow's fine!" She undressed by the door, watching him toss handfuls of powder into the air to sift around him. "Hurry up!"

Naked, she stepped out on the porch, soles cramping with cold, the air colder, and tiptoed down the steps starting to shriek, dancing with him in a circle. He somersaulted into a powdery drift. Picking a deep spot, she pretended to be a tree and fell sideways, the shock lifting her back into the air screeching while Walt laughed and howled, then he was hugging her and they rolled over and over, kissing between yelps before leaping to their feet to race inside, running with one mind upstairs to the shower. Hot water felt tepid against the rush in their skins, Walt ecstatic, whooping and jumping around, while she laughed at his delight.

"What do you want drugs for?" she said as they dried off. "You're already tripping."

"I take this moment—" he drew a frame around them in the air, "and paste it in the scrapbook of my heart—" spreading his hands against his chest. "This moment justifies being alive: all the goodness, effort, and shit I've gone through to get here. This moment is divine and you are its god. Thank you thank you thank you." He put an arm around her shoulders and turned her to face the shower, gesturing. "We stand by the cosmic door and push it open just an inch, and the golden stream flowing out is—" eyes like suns, he flung open the shower curtain, "—is laughter."

"It must be," she said, overwhelmed. His radiance made her think of when she'd gone to see the Ceremony of the Black Crown, a ritual performed by high-ranking Tibetan Buddhist holy man the Gyalwa Karmapa. His slow gestures and bass chanting had lasted forty-five minutes, incomprehensible but calming. Afterwards several hundred people lined up to be blessed, the Karmapa draping a strand of red yarn on each person's neck in turn. He took his time—seemed to have nothing but time—and she waited over an hour to stand before him. Most bowed their heads when they reached the platform where he sat, but not being a follower, she looked up into his face—and saw all faces there, shifting and fluid. Meeting his gaze she saw love, wisdom, infinity. What a shame so few dared to look. Ever since, she'd see that brilliance sometimes, flowing through his forehead, through his eyes, from some other world. She saw it now, in Walt's vast smile.

Her knees went watery; sure she stood in the presence of God, she groped for the doorjamb and sank to the footprint-spotted bathmat. Eye level with his kneecaps, she abruptly remembered Cory demanding that she start at his feet, kissing her way up to—abject, lost, worthless, she began to cry.

Squatting, Walt saw her tears, tried to pick her up, but she clutched in a fetal ball so he gathered her onto his lap, stroking and soothing while pain and humiliation rushed over the spillway in her heart. He wrapped her in a towel, still hugging her, kissing her hair, shushing her. As she intook breath to speak, he set his fingers against her lips.

"Don't apologize, whatever you do," he said. "Cory?"

She nodded.

"If it helps cry, but no guilt, OK?" She clamped her arms around his neck to release another volume of grief. His embrace was a garment against the cold; she sagged into him. When she grew quiet, he ventured, "Y'all right?"

She hiccupped and scorned herself for that—what a baby.

He held her awhile longer, then said, "Are we going skiing?"

"Oh yeah," in a normal tone. "What time is it?"

"Christmas—don't need a clock today. But we should call Harold and Tom so they'll be ready."

Four pairs of skis in the middle of the car were going to slide around and interfere with his driving, so from Harold's he called home. Stu answered.

"Hey," Walt said, "think I could borrow Romo's ski rack?"

"We're talking about skiing."

"Who's 'we'?"

"Barbara flew to California yesterday, Terry doesn't ski—just us, I guess."

"Come with."

When they got there with Tom and Harold, packs and skis and everything, Romo shook his head.

"The Blues Bus is bigger."

They loaded gear, put the skis on the rack, then Romo, Stu, and Tom sat in front, Harold and Walt on either side of Anna in the backseat, and Romo aimed the big car up the canyon. Rock faces were bare, but every ledge and protruding tree was blobbed with white. The road twisted between sun and deep shade, margins piled with ridges of plowed snow. Sun dazzled off the frozen creek, catching open water between ice-fringed boulders twenty feet below the pavement.

In the shadows ice glazed the road and as they came around a long curve, the Blues Bus kept turning, executing a complete three sixty. They all watched helplessly as the view through the windshield spun by—creek, back down the road, the canyon wall—and when the car came to rest against the guardrail in the wrong lane, they breathed again, looking down into the drop just a few feet away.

"Sorry folks," Romo said. "I will now drive *very* slowly," easing back to the right lane. Just as he crossed the yellow line a flatbed truck came around the curve, headed down the canyon—as it rumbled past, they sent up a collective gasp.

• • •

ANNA AND WALT PAUSED on the trail, well ahead of the others who'd stopped for a joint. He said, "Did you feel the hand of the cosmos back there, lifting us gently out of the path of destruction?"

"If it's so gentle, why was the road icy?"

"Fortune doesn't change circumstances, just our relation to them. That was perfect—perfect spot, where there's a guardrail, perfect moment, when that truck was far enough away, perfect outcome. A scare's useful—it wakes us up, reminds us what's important."

"What is?" meeting his eyes.

He knew she was afraid to hear it, but their brush with death nudged him. "You. I offer you—" pulling off his right glove, "my hand." He puzzled, "Why do they say 'offering his hand' or 'giving her hand' anyway?"

"Because our hands do everything for us. They work, play, attack, and caress—they stand in for our whole selves."

"They join." He tugged off her glove to put his palm to hers, fingers lacing together. "I offer my hand, my heart, my future. Will you accept them?"

"Are you—" she faltered, "are you asking—"

"Yes. Please be my wife."

"Oh Walt, I can't do that. Where, how?"

"In Boulder—we'll find a judge—on March fourth."

"Huh?"

"One of my favorite days—march forth! A call to action."

"To arms maybe."

"To my arms, to yours," releasing hands to hug her. She pulled back, which unbalanced him, and they fell into the snow, powder fluffing up then settling in their collars and up their sleeves, all over their faces. He grinned.

She smiled faintly back. "Don't push me, don't rush me."

"By then I'd like to know."

"What if—"

"No 'what if'—that's a game I don't play anymore. I want to send my light into all the little corners where your doubt is hiding, and obliterate the shadows, and convince you I not only mean what I say, but I know myself well enough that it's true."

"All I know is my hand's frozen." Getting upright turned out to be a project: the hole they'd made was too big and soft to climb out of, and floundering only enlarged it. Finally they took off their skis, set them edge to edge, and pulled up onto them like swimmers boarding a raft. Upright at last, covered with snow, they clipped back into their bindings. "Here," he offered, lifting his shirt. "Put your hand in my armpit to warm it." She guided his bare hand under her arm as well, which was how they were standing when the others came up the trail.

Romo broke into a grin. "Snow sex?" Every time he looked at her she blushed—why couldn't it have been Walt who opened the door last night?

"Thawing our hands," Walt explained.

"And somebody else's heater's bound to be hotter than yours."

"Bound to be," Walt agreed, but Anna looked away. Cupping her hands in his, he blew warm breath on them. "Better?"

She nodded slightly, feeling everyone staring at her.

"What a couple of idiots," Harold said. "Don't let all that melt on you."

Walt brushed off as much snow as he could and Anna, snapping out of her trance, shook her pant legs and parka. Once Romo, Stu, and Tom were up the trail, Harold pulled a plastic bag from his pants pocket

"Here's the shrooms—still want 'em?"

"Yeah, thanks," Walt said. "Just a few." He lay his backpack on a snowcapped rock, spread his bandana between the straps, then pinched dried mushrooms into the center. "This good, Anna?"

Her face was blank. "See you up the trail." She pushed off.

He gave the bag back to Harold, carefully folding the bandana and tucking the lumpy square into his coat pocket.

"You and Anna are pretty cozy," Harold said. "You know she's been hurt."

"So've I."

"When she came home from London, she couldn't even look me in the eye—afraid of everything, no self-respect, didn't trust anyone." He leveled a hard look at Walt. "Don't send her back to that."

"We're helping each other," Walt said, then he asked, "Has she always been shy?"

"It's funny—when we were growing up, the neighborhood kids were mostly boys, and even though she'd get pushed around for being the youngest, she held her own. Girls made her shy, making fun of her glasses. You might think she feels out of place skiing with five guys, but it's you that's embarrassing her."

"Me? How?"

"Around you she can't be just another guy."

• • •

AT LUNCH ROMO OPENED a bottle of retsina, Greek white wine flavored with resin. "It tastes like a forest," passing it around. Walt thought it was weird, but Anna liked it.

"Like drinking pine trees," she said. "I love the smell. Where'd you get it?"

"Liquor World, where else?"

"I don't think I'd want it with dinner, but it's perfect out here." She took another swig and passed it to Harold, who was watching her very closely. The way his eyes jumped from her to Walt she was sure he misunderstood—seemed ready to heroically drive him off if she so much as grimaced.

"Hey Harold, let's telemark on that slope we passed," her eyes ordered him to agree, so he followed.

Once they'd cut a few curves, they sat on a downed tree. "Don't interfere," she said.

"I'm not gonna stand by and watch you get hurt."

"I'm stronger now—this is OK."

"You damn near lost your mind—you can't—"

"I'm old enough to decide for myself." She didn't mention Walt's proposal—even seeing it coming, what a jolt. "Look at me, Harold." Their eyes met—her protector. Once he'd beat up a guy who harassed her in high school. "If I need help, I promise I'll ask."

"Are you happy?"

Her face relaxed into a wide smile.

"All right," smiling too, "gimme a hug."

As they climbed back up to the trail, the others were arriving to carve some turns; they all telemarked till the slope was too potholed to ski down without wiping out. Romo sent around the retsina again to kill it.

"Last one to the car's a rotten egg," Harold said.

"You'll never catch me," Anna declared, and the others watched as with a flash of ski bottoms she and her brother took off in flying strides. Tom went next, then Walt, with Romo and Stu bringing up the rear. As Walt neared the end of the trail, Anna passed him going up for another run, grinning wide, and calling, "See you at the car." When she reached Stu, she turned around and swished back down the trail, rapid and graceful as though her speed elevated her to a different sport. Harold was lying on the Blues Bus hood when the rest of them crunched across the gravel carrying their skis.

"Who won?" Walt asked him.

"Are you kidding?

She opened the ski rack with a grin. "It's like flying on the ground."

chapter 15

Fear Is a Doorway

ROMO SPOTTED THE black Ford with square taillights in the parking area, and kept driving.

"Anyone with anything illegal on 'em, get out or get rid of it,"
he ordered when they were two blocks past.

Torn from his post-exertion stupor, Harold panicked. "What do
you mean?"

"I mean the narcs are back with a warrant to search this car.
Christmas Day man!" He pounded the dash, cutting loose with a
long string of curses.

"Start walking on Arapahoe," Anna told her brother. "Walt and
I'll pick you up." Romo looked at her gratefully—at least someone
was thinking. Seeing a trashcan on a side street curb, he pulled over
and cut the engine.

Harold got out. "These ski boots aren't good to walk in—"

"Enjoy your freedom," Romo growled. Blanching, Harold shoul-
dered his pack and headed down the street. Tom got out too, then
Walt had to choose.

"Anna, let's either eat these shrooms right now, or ditch 'em."

She hated to waste anything, but being pushed into a decision
was even worse.

He unwrapped the bandana. "Romo? Stu?"

"You gotta be kidding, man. Trip with narcs?"

"We're not sticking around," Walt said. "Gotta get Anna back to Hunt Ridge."

He popped two caps into his mouth, munched and added a couple more. Anna fidgeted watching, and finally ate two. With no more takers, he shook the rest into the trashcan, then dug the crackers out of Stu's pack, pulverized several in the bandana and brushed the crumbs off. He shared an orange with Anna to clear the evidence off their breath and fingers, nibbling peel, then throwing that away.

"All clean—let's go home."

Romo drove back on a parallel street so he could approach the house again as though from the canyon, and parked this time. Three narcs climbed stiffly from the unmarked cruiser, flashing badges.

"Last time we didn't get a chance to look in your car," their leader said, dangling the warrant like a bully daring you to grab your lunch money back. Romo read it, then unlocked his trunk and popped the hood.

"Be my guests," resignedly, opening the roof rack. Walt loaded skis into Plug, then he and Anna got in, but when he started the engine the biggest narc came over. Walt rolled down his window.

"Where d'ya think you're going?"

"We're house-sitting—it's time to feed the animals."

"This car's going nowhere till we've searched it. Get out."

"The warrant's for—"

"This property including all vehicles."

"Well, we really do need to get back." Walt concentrated on his breathing, pushing down distress poised to flip over into panic. He unlocked the trunk, lifted the hood, then handed Romo his car keys, saying, "Later, man," under his breath. Romo nodded grimly. Anna put her pack on one shoulder, moving toward the sidewalk; once all three narcs were busy, Walt joined her and they backed up then sidled then turned and walked away casually, rounding the corner, speeding up once the house was out of sight. Five blocks away, they started thumbing in sparse traffic. A guy in a pickup stopped and they crammed into the cab beside his dog. Anna worried how Harold was getting home, but in half a mile they didn't see him. She told the driver Jill's address.

"I can drop you at Hunt Ridge. Merry Christmas—I'm Norm."

After brief greetings they settled into silence, Walt and Anna coming on to the mushrooms while the truck proceeded east. Dashboard and floor were cluttered with papers, beer bottles, soda cans and fast food wrappers; Anna in the middle couldn't see much else, the world shrinking toward her. She longed for a shower; a crust of sweat had stiffened the skin on her face and neck. Harold was right—these boots were uncomfortable. She wished she'd thought to grab her hiking boots from Walt's trunk.

She vibed on the husky: its panting tongue scattered drips on her, wolf just under the domestic surface. It grinned at her, asking how strong an animal she was, and a cringe of fear ran through her. She and the dog made eye contact, then without so much as a warning growl, it lunged at her, their bodies colliding, paws and strong legs against her chest—and she felt knives rake her jaw seeking her neck. Reeking breath, heat, stabbing, wet—saliva? blood?—her mind shrank away, desperate to hide. Pain flared along her nerves.

Walt's energy interposed, he shouted as he pushed her down, a confusion of hands and arms fighting off the dog. A sawing noise erupted from the animal's throat. As she clamped her hands over her torn face, Norm's voice joined the racket, high and alarmed. The truck jerked sideways and stopped.

The dog was out of the cab now—she didn't even have to open her eyes to know: this space crowded with chaos was suddenly ringing empty. *He attacked because he was cornered—not enough room in here. Now he can breathe—he's done. I was the weakest one—that's why he went for me.* Her skin reported every impact point where the dog had hurled not just body but its whole being against her. She heard magpie cries—"Aaa, aaa, aaa"—and noticed her own larynx, her own lungs voicing them.

"Let me see, let me see," Walt urged, prying her hands off her face for an instant, then letting them clamp back into place.

"Oh, god." Norm was next to her again, he slammed the door, his voice high pitched with panic. "He's never done that, I—"

"She's bleeding," Walt said, but not to her. "Take us to the Emergency Room."

The pickup lurched around, engine roaring like another angry animal. Anna couldn't stop wailing, clutching her face to hold it together; warmth dribbled toward her wrists. Walt pulled her close, chanting, "You'll be OK, I'll take care of you, don't be afraid," over and over, as if undoing a curse. The truck wheeled around corners, throwing her from Walt's shoulder into Norm's, as though whatever magnetism each exerted was immediately counteracted by a cosmic force intent on isolating her.

In the Emergency pull-through, Norm cut the engine. Walt helped her out. She glimpsed the dog standing in the truckbed, mouth open, smiling. *Sorry I got in your way*, she said to the animal, mind to mind. It gave her a triumphant look, gladiatorial, self-possessed. It could have lunged again, to finish her off, but chose not to—she was conquered. That was the point.

Walt and Norm were half leading, half carrying her through the open glass doors, then the dog was in the past and she was in a room that smelled of fear sweat, urine, antiseptic, and coffee.

"Should I stay?" Norm asked Walt.

"Let's get her checked in first."

At the Triage window, they faced a desk scattered with papers, an empty chair—she cast her eyes around bewildered. A door opened, a nurse came out eating a Christmas tree cookie with green sugar sprinkles, laughing over her shoulder. Seeing them, her cheer stiffened; she beckoned, the guys moved Anna into her cubicle and pressed her into the armchair beside the desk.

"Come on, sweetie, I have to see."

At the kind touch brushing her knuckles, Anna's sticky hands fell loose, dropping to her lap.

The nurse recited, "Two lacerations here—tilt your head honey," one finger on her chin and another on the top of her head angling her face to one side. "Punctures on the jaw," fingertips identifying, "and two, no, three on the neck, and a welt, but the skin's not broken there." She released Anna's head and wrote on a form while Walt and Norm stood watching.

"What about you, sir?" She turned to Walt's red palms. Examining, she remarked some of this blood was his. "Dog bites," she said, "Where's the dog?"

"In my truck," Norm said.

"Has it had rabies shots?"

"Yeah—lemme think when."

"It'll say on the tag."

"Right, I'll go check."

● ● ●

BUT HE WAS GONE so long Walt figured he'd split. He talked to the billing people, signed pieces of paper, then an aide walked him with Anna into the back. They sat in a partitioned space together, the mushrooms cuing them to other injured people behind curtains. This ward was a collection point for misery. It struck Walt as very strange anyone would choose to concentrate psychic distress this way, magnifying its power to defeat healing. It should be dissipated by open air, not compounding itself—people who worked here must get sick from it. He remembered one of the nurses after his California car accident: she carried herself as though she'd been stabbed, hunching sideways, her stride off-kilter. At the time he'd thought she had a deformity; now, psilocybin told him the hysterically negative Emergency Ward energy had crippled her.

He projected radiance toward Anna—her vibe was dark as clotting blood—but she just looked at him, blank and empty, as though she deserved the attack. His mental images of sun on snow where they'd skied today couldn't get in: her spirit resisted. Was he to blame, not just because she was the one sitting next to the dog, but for being in that situation at all? As though the cosmos had reversed course to maintain equilibrium, this morning it spared them from an awful wreck in the canyon, then this afternoon turned their flight from his household into something worse than the narc raid. Hairline cracks of doubt spread—had the universe enlisted him to deliver the next blow to her shaky confidence? He sat in silence, holding her hand, and finally the medical team arrived. Walt described the attack while the doctor cleaned her wounds with a sterile swab; the Triage nurse interrupted to report the dog's rabies shot was last May.

"Well, that's fortunate," the doctor said, returning to his task. "I think she'll need stitches along the jaw—the wounds are deeper against the bone than on her cheek." Anna stared while the aide selected sutures and gauze pads to soak in antiseptic. The doctor pressed a hypodermic into her cheek to numb the area; while that was taking effect he turned to Walt's injury.

As they cleaned off blood, a long deep slash was revealed, running the length of the heel of his hand from wrist to pinky, along with three puncture wounds by his knuckles. "Have to stitch him too." The doctor spoke only to his aide, as though Walt and Anna were just pieces of meat. He injected Walt's hand, then tapped on Anna's jaw—numb. He inserted the curved needle into her skin; when the point poked through, Walt went light-headed, and bent forward breathing slowly, trying not to pass out.

The aide touched his shoulder. "You all right?"

He didn't answer—his vision was going spotty, ears zinging, face clammy. Anna's hand rested on his forearm. Focusing on her touch he swam back, nudging his temple against her wrist.

"Expect some bruising," the doctor said, applying narrow tape to Anna's cheek above the stitches, "particularly under your jaw. I'll leave prescriptions for an antibiotic and painkillers. Keep your face dry for four days," as he pressed on another strip an inch away, parallel to the first. "No exertion sufficient to cause sweating, don't wash it, don't eat spicy foods. Wear these bandages as long as possible, and trim the ends when they start to peel back. Make an appointment to have the stitches removed in a week—that'll be after New Year's."

The aide offered the doctor a longer suture. Walt looked at the hand he was preparing to stitch—numb and bloody, a glove they should throw away—waste of time to mend it first. Anna's pain was vivid to him; why could he feel nothing below his own wrist? Her stitches had been impossible to witness, but the doctor's task now meant nothing. He glanced at Anna. Her eyes were dull, energy sunk inward. He tried to remember the dog's teeth: The jaw across his hand, yes. This long slash? No. Maybe he'd cut himself on part of the truck? All he could recall was the dog's roar, then Anna's face, blood between her fingers—

He wasn't sure how they'd got here. When they played bounce-ket-ball a couple blocks from here, Anna'd told him her grandfather served on the hospital board. Was that why they were in this big cold room capped with flickering light, in a curtained alcove where fear and misery rebounded like superballs? He felt tugging, and thought a child was trying to get his attention, help him escape. But it was the doctor, tying off another stitch. A row like a spiral binding decorated the heel of his hand. Weren't they done yet? He wanted to get away before something worse happened—the air was thick with agony.

The doctor removed his latex gloves and wrote on a pad, tearing off one sheet, two, a third, handing them not to him but to the aide. "Be sure to make a follow-up appointment," he said, and left. The curtain was open now—fear and pain belonged to the figure on the gurney across the way—victim of a beating, it seemed, with damage as much psychic as physical. He had to free Anna from this misery trap. The aide was trussing his hand with gauze, telling him how long to keep it in place, giving him other orders that were slipping between his thoughts like tires sliding on ice. It was a surprise to find himself back in the waiting room with a fat envelope in his good hand, Anna leaning into him as they wobbled to a phone.

Romo picked up on the first ring.

"Hey, it's Walt." But the noise behind his housemate slapped him present—the narcs. "They're still at it?"

"Gotta be done soon—they're running out of things to break."

The cosmic egg-beater was cranking furiously, and everyone he touched was spinning in the blades, savaged. Why? What would make it stop?

He was ashamed to ask a favor but Anna needed help. "We're at the Emergency Room—could somebody pick us up?"

"My car's trashed but yours isn't as bad—I'll ask Stu."

Walt and Anna sagged into each other on a bench outside, his arm around her shoulders. Bad energy dispersed into the chill. At last, he trusted his surroundings enough to take several deep breaths.

"Hey sweetie," he ventured, "you gonna be OK?"

"That dog exploded in my face."

A *doggone dog-bomb*, he thought, but he couldn't say that without sounding heartless so he kept quiet while they waited for Stu.

When they got home the narc car still sat in the lot.

"Stay put," Walt told her, following Stu into the house. The lead cop said they were done with Plug—he could take it. Romo sat in the kitchen staring at the mess. As Walt offered scattershot details of the dog attack, his housemate regarded him dully. Waving his hands, Walt concluded, "I'll be home tomorrow." Romo just nodded from far away.

• • •

WALT DROVE OUT TO Jill's in a daze. Hadn't even looked at his room—Christmas! But he should've thrown away the mushrooms— Anna might've been OK with the dog otherwise. He kept following his instincts dealing with her, but the very acts that worked and made sense for him wreaked havoc on her. Maybe she was right to retreat into her shell. Every time she stepped out, harm dropped on her like a hunting hawk.

Feeling battered, he fed Doc, the cats, the chickens, then mechanically chopped onion and bell pepper for rice and veggies while she phoned Harold. Her brother had hitched a ride home— when she told him about the dog, he said he'd come over.

"What for? Walt's looking after me."

The silence on the line was cold with judgment. Finally Harold said, "Why do you trust this guy?"

"He shielded me so the dog bit him instead—you're wrong about him."

He hung up on her.

Dinner was ready but her face hurt—she couldn't chew, could scarcely drink. Walt offered to make broth but she said not to bother. "I'm going to bed."

"Call your boss," he said. "You can't work tomorrow."

"I'll manage."

"I'm off this week—it's winter break. I'll sub for you."

She trudged upstairs, shed a layer, and though she still felt grungy, slipped beneath the covers in her long underwear. He sat beside her in the dark, stroking the long bones in her hand as she receded into sleep. He kissed her forehead. No doubt his marriage proposal had been swept away in the avalanche that followed. Her surprise visit this morning—and the ski trip—were so wonderful, then the day turned nightmare. What was going on?

In the living room he found a copy of the I Ching on a bookshelf and sifted through his pocket change, picking out three nickels. Composing himself on the rug he shook the coins in his cupped hands, threw them, noted heads and tails, gathered them, concentrated and shook again, six times in all. Drawing whole or broken lines from bottom to top, he formed Hexagram 25, Wu Wang (Innocence/The Unexpected), which changed to 21, Shih Ho (Biting Through). The commentary for Innocence said that something external in origin was certain to pass on its own, not being connected to his behavior—but also said that motiveless action resonated in the larger world, while attempts to influence events on his own behalf would fail. The near-miss in the canyon bore that out, but so did the psilocybin trip. He should've given the shrooms back to Harold. What were psychedelics going to show him and Anna about each other that sex hadn't already?

• • •

IN THE MORNING HER face was blue and purple along her jaw, but she did rinse off, aiming the shower head low to keep her head dry. With clean clothes on, her body from the neck down felt almost normal, but she winced at every swallow. Walt phoned Perfectly Clean. Stefan was alarmed at his report; Walt knew his next thought would be about her jobs, so he cut that short by offering to do them. Then he cooked up a batch of Malt-O-Meal.

Anna slurped a few bites of the cereal then, as it cooled, toyed with it, shaping a pyramid with the back of her spoon. Considering that, she plopped another mound into her bowl, and with a chopstick began sculpting a sphinx. Walt stopped eating to watch, then served a jellied lump onto a plate and trimmed it with a tableknife to a sarcophagus shape. As he put in details, she added her own embellishments with her chopstick. Clearing away the trimmings they looked at their handiwork—she couldn't smile without hurting, but her eyes crinkled with humor. Getting out pads and pencils, they drew the miniature Egyptian still life, and when they were done they looked at the drawings. She'd included tabletop, bowl, and plate to provide context, while Walt's pictures floated on the page. She liked his bigger images, he liked Egypt in dishes: absurdity enhanced the effect.

• • •

WHEN JILL CAME HOME midafternoon they left, stopping by Harold's to deliver his ski gear and hiking boots. Her brother made a critical inspection of Anna's face, and scolded them for not filling their prescriptions yet. Herding them into his dim living room where Boston blasted on the stereo, he went to the pharmacy himself. Walt turned off the music, holding Anna's hand in silence while they waited. Once Harold returned, he made them each take a double dose of antibiotics, then ordered Anna to give him daily progress reports. By the time they were back in Plug heading for Boulder, the sun was gone and cold was sharpening.

"Drop me at home," Anna said. He helped bring in her gear, and once he'd set down boots and skis, she snared him with one arm for a strong hug. "Thank you." As his ears strained toward the words, she mumbled what might've been "I love you."

"I'll come by tomorrow and make soup," he promised. His hands shook all the way home, the left pulsing with pain, the right spastic with ecstasy.

When he walked in the kitchen and saw broken drawers and the dismembered toaster, it was as though the narcs had just left—every glance raked him further. Romo was sorting tapes in the living room. His six-year collection of Dead concerts was strewn, quite a few cassettes snapped apart with the tape spiraling out, splintered plastic boxes everywhere.

"Hey Romo, I'm back."

"Hey Walt," flatly.

"What's the most urgent repair? I'm subbing for Anna at nine thirty, but I'll fix things till then."

"Look around—I'm sure you can find something broken."

"You OK?"

"Why wouldn't I be?" Romo snarled. "Doesn't the law say they can come in with their piece of paper and destroy our space? Doesn't it say they can do this till they find something? I'm tempted to shit in a bowl, stick a roach in it, and invite 'em to go fishing."

"What'd they do to your car?"

"Slashed the upholstery, tore out the headliner, broke the glove box. They yanked loose some wiring and pulled out the fuse panel."

"Tom knows a guy in auto electric—"

"I'm done with that car. If I fix it enough to sell maybe I can break even."

"I'll copy my car keys and give you a set. It's not like I drive a lot."

"Thanks man. Better check out your room—they spent a long time in there—you're probably wired for sound."

Walt went upstairs. His mattress was worse this time: a long diagonal gash showed springs torn from their casings. His clothes rod was on the floor, plaster ground into his one suit, the peg rack pulled down again, the holes in the wall bigger than before. The back of his dresser was ripped away, tracks for two of the four drawers broken. The narcs hadn't done much to his bookshelf on their previous visit so they made up for that. Every book had been pulled off, many of them obviously flung, covers torn and spines cracked, loose pages visible in the heap. He pushed books and clothes out of the way and turned the mattress over. The underside was slashed too, but no springs were sticking out. He got the duct tape. Once that side was patched, he shook the plaster off his blankets and lay down to close his eyes just a moment.

• • •

STU WOKE HIM. "HATE to bother you, but Anna's boss is here."

He sat up woozy, then stumbled down to the kitchen where Stefan and Terry were talking.

"What's with your hand?" Stefan asked.

"Got some stitches."

"And you think you're working tonight?" He turned to his window washer. "Help me out." Terry grabbed his workshirt and they left. Walt went upstairs, turned out his light on the chaos and went back to sleep.

In the morning Lloyd was there.

"I'm ready to sue," Romo said. "They've gone too far."

"You have to document the damage," Lloyd said. "Everything—every room, your car—then write out a statement. Oh hey Walt," he acknowledged him. "Housemates can corroborate what they did last time—we'll play up that they ripped into your home on Christmas—no jury'll stand for that. A warrant isn't carte blanche—they're pushing you around 'cause they think they can get away with it."

"I'll help," Walt offered, then Lloyd asked about his hand.

Once he'd heard the gist of it, he remarked, "Not very lucky are you?"

"I have tons of luck," Walt said. "Some of it's bad, that's all. I can move out—"

"Don't," Romo said. "I need you here paying rent. I'm worried Barbara'll leave."

"How bad's her room?"

"About like last time. Find any bugs upstairs?"

"Didn't look yet."

"Check for wires around your door and windows, or in the holes in your walls."

"Count me in for your lawsuit," Walt said. "People don't realize narcs do stuff like this—the only time you hear about searches is when they find something." He turned to Lloyd, "Can they hit us again after coming up empty twice?"

"If they have probable cause and a sympathetic judge."

"Then let's publicize," Romo decided. "Can you handle the exposure, Walt? I want to call the media, get a photographer in here and make a splash. Lawsuits move under the radar—I want the word out."

Walt thought about Anna's family—how would the Brubakers react, seeing their daughter's friend they'd just met front and center in a failed drug bust? But his choice came down to comfort versus right: he had to support Romo. "Yeah—get the press in here. Let's make a big stink."

"Good. Stop cleaning."

"Think I'll check up on Anna."

Romo squinted, worried. "Stu said she looked pretty bad—will she be OK?"

"Hope so," whispering past the knot in his throat.

Romo embraced him. "Go on," he said, rubbing Walt's shoulder.

"We'll nail 'em to the wall, buddy," Walt said. "They won't get away with this."

chapter 16
Not Gonna Take It

WHEN WALT GOT home, a TV crew was filming in the living room. Romo waved him over to meet the reporter.

"They just got here—show 'em your room."

The camera guy looked stricken as Walt turned over his mattress to show the side he hadn't duct taped. He pointed out his suit on the floor, plaster stomped into the dark wool, then held up some damaged paperbacks.

"Did they really have to tear my books in half? Was it necessary to break my dresser? Is it reasonable to come in and do this on *Christmas*?"

They toured the bathroom, which Terry had cleaned up just enough to use.

"They've been here and found nothing *twice*—we're being harassed. We don't have high-paying jobs, but now we have all this stuff to fix, and if people move out because of the raids, we have to pay more rent to cover their share. Did you see Romo's car? It's not legal to drive—have you priced auto electric service? Maybe you could afford this, but we can't."

"Consider the economic angle," the reporter said to the camera. "So you have no recourse?"

"Far's I know," Walt said sarcastically, "disaster relief doesn't cover narc tornadoes. That's why we're suing."

"For damages?"

"To publicize abuse of power—the Constitution prohibits unreasonable search and seizure—we think this qualifies."

"Thank you, Walt Sanders. This is Channel Five On-the-Spot News, from Boulder." Camera packed up, they went out to their van. More people stood around in the parking area: newspaper reporters and a guy from public radio. Romo toured the wreckage with them, then answered questions in the kitchen.

When they'd finally left, Walt asked him if that was everybody.

"Close enough," Romo said. "Things cool with Anna?"

"Yeah—thanks for asking."

She'd insisted on visiting her grandparents this morning; their affection was some security blanket. He wondered how she'd explain the dog attack, but she assured him it would all make sense. Turned out she was after her grandma's home remedy for wound care, and for someone who changed her mind like the weather, she was surprisingly stubborn. He wasn't going to join her but she wanted a ride, and when they arrived, her grandpa was outside—Anna's conversation pulled in Walt, and next thing he knew he was in their living room. Her grandma gave her a small tin of lamb fat, saying it was pure lanolin, and instructed her to rub it on the gashes every few hours. "Don't keep the stitches in longer than seven days—by then they're not helping, and they'll leave marks."

On the drive back to Anna's, he mentioned the doctor's office wouldn't be open till the ninth day. To him that didn't matter, but for Anna her grandma's advice was gospel. He shelved what was turning into an argument. Once New Year's rolled around, she'd see it was no big deal to wait another couple days. He couldn't imagine she'd go back to the ER to get stitches out—and who else would be open?

He apologized for pressing her to do mushrooms—his expectation of what would happen had blinded him. Anna wouldn't talk about it, and he worried she'd never trust him again. He remembered a dumb stunt he'd pulled as a teenager: afterwards his mom observed that a mistake was only innocent if nobody got hurt.

• • •

IN HIS ROOM HE shelved books, arranging the fiction by style and era, nonfiction by subject. Many were too torn up to keep so he started a list, also noting time he spent on repairs. His mattress was really trashed now, but why get another if the narcs might come back? They'd ripped his sheets too. His sleeping bag was still in one—dirty—piece; he'd just sleep in that. He spread his blanket on the mattress, the bag on top, then put his clothes rod back up. Before patching the wall he shone his flashlight into the cavity, clipping a wire much thinner than the old fabric-wrapped house cable. He recalled Coppola's film *The Conversation*: at the end, Gene Hackman, a surveillance man, ripped apart even his walls and floor, knowing he might never find the bugs in his apartment.

Much later, Anna called. "Coming over tonight?"

"I'm pretty busy."

"How's your hand?"

"Not too bad."

She paused. "Are you depressed?"

"Well, yeah. Watch the news—we should be on tonight."

"I don't have a TV."

"Barbara's friend Rita does. We're going over there for the 11:00 news."

"I'd like to see it too—I'll walk over."

"Sure that's safe after dark?"

"I've walked around Boulder at all hours since I was a teenager— I'm fine."

He resumed repairs, and twenty minutes later she stood in his doorway. His half smile invited her in. She dropped her pack and coat on his mattress and began sorting scattered clothes—a pile to wash, a folded pile that was still clean. He was fixing his dresser, sandwiching the torn edges of the masonite backing in duct tape.

"Here," he said, "hold this while I tack it." She helped him position it. The dresser's sides wanted to lean without the back to hold them upright; he shot in staples around the edges. After he'd taped the splintered drawer tracks one by one, Anna held them in place while he drove in screws. He slid in the drawers and filled them with his clean clothes, then checked the time.

"Let's go catch the news." They went over with Romo and Stu, crowding Rita's living room. The three-minute piece had good visuals including interviews with Romo and Walt—seemed likely to create the level of outrage they were after.

"Brace for a counterstrike," Romo said. "The narcs will try to justify this by making us look bad."

Anna said Jill was having a New Year's party, and some of the people she'd invited worked at the new public TV station. Romo said maybe he'd come.

• • •

THE NEXT DAY HAROLD called Anna—he'd seen the news. "Mom and Dad musta heard by now—it's in the paper too. Better call 'em."

She couldn't bring herself to—they'd just met Walt. She figured it was better to say nothing. But that was before the police department huddled and came up with their response. In a TV interview that night, they said Walt had been jailed in November in connection with a sexual assault.

"Law-abiding citizens have nothing to worry about," the police chief said. "This young man had drugs on him when we brought him in. We had probable cause to search that house." That was slanderous, but even if Walt managed to clear his name, the idea was planted that he deserved what had happened.

In the morning Walt contacted the TV station; the reporter said he'd have to ask his manager whether this story was worth any more airtime. The guy got permission for an interview so they met, and Walt explained he'd never been charged with anything. But the story didn't have the dramatic pulse the station manager wanted, so he killed the piece. Walt talked to a gaggle of newspaper reporters too, but when they realized he'd had the knockout drug in his pocket, he felt the tide moving against him. Sure enough, their stories played up the drug angle.

Anna came over New Year's Eve morning, and they had coffee while she read one article after another. "These are so inaccurate," she raged.

"That's what the world knows—nothing I can do about it."

Tapping her cheek she said, "It's seven days today. I'm going to have Grandpa Francis take my stitches out. He could do yours too—want to come?"

Why'd she suggest that, with the newspapers depicting him as some degenerate? Parents—and grandparents even more—didn't want to know everything. His sure didn't. She couldn't prevent them reading about this, but by visiting she'd be inviting them to probe deeper. "No. I'll do it." Picking up a paring knife he sliced his first stitch.

"You shouldn't do that on yourself."

"Then help me." With needle-nosed pliers and the small scissors on his Swiss Army knife, they sat at the kitchen table, his hand outstretched while she snipped the cords and gently pulled them out. When she was done, he looked at the stiffly curled sutures on the table, then his hand. "I'll never get a job teaching in this town now."

"You didn't do anything." Her hand rotated over the newspapers as if to rub their noses in their own lies. "They're all wrong."

"To which the world says, 'So what?' Talk to Harold?"

"Not today."

"Call him—see what he says."

She gingerly punched in digits, as though the number pad might deliver electric shocks. "Harold? It's Anna."

"Is this shit in the papers true?" he boomed. Walt heard him clearly as she held the phone away from her ear.

"No. Well, some of it. The drugs were a coincidence—he wasn't charged."

"He's really marginal, Anna. Stay away from him."

"Walt's a good—"

"You're a fool." He hung up. She looked at the receiver, then at Walt staring into his coffee mug as though the future were written there and he could finally read it.

"I'm outta here," he said, standing up.

"I was going to call—"

"Call from someplace else. I'm leaving."

"Where?" she asked, confused. "When?"

"Now. California maybe."

"You're just running out? Don't you think that makes you look guilty?"

"Far's the papers are concerned, I am. Telling the truth just made it worse. I need to let the mud settle, come back when the water's clear again." He put his hands in her hair, tilting her head back to look her in the eyes. "I'll be back by March fourth." They hadn't kissed since the dog bite, but he put his mouth to hers now as if to store her inside him. A hard squeeze, then he let go. She followed to his room where he collected sleeping bag, tent, and winter clothes.

"What about all this?" Her gesture took in his books, his dresser.

"I paid January rent—that's all I can do."

"What about New Year's?"

"I'm not staying another minute."

"Please?"

Alarms were going off in his head, so loud he couldn't think; her voice was a steady point to focus on. He slowed his breathing, closed his eyes listening for silence beneath the clangor, and gradually he could hear it, easing his mind to stillness. When he opened his eyes he gave her a wry smile.

"I don't have to dash out the door this second I guess. I'll come to Jill's party tonight, but tomorrow I'm on the road."

"How'd you do that? You were all wound up, then you just—"

"Shut your eyes. Under your heartbeat, under your breath, inside your rib cage, there's a seed of silence. Find it, tune in to it."

She was nodding, eyes closed.

"Listen to it—it's always there—sometimes all you need is to step back."

She looked at him sharply. "How does that jibe with leaving?"

"Sometimes you have to step further back."

"Then I'm coming too."

"You don't even know where I'm going—what'll you do?"

"Whatever you do—scrounge work—I'll bring some window washing gear."

Hitting the road again was natural for him, but it bothered him that she'd drop everything to come along. He thought about Ray, his housemate in Santa Cruz and possibly the sanest person he'd ever met—what would he suggest? "So what do you think of me running away like this?"

"You're cornered—I understand. But there's other ways to—"

"Anna, if I didn't love you, I wouldn't be doing this. I'm accepted in my community—my housemates, people with lifestyles like mine. But your family wants someone respectable and decent for you. I saw the way your grandparents look at you—you're the light of their lives. How could I sully that?"

"They trust my judgment. If I tell them I love you, they'll be happy for me. And Dad's used to young people in trouble—"

"Doesn't want you to marry one, I'll bet." He sighed, touching her jaw. "We didn't take out your stitches."

Back in the kitchen she sat on the table where the other sutures still clustered, and one by one he clipped and eased hers out. Setting down pliers and knife, he swept the curls into his palm.

"Let's bury these." The snow was gone from sunny spots. She held the stitches while he dug into damp ground, turning over a wedge of clay with half an inch of soil on top. He pinched tiny knots off her palm, sprinkling them into the hole.

"Let wounds be buried and healing grow," he said. She shook the rest from her hand. He broke up the dirt and tamped it down, then turned her face toward the sun—the bites weren't nearly as bad as they'd looked in the Emergency Room. He kissed up one line then down the other before her mouth found his.

"What are you burying there?" someone accosted them. They separated, turning—another TV reporter with a cameraman.

"Misery," Walt said. "What do you want?"

"I'm with Channel Seven News—I got a call from Sean at Channel Five, said he interviewed you but his manager never aired it. He saw some of the stories in the newspaper and thought he should've followed up."

"On what?"

"The whole innocence angle—there were no charges, right?"

"None."

"I talked to the detective who questioned you—he said he knew right off that you weren't the man they were after."

"They held me almost a week anyhow."

"They were hot to charge somebody—once they had a better suspect they had to let you go. But he told me more—did you know the lab found fingerprints on the inside of that bag of white powder?"

"No—they didn't tell me anything."

"The guy they charged was a match—apparently he dropped the stuff where you picked it up. Your prints were only on the outside. They searched his house and found more of the drug."

"So after they arrested him, why'd they come back here?"

The reporter smiled broadly. "Pure harassment. No reason, except you guys like the Grateful Dead."

"I should talk to that detective."

"This your girlfriend?"

Was she? Could he say that?

"He's my sweetie," she said. "And you need to get the true story out—my family lives here in town—why should they have to hear all these lies?" Her eyes flashed with indignation. The cameraman said something in an undertone.

"Were you recently injured?" the reporter asked.

Suddenly Walt was furious. "She got bit in the face by a dog, because we were hitchhiking, because the narcs were ripping through my car—if they'd left us alone she never would've got hurt!"

The reporter addressed the camera. "This young man's girlfriend is scarred, his possessions damaged, his reputation destroyed—all in a day's work for a system of selective law enforcement that deserves scrutiny, and then reform." The cameraman nodded, the reporter's on-air expression vanished.

"When will this be on?" Anna asked. "I'll tell people to watch."

"On the local news at six and eleven tonight," the reporter said. "And the papers'll pick it up, I guarantee."

"Gratitude might be premature," Walt said, "but this could help. Thank you."

chapter 17

Getting a Lift

"THAT DETECTIVE COULD save my butt," Walt told Anna. They were at her house, sitting at her new table and chairs—courtesy of her grandparents—waiting for Burke to come. They planned to go to Jill's party together that evening.

She phoned Harold to watch the Channel Seven news.

"Talk to the folks yet?" he demanded.

"I'm about to."

"That's what you said this morning."

"I really am now—this news report should answer a lot of questions."

"I've only got one: why are you still hangin' around that guy?"

"Bye, Harold." She hung up on him, and called home. Dad answered. She told him to tune in, then asked which stories they'd heard.

"We understand you like...Walt," his voice strained, "but do you know how difficult it is for us to accept your...'friendship,' or whatever it is?"

"The papers have it wrong. The news tonight will clear up everything."

"Your mother may not even watch—she's very upset. Where did you meet this fellow anyway?"

"At a drawing class."

"Through Adult Ed?"

"The Free School."

He sighed loudly—he didn't even have to say *it figures.* "Well Anna, I can't dictate, but I do wish you weren't involved with him."

"Will you please suspend judgment till you see the news tonight?"

"Suspend disbelief you mean? It isn't rule-breakers who gall me, it's their fan club—'the world's against him—he's been wronged.' Logic can't penetrate a fortress like that."

"Facts, Dad—facts will exonerate him."

"Is it a fact he had that drug?"

"It wasn't his—he found it on the floor when he was cleaning."

"Anna," his voice grew thin and tight, "I hear stories like that every day. I never thought I'd have to listen to that crap from you."

"Bye, Dad," she said faintly.

Walt had that ready-to-flee look again. "My credibility's in shambles. If your parents think I did any of that, a new twist won't change their minds. As the world gets complex we gravitate to the simple—that's human nature."

"Is that what I'm doing?"

"Sure. Didn't you wonder why I had that stuff in my pocket?"

"I did wonder, Walt. That was one of the worst moments of my life, thinking those things the detective said might be true—not just because of you, but because of what that would say about me—whether I could trust my own perceptions."

"Right. Now do you see why your dad's unhappy?" He grimaced. "I'm just being realistic about my prospects."

"Which prospects?"

"The ones that matter to me—getting the work I want, having you—" But he didn't finish the sentence. He paced, then went out to the street, watching for Burke.

When her friend finally arrived, they came back in together, Burke remarking, "You're getting some very strange press."

"Not all of it's lies," Walt said.

Burke laughed. "Which stories should I believe?"

"Ask Anna—at this point she's more sure than I am. But don't miss tonight's episode—it should cast all your doubts into doubt."

"But I thought we had a party." Burke turned to Anna. "What are you bringing?"

"Oh, shoot, I didn't even think about it. What've you got?"

"A six-pack and a loaf of bread. Walt?"

"I'll see what's in my fridge—I'm feeling broke at the moment."

Anna said, "I have an electric wok, and red bell pepper and purple cabbage we can use for a rainbow stir-fry. Have you got carrots and something green?"

"Carrots and broccoli," Walt said. "That should work."

• • •

"WHAT ABOUT THE 6:00 news?" she reminded them when the stir-fry was done.

"I have a TV," Burke said. "Come over, then we'll go to Jill's from there. She could probably use help setting up." They all piled into his truck.

"I have to give other people a ride to the party," Walt said when they got to Burke's house.

"I thought Romo was coming," Anna said. "Can't he bring them?"

"Yeah, I guess he could pick up Tom, and maybe Stu'll come too." But when he phoned his house, nobody answered, so they snacked and played with Burke's keyboard and pedal steel. The 6:00 news report was better than Walt had hoped; his anger came across well—a man wronged. He called home again, and Barbara answered, getting ready for some hotel shindig.

"A bunch of Car's work buddies are going," she said, "and it's the kind of thing where you bring a date. That's me I guess." She didn't sound too thrilled.

"Pretend it's fun," Walt said.

"I'd rather go to your party—will Lloyd be there?"

"Romo might've invited him—it's pretty open. You could stop by if the hotel's boring—it's out on 104th."

"That's too far—I won't make it. But tell Lloyd—"

"Yeah?"

"No don't."

He laughed. "He asked me to put in a good word with you."

"Walt? Are things all right with Anna? Romo said she—"

"Her family's freaking out—this story might help, or it might be too late."

"If there's anything I can do—"

"Thanks Barbara."

He rejoined Anna and Burke. "Drop me at home on your way to Jill's. Romo's not there, and I don't want to leave Tom stranded."

Anna gave him a probing look. "Sure you're coming?"

"I said I would. I can't guarantee I'll enjoy myself, but I'll be there."

"When?"

"I don't know where Romo is, so I don't know when he'll show up."

Anna clung to his hand on the drive to his house, then got out with him for a hug and kiss, reluctant to let go.

"I love you girl—don't worry." He disengaged, she climbed back in Burke's truck, the headlights crossed Walt's legs as he unlocked the kitchen door and stepped in, standing a moment in the darkness. His urge to leave was strong now. Collecting the gear he'd thrown together, he loaded it in his trunk and counted his traveler's checks—$180 should last awhile. Hadn't said anything to Romo yet—he owed him that—but the person he really wanted to talk to was his friend from Santa Cruz, Ray. Directory assistance didn't have him at his old East LA address, but they did have a Raimundo Esposito—turned out to be Ray's dad. Through the man's fragmented English, he got his friend's phone number.

"Ray, it's Walt, from Santa Cruz."

"Hey man, I was thinkin' about you this week—how's your life?"

"Up and down—met a woman. I'm about to do some traveling—can I drop by and see you?"

"I won't be in Indio—we're goin' into the desert next week in Joshua Tree."

"Cool place."

"If you meet us there, we could hang out."

"Who's with you?"

"Oh, allies." Ray laughed.

They picked a time and place to meet, then an alternate, then another alternate—Walt didn't want to drive that far and not be able to find him. Having a defined plan made him feel more solid. He went over to Tom's and they smoked a joint and listened to music, not saying much, just kicking back in his microscopic apartment. He always managed to find places so tiny there was barely room for a cot. Walt was planted on his bed.

"When are we going to this party?" Tom asked.

"I have to see if Romo's back—I'm giving him a ride."

"What if he doesn't show up?"

"He will." But as they listened to one album after another, the phone at home kept ringing to empty walls.

"Hey, it's 10:30," Tom said. "Thought we had to catch your big broadcast—shouldn't we get going?"

"I guess—let's go by the house—maybe Romo's trying to call me there."

No one was home. Tom got antsy. "Let's just go man. I know you didn't do all that shit. I can skip the news, but the party'll be over."

Walt aimed Plug east, preoccupied wondering where Romo was. The car ahead suddenly braked. In the headlights, he glimpsed a coyote bounding away, but he was coming up on the other guy too fast. Rather than rear-end him, he swerved onto the shoulder softened by snowmelt—his wheels sank and stopped. The other car sped up, gone in a moment.

He and Tom climbed out to see how bad it was; mud dragged at their boots. They were on a low dark stretch between empty fields, clouds scudding across the stars. The front tires were maybe four inches into the mud, the rear nearly to the axle.

"Got boards or anything?" Tom asked.

"There's a box I can sacrifice, but I don't know what good it'll do."

"Which is your driving wheel?"

"Right rear."

"Let's work on that one."

Walt popped the trunk.

"What's all this stuff?" Tom demanded. "Going someplace?"

"Yeah, actually—later tonight."

"Where?"

"California desert."

"When'll you be back?"

"Early March, maybe sooner."

"*March?* What about your classes?"

"I'm dropping 'em—never get a teaching job in Boulder now."

"You can't just run away when the going gets a little rough."

"It's not 'a little rough'; this is bad."

"Well, I'll tell you what I'm doing," Tom said. "I'm hitching to this party, and if I can find someone with a winch we'll be back to pull you out. But if that means you're taking off, it's tempting to just leave you here in the mud."

"Thanks a lot!"

"I'm helping—thank me later." Tom moved down the road watching for headlights, and when a car came along, he flashed his Hawaiian shirt. A jovial quartet of teenagers crammed him in. When they dropped him at Jill's, the party was in full swing—animated conversations, people dancing to the Talking Heads. Anna came over immediately; she'd been watching the door all evening.

"Tom, you made it." But he was alone. "Where's Walt? And Romo?"

"Never found Romo. Walt's stuck in the mud a couple miles from here."

She rolled her eyes. "Burke has a truck—I guess we could pull him out."

"Well, I wouldn't be in a big hurry—it's pretty soupy right now. Why don't you just pick him up, and leave his car there till tomorrow?"

He told her the approximate location; she put on her boots and coat and went out. Nervous energy was unbalancing her. She needed to think. The news story was good but people kept asking about Walt—wasn't he coming? As she walked, shreds of cloud flying east kept hiding then revealing stars. The air wasn't really cold—low forties maybe—but she could feel it chapping her cheeks and lips, attracted to the recent wounds on her jaw. She turned up her collar—people made fun of this old coat but it sure kept the wind out. At the four-way stop she turned west, and topping a rise saw Plug a long way off. She had to keep to the road—the shoulder was mucky. Nearing the car, she couldn't see Walt—maybe he'd hitched a ride?—but as she came alongside there he was, sitting slumped on his trunk lid, shaking his head to an inner conversation.

"Walt?"

He slid off to stand in the mud.

"I came to give you a lift," she said.

"Got a car someplace?" He looked around, puzzled.

"I don't own a car, you know that." Then as he stepped onto the asphalt, she bent her knees, put her arms tight around his waist, and straightening her legs lifted him six inches off the road. "C'mon," she said, setting him down again. Getting the joke, he began to laugh.

"Oh Anna thank you—I needed that."

"Yes I know." She scrutinized him. "You have all your stuff, don't you?"

He nodded.

"Think you're going somewhere real soon, don't you?"

He nodded again.

"Well I've got news for you, buddy," starting to walk. "Either we're taking a little short vacation together, or you're going nowhere."

"Are you sure?" He swung into step beside her as they crossed the road to face any oncoming traffic.

"Yep—me and that mud, we're in cahoots."

It was a few minutes before he spoke again. "I'm sorry Anna, I don't know how cutting out was supposed to help."

"It wouldn't. It would confirm everything my dad and Harold are already thinking, and make it pretty hard for me to take your proposal seriously."

"A short trip then—there's someone I want you to meet."

"You really want me along?"

"Yes. And we'll come back together."

They held hands as they walked, the wind pushing at their backs. At 104th they turned south; soon the lights of the big house came into view. In the yard full of vehicles, they had a long kiss, and heard the crowd inside counting down.

Rubbing foreheads they chanted, "Four, three, two, one, happy new year," then kissed again. The door banged open, someone leaned out to blast on a plastic horn, in the background corks and party poppers were going off amid the shouting.

"Shall we go in?" sticking out her elbow. He looped his wrist around her forearm and they came up the steps, catching the door as it was swinging shut. Inside they blinked at the brightness while people crowded.

"Anna, where've you been?"

"We saw the news—was it true?"

"Is your house bugged?"

Dazed by the onslaught, they wished they were back out in the windy night.

"Champagne?" Plastic cups were shoved into their hands.

Walt raised his, nodding to Anna. "To you."

"To silliness," she said, then clicking rims, they drank.

"Speech, speech!" someone shouted, and the music stopped. Walt raised his hands, slopping champagne.

"All right, let's get this over with. There's a lot of distortions and outright lies circulating, but tonight's newscast was not only fairly accurate, the reporter provided me information I should've had access to a month ago. I'm co-plaintiff in a lawsuit against the narcotics squad of the Boulder police department for exceeding their constitutional authority. A warrant isn't license to do whatever they feel like, but only the vigilance of the public can change things—that's you. Any elected officials who think this behavior seems OK, vote 'em out. Remember which judges signed those warrants, and vote not to retain 'em. And challenge the Ed Meese mentality that if you're stopped or searched, or picked up, you must be guilty. I was jailed six days without being charged—if they can do it to me, they can do it to you." He took a long breath. "That's it—stay tuned for our lawsuit."

People clapped and cheered, ushering him to the food tables. As he heaped what was left of Anna's colorful vegetables over noodles, he bumped into Tom reloading a plate.

"Get your car unstuck?" Tom asked.

"Later. Anna and I are heading for Joshua Tree."

"And then—"

"In a week I'll be back here driving a school bus again."

"That's not the tune you were singing an hour ago."

"I know—she made everything clear."

● ● ●

WHEN TOM FIRST KNEW Walt as a sophomore, he'd been impressed by his steady nature, and watched his deepening affection for Laura mature him—till they went to California anyway. But at least the guy who came back damaged last fall knew which way was up. Anna had severed his connection to the ground. He might enjoy being tossed into space by this turbulent love, but in Tom's view it wasn't doing him any good.

These private types were the worst for monopolizing a guy's time and energy. But there was no telling Walt anything—he was enthralled. At this party where he should be circulating, talking up his legal action, what was he doing? Going off to sit on the stairs with Anna as though they were the only people here. At least when Laura showed up, she'd open his eyes...

Tom thought back to his trip to Santa Cruz three years ago, to visit Opal and Walt and Laura—except Walt had unexpectedly gone to Maryland, so it was just the two women. He'd relaxed first into Opal's embrace—she was Home, what the I Ching called The Enduring—they'd known that since the day they met. She made her living as a hairdresser and the holidays were busy so he'd worked Walt's projectionist gig, and between shifts hung out with Laura at Walt's house. The night before New Year's Eve, Opal was sleeping off a touch of stomach flu at home, and when Laura headed for bed he said, "You don't have to sleep alone." She gave him a long appraising look.

"I know," she said coolly.

"Walt's our friend, Opal's our friend—complete the square."

Laura looked right through his BS and recognized lust—but all the same she led him to his room and put him through his paces. He didn't understand how, but she wasn't the not-bad-looking woman who'd left Boulder with Walt a year earlier to check out Berkeley. She was devastating, every curve of her exactly right, her taut belly and perfect mouth his for a night. She'd haunted him like a succubus ever since—Walt thought he'd just walk away, huh? Who was he kidding?

Opal liked to talk about All Possible Worlds as though you could live in more than one—the world of Laura and the world of Opal? Tom knew better. If Laura wanted him, all bets were off. Even knowing that would hurt Opal, even knowing Laura would ditch him, he'd go for her anyway. But he was conscious that would be a mistake, understood how much pain would follow. Did Walt have an inkling he was screwing up with this girl? Did being in love exempt you from common sense? Could it shield you from its own consequences? Not fucking likely. Walt was a fool and he was gonna get it in the teeth and end up alone—no Laura if he chased her off, and no Anna either if Tom was reading the girl right. Their relationship petrified her—couldn't he see that?

• • •

WALT TRIED NOT TO eat too fast—one bite told him how hungry he was. Anna leaned into him, a hand on his thigh, nibbling off his plate. "Jill said we can stay here tonight."

"What about my car?"

"What about it? It's not going anywhere. Burke can winch it out tomorrow."

"We have to leave tomorrow to meet Ray—it's a two-day drive."

"But when my parents—"

"Once the flap dies down I'll talk to 'em. Now that the truth is circulating, I don't feel quite so far out on a limb." He shook his head. "Why's it like this? Nothing works till I give up, then I get what I want."

"Is that what you mean by 'spineless'—giving up?"

"Maybe. Or maybe I just don't like to force things, after being pushed around."

"Burke was telling me about Schrödinger's cat," she said. "It's inside a box, alive and also dead. But as soon as you look at it, it's one or the other. The act of observing makes it take a state. If you didn't look, I guess it would stay undefined. If somebody asks how the cat's doing, you peek—and probably kill it. We can't leave the universe alone, but we can't choose what's going to happen either—things just jump."

Walt nodded. "I feel like that cat being looked at—cruising along, everything's cool, then suddenly *whomp!* I'm dead. Then *whomp!*, alive again."

"Like a superball," she said, and he grinned and kissed her.

• • •

IN THE MORNING, ANNA talked to Harold—he'd been impressed with the news story but still considered Walt bad news. Then she called her parents—Dad's opinion of him was slightly higher, but he wasn't buying the coincidence of the drug in his pocket. Mom said she was going to call the highway patrol in six states if Anna wasn't back in a week, and made her recite Walt's license plate number and a description of his car.

It was afternoon before Burke got his winch and cable and truck and his hung-over self together to meet them at Plug, but in the interim, sun had stiffened the muck. Burke hooked the cable to his rear bumper, they pushed while he winched, and the mud slowly released the car.

After a stop at a car wash to hose off the wheels and under-carriage which were making a new grinding noise, they swung by Anna's apartment to collect her sleeping bag and duffel. Seeing her drawing stuff, he realized he'd forgotten his. Stopping at home, he encountered Barbara in the kitchen.

"How was your evening?" he asked her.

"I've had more fun at the clinic, but Car had a great time. He asked me to move in with him—has a really nice place, all to himself."

"Going to?"

"Last night I realized how little I actually like him," she twisted a smile.

"So are you shopping?"

"If Lloyd asks me out I won't say no, let's put it that way. But you—" poking him in the solar plexus with a manicured finger— "change so fast you're a blur. What's up?"

"Anna and I are off to the desert."

"Then you're coming back, right?"

How'd she know so much? "Yeah," he agreed, "but I wouldn't have said that yesterday—that girl's saved my sanity."

"Don't spend it all at once."

chapter 18

Sage

ANNA WAS USED to starting trips before dawn, getting in at least a hundred miles before breakfast—it felt wrong to be hitting the highway as the last light abandoned the sky, but Walt's concern was making miles. They had US 285 to themselves southwest of Denver, and once they'd left the curving stretch through the mountains, Plug went faster on the flats of South Park till they climbed Poncha Pass into the San Luis Valley. By then it was midnight, a long day. The cold that pierced through gaps in the weatherstripping wasn't stirring her hair, but the whistling of the wing mirror made her feel she was sitting in a breeze.

"Let's camp at Sand Dunes," she suggested, so they drove south then east to where those nestled against the mountains, pale and frigid. Past the closed dark entry booth, they aimed for the campground, the brilliant wash of stars revealing only scrubby trees, no tent shape nor gleam of a vehicle. Parked near the outhouse, with Plug's engine cut off and the metal ticking as it cooled, they stepped out to set up camp. Now that the headlights were off, the Milky Way cast shadows—no need to rummage for a flashlight.

By the time Anna paused to put on gloves, her hands were stiff and the extra layer just trapped in the cold. The sand was frozen so hard it might as well be rock, and hammering only bent the stakes—they had to run guy lines to bushes to make the tent stay up. They unfurled pads and a thick wool blanket, spread their sleeping bags on that, and topped those with the other blanket, but even swaddled in coats, sweaters, and heavy shirts, huddling in their cocoon of layers, they couldn't escape the cold into deep sleep.

They nodded, woke, shivered, and catnapped through the hours, but when the sun came up, the shadow of mountains lying across their campsite felt even colder than the night. They watched the sky silvering and hugged each other, telling jokes, but finally couldn't lie freezing another minute. They bundled everything into the car, pulling the guy lines loose with sage attached. The starter chittered—they held their breath till the engine groaned, then flapped their arms and bounced on the seat till the valves stopped clattering. Walt eased Plug into gear, and as they circled the campground loop on their way out, they caught a view of dunes pale and smooth as snowdrifts.

"Too bad we don't have a thermometer," she said.

"I don't want to know," he shivered. "How would putting a number on it improve the experience?"

"It'd justify being numb-er, that's all."

She laughed and he moaned.

The defroster labored to clear semicircles at the base of the breath-fogged windshield, and finally Walt had to crack his window so he could see. The fresh breeze snapped at their cheeks, defeating the heater entirely. At last they drove into Alamosa, too early—nothing was open.

"I seem to remember a pueblo down by Tres Piedras with a gas pump and grill," he said. "Let's just roll. Eventually we'll thaw." Clusters of antelope off in the brush turned heads to watch them pass; near the New Mexico line, Walt stopped. "We have to look."

They got out, hopping around to get their blood moving then facing north to admire the San Luis Valley: a broad expanse of gray-green sagebrush, edged by peaks bright with snow above timberline and dark green below, under a sky pale as old denim. He ducked with her through a barbed-wire fence into pasture, where he picked some sage. Baring his fingers to rub it between them, he held it to her nose. The scent was like the view, wild and cold, and she felt ashamed that a nomad from Maryland was pointing out these beauties—she ought to be showing off her home state. He fished in his pocket for the antler pipe and broke sprigs into it, took a hit, and offered it to her. She drew in the pungent smoke, coughing.

"Does sage get you high?"

"Not like pot, but—yeah. I love this."

"To me it smells like home."

"You're the most home I've had in years, know that?" He pressed sage to her temples and jaw, his nose following. As he brought her close she felt his hard-on.

"It's too cold here," she said.

"I'm not cold anymore."

"Waa-alt—"

His eyes snapped with mischief and desire. "Thought Colorado women were hardy," he growled, hands busy on her jeans. The fresh morning, the scent, his heat conspired against her practicality as he slipped off his coat to sit on, then tugged her down astride his legs.

Their coupling amid the sage was quick and energetic, then she climbed to her feet yanking up her jeans—the cold was arriving fast from wherever they'd chased it off to. He pulled on his peacoat, then stood twitching his shoulders. "Shoulda used your coat—bet cactus wouldn't go through that," turning so she could pick spines from his back.

She drove while he stretched out as much as the front seat allowed, head on her thigh. "What's the difference between men and women," he asked, "when it comes to sex?"

"That's quite a question."

"No no, it's a joke."

"All right: what?"

"Women need a reason for sex, men only need a place."

"Except you," she laughed. "You don't even need that."

"You don't consider wild untrammeled nature a fine place? That one goes in my heart scrapbook."

She rested her right hand over his heart, imagining his pulse against her palm through shirts, coat, and gloves—her fingers warmed just being there. He fiddled with the radio till he located a country station, which treated them to "Drop Kick Me Jesus through the Goal Posts of Life" followed soon after by "Thank God and Greyhound She's Gone," worth miles of laughs. He was right about the truck stop in Tres Piedras. After tanking up, they had breakfast in the low-slung reddish building.

"Let's take 64 to Farmington and go past Shiprock," he suggested. "The interstates are so boring. A two-lane road only occupies about fifteen percent of your windshield view, but a divided four-lane highway fills more like sixty or seventy percent. They're for people who'd rather fly."

"I remember when they put I-70 through Vail," she said. "What a huge gash they cut to grade and widen. Now it's got grass and aspen trees on it, but when it was slopes of red dirt it was so awful—like the Earth was bleeding."

The road climbed through piñon-covered hills, north to Chama then west through Apache reservation, on toward Bloomfield and Farmington and the larger Navajo lands.

"This whole country was theirs," Walt said, "and look what they ended up with."

"But only till someone finds uranium or oil—then they'll have to move. The moon seems like the next logical spot to push them to: first they had soil taken away, then water—why not air?" But the land was beautiful in its inhospitable way. Odd formations of pink and off-white and deep red stone reared above dusty arroyos that only saw rain in flash floods, the water gone so fast the ground was only tantalized.

In Farmington they gassed up before the next reservation. Walt drove again, past Shiprock rising black out of the plain. The sign at Teec Nos Pos reminded them they'd crossed into Arizona. He parked at the trading post and they went in, admiring the expensive blankets then checking out the jewelry.

"Want something?" he asked casually, and since she liked turquoise she looked over the trays set out by the Navajo woman working the counter. She was a display herself, laden with squash blossom bracelets, necklace, and earrings, strings of turquoise chunks dangling against her loose purple blouse, rings on all her fingers, a wide silver clasp in her straight black hair, a silver conch-studded belt around her thick waist. Anna tried different bracelets, not liking any, then Walt put on her finger a silver ring with a narrow turquoise inset all the way around. She fiddled with it, slipping it on and off.

"Does this mean something?" she asked.

"Sure, it means I have no sense—I should be saving my money."

"Want a ring?" Her voice lilted with tease.

He admired one with a square setting, reversed quarter circles of turquoise forming its corners, outlined in silver. In the middle between the arcs, jet-black fragments were inset. It fit well on his right ring finger, so he tried it on his left—that was good too. "I like this," moving it back to his right hand. The one he'd chosen for Anna was still on her finger. Grinning, each bought the other's, then they went outside. Sun streaked the cloudless air from behind mountains, the temperature dropping fast.

"What does this mean?" she said, waving her hand around.

"It means they can afford gas today."

She just looked at him.

"It means your finger can't stop thinking about me."

Still that scrutiny.

"It means you can't stop thinking about your finger."

She whopped his shoulder with her gloves—he half raised his arm to protect his face. "What do you think of your finger anyway?" he said.

"I think it's a stand-in for my hand."

He nodded, pleased. "It is. And you've honored me, wearing that. Thank you." Their westward travel prolonged the sunset, the shacks and broken trucks of the reservation gradually fading into darkness. They went through Tuba City, then picked up US 89 south to Flagstaff.

"We don't have time to see the Grand Canyon now," he said, "but we could on our way back—want to?"

"I've never been there; sure."

"It's another hour into Flagstaff—we could take a breather, or just haul to the California line."

"How far's that?"

"Another four–five hours."

"Let's keep going—I can spell you." She put on the tape he'd made her, and they rolled down the road to Joni Mitchell's serenade. With the instrument panel lighting the planes of his face, she watched his expression change with the music.

"Walt."

"Hmm?"

"Tell me about Laura."

"What do you want to know?" Casually.

"How'd she hurt you so bad?"

"Love can't hurt you if you don't let anybody in, right?"

"Right."

"I did love her, Anna—we thought we'd marry once she had her master's degree. But while I was avoiding Berkeley, Cob the Testosterone King showed up. He loved her, as much as a person that selfish could love anyone, and after months of keeping me on call, she decided she loved him. We all played that game, pretending our threesome worked. If she hadn't dropped me, I'd still be waiting, telling myself that the way her karma rode mine didn't affect us. So I should thank her, I guess."

"Or I should," she said huskily.

"But I won't—she knew that note was murder and she sent it anyway. Ray saw her before that—she looked after me when I broke my leg."

"You never said how that happened—"

"I was driving in the rain to see her, and some guy ran me off the road. Totaled the car—Onion was a good little car—and broke my right thighbone in two places." He laughed, "You'd think I coulda taken the hint. From the minute we got to California her energy was pushing me around—or maybe she was channeling Cob's at me—I don't know. Doesn't matter anymore—he's dead and she's behind bars feeling sorry for herself."

"So when she shows up and wants you back, how are you going to stop her?"

"Tell her I'm in love."

"That won't work," she said flatly.

"I'll tell her better luck next life. See, we tripped, before she ever met Cob—we'd known each other in previous lifetimes."

"Is that why you wanted to trip with me? To see if I'm in your past?"

"I don't think you are. I started over, and you're part of my rebirth. I don't care how many times I knew her—that connection's cut now. You're the box of rain she said was empty, the future she couldn't see. You and me, sweetie, we're the punchline of the cosmic joke."

She had no answer, listening instead to the music. When it ended, the only sounds were tires on the road and wind rushing against the car. He draped his arm across the seatback, fingernails brushing her neck, smiling with distant contentment while she wrestled with her insecurity. Her urge—her need—to trust him overpowered her, but when Laura showed up Anna would be in the losing corner of that triangle, as surely as Walt had been dealing with Laura and Cob. She looked up at the stars. Every time the headlights picked out a tree or rock, the gleam off her glasses threw her reflection against the windshield, blinding her to the sky. If a vampire had no reflection, what would the world call someone who was nothing else—an illusion? An imperfect cleaning, to be polished away like squeegee tracks?

She'd co-opted Walt, reducing his getaway to a visit by inviting herself along. He didn't want her to come: because she'd be an emotional burden? He'd deny that. Kindness made him overcompensate, made him think he loved her when he was only seeking refuge. And convincing her too, in those wonderful moments—oh god, her heart was in fragments flung wide as the speckle of stars—she'd never retrieve all the pieces and feel whole.

He took the exit to Seligman, picking up old Route 66, and parked where a gravel road crossed a cattle guard. Cutting the engine he got out, stretching and gazing upward, his coat on but unbuttoned. The Milky Way was a highway, wide and bright, and the clean breeze kept him looking. Finally she got out too, standing on the passenger side, marveling at how much warmer it was than last night at Sand Dunes, and turning to the tree-pricked horizon. He walked up the side road crunching gravel, singing lines from "Cassady" to the trees that grew close. Anna followed, about five paces back. At a break in the trees, stars picked up flecks of mica and quartz in the scattered rocks, and the shanks of grama grass shone faintly. He stopped; she faced him.

"Wish I could draw you now." His fingers outlined the light on her hair, his near-touch conjuring gooseflesh on her scalp and the back of her neck. He gave her a ghost kiss, his mouth a centimeter from hers. Her raised hands hovered near his cheeks, he moved his around her coat. His breath stirred the tiny hairs on her upper lip, she breathed back to him, they traded warm air a dozen times before her lips contacted his. Still only the slightest touches accompanied their exchange of breath. He laughed from somewhere low—his knees, or the earth he stood on—then they clasped, eyes reflecting the sky, kissing slowly.

Releasing her lips he said, "Anna Karenina, you're better than acid," pressing her to his chest, the silence spreading inside as though he was a Magritte painting of a man, an outline full of airy clouds, in his arms a woman outline of sagebrush and stone. "I want to merge with your head and look out through your eyes."

"Will Ray have something?"

"We shall see."

Well, maybe then he'd understand he was lost in wishful thinking. That mauling had destroyed her enthusiasm for drugs. She didn't even know animals had minds, then suddenly that dog was inside hers. If she wasn't strong enough to deflect that, how would she defend herself from Laura? Walt probably imagined he was going to—like he did in that pickup? Carting her off to the Emergency Room slashed and bleeding, too late?

Taking the wheel for the next stretch she continued south, past Lake Havasu to Parker, across the Colorado River into California. Out on that empty road leading west, one bare mountain range after another stood behind flats studded with rocks but not even cactus. After Plug topped a low pass, Walt said the hummocks north of the road were the Sheep Hole Mountains. At that point Anna could see what he already knew was there: the Lost Subdivision. Acre lots, each with its bungalow, were arrayed three deep on both sides of the road, regular as a field of corn. Though a handful were fortressed, most were abandoned—just open to anyone who might drop by.

"Imagine the ads in the late '30s in Chicago newspapers," he said. "'Buy a vacation home in Sunny Southern California—Escape winter on your own acre of Paradise. Act fast—they won't last!'"

She laughed. "Sight unseen."

"Must've been an awful shock when they first visited 'paradise'—there's nothing green for miles except what they've stuck in the ground and watered."

Another hour brought them to Twentynine Palms. Walt told her where to turn, south to Joshua Tree National Monument. She could see joshua trees—small for trees, big for cactus—with clusters of spikes sprouting like hands from their branch tips. Driving in past the closed gatehouse, she parked at a vacant site in the camping loop.

Walt said, "I'm supposed to meet Ray at 10:30 at the gatehouse."

Under the cover of sleeping bags they relaxed skin to skin, loving leisurely till they drifted to sleep spooned, her head on his arm, his other holding her against him, the sage he'd rubbed on her temple hours ago wafting through his dreams.

She was an antelope. He was small enough to ride on her back; she ran so fast through the sagebrush, the wind tore his clothes away. She became a centaurlike creature and carried him through fields of cactus to a river. They swam side by side, but her thin legs couldn't propel her through the water. As she tired he held her, swimming hard, but the current increased, pulling her downstream. He clung to her, thinking they might as well drown together, but she struck his arms with her sharp hoofs then rolled into fast water, gone. Stranded on a flat rock, he lay panting. Recovering breath, he swam the rest of the way across, then walked downriver where he found her body, now a broken cactus-tree. He cried, "Don't leave me," but she was disintegrating into spiny strips of papyrus, which turned into books begging to be saved from the flood. He was stacking those on the bank when Laura came up. "Well, I see you found a use for your life," she said coldly, and walked away. He tried to follow despite the sharp rocks gouging his feet, but her shadow became Cob, too tough to need shoes, taunting that Walt had never been man enough for her.

• • •

WARMTH WOKE ANNA. SHE looked at Walt's face, slack in repose. What could be more frustrating than lying wide awake next to someone sleeping? She inched out of his arms, into clothes. In daylight she got a good look at a joshua tree—if a person turned into a yucca, this might be the result. She got out her drawing pad and sat on the picnic table, roughing in its shape before working on details. She'd got pretty far along when she felt someone watching.

"Hey, that's good." A thirtyish Chicano man stood there, smallish and slim with lively eyes, a clipped moustache, and a ready smile. "Draw anything else?"

"A few things—I took a class last fall. The teacher said first you have to see, before you can put it on paper."

"I draw a calendar diary—a month per page, with a box for each day, or if a week's had a consistent tone, maybe one long picture. It's a memory book."

"Good idea," she said, inspired to show off her drawings. Thumbing one corner of her pad, she let the pages fall in quick succession.

"Know him long?" he asked.

Realizing he'd seen her drawing of Walt's hard-on, she blushed. "A few months."

"Are you happy, or heavy?"

"Happy mostly," wondering why having such an intimate conversation with a complete stranger seemed perfectly natural.

"Women know so much more about love," he said. "Men are afraid, so we take refuge in how our bodies feel. We get tangled up in longing, and stumble in and out of love without understanding what's good or hurtful about it."

"How can anyone tell?"

"I think it's a matter of how much of the time you feel light, versus how often your heart's dragging you down. Cosmic love lifts you— like Christ walking on water. The murk of possession drowns you."

"It does." She thought of Cory. They'd started bright but didn't stay that way long, and once she'd moved in with him, they were never lighthearted again. "What about you? Is it really easier if you know the pitfalls?"

"Oh, we fly around the sun sometimes, we travel so far—five of us. Keeping it light's a challenge—no room for 'he loves me more' or 'I only want her.'"

"Are all of you here?"

"Yeah, drove in this morning. I'm hoping to meet up with an old friend—when he called I'd just been thinking about him. I brought him something."

"Are you Ray?"

He beamed. "Are you Walt's friend?"

She nodded. "We drove most of the night—he didn't want to miss you. He has some stuff to sort out."

"Don't we all." His smile was warm as the new sun. "What's your name?"

"Anna Karenina Brubaker."

He whistled. "I haven't read it but—didn't she throw herself in front of a train?"

"Under it, yeah. After eight years in a loveless marriage she met an army officer. Having an affair was acceptable, but the depth of their love broke all the rules so they were ostracized, and finally every moment out of his arms was such torment she killed herself. And that destroyed him—he went off to war hoping to get shot. Everything he could've achieved he gave up for her, and she sacrificed her relationship with her son, her place in society, and her sanity for him."

"Don't do that," he said. "Walt doesn't want that, does he?"

"No. He's been hurt bad, and says he's through with that."

"We all wish we were," he said, shaking his head. "Do you love each other?"

She smiled.

"When the pain pulls on your shoes look up—even at night there's light."

"That you Ray?" Walt said from the tent.

"Don't let us disturb you."

"I came a long way to see you." With a shudder the tent opened. He climbed out buttoning his jeans, and sticking feet into boots, stumbled forward. Ray caught him with a hug. They held on a moment, feeling time pass and bring them back, then stepped apart. "Excellent," Walt nodded. "And you and Anna have met—also excellent."

"Join us for breakfast."

A silver van with blue and white striped curtains was parked by a picnic table where a guy stood pumping the tank of a two-burner gas stove. One skin shade lighter and a head taller than Ray, he was sturdy, with a burr of black hair and a goatee. From the van they heard laughter, then a woman came out, gathering her long straight dark hair into a band. Her face rounded with a smile. Ray stepped up and they touched lips in greeting.

"Walt and Anna, this is Luisa, and setting up the stove, Mario." He stopped pumping to shake hands with them, a firm friendly grip. Luisa embraced Anna then offered Walt a long-fingered brown hand, her pair of silver rings flashing.

"Ray told us you were housemates," she said to Walt.

"He helped a lot after I broke my leg."

"People are supposed to, aren't they?"

"And hardly ever do," Mario said. "But we try."

"Want some *platanos*?" Ray asked.

"Plantain?" Walt said. "Sure."

"We're eating light because we're traveling with mescal today. Coming with?"

Anna'd decided last night to refuse, but Ray's offer was part of the moment, arising as effortlessly as their meeting this morning. "We'll join you," she said.

As Mario fried plantains, the others emerged from their van—a small barrel-shaped older woman introducing herself as Marisa, and a man with lined dark skin and intense eyes and a thatch of black hair with silver in it, his body so well knit he might be forty or a very fit sixty—Tonio. The touch of his hand was dry and quick, as though he didn't want her to think they'd met yet, while Marisa was bubbly and gregarious, rubbing Mario's back, playfully tweaking Ray's ear, whispering to Luisa, surprising Anna by leaning to her ear then kissing there. She put her finger on Walt's jaw.

"Forget to shave?"

"Use my razor," Ray suggested. Standing on the far side of the vehicle from the table, Walt plugged it into the van's cigarette lighter, as he shaved glancing through the windows at Anna who seemed to have left her shyness someplace. She was peeling plantains for Luisa to slice, then took a fried one, tossing while it cooled.

"We have fresh tortillas," she offered.

"We'll be hungry tonight," Marisa said. "We'll roll them with beans and rice."

When Walt joined them, Tonio cleared his throat. Conversation stilled as though they'd all been a vibrating tuning fork he'd placed his fingers over.

"We will go a different place today. Do not talk in the presence of Señor Mescal. As we walk, sense the stones, the earth, the plants around us—your animal being, not your busy mind. Bring water." Ray handed around water bottles, then locked the van and put the key on the rear tire. He moved near Anna as they walked.

chapter 19

Señor Mescal

THE SILENCE MADE her aware of cold, sun, the rasp of sand on their boots, and the far-off soughing of air moving among the joshua trees; she also felt Ray's energy, alive as a current flowing through her. She didn't sense Walt, a few paces behind. The cold and warm pockets of air they passed through reminded her of swimming in a lake. In the warmest, Tonio stopped. The ground was dished; here the campground was out of sight, the rock formations distant.

Standing in the lowest part, Tonio gestured the others to encircle him: Walt, Ray, Anna, Marisa, Mario, Luisa on Walt's other side. They all knelt, carefully avoiding rocks and cacti, while from a cloth bag Tonio removed four peyote buttons, then handed the bag to Ray who took three, passing to Anna who took two and a broken piece of a third. Marisa chose three, Mario four, Luisa three, and Walt two and another broken piece. The buttons resembled desiccated figs—flat, wrinkled, and brown, an inch and a half in diameter. Tonio put one in his mouth and began to chew; the others did likewise.

The cactus fruit was bitter and tough—Anna sipped water as she chewed, gradually grinding it fine enough to swallow, the others already on their second button. She was the last to finish, but once they were done eating they only drank and sat back on their heels, Ray and Luisa with eyes closed, Tonio looking at something far off behind her, Mario's gaze skyward, Marisa looking at each of them before concentrating on Tonio's back. Walt's eyes met hers a moment before wandering on.

Anna became aware of every pebble indenting her shins, the two-inch barrel cactus a few inches from her left knee, the prickling then numbing of her feet as the circulation in her legs failed. The wounds on her face, becoming scar, ached in her skin and the flesh beneath, still sending messages of damage and distress though the surface seemed healed. Two hot stripes of pain lit her jaw, the dog's teeth even now tearing at her from the inside. She felt in her throat a roar of anger matching its deep growl, and those snapping jaws pulled back, not dragged off by the animal's owner but pressed away by her answering threat. She sagged, feeling she'd finally rescued herself.

Her back was to the sun and she felt warmth there, and coolness on her shadowed fingers, and lines of cold now marking where her cheek had burned. Nausea brought her eyes open again. Drinking, she noticed rock granules patterned like heat waves in the sand, and the cactus by her knee shimmering. She thought of Van Gogh's later paintings—trees that emerged from earth and dissipated into sky, fluid. She considered her hands resting on her thighs—fingers elongated then shortened, turned to talons then cat claws then dog paws then the feet of a lizard. Those hands were impossibly far away—she must be a giant to be connected to them. Awareness moved to her throat where blood pushed with effort into her head then dropped easily to her heart, breath journeying through her nasal passages, sussing past her upper lip to spread into the air, like water from a river delta merging with the sea. In the heat of her veins and arteries, cells hurried like ants at their tasks, serving the colony of her blood.

As though someone had touched her ear, she felt a presence there—Ray, tapping on her mind. He'd become a coyote with wary widespread ears, nose lifted to the breeze, eyes sharp. His mouth opened laughing and she remembered how the dog had smiled. She recoiled, and his face turned snarling into a demon dog's; fleeing her senses, she huddled around her inner stillness, her face throbbing. Slowly her muscles unclenched. She looked again, this time past Ray, at Walt—a songbird—she thought the demon dog would hurt him but Ray was now a desert mouse. Reassured, she looked the other direction—Marisa was a large fierce owl, Mario beyond her a slow bear. But she dared not look at Tonio, or even at Luisa because that would bring her eyes too near—she knew he'd terrify her.

She turned back. Now Walt had Cory's face. Involuntarily she started crying, that loss fresh, her insides reduced to a slurry through which emotions bubbled. Sweat came out on her forehead, all the liquid inside her trying to leave, blood pounding in her skin as though at a door it begged to open. She looked at Ray again; the steady warmth in his eyes soothed her dissolved heart. Abruptly she felt her interior solidify, taking on the angles of a crystal, shifting as it grew till all her substance was part of it, her skin aglow, light filling her. That brightness drew Walt's attention, his face changing but eyes calm; he raised his hand so she could see the ring she'd given him. Her ring finger pulsed, she let her hand rise to answer. He stretched his toward her, she felt their energy touch. She invited him into her newly crystalline heart where his light refracted into slivers, scattering through her.

She tried to get up, but her feet had gone to sleep. She fell back, aware of that small cactus so she neither sat on it nor put her hand in it, and rubbed her calves to restore circulation. Walt helped her stand. While the others remained in their circle, motionless but completely present, he picked up her water bottle and they walked.

In the lee of a rock they sat, the sun high now, warm. He sandwiched her ring hand between his, lightly as though it were fragile, spreading his fingers to kiss hers beneath. He met her eyes.

"Merge with me?"

"I don't know—"

"Sure you do." He began unbuttoning her coat.

She blushed. "Here?"

"Where else?" He spread her coat on the ground, straightening to take off his clothes. She undressed where she sat, leaning against the rock to pull down her jeans. Where sun struck them it was already warm, with a promise of unwanted heat. Clothing seemed unnecessary. As he lay back naked she could see his energy flowing to twin centers, his heart and his sex. His body neither demand nor threat, he was an invitation, hiding nothing. She thought fleetingly of how she'd spread herself like a picnic for Cory, to shut him up and to silence her own proliferating doubts—Walt's surrender was an opportunity to visit herself from the conqueror's vantage, to understand how it felt to master someone. Her hand coaxed his hard-on, his faster breathing triggered hers, but when she took him inside she felt them change—he was her, she was Laura.

Her hands flailed and he caught them in his, the flow of his vitality sweeping up her arms, into her center. She felt the immediacy of his love, and in its shadow the pain he'd tried to outrun. Her palms became the positive and negative poles of electrical flow, their sexual contact the grounding. As her self-doubt and yearning engulfed them both, he sat up, her legs around his hips holding him inside not for the friction of pleasure but to feel him occupy her, connecting them. They joined hands, eyes too close to see anything, then kissed, energy moving through her in an arc, her tongue in his mouth completing that circuit.

"Let me convince you that wasn't all your fault," he said inside her mind. Then he was Cory. He laid her down hard, one hand imprisoning her crossed wrists above her head while his other gripped a handful of her hair, his mouth and thrusting rough, and she was back in that flat, frantic for the affection Cory wouldn't give her, taking instead the abuse he dealt out as a substitute. Finally ready to fight back, she wrenched a hand free to slap his face, and comprehension flashed through her—soured by differences they couldn't bridge, Cory took her submission as an invitation to dominate, punishing her for their failure.

Walt, feeling her change, released her.

"What about Laura?" her mind asked him, but already they were there, the misery as strong as if he'd just opened that letter. But it didn't work—Laura had summoned and dismissed Walt, but Anna had too. And he'd allowed that, even encouraged her. She was wretchedly sorry she couldn't heal him the way he'd helped her. Feeling her dejection, he hugged her; sun warmed their skin while their hearts warmed each other. A crow flew past, its shadow crossing them—as though at a signal they disengaged, put on clothes, and walked back to the others.

Tonio and Mario knelt touching foreheads, swaying side to side; Marisa, Luisa, and Ray with joined hands encircled them. Anna could see the group's energy flow skyward, as distinct as a column of smoke. Ray nodded to her and Walt, then they walked away.

Walt held her hand as though by letting go they'd lose each other; they didn't speak. Anna gripped suddenly. Following her glance he saw a rattlesnake gliding toward them, enlivened by the heat of rock and sand. They stood perfectly still. Her inner silence spread, and the snake moved swiftly beyond them, head and tail off the sand, spine flexing, leaving S-tracks. Calmness filled her—right now she could handle anything. They headed for the campground, its location tangible in waves of activity rising there.

• • •

"LET'S DRAW," HE SUGGESTED. Didn't think he could do anything else with the mescaline sliding around in his nerves. Seated on the picnic table, Anna selected a nearby rock as a subject. Walt chose their tent, which he expected to be simple—but it wouldn't stop flowing, every edge wavering off into the surrounding air. He closed his eyes. When he looked again, those flow lines were still there, so he penciled them in, wondering what Luna would say.

Finished drawing, he and Anna lay head to foot on the table, staring at the sky. One moment the clear air was a blue ceiling, the next, infinite space into which he could see far enough to detect stars. His hand found Anna's, their fingertips curled together as he tuned in to heart and breath, his buzz of thoughts fading off, the sky pulsing in and out, closer then more distant.

In a waking dream he saw he should've sat next to the dog in the truck. Anna's father frowned at him, arms crossed on his chest, saying he'd brought harm to her: no amends were possible, the best he could do was leave her alone. Then like a film clip he watched Laura seeing him off at the airport—her body, her kiss—even now that memory conquered him. What could he really do when she reached for him? Months awaiting trial, then two years in prison—what had that done to her? He thought of Stream, the girl he'd never met who'd wrung Cob's heart—Laura's arrival had triggered her downfall. He felt suddenly afraid for Anna. He'd been deluded thinking Laura would just leave him alone. She'd had plenty of solitude to hone her desire.

• • •

IN ANNA'S DREAM, A woman *with a lean and beautiful face was shuffling a tarot deck, and after she cut the cards began laying them*

out face up. "Let me tell you what happens to innocence," gesturing
to her right. Anna following the sweep of her arm saw a young woman
with hair like Walt's before he'd cut it—thick, sun bleached—framing a
naïvely smiling face. She looked so peaceful sitting there with her eyes
closed. Glancing lower, Anna saw blood on her wrists, skirt, pooling
around her crossed legs. Heart freezing with fear, Anna looked back
at the woman holding the cards, who nodded knowingly. Tapping
the King of Cups in the center of her layout she placed the next
card across it—the Queen of Swords—and said, "He's mine. Don't
interfere." Anna's tongue couldn't move; little meaningless noises
escaped her throat. The woman became a rattlesnake, her head
swaying slowly side to side—it struck. Anna woke with a terrified jolt.

Walt lay asleep on the table; his fingers falling loose had released
hers. She moved away, walking faster till she found herself running
despite the tightness in her lungs and heart. Panting, she stopped
to lean against one of the rock formations jutting like icebergs, and
looked down. In the coarse sand, one line after another became
rattlesnakes. "They're not there, not there," she said over and over,
and at each assertion they became sand, but new ones kept appear-
ing, more threatening. She scrambled onto the rock and perched six
feet up, watching them circle and vanish, longing to leave this spot
but afraid to set foot on the ground. She'd been crouched there longer than daylight seemed capable of lasting, when someone spoke.

"You can come down if you want." Ray had dead snakes under
his boots.

"But they—I'm—the snakes—" She met his calm gaze. "They're
not there, are they?"

"Nope—not here." He reached to her, and as soon as their fingers touched, the rattlers were gone—nothing but sand, not even
rippling anymore. "Your fear is what's real."

She glimpsed it, crouching like a cornered beast beyond him—
but when she looked full at it, the shape was a joshua tree.

"You make them," he said. "That means you can make them
go away."

"But fear's a warning," remembering her dream: the young
woman sitting in her own blood.

"Fear paralyzes. It loses its power once you accept death."

And she recalled the bleeding woman's serenity—dying, she wasn't afraid. But the woman dealing tarot cards wasn't a fear-snake, she was real—she was Laura, coming back to claim Walt, and being fearless made no difference against her. Anna's heart felt very small and vulnerable. Walt's love couldn't protect her; the weight of karma drove Laura's intention. "What should I do?"

"Base your actions on what you want, not how somebody else might treat you."

She walked back to the van with him. Luisa and Mario were roasting dark green chilis in the skillet, heating them till the semitransparent skins blistered away from the pulp. Taking refuge in routine, Anna helped peel then chop them, and once those were done, Luisa started frying beans, adding the chilis and cumin. Anna had felt the group's expectation that she go get Walt, but convinced now she needed to stay away from him, she kept busy.

• • •

WALT SET A STACK of tortillas next to the camp stove, his retreating hand lingering on Anna's forearm. "Hey, I missed you."

She took a deep shuddering breath. "You should stay away from me. We're just going to get hurt—both of us," looking him full in the face. Her pain was as shocking and hard as hitting that tree when the van pushed him off Highway 17. They'd been so light—

Ray put his hand on her back between her shoulders. "Walk with me Anna." They moved away.

Walt stood frozen, fracture patterns spreading in his heart like Onion's honeycombed glass—that entire experience was still in him. Every detail he'd willed to vanish rose up like the sight of tree bark suddenly too large and close, before his windshield broke and went opaque, the scream of collapsing metal, the stench of skid-burnt tires and sprung radiator, the scald of his pinned and fractured leg. The ache in his chest where he was thrown into the seatbelt, the warm salt of his nosebleed triggered by the force of his head snapping forward, cold rain hitting his hands and soaking into his lap as the windshield sagged apart—everything had healed except in his soul where the collision waited, unchanged, to ambush him again in a moment of weakness.

• • •

SAYING NOTHING, ANNA LET Ray lead, feeling the breeze move and slack like breath. In a cluster of joshua trees they stopped.

"Tell me about Laura," she said.

"The first time I met her he was rescuing her—that other guy worked her over pretty hard, and Walt brought her home to recuperate. You know how generous he is—she'd told him to stay away, so he did till she wanted to see him, then he took her in as though she'd always been loyal. But she had that Berkeley edge—people who look out for themselves because nobody else will. She was hard."

"And beautiful?"

"Is that what you're afraid of?" Ray squinted knowingly. "He was twisted in a knot, trying to be her man. He seems happier with you."

"But she wants him back."

"Maybe she's out to reconstruct her sanity—killing someone's a lot to atone for."

"So Walt's still supposed to be her soft landing?"

"Not necessarily."

"But he's having all this bad luck." She told him about his detention, the drug raids on his house.

"I've seen this before," Ray mused. "People who are more awake become lightning rods for systems of abuse. It's like a tempering process." He looked at her warmly. "How's he been with you?"

"Kind and funny and playful—but now I know what she's capable of."

"If she met you first, maybe she'd leave him alone."

Her wide eyes told him how afraid she was.

He laughed. "Show her your drawings—she'll figure it out."

When they got back, everyone was sitting around the picnic table eating beans and rice wrapped in tortillas, washing that down with amber beer. Walt made room beside him but Ray sat there. Anna took a place opposite, while Mario and Marisa led a discussion of plans once they returned to Indio—they ran a retreat center there, and also rented a house in East L.A. where they worked with poor families terrorized by police and immigration authorities.

"A hard life *en El Norte* is still much better than the struggle in Mexico," Mario explained, "and some of the people who come here are powerful beings. We team with them to bring order to the *barrio*, to teach people skills and solidarity. In Mexico there is a strong spiritual tradition—when they feel like mice, people go along to avoid being noticed, but we help them remember they are hawks and jaguars and coyotes, then authorities can't push them around so easily."

"Do you have trouble with the police?" Walt asked.

"At first we did," Mario said, "when they weren't sure what we were up to. But where we work violent crime has gone down, so they leave us alone—as long as we don't have a political agenda."

Ray laughed. "We do, but they don't understand it. We're spiritual anarchists—people living by internal rules, aligning life with spirit."

"What about the drugs?" Anna asked.

"We're organized as a church—the peyote ritual's part of our worship. We invited some investigators to participate and they called off the cops, but part of the deal was to base the center outside the city. We like Indio—it's not too far from here—and Joshua Tree is a place we favor—and we can get into East L.A. easily."

"How big's the center?" Walt asked.

"We have two adobe buildings, and a third under construction. They're small, but *los pobres* are used to that—if you take them from ten to a room into a gym, they get very nervous."

"We close from Christmas till the second week of January," Luisa said. "This gives us time to work out our program for the coming year, and clean the center, and get away. When we go back, two of us will stay in Indio, three will go to L.A. When we have a new group for the center, one will come back with them."

"Do you have certain roles?" Anna asked.

"I stay at the center," Tonio said. "In the *barrio*, people are too wretched. By the time Ray sends them to Indio they have enough dignity I can help them."

"I spend most of my time in the *barrio*," Ray said. "I'm not so scary looking."

They all laughed.

• • •

AS WALT AND ANNA walked back to their campsite in the dark, she said, "Walt, let's not have sex."

"Why not?" Trying to deny this looming emptiness.

"I think we're sowing confusion where we need clarity."

"You mean you can talk yourself out of love if I'm not holding you."

"No."

A high thin cloud cover masked the brilliance of the stars—all he could see was shimmer in her eyes.

She said, "Maybe I can't explain without sounding stupid—"

"Don't apologize. I'm glad you said something, if that's how you feel."

To which she was silent.

"Want to go home soon?" he asked.

"But you've hardly talked to Ray—isn't that why you came?"

"Yeah—maybe tomorrow, then we can leave." Every time she shut him out, it hurt more, got harder to come back from. He thought about her parents waiting for her; Harold who by now must be ready to beat him up for the misery she couldn't hide; her grandparents' open sweet nature. It wasn't fair to show how her decision lacerated him—he didn't want her capitulating out of guilt. She'd closed the door, he could feel deadbolts and chains sliding into place. *Give up, Walt.*

In the tent he shifted his bag to one side, listening to her a couple feet away, her breath slowing as she dropped off. He still felt her resounding slap on his face when he'd loved her as Cory and she found the will to resist him—maybe in her heart he was just like him? Ultimately had he used affection to coerce her, the same way he'd been bulldozed by Laura?

chapter 20

Deserters

AT FIRST ANNA thought the whimpering was a coyote pup near their tent, but waking more, realized Walt was keening in his sleep. She lay making plans until the first hint of light, then moved stealthily from the tent, pulling her sleeping bag after her. She stuffed it, got her knapsack from the car, took a quart of water, and walked up the road toward Twentynine Palms. It was several miles but she strode quickly. Reaching the desert highway, she tore a flap from a weathered beer case to make a sign. Lettering COLORADO, she stood on the shoulder holding it out. A dusty blue two-door Pontiac stopped, two Marines in it.

"'At's a long way," the passenger said, leaning out his window.

"I know where it is."

"We're goin' out to the base or we'd give y' a lift." He turned to the driver to consult, then leaned back her direction. "Hey listen, we can take y' across the base and drop ya on I-40. Nobody uses this road—you'll be here all day."

Not wanting Walt to find her, she nodded acceptance. The guy stepped out, and in the brightness she could see days-old stubble on his cheeks, his uniform sweat stained and reeking of cigarettes. He tossed her sleeping bag into the back while she kept hold of her knapsack and sign. As she reached to flip the seat forward, a quick sweep of his forearm deflected her hand. "Jus' git in."

Her stomach tightening, she scooted into the middle. He sat beside her and pulled the door shut, and the car roared up the road. Both guys smelled like her brother Roger after he'd been playing basketball—harsh male sweat steeped in cigarette smoke. She sat straighter—she was done taking crap from him.

"I'm Rance." The passenger's olive-drab short-sleeved shirt was stenciled R. MORGAN above the pocket.

"Dave," said the driver, nodding to the windshield. His said D. BELLOWS.

"I'm Anna."

Dave grabbed a white pastry bag off the dashboard to pass, and she chose a glazed donut—either yesterday's, or the bag had been left open—it was not only stale but kind of gritty; while she chewed, the roofs and trees of Twentynine Palms became more distinct. Near the outskirts Dave turned abruptly off the road, following tire tracks in the sand. The car rattled and bounced across open desert, and soon they drove over a wire fence lying flat. Another quarter-mile of bumping and sliding brought them to a dirt road.

Rance offered her a can from the six-pack at his feet, but she declined, glad to have her water to wash the after-tang of sugar from her mouth. He opened the beer himself; it spurted and he blew off the foam, spattering the windshield. Despite the road's washboarding—from tank treads maybe—Dave drove fast, the car bounding upward and slamming down on its way. She couldn't see to either side very well but the road ran straight till it faded into the desert. Rance pushed a Lynyrd Skynyrd tape into the deck and turned it up; as it played "Free Bird" she thought she'd never been so trapped.

"Like this song?" A note of lewd arrogance lit his voice.

"It's not my favorite," she said steadily.

"What is?"

"Joni Mitchell—she wrote a lot about the desert, and traveling."

"Think you're Joni Mitchell?" Scornful as Roger.

"No, but I understand her."

"Hey Dave, she's sen-si-tive," he laughed. Dave's face was impassive—he still hadn't looked at her. "Hey Amy, I am too. I wanna share my sensitivity with you." His left hand holding his beer moved to the seatback behind her, his right to his crotch.

"No that's OK," she said flatly.

"Last chick I did cried, then she screamed and I hadda break 'er jaw. What about you?" leaning close to leer at her—he had blackheads across his sunburnt nose, and now she could see how young he was—maybe not even twenty-one. His body might be a killing machine but he was a kid inside it. The rattlesnake woman in her dream was thousands of years old—now *there* was someone to fear. She thought of the beatific face of the girl sitting in her own blood—maybe Richard Brautigan was right in *The Hawkline Monster*, and death was just a game of musical chairs spirits played with bodies.

Rance's energy was jittery, swarming over her like ants, an itch on the surface of her skin. But within her she felt a massive calm that bloomed large, filling her, pushing outward. All her life she'd absorbed whatever was around her, beautiful or ugly, unable to keep it out, but now serenity had settled inside. Nothing could harm her anymore, nothing could make a difference. *I'm dead. At last. And free.* Whatever they planned to do to her, these Marines had showed up just in time to save her from far greater pain. She met Rance's eyes. "I'm already dead."

He blinked and sat back, baffled, spooked. "Dave stop the car," he barked, sharp as an order. The Pontiac slewed around, skidding to a standstill in a cloud of dust. "Git in the back." He flung open his door, jumped out, and flipped his seatback forward. She half climbed half dived over, he sat back down and slammed the door, turning the tape deck as loud as it would go, sitting rigid.

The Pontiac with another churn of dirt was back in motion. On the long ride she felt dust thickening in her nasal passages, watched minuscule particles vibrate on the seat as the car shook and jarred on the rough road. Through the narrow side window, she could make out reddish strings of hills like big dirt piles, scabbed with rocks or cacti—she was jostled too much to tell which.

"Giddown," Rance snapped; she glimpsed a gatehouse, and hunched on the floor. The car slowed but kept moving as the Marines exchanged greetings with the guard on duty. A few minutes later the car stopped. "Out!" Rance ordered. As she walked away he wolf-whistled, but she was free. She knew—she had known—that Death was in the car, in the harsh music, in the stench and the soldiers' roughness, in sitting between them. The only reason they hadn't hurt her was that she welcomed Death. The peyote had showed her how she created her own circumstances—misery and joy. If she projected fear, the world would oblige by scaring her. If she projected certainty, occupying her own space, the world would meet her on equal terms.

At root, all fear was fear of death. And when something in her died yesterday, fear died with it. Regret was an indulgence; by standing up for what she wanted and rejecting what she didn't, she needn't ever wallow in it again. Being physically strong wasn't the only way to have power. Rance had been afraid of her because she didn't respond as expected. He was waiting for her fear, and when she showed she was dead to his harm, that rebounded back on him. *Like a superball*. And now she could even smile at that thought, dissociate it from Walt, happily picture a neon-colored superball caroming through space. *After death is birth*, she thought, and approached the highway interchange with light steps.

Hitchhiking was illegal on interstates, but she wasn't going to wait at this middle-of-nowhere on-ramp all day; she walked up to the merge point with her sign, the glare of sun on bare landscape making her eyes water. A semi passed, its wake flinging grit and rousing dust slower to settle—she closed her eyes to keep it out, then held up her sign again. A bulbous sedan with faded green paint stopped—a Rambler or Studebaker—the chrome name was gone. A small man, sunburn peeling on his bald spot, leaned toward her.

"Where in Colorado?" he asked in a reedy voice.

"Boulder."

"I live in Lakewood—I can give you a ride that far."

"Thanks." She put her sleeping bag on the floor between her feet and rested her pack on the eroding seat whose material had split into strips, wisps of stuffing working their way out the gaps. "I'm Anna."

"Orland Kavala—I'm 'O.K.,'" laughing at his own joke. He'd told her he'd been at an astrology conference in San Bernardino. A shoe repairman by trade, he had a passion for interpreting horoscopes. When she told him her birthdate and time of day, he nodded.

"You're a Virgo—good with details, precise, careful about your health, like to keep things neat and orderly. You worry. But the Gemini ascendant's challenging—the twins—two personalities changing places, quick-witted but restless. Square to the Virgo, I'd say that makes you moody. I need to look up your Moon sign—that'll be important in balancing your impulses." He stole slightly awed, slightly greedy glances at her, as though she were a box of treasure. He sprinkled his comments with words like "destiny" and "transcendent," and she began to relax, letting her encounter with the Marines fade.

She had no doubt they—well, Rance anyway—intended to rape her, but when she'd said she was dead, his eyes changed, as though she wasn't a corpse but Death itself. Now she wondered why they'd let her stay in the car clear to the gate. Probably because her discovery on the base would have got them in trouble. Riding with O.K., she felt as though she'd gone from one reality into another, from a visceral immediate world of pain and trouble into an abstract place where events were put in motion by forces far beyond Earth.

Later when they traded off driving, he opened his valise, pulled out a sheet of paper with a twelve-part pie outlined on it, and thumbing a booklet began to draw symbols, first around then inside the circle.

"Your Libra Moon calms those Gemini urges with a sense of fairness—you can't help seeing the other side of a question, appreciating its merits—you're very broad-minded. But respecting divergent points of view makes choosing one difficult. With Gemini changing its face constantly and Libra vacillating, I'd say you have trouble making decisions, or sticking to them." He smiled at her nods of confirmation. "If it wasn't for your Virgo, you'd blow away with all that air, but you're well anchored with Sun and Venus in an earth sign. It's curious that your Saturn's the only planet above the horizon—that governs your relation to work. You're bound to succeed, Saturn being in its natal sign, but how you do that must seem a mystery to those around you—you're hard-working, but I think you're lucky too, and you find opportunities most people wouldn't."

She wished she knew Walt's birthday. "What about my love life?"

"Venus in Virgo's, well, virginal. Shy, innocent—maybe a little naïve. People might take advantage of you."

"Yeah," thinking of Cory. But she'd taken advantage of Walt when she should've stayed aloof, and now they'd both have to pay.

• • •

WALT FELT HER ABSENCE, not conscious enough to draw a conclusion, just stretching out more and sleeping deeper. The tent was stuffy when he woke, the sun like a dot-pattern newspaper image against the canvas. He pulled on his jeans and crawled out, looking around—didn't see her. Checked in the tent—her sleeping bag was gone. *Oh.* Now he remembered sounds associated with her departure.

Not so warm out here. Buttoning his shirt and putting on his coat, he walked over to Ray's van. His friend and Marisa were making pancakes studded with plantain and orange slices.

"Seen Anna this morning?" he asked noncommittally.

"No." Ray looked at him. "She reminds me of a cat my mom had—shied at every noise. The only person he liked was Mom, and then only when she was sitting down to watch TV. He'd curl up on her lap, but if she so much as crossed her legs he was gone."

Walt sagged.

"But he stuck around fifteen years. She loved that cat."

"I won't last that long," he mumbled.

"Think of her moods as a pendulum—look for the center, the point she always crosses—that's where she really is. All this back and forth is just the swing that keeps her ticking."

"I asked her to marry me," he said forlornly. "Gave her till March to decide."

"Think she will?"

"No. I can't uproot her, and her family won't accept me."

"Want me to give you a reference?"

Walt smiled wryly. "I have no credibility—why would my friends?"

"Have a pancake." Ray extended the spatula, Walt lifted one off, taking bites with teeth bared as it cooled. Ray ate one then turned the spatula over to Marisa, rapping on the back window of the van, calling, "Breakfast."

To Walt he said, "Let's walk."

Away from the campground, pivoting in a circle Ray nodded at the far-off mountains, climbing sun, joshua trees—surroundings untouched by individual misery. But this place with its sere loveliness—brown, yellow, gray-green, and black against the immaculate blue dome of sky—gave Walt no comfort. Walking over to a joshua tree, he tapped his fingernail on a spike.

"Ray, Anna just left in the middle of the night—never said anything. Where'd she go?"

"Home," Ray said immediately. Shaking his head, he continued, "I can't untie this knot for you, I'll just say that making someone's life better's a good thing—she's stronger since we all tripped yesterday. Now it's her turn, to meet the world and test herself."

Walt's heart was a lonely hole in the middle of him. He forced himself to think of it as a seed that needed patience to germinate, while he focused elsewhere. "I wanted to be a teacher, but I got switched off that track so fast—"

"There's other worthwhile work—look around."

"And what about Laura?"

"I don't know," Ray said. "Maybe you still love her, or want her or something. That guy abused her but she wanted him back."

"If I'm making progress, why are my hands empty?"

"Maybe they're not. You told me about the box of rain you found in Santa Cruz, under the jasmine by the steps. That was a great omen, coming just when you thought you were destroyed—take another look."

Walt might've killed himself before he saw that, but it seemed such a fine joke he'd had to laugh. Maybe joy would save him again. "All right, thanks."

• • •

HE REACHED GRAND CANYON after dark, driving in till he found a graveled spot to pull off. Moving to the backseat, he crawled into his sleeping bag, cracking open the window by his feet, folding his coat for a pillow. He woke early, nose and cheeks cold, hamstrings and calves tight. He hustled into clothes as stars disappeared, then walking away from the road, realized he was quite near the rim. He paced while he watched colors emerge on the cliff walls across the chasm. Clouds and canyon took on scarlet, fuchsia, orange, yellow, then the red ball of sun edged up casting blue tree shadows, flaring as it climbed free of the plateau, paling through the spectrum. In twenty minutes, glare had washed out the dawn colors.

He thought, *Anna would've liked this*, then stopped himself—*he* liked it. That would suffice. Driving around to a parking area along the rim, he found a vacant space and got out, walking down the row enjoying not just the canyon but the people visiting—U-Haul trucks, pickups full of furniture, men and women looking tired and rumpled while excited kids raced, fragments of their shouts rebounding off the walls of stone. He paused in front of a car that had a rocking chair lashed to its trunk, and admired the way it was mounted—with runners up and its back slanting to the rear window, it allowed the trunk lid to open. A woman sat on the hood, looking across the canyon through binoculars, her loose long brown hair lifting from her shoulders in the breeze that flowed up from the river.

"Moving?" he asked her.

"Yeah." She tossed her hair. "As long as I have my rocking chair and books, I'm home anyplace. How about you?"

"I've moved around more than I've moved."

She laughed. "How do you manage that?"

"Moving implies stopping, staying someplace. Moving around has no endpoint."

"Like a circle."

"Or a cycle." He'd been here two and a half years ago, and now maybe he could finish scattering the ashes, let it be.

"Great place to get high—want to?" another invitation in her eyes: the remedy for his loss.

"Let's go."

In her car they drove the rim road, then turned down a campground loop and parked on a remote curve. Carrying a foam pad and blanket they walked back among the trees; in a piñon-veiled spot with a vantage of the canyon, he spread the pad on the ground and they sat. She offered a brick-colored stone pipe carved in the likeness of a crested jay with open beak. They smoked two bowls to fine ash, then she knocked and blew the pipe clean before putting it away. They took in the view in silence. As Walt came onto the grass, the mescaline surfaced to meet it, revealing vibrations in everything—trees stroked the air, the colors on the canyon walls shimmered, sheets of energy crossed the void of sky like auroras. She wore a halo of white flowers; her skin was gold, eyes turquoise. His head swam. She was a goddess, her energy clear as sunshine. Eyes on hers, he took her hands.

"May I?"

She inclined her head. "Please."

• • •

RELEASE FILLED HIM WITH light. He lay looking up at the pine needles. Beneath this thin pad and the skin of soil, millennia of stone supported them resting together in contact—red layer, yellow, white—not so different from her body on his, the blanket over them both, the skin of her back smooth as polished metal beneath his arms. His eyes slipped shut in a dream.

He had Laura's rejection in his hands again, but this time it turned to dust as he tried to read it. Laughter sounded as a gust blew it swirling away then down, its particles turning and spreading the way a flock of birds moves, clustering and dissipating, changing direction together. The laughter came from the canyon. He knelt on the very rim to look down; a pair of bright eyes in the depths gazed at him full of joy, and he laughed back, then pushed off, soaring into the great empty space above the river. Five swifts touched him with their wings, each contact making him lighter and faster. "How can your pain let go when you're hangin' on so hard?" one asked—Ray. So Walt reached inside his throat to pull out a hot dark-red clump he let fall, and in that moment, became a swift himself.

He opened his eyes, heart flying, and he and his sojourner shared a kiss tasting of apricots. They sat up, put on clothes, folded her blanket. She touched the tree they'd lain under, her finger coming away sticky with resin she rubbed at the base of his nostrils. Humbled, he touched his forehead to her shins, then inhaling the pine scent looked into her eyes expansive as desert sky. Fingers linked, they walked to her car and she drove back to the parking area.

"Thank you," she said, face and voice warm with delight. They held eyes another moment, then she drove away. He got in Plug and left the Grand Canyon. Ray was right—the box didn't ever have to be empty. When he found his own renewal, his life would manifest it everywhere he looked. Flow wasn't just a notion, it was the way of things, and as long as he was in the current he'd encounter what he needed next.

book three

Spring 1982

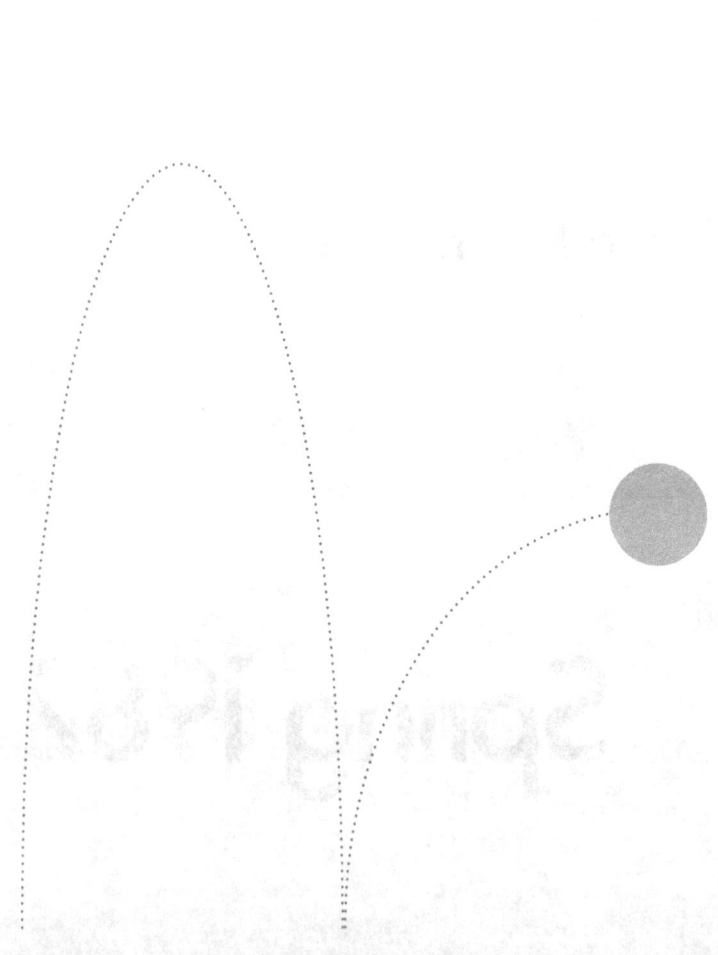

chapter 21
On Your Toes

TEN MINUTES LATE, Walt grabbed a booth at Tom's Tavern, then while the neon hands traveled the clock face, he waited, wondering if he'd missed Burke. Walt hadn't seen or heard from Anna since returning a month ago, but her friend was surely an emissary. He looked around. Locals not college students, relaxing as though they owned the place. From what Anna said, only a few old-line establishments remained. Anywhere you went, time left some things standing while demolishing others, but it happened faster here. Roger had touched a nerve at Christmas, teasing her about invaders—her brother had embraced the region's booming economy, but she hadn't. Though she might be happier someplace else, she must sometimes feel she'd moved anyway.

After another fifteen minutes, Burke arrived. "Sorry," he said as he settled opposite, that apology belied by his unruffled demeanor. "It's impossible to park downtown anymore. I should've walked."

They agreed to split a pitcher. The waitress delivered it, poured their beer, then left. Lifting his glass and taking in the place with a sweeping gaze, Walt said, "Here's to what remains."

Burke clinked rims with him. "Boulder you mean? To whatever's left—yes."

"So, tell me the occasion."

"When's the last time you talked to Anna?"

"The night she left Joshua Tree without telling me."

Burke sighed. "That's what I thought. She asked me to find out your birth information: date, time, place. She met some astrologer and wants him to do your chart."

"Tell her I'm a Possum with my Moon over Pueblo."

They laughed.

"No, seriously—"

"Is she gonna make some decision about me based on what this guy thinks?"

"That's my guess," Burke said. "Might be as good as any other decision she makes, too."

"*Indecisive* you mean."

"Exactly. That's what the guy told her about herself—changeable and also vacillating, and shy and moody."

"All the right buttons. So now she wants to locate mine? I'll tell you where they are: here—" finger to his forehead, "here—" on his heart, "and down here—" pointing at his crotch. "She doesn't need an astrologer to figure that out."

"I think she's looking for an opening, personally."

"She can talk to me anytime. I'm not the one who walked away."

"She thinks you're mad at her, or fed up or something."

"Maybe I should be, but I feel sorta neutral."

"Walt, this pains me. I really like Anna, we've been friends for years—but she makes simple things so complicated."

"If she's confused, that's her. I'm just waiting."

"She's scared of your old girlfriend."

Walt laughed. "You'd think Laura was evil—she was wrong for me but she's not a bad person. She's not gonna scratch Anna's eyes out."

Burke put down his glass, announcing, "This is too much beer for two people," and left for the restroom. During his absence Walt asked for a glass of water, and listened to the couple in the next booth having a loud argument. The guy's assumption that she had nothing better to do than look after his dog all weekend angered her—he didn't care how she might choose to spend her time—and also pissed him off, because he'd already made plans based on her help. A little communication goes a long way. But as they took turns ranting, Walt began to hear it as performance: no effort to resolve the argument, neither one walked out—this wrangle was for public consumption. The waitress went by with a plate of French fries. As the minutes lengthened, she even brought his water.

When Burke finally got back he poured himself more beer, and they talked on, below half the pitcher, then Walt excused himself. On his way to the restroom he passed a young woman having an earnest conversation on the pay phone. *Hmm.* So he wasn't that surprised when he came back to the table, and Anna was sitting in his spot.

"Siddown," Burke ordered, so he did, on her side, just far enough into the six-seater booth to be out of the aisle. Her hair, chopped short, made her look like a fifteen-year-old boy; her eyes were huge and worried.

"Hello," Walt said matter-of-factly.

"Hi," she hesitated, "I'm—"

"If you say you're sorry, I'm leaving."

"OK I won't," she shot back.

"Good," he smiled. "How was your trip home?"

"I learned some things—got a ride through the middle of nowhere with a pair of Marines. It was like sitting next to that dog in the pickup truck."

"Did you get bit?"

A smile of inner satisfaction stole across her mouth. "Nope. They gave me a ride to the Interstate and that was that."

"Because you weren't afraid of them?"

"That's right." The glint in her eye was new—she was definite, she was assertive, she was fearless. God how he'd wanted that.

"That," he smiled, "is excellent," and kissed her, keeping his hands to himself. She could retreat if she wanted, but her mouth responded with the warmth he had come to love and ceased to expect. When their lips released, Anna blushed, and Walt spread his right hand on the table, looking at the ring she'd bought him. She covered it with the ring on her middle finger, then looked away as though they hadn't made contact. He took the opportunity to study her face—the bites on her jaw had faded to hairlines, like cracks in porcelain. He traced one.

"You've been using lanolin, haven't you?"

"Yeah—Grandma knew what she was doing, giving me that."

"What does she think of me?"

After a glance at him, she spoke to the table. "She didn't understand all that police activity—she and Grandpa are worried it might happen again, and they think maybe the cops had a reason to pick you up."

"They thought so. What about your dad?"

She closed her eyes. "I can't mention your name."

"That's about what I expected." He drank the rest of his water, filled the glass with beer and set it in front of her. "So why do you want some astrologer to tell you who I am? You already know more than he's gonna see in a chart."

"I've been wrong though." She was looking at Burke.

Walt said, "But you were afraid of what you'd find out so you drew in all these lines that aren't there. 'Erase, erase, erase. Draw only what you see.'"

She laughed. "I picked up the Free School bulletin—Luna's teaching colored pencil Wednesday afternoons three to five, starting March tenth."

"Gonna take it with me?"

"Yeah."

He lifted her hand and kissed it. "We can start over." In a commanding voice he barked, "Forward! March forth!"

At his reminder, distress rushed into her face; she stared at her beer.

"April Fool," he murmured.

She blushed.

"Mayday, mayday, plane going down," in a nasal imitation of a WWII cockpit radioman.

Burke shook his head, laughing.

Anna turtled into her coat. Walt rubbed her back and kissed the top of her head, trading looks with Burke, who said, "You should go."

"Thank you." Walt dug in his jeans pocket.

"No no, my treat."

"Anna said you don't have any money."

"I generally don't. So let me pay."

"I'll leave the tip." Walt put down a single and a heap of dimes and nickels. "C'mon Anna, let's go."

"Go where?" letting her coat drop to her shoulders.

"Your place—my mattress has disintegrated. Burke, when can we use your pickup to go to Old World? I can't sleep on that thing anymore."

"Saturday."

"Good—I'll call."

Anna slid over, giving Burke a grateful smile. "You were right."

"Of course," he huffed. "I'm frequently correct."

As soon as Anna and Walt stepped outside, cold wind swept against them, coming off the foothills like a tide of ice. They hastily buttoned up, and pulled on hats and gloves.

"So," she said, "you think I'm taking you home."

"You could. That'd be—"

"What about March fourth?"

"That's a month away. You're probably not done changing your mind."

"O.K.— the astrologer I got a ride from—was so accurate," she enthused as they walked, leaning into the wind, squinting. "Gemini Rising making me switch around all the time, and Libra Moon—the scales, you know, see-sawing before they balance—up and down, back and forth—" her hand waving in illustration. "That's exactly how I feel."

"Anna, I've met lots of people into astrology. Insight's no substitute for your own perceptions. I'll tell you my birthdate if you really want to know, but don't let what he says blind you."

"All right—when is it?"

He grinned. "Make it worth my while."

"I said no sex. I still mean that."

"Can I play with your feet?"

"Huh?"

"I'd love to massage your feet—you might like it too. Then we'll go walk."

When they got to her apartment he took off his coat and boots and sat with his back to her dresser, legs stretched along her bed.

She removed her boots. "What about my socks?"

"I'll take care of those. Just put your head back and don't think so much."

She lay the opposite direction, staring upward.

He started with gentle rubbing, rolling the tops of her socks, working one then the other down to her heels then tugging them off altogether. He put his teeth against the inside of one arch, biting gently, moving up to spread her toes, and checked her expression— now her eyes were closed, her nostrils widening and mouth quivering as he kissed just below the ball. Her foot curled in his hands. As he kissed slowly up the inside of her ankle then back to the sole, she flipped her head from side to side.

"I said no sex," her voice cracked.

"This isn't sex—it's a version of boko-maru. Didn't you read *Cat's Cradle?*"

"Vonnegut? Not that one."

"It's required reading. We'll stop by my house and get it."

She sat up looking peeved, dangling her feet off the side of her bed. "So now that Burke's done his little peacemaking thing, you just pick up where you left off?"

"Anna, don't you want me to care about you?"

Her face scrunched tight.

"Did your astrologer say you're into guilt?"

"He didn't put it like that."

"All right, listen carefully—I'm only saying this once: I was born May 11, 1955, at 3:55 p.m. in Silver Spring, Maryland."

"Hold on, let me get that down," scrambling for paper and a pen. "Shoot, what time?"

"Unh-unh, I said once—that's it. But since you're writing down important things you should add a few."

"Like what?"

"'I love you,' and 'Be silly,' and 'Please can I kiss you?'"

"Those aren't—"

"To me they are. C'mon, I'll help you spell—I, I-o-v-e, y-o-u," his hand around hers guiding the letters. Resisting, she scrawled over his birthdate and exclaimed in annoyance, releasing the pen. He fixed the two to a five in the time, then printed neatly BE MY VALENTINE. "There. It's perfect. Valentine's Day is a week from Monday. May I spend the night then?"

"Walter Sanders, unplug your ears and listen—I said NO SEX."

"OK fine—let's walk."

The trek to his house was easy, the gale pushing at their backs hurrying them along. She waited in his kitchen while he retrieved *Cat's Cradle*, then they kept going, bent against a side wind, climbing the 17th Street hill. The university campus was deserted at this hour, wind roaring among the trees. Past the Atheneum in the lee of the blast, on they climbed, buffeted again, toward Chautauqua, then up and west. At the shelter behind the mesa he unbuttoned his coat, welcoming this small zone of still air.

"I liked your story about the Marines," he said. "They would've hurt you, wouldn't they?"

She nodded. "It was strange—the aggressive one just wanted me to be afraid of him, but after the peyote and walking out on you, I was ready to die—nothing could touch me."

"Then what's so scary about me?"

"I've been badly hurt, you know."

"It's only present pain that hurts—like what you said today."

"What, 'no sex'? Why's that matter so much?"

"When I'm with you, when I'm in you, you aren't hiding from me—might be the only time."

"O.K. said people take advantage of me, in love."

"Have I?"

"You want to."

"For what purpose?" He dropped to a squat, hugging his knees, rocking from toes to heels, intent on his balance. It was easier to listen to her justifications if he didn't have to watch her face contort trying to make them plausible.

"To make me love you." She squatted in front of him looking defiant, but he nudged her shin with one finger, and she sat.

"See how easy it is to get knocked on your ass?" he said. "Go ahead, do it to me." She reached but he hopped backwards just far enough to elude her. On her knees she swiped with a hand, but he hopped again. She lunged flat out and made contact, which rocked him onto his back. She was trying hard not to be drawn in, but rolling from side to side he looked like a pillbug—hilarity burst out of her.

"I fall on my ass when I'm not on my toes," he said, tipping toward one elbow.

"So if you make me laugh you think I'll change my mind?" she said severely. "I just don't see how you can be in my future, so it's better to keep you out of my present. See, after the peyote, I felt solid for the first time—full—like the only thing inside this skin was me. But this new Anna is still figuring it out. The person so clear about who she is is already fading. So I need to dig into these changes, and make them permanent. To do that I have to be alone. Uninvolved." She looked at him mournfully, just a moment.

But he'd seen this before—he believed her and he didn't. How could loving each other feel so right, if it was completely wrong? "Why'd you come to Tom's Tavern? Burke told you I was there, right?"

"He didn't say but I knew." Standing, she brushed off her hands and knees. "I have to isolate myself till I know I'm solid. Walk me home."

With a sigh, he got up.

Back in the gale on the way downhill, she said, "Know why it's called Baseline Road?"

"Because it's forty degrees north."

"Close—the fortieth parallel was the baseline of the great survey of the West—all the other latitudes were calibrated off this. And here it is, like it's printed on the ground." She swept her arm eastward where the road ran straight to the horizon, interrupted only by a lake. "I crossed that to get to school, from third grade on. It made every day an expedition." They trudged on.

"You like the wind," Walt watched her face as she leaned into it.

"Yeah—the air's so clean afterwards—all the grit and smog end up in Kansas."

Arriving at her house, with her back to him she said, "Thanks Walt. If you want to walk sometime, that's all right. But you can't stay—please don't ask."

"What about Valentine's Day?" he asked her. "Will you come over for soufflé?"

"For dinner, but don't expect me to stay."

"OK," he said, kissing the sweaty spot behind her ear. "G'night."

• • •

SATURDAY ANNA SHOWED UP with Burke for Walt's shopping expedition.

They drove out to the edge of town where Old World sprawled, stuffed with furniture, dishes, appliances, and junk. Anything electrical or mechanical had to be tested on the spot—No Refunds No

Returns. Walt chose four salad plates at a dime apiece and a fine old two-burner waffle iron for a dollar, then went back to the mattress wall. There were lots of twins to choose from, some expensive for being secondhand. The best bargain turned out to be a child's mattress decorated with space ships and stars against an outer space blue background—fifteen bucks, hardly used.

"My sheets aren't even good rags anymore," he said, "but the bedding here looks straight out of a dumpster—I'd rather buy new."

A stop at the dime store completed his shopping trip. Anna still hadn't said anything about why she'd come. Walt didn't want another rebuff so he kept his curiosity to himself.

He invited her and Burke to stay for lunch, to test out his new waffle iron. He scrubbed and rinsed the insides then plugged it in, and as it warmed, the last water droplets hissing, he pulled from his fridge bin a plastic-wrapped package six by nine inches by half an inch thick. The light-brown stuff looked like a ceramic floor tile. He quartered it, sliced one piece edgewise into a pair of thin slabs, and placed one in each compartment of the iron.

"This is mochi," he explained. "It's a very sticky type of rice that's cooked then pounded flat. When it's heated it swells and gets gooey inside—some people bake it in a toaster oven, or nuke it, but I think it makes unbeatable waffles."

"Won't it stick?" Anna asked. "You didn't oil the waffle iron."

"The trick's to let a crust form—I guess it could make a mess but that's never happened to me."

An aroma like toast soon warmed the kitchen.

"Where'd you ever hear of this stuff?" Anna asked as he opened one iron, pulling hers loose with a fork—more cohesive than a batter waffle—airy, crunchy, chewy inside.

"I used to eat it in Chico, California—they grow rice in the Sacramento Valley, and a guy in town makes mochi." He offered Burke the other waffle and started a piece for himself. "Try it with tahini."

"What the hell's tahini?" Burke said.

"Sesame butter."

"See, Californians are different," Burke told Anna. "They eat all this material you didn't even know was food." Having smeared tahini on his, at Walt's suggestion he daubed cream cheese on top, then took a bite. "And it's good too."

She felt she was being coerced at a deep level, as though Walt were a lakebed where she was always going to end up, flowing into him, losing her identity. Whichever direction gravity moved her, there he was, holding her, capturing her. Complete embrace. Which was its own kind of wonder, the brightest spark in the gloom of her heart. He wanted her to be strong, and encouraged her to walk away, but her attraction to him, stubborn as an instinct, didn't care what her brain had decided.

chapter 22

O.K.'s Insight

WHEN ANNA ARRIVED on Valentine's Day at the appointed time, Walt explained it would be just the two of them. "I asked for some space, so my housemates are out." He set four eggs on a kitchen towel. "This'll be a small soufflé. Want to uncork the wine while I start?"

"You're trying to get me loaded." She oozed suspicion.

"You don't have to drink." Getting out mixing bowls, he looked at her. "You don't have to be here at all. Go now, if this is such a drag."

"It isn't a drag."

He arrayed his utensils. "So did your astrologer pigeonhole me yet?"

"You have Mercury and Mars in your twelfth house."

"What's that mean?"

"Well, Mercury there makes your actions intuitive."

"Are they?" He started the roux.

"I think so. And he said the home spot for Mars is the first house, so if it's in the last, you've gone all the way through the cycle. He said your conflict energy is directed toward righting wrongs, not on your own behalf."

"What else?"

"Your Venus is in Aries at Midheaven—he said that's really important to you. With your Sun in Taurus, he said love is the governing impulse in your life."

"And?" At least she was comfortable talking.

"He said Aries—your Midheaven—isn't just a warrior, it's a child, seeing the world in new ways. He said it's a natural fit with my Venus in Virgo." Separating eggs, Walt smiled to himself—it took some bullshit artist to convince her they were a natural fit?

"Choose some music," he suggested.

She went to the living room, and soon Glenn Gould was playing a Bach partita over the kitchen speakers. Returning, she stood where she could watch him beat the egg whites. He carefully blended those with the sauce and eased it all into a small mixing bowl, setting that in a pan of water in the oven.

"I'll give it forty minutes. Help with the salad?"

She washed, dried, and tore lettuce while he chopped purple cabbage and carrot to put in. He cut thin slices off a baguette, heaped them in a soup bowl, poured himself more wine, and got another glass.

"Let's take our appetizers to the living room while it bakes."

He upped the thermostat on the gas heater—usually kept at fifty—then turned circles to the music, his glass extended like a partner. Glancing at her, he said nothing. She was poised to leave the minute dinner was over, still hadn't touched the wine. Her fingers shredded a piece of bread while she paced.

"Walt?" she said finally, so low he could barely hear.

"Hmm?"

"He didn't think we'd make a good match—you're more advanced than I am."

"What do you mean?"

"You're a—higher being."

He froze. "A what?"

"A—higher—"

"Anna, don't you know bullshit when you hear it?"

"I think it's true. I've never seen so much light in anyone."

"Haven't you learned anything washing windows? Light comes through when the glass is clean. If you don't wash away the crud, how can it?" He set down his wine and came closer. Her eyes were swelling with tears. He put his arms around her and stood very still, the heat and wet penetrating to his t-shirt and skin, his heart flip-flopping like a shot rabbit. Her arms hung limp at her sides. He rested his temple on her hair, wondering that he could love someone who put herself so far away.

"Anna," he said gently, "maybe you shouldn't marry me, but don't ask me not to feel. Your astrologer got that right—love governs my life."

"I'm wasting your time," she said into his shirt. "I wasn't Cory's equal, and I'm not yours either. The only part of us that's equal is sex."

"I asked you to marry me. I never did that before."

She backed up far enough to see his expression. "You didn't ask Laura?"

"Nope." He shrugged. "We assumed we had a future, but I never proposed." Leaving her to ponder that, he went back to the kitchen and opened the oven door a crack—the soufflé was high and gold. Opening further, he tapped the side of the bowl—the spiraled top didn't wobble. "Come and get it." She brought glasses in one hand, bottle in the other, the bread dish in the crook of her arm. He collected things from her, and she put out plates while he set silver at their places, and washcloths for napkins.

"Wine?" he offered again.

"I'll just drink water."

He corked the bottle and poured water for them both, and when everything was ready took out the soufflé, already sinking. It was a little dry—liked a bigger dish, he decided—but airy. Sitting across from her, watching her eat, he realized how much he'd enjoyed living with Laura in her pre-Berkeley days: sharing a kitchen, a bed, time. He wanted that with Anna.

Between bites she asked, "How's your new mattress?"

"My room feels like home again. I've slept some weird places, but crashing in my own house lately has been the strangest. Got my walls patched finally—just about ready to paint."

"When we're done with dinner, I want to see." She took another bite. "This soufflé's really yummy."

"Thank you. Happy Valentine's Day."

Four eggs was just right—they ate it all without feeling stuffed, refrigerated the rest of the salad, and went up to his room. He'd put everything back, found a new print—a Ralph Steadman poster of *Fear and Loathing in Las Vegas* to replace the poster the narcs had torn down—and his bed was neatly made—blankets, several inches of top sheet visible, a new pillowcase. She picked up a quartet of paint color strips from his bookcase, squinting first at those, then at the grayish walls, which looked grungy beside the sizeable white areas he'd patched and sanded.

"I was thinking maybe this color." He tapped the buttery gold.

She studied the paint strips as though she were reading tarot cards.

"A penny for your thoughts, Miss Busy-Brain Brubaker." He laughed. "Try saying *that* five times fast—Busy-Brain Brubaker, Busy-Brain Brubraker, Brizzy Brain Boo—" He stopped, eyes glowing warm.

"I was just thinking—" she swallowed, "how much fun we had, playing in the snow naked."

"Some things, if you do 'em alone you're crazy, but if another person joins in, you can touch God." He rested his fingertips on the sleeves covering her forearms. "That's why I belong with you. Alone, I'm someone they should lock up, but when we do silly stuff together, it's divine nonsense."

"Where's my penny?" she said.

"In my pocket. Help yourself." They eyed each other.

"I think I'll go home."

"You didn't have dessert yet—I made chocolate mousse. Want coffee with it?"

"Better not—I have an upholstery job in Denver tomorrow."

"I won't keep you—mousse but no coffee, then I'll walk you home."

They ate fast—with no drinks and her exit planned, he felt cheated, the richness of the moment squandered in their power struggle. And yet, optimist that he was, he went around with a pocketful of condoms.

chapter 23

YES

" **L E T M E H E L P** with the dishes," Anna said, taking hers
to the sink where bowls and pans were piled high.

"No, that'll give me something to do with the rest of my evening."

She winced, and silently put on her coat as he got his fedora.
They walked briskly to her apartment in the chilly darkness, barely a
word exchanged. Approaching her door, she got out her key.

"Oh hey," he said, "look at this untracked snow." She followed
him to the side yard, where one white rectangle remained from
three days ago. He walked out into the middle and flopped back,
sweeping arms and legs to make a snow angel. Sitting up with snow
caked in his hair, he said, "Help me so I don't wreck it." She took his
extended hands and braced to pull, but he hooked the back of her
knee with one foot and she fell on him, his arms around her, kissing
her, and all her resistance just ran out—one more cracked egg that
didn't make it into the soufflé. She kissed him back, gripping his
legs between hers.

He rolled over onto her, took a slow deliberate breath, let it out,
then took another. "Should I go?"

She sank her fingers into his hair, snow melting on her hands as
she brought his mouth back to hers. Maybe in O.K.'s world she and
Walt weren't suited, but this match could start a bonfire.

Eventually she said, "Want to come inside?"

"Well, I do kinda like the snow—"

"Where all the neighbors can watch us?"

"Are they?" he grinned. "Can you see 'em?"

"You're embarrassing me."

"Mmm—bare ass. In me?" He beamed. "In you." Scrambling to his feet, he gave her a hand up, and they went in.

• • •

BY HIS COUNT IT had been six weeks. "It's good to be back."

She put her ear to his chest and listened to his heart thump and rush. "I shouldn't have done this—now you think the door's open again."

"I," he said, stroking her back, "am not thinking. Period. Why are you?"

"Because this could all be wrong."

"Trust your instincts. Your astrologer may understand your chart but—" finger tracing her cheek, "does he feel this?"

As he moved to kiss her, she averted her face. "Happy Valentine's Day, Walt. Now get dressed and go."

Reluctantly he sat up. "I miss sleeping with you, sweetie."

"Don't—you got what you want."

"I did? You think I just wanna jack off? Don't you get it, girl? Sex is just the completest expression, the one you join me in and forget all the BS. I want you to feel not just my dick but my heart inside you, warming you, treasuring you, making you feel whole and loved and wonderful. But if you're in such a hurry to kick me out, I don't think we got there, do you?"

She felt boxed in. His perspective made more sense than hers, which meant she was mistrusting herself. Where was the balance in that? "I guess I want reasons," she said at last. "Why should you love me?"

"Because we're here. Because the cosmos put you next to me and told us to look. Because otherwise we'd be wasting away in our separate little jail cells of misery."

"That's it?"

"If you don't like those reasons, make up your own." He winked, "Know what I want?"

She shouldn't, but she'd already crossed that line—might as well make a night of it. "You can stay, in honor of St. Valentine."

• • •

WALT'S SKIN SLIPPED PLEASANTLY against hers, and he thought about friction: too much would pull, catch, drag, and ultimately bring a relationship to a halt. Its absence however, gave a man no purchase. By now his love for Anna should have gained some traction, but here they were, months after he'd given his heart, and he was still sliding as though she were a patch of wet ice on a barely detectable slope. It didn't look insurmountable, but it was turning out to be.

The friction in their lovemaking was perfect—just enough grab to raise the heat—a toastier dynamic he could not imagine. But when they were two people, one was dodging, eluding, and at heart he knew that however fine he made her feel, he was carrying the commitment for both of them—possibly a sin, since he wanted her while she continued to want her aloneness. He would've felt more at ease if she wanted another guy: that would give him grounds for proving the superiority of his affection, his greater ability to please her and create a life that would delight them both. But if what she really wanted was Nothing, and he was something, his rival was unconquerable, her heart inaccessible. He kept flinching from that recognition because it was a pain without solace. *Put it away Walt,* he told himself. *We're together now—that's all there is.*

In the summer between freshman and sophomore college years, he'd taken a canoe trip with a couple of high school buddies. Floating down a river in West Virginia, they were led through the massive quiet by a kingfisher who flew ahead thirty yards at a time, waiting for them to catch up before continuing. Walt, watching the water curling against his paddle and around the angular gray rocks in the river, thought about time. The kingfisher, swooping off toward the next branch, conducted them into the future while their wake gurgled into history. Time was a moving point, the past a construct of synapses and assertions, the future nonexistent—the present was the only reality.

That understanding had given him a great sense of peace, but now it felt like a tenuous refuge, the skin of a bubble that would pop on contact. He nuzzled the back of Anna's neck, inhaling sweat—he was infused with her now, but that couldn't last as long as he needed it to.

• • •

HE SET HER ALARM —had to be at the bus lot at seven. Usually he caught a city bus, but tomorrow morning he'd walk home then drive. Though 5:30 seemed brutal, he didn't want to screw up his day.

But his calculations were moot. She wanted him. He knew it was morning, he had to get going—couldn't let go. He looked at the clock finally—almost 6:30—and phoned Romo, who was getting antsy. "Hey man, can you pick me up at Anna's on your way to the lot?"

"Wasn't sure where you were. This your mess in the kitchen?"

"Yeah—sorry—I'll deal with it this afternoon." With another ten minutes stolen from the world of obligations, Walt came back to those open arms he'd missed so much.

When Romo honked, she finally let him loose. Eyes on her, he threw on clothes, kissing as he pulled on his boots, casting a brilliant smile her direction as he ran out, forgetting his hat, laces flopping, shirt unbuttoned—

Romo laughed as he got in the car. "Sorry for interrupting."

"Time interrupted—you're just doin' your job. Thanks for the ride."

"Better assemble yourself—those kids'll be murder."

"I know." He could still smell her, feel her; when he closed his eyes, the weight of his coat was her hands. Romo pulled in to a convenience store, came out shoving a cup of coffee at him, muscled his way back into aggressive morning traffic.

At the lot, Walt did what he could with a comb—had better luck with a brush—then straightened his clothes, grinning as they went inside to punch the clock.

"Don't run any red lights," Romo teased, and they started their buses, doors shut against the fumes.

Walt's morning was a blur. The kids, picking up on his distraction, entertained themselves shooting tightly rolled paper bullets at him with rubber bands. Those mostly hit his peacoat but one stung him in the neck, possibly from short range. Once he'd parked at their school, he stood to address them, holding up the offending ammunition.

"Whoever shot this, I'll just tell you—it hurt. If you do that again I'll assign seats." He scanned their faces, not sure they cared—what did they know about harm? Opening the door, he watched them clomp up the aisle and turn to go down the steps.

"Sorry Mr. Sanders," one boy said under his breath, and Walt nodded. They were the age he might've been teaching—junior high. Everything Anna's father had said about them was true. They were like Kipling's *Just So Stories* rhinoceros, cake crumbs tickling under their skins driving them crazy.

Between runs Walt zoned out in his bus, back and butt on one seat, calves and feet across the aisle, dipping in and out of sleep, mind still fogged, his body humming. He wondered what kind of day she was having. With so much practice shutting down her feelings, she'd probably be fine, but how long before she admitted him again?

He remembered a picture he'd seen—the word YES formed by hundreds of NO's—that was Anna. He went into the bus office and got a piece of paper, penciling YES as big as the sheet permitted, then with a pen began filling the Y with NO after NO. Pretty soon rows got boring, so he let the NO's snake around, curling and flowing. By the time he got to the S he was laughing, and when he finished, he carefully erased the penciled outline—YES! Cadging a nine-by-twelve envelope from the supervisor, he printed her address on it, then peeled a sticky note off a pad and wrote

> Anna my love—
> Isn't this true?
> Thank you thank you thank you.
> Love you, Walt

He stuck that on his drawing, slipped it into the envelope, and sealed the flap. The supervisor told him about a post office branch not far away, so he strolled over to mail it. The day was bright and warm, water spreading from beneath snow mounds piled up by plows. Off westward the Indian Peaks all in white dazzled against the blue.

When he got home he cleaned up his dirty dishes then went on to sweep and mop the kitchen floor, whistling.

Romo laughed. "You're like a little kid."

"She blows me away—I feel so incredibly alive."

"At the moment," Romo said skeptically.

Walt moved the chairs. "Hey, I'm gonna paint this weekend—want to do your room too?"

"Sure—I'm tired of looking at drywall patch."

"Time for renewal," Walt said, "moving on from that shit."

"I still think—" Romo raised his voice to a shout, "THIS HOUSE IS BUGGED, DON'T YOU?"

"YEAH, I'D BE AMAZED IF IT ISN'T."

"DON'T THEY HAVE ANYTHING BETTER TO DO?"

Walt shook his head then blared, "WE'RE THEIR BIG ENTERTAINMENT. IMAGINE HOW BORING THEIR LIVES MUST BE."

● ● ●

THE NEXT AFTERNOON ANNA called. "Walt, I got the best thing in the mail."

"You like that?"

"I'm getting a matte and frame for it."

"Hey listen, I'd like to take you out for dessert tonight—want to?"

"I guess."

"I'll come by for you—how's seven?"

Walking from her apartment, she tried to find out where they were going. He wouldn't say but they kept getting closer to his house. Her wariness returned. "You said you're taking me *out*."

"To a café."

He walked her to his door and held it open.

"Walt…"

"Right this way," escorting her through the kitchen.

Just past the inner doorway Barbara met them, wearing a knee-length black skirt, white blouse, and half apron, blonde hair twisted into a bun secured with a pair of lacquered black chopsticks. "Two sir?"

"Yes, thank you," Walt said.

She disappeared into the living room a moment while Walt took Anna's coat and removed his own. Returning, Barbara said, "Follow me please." The heater glowed, a Bach concerto was playing. On a small table near the window stood two wine bottles, a lighted candle in one, an arrangement of dried grasses in the other, both resting on a white cloth remarkably like a pillowcase. Walt pulled out a chair for Anna, then seated himself.

"Our dessert special tonight," Barbara said, "is chocolate mousse. Would you care for something to drink with that?"

"What do you have?" Anna asked.

"Coffee—decaf if you prefer—with a splash of Grand Marnier?"

"That sounds good—with decaf."

"And you sir?"

"What the lady's having, thank you."

Barbara left the room. Walt's eyes were so affectionate Anna had to look away—she watched her finger moving on the tablecloth.

"I really like that drawing you sent," she said.

"I forget where I saw that, years ago, but it seemed fitting." He slid his fingers over to bump hers. "Think I could talk to your dad?"

Her insides lurched—she'd thought her feet were firmly planted, then just like that he whisked away her support. "Wh-what for?"

"I should tell him my intentions. He doesn't need any more shocks from me."

"Last time your name came up, he was pretty blunt." He'd said Walt was rootless, anarchic, bound to hurt her. She traced a spiral on the cloth. She'd never found Dad intimidating, but people who dealt with him in his official capacity sure did. She had no doubt he could make Walt feel unwelcome, but once again at the cost of her autonomy. She didn't want anyone protecting her—not Dad, not Harold. Not Walt.

Barbara came in with a tray and set out a shotglass of cream, spoons, and neatly folded washcloths. "Coffee will be out in just a moment."

Anna twiddled her spoon. Walt went to these ridiculous lengths to woo her and took such joy in it. She felt like an ingrate.

The concerto ended; Barbara flipped the record then returned with her tray, placing dishes of chocolate mousse and mugs of coffee in front of them. "Anything else?"

Walt dismissed her with a nod.

They creamed their coffee, then Walt tasted his dessert.

"Is it good?" Anna asked.

"Try it," extending a bite on his spoon.

"Hm," she said. "Might be a few days old. Taste mine."

He considered before swallowing. "Maybe." He fed her another morsel.

"You know," she said, "I had something similar recently."

"And how was that?"

"Not as good. It seemed—bare."

"Yeah it did," he agreed. "I'm glad you came back."

When the mousse was gone, they lingered over coffee.

"I have an early job tomorrow," Anna said, lifting her empty mug to her lips the third time.

They were quiet on the walk to her apartment while she thought about him talking to her dad. She'd convinced herself he'd given up on March fourth—hadn't she made clear over and over she couldn't possibly marry him? But here it was again, like the third resurrection of Frankenstein's monster—would it never die? At her door, she tensed. Her pulse was speeding but she didn't want him to stay.

"If you wouldn't mind a kiss," he said, "I'll be going."

Her shoulders slacked. "You left your hat."

He laughed. "If I'd run out naked I wouldn't have noticed."

He stayed in the stairwell. Handing over his fedora, she put her arms around him, offering not a fast little *get-out-of-here* peck nor the flame of *come in*; just a friendly kiss. He stepped back, pressed his hat down onto his hair, and headed home.

chapter 24

Facts and Figures

WHEN FRANK BRUBAKER got to the Rose and Crown at 4:30, the only people in the pub were a waitress doing setup and Anna's young man, sitting at a table with a clear view of the door. With an exchange of nods, he took the chair facing Walt, and the waitress came over. Frank had never sampled English or Irish beer, but he'd heard of Watneys so he ordered one.

Walt asked for a black and tan.

They sat back. Years of dealing with students in trouble had taught him the value of patience. Once he'd got their minds going with a "Tell me what happened," he'd wait them out, and pretty soon the whole story would roll off their tongues.

Neither he nor Walt said anything. Soon the waitress came back and set down cocktail napkins then, carefully, tall slope-sided glasses, as though her presentation was why they'd come. Walt's had light beer on the bottom, dark beer floating on it; Frank thought of salad dressing that had separated, and just for an instant wondered if the dark beer was oily. It couldn't be, but plainly they had different densities. His own beer was ruddy—he sipped. Not clean-tasting like Coors.

"Mr. Brubaker—"

"Please call me Frank." He didn't want Walt on the same footing as his students. Treating him like a teenager would be depressing, knowing his daughter was involved.

"Frank, I've asked Anna to marry me. I thought after my—experiences—with the law, I should spare you further surprises."

"Thank you." He'd figured when he got the phone call the other night it would be something like this. He appreciated Walt seeking him out, but he sure didn't want Anna to marry him. She was just going to get hurt—if she hadn't already. "As a father," he said heavily, "I have my duty. She's an adult so I can't stop her, but—" he went on to quiz him about the dog attack, that drug in his pocket.

Though Walt answered earnestly, Frank couldn't stop his sense of desolation—this fellow meant well but would she always be in his shadow? He and Carolyn had trusted her judgment when she went to London to stay with Cory, but instead of looking after her he'd exploited her. What kind of father would stand aside while that happened again? He said, "You're older, more experienced, and she's still an innocent—I've met more worldly fourteen-year-olds. Marriage should be between equals to last."

"We are," Walt said. "My heart and hers are a match."

Whatever that meant. It seemed to Frank they just had a strong sexual attraction that Walt was mistaking for something more enduring. Attraction was necessary, of course—otherwise who would make it past the first dozen disagreements?—but it was one factor of many. And he wasn't seeing those others that kept a marriage going: financial compatibility, accord about child-rearing, similar life goals and attitudes, some balance of experience. Partners facing the world together, supporting each other, each knowing enough to contribute to decisions. Anna seemed so *young.* He took refuge in rote questions. "What are your prospects, Walt?"

"Well, I can't teach around here—"

"You don't think the school system would give you a fair shake?"

"Even if they hired me, if you were a parent of a junior high school girl, would you feel comfortable having me as her teacher? It's not the facts that stick in people's minds, it's their first impression—a man slips a woman a drug, then rapes her. Parents wouldn't stand for that, and I can't really blame 'em."

"You gave up awfully easily."

"I altered course. When I was a teenager I did some sailing on the Chesapeake Bay. You can't sail into the wind, you have to tack, zigzagging across it."

Frank hated sports metaphors—people of limited imagination compared football to war, marketing, religion. To him it was a sign of flabby thinking. He avoided Walt's reference, saying instead, "I know an excellent career counselor." He fished through his wallet. "I should have her card here." Pulling one out, he handed it to Walt.

ABERNATHY COUNSELING
DIANE ABERNATHY—CAREER AND EMPLOYMENT SERVICES

"Tell her I referred you, that you're to get the student rate."

"Thanks very much—I'll call her." Walt put the card in his pocket.

Either the young man was trying to flatter him, or he'd run out of ideas of his own. *Or maybe*, Frank told himself, *I'm being cynical. Maybe he really is ready for a career, and wants some guidance.* "What's your background, Walt?"

"My dad's in real estate in Maryland. My mom's a book-keeper—she went back to work when my younger brother finished high school."

"And he's—" raising his eyebrows.

"Grant's into punk music—has a mohawk and raggedy clothes. He freelances music reviews and articles, which means he's usually broke. He's in Baltimore, and if there weren't ten people splitting rent, he'd probably be living in a refrigerator carton."

"No more aimless than Harold I suppose," Frank said, shaking his head. "Someday Walt, you may have children of your own, and when you do, I hope your luck's better than ours."

"How do you mean? Harold's a good person—very protective of Anna. And your older son's successful, and Anna—" he smiled at Frank. "Anna's my love."

The comment about Harold caught Frank flat footed—why was he running down his own son? Harold was only twenty-five. What did it matter if he drifted from job to job? He was self-supporting, and apparently looked after his sister, which Frank hadn't known. By defending him, Walt showed a sense of honor or respect—although clearly that old-fashioned morality didn't extend to chaste relations with Anna. "Are you—ahem—using birth control?"

"Absolutely—she should decide freely, not because she's pregnant."

"You realize that girl changes her mind continually."

Walt smiled wryly. "Yes sir, I know that."

"And you want her anyway. God help you."

"I think it does."

"'It'?"

"To me, God's not male or female—it's beyond human limitations."

Kids hardly seemed to think about God. "But you believe in a higher power?"

"Oh yes I do."

"So where was God when you were in jail?"

"Setting me up with time to read *Anna Karenina*. It's a long book."

Frank laughed. "I see why she likes you—you're pretty funny, young man."

"Thank you."

"When she was younger, something would start her laughing," he remembered with a smile, "and she'd keep it up so long she'd fold up against a wall." His cheer dropped away. "When she came home from London, I wondered how long it would be before she'd laugh again." He gave Walt an appraising look. Perhaps he'd underestimated their attraction. A shared sense of humor sustained plenty of marriages. "It's good to see her happy."

"I'm glad if I've helped her."

They drank in silence. This beer was going to leave quite an aftertaste—trying it once was all right, but he'd stick to Coors.

"Should I talk to Carolyn too?" Walt asked.

"She'll get all worked up—wait till Anna decides." He considered. "I hope you gave her a deadline."

"March fourth."

"That's pretty soon—why didn't you wait to talk to me?"

"I thought I should clear the air, so we wouldn't show up with rings on our fingers when the last you heard of me was that circus after Christmas."

"Circus is right," Frank growled. "Anna insisted I watch the interview with that detective, then I saw another one a few days later where he really stuck out his neck for you—he said incarcerating you was a mistake and he regretted the trouble it caused you. Apparently he didn't know about the narcotics squad's search warrants."

"I missed that second interview—that's when we were in California."

Frank sat back. "Every day I hear 'That isn't mine, I don't know where it came from, I just found it'—when Anna told me that, I felt terribly disappointed—in you, and in her for believing you." He gave Walt a sharp look. "Next time throw it away."

"Right," with a twist of a grin.

Frank drained his glass, then pulled out his wallet.

"No no, I'll pay," Walt said. "I asked you to meet me."

Frank put a dollar on the table, looked at it a moment, then put another on top of it, and extended his hand. "Good luck."

Walt stood to shake hands. "Thank you sir. Sure her mom won't be mad if we show up hitched?"

"If you tell her you're engaged, she'll plan your wedding." Carolyn wouldn't get another chance for a big to-do. They'd done almost nothing for Roger's wedding—hosted the rehearsal dinner and showed up in the right clothes, at the arranged place and time—then that marriage lasted only three years. And Harold didn't even have a girlfriend. But for a daughter? He didn't begrudge what it would cost to provide Anna with a send-off that would make her happy, but all that fuss—months on end—the prospect exhausted him. Besides, Anna preferred looking grungy. At Carolyn's insistence she'd worn a skirt to her high school graduation, but changed into jeans for the family party afterwards. He couldn't imagine her in a satin dress and veil. Weddings were a big deal: mother and daughter would fight endlessly about what was appropriate. "You don't want that."

"Don't I?" They were both grinning now.

"Trust me."

● ● ●

WALT MADE AN APPOINTMENT with Diane Abernathy, who asked him to bring his résumé. Writing out everyplace he'd worked longer than a month, he produced quite a list. Had he really done all that? Eleven months at his Santa Cruz projectionist gig was looking like a steady job. He wrote up a clean copy, then borrowed Barbara's typewriter. That ran three pages so he did another, condensing the period between Santa Cruz and his return to Boulder into a Miscellaneous Work paragraph. As references, he listed the Atheneum manager even though he'd fired him, Tom who'd trained him as a projectionist, and the bus lot supervisor.

Before the appointment he shaved, then tamed his hair as well as he could—as it got longer it kept fighting its way out of restraints—maybe by late summer he could band it into a ponytail… Dressed in a light blue oxford shirt, black suit, and burgundy tie, he checked out his reflection in Barbara's long mirror. The jacket fit his shoulders but his pants were loose. He gathered a couple of excess inches from the waist, shifting it to the back then snugging his belt. Overall he thought he looked like someone to take seriously.

Abernathy Counseling occupied a square room that would've seemed larger if it weren't so full—shelves filled both side walls, stuffed with directories, books, and binders in five or six colors. Her chair was near a window flanked by filing cabinets, the big desk in front of it heaped with papers and two ashtrays. The glass was hazed and the air bluish, reeking of cigarette smoke—his clean suit was going to stink. Diane Abernathy was a stout woman with a gray pageboy haircut, piercing blue eyes, and a cigarette she switched to her other hand to greet him. Her grip was damp and firm.

"Sit down," she rasped, and he took the upright chair facing her desk. She moved a sandbag ashtray close and tapped ash into it. "Frank Brubaker said he was sending you over. How do you know him?"

"I—uh—know his daughter."

She smiled. "How is Anna? I never see her anymore."

"She's doing OK—she's in the cleaning business—upholstery and windows."

"I could use that," she chuckled—a wheezing sound. "The building service cleaned this window six weeks ago, but you'd never know it. Smoking's a foul habit, young man, don't ever let anybody tell you different. But if I quit now it'd kill me."

"I've never smoked, myself," he said.

She pulled a pad close. "So what are your thoughts about a career?"

"I've never held what you'd call a real job, but it feels like time to start. I brought my résumé—a couple versions actually." He handed those across. She leafed through, nodding, then settled with the single page in her hand.

"You've done quite a bit—do you like fixing things?"

"Don't know that I *liked* it so much—that was just work I could pick up on the fly. I didn't stay anyplace very long, the last couple years."

"So you saw a lot. What were other people doing you thought you might enjoy—or you'd absolutely hate? Might as well cover both sides."

"I guess desk jobs always seemed awful to me—being trapped indoors, pushing papers, answering the phone. That has no appeal."

"Well, not if you put it in those terms," she laughed—another wheeze. "Maybe that's how you'd describe my job, but I don't think of it that way. Want to work by yourself, or with a group? With your hands? Your brain? Help me out here, Walter."

"Outside—I'd like to be a park ranger, something like that."

She half closed one eye and looked at him hard through the other. "You know, rangers spend a lot of time telling people what they can't do, and pumping out latrines—sort of a combination policeman and sanitation worker."

His face pinched.

"I've counseled plenty of young people who consider that their dream job, but I've also advised park rangers who are sick of the difference between what they expected and what the job actually turned out to be—they just want life in the woods with a paycheck." She took another deep drag on her cigarette and let the smoke out slowly.

"Why don't you fill out some personality tests I have here? Then we'll see what the books say." Seeing the disgust he tried to hide, she smiled. "It's a place to start, Walter. It's possible you've had no exposure to the type of work that would suit you best—we're here to explore." She rummaged on the shelf to her left, pulled out a thick green binder and opening the rings, handed him four sheets. "Got a pen?"

"Yes, thanks."

She offered a clipboard and he worked his way through the questions. Was he analytic or intuitive? Depended on the situation—but he was supposed to choose one. Though he felt his work energy and interests weren't being addressed by these forms, he pressed on, setting the first completed sheet on the desk; she picked it up while he continued. On graph paper she drew X and Y axes and made dots in one quadrant then another, adding from each page he finished. He didn't have to wait long till she'd marked the last dots and laid her chart down in front of him.

"This area is 'people,' this one's 'manual work,' this is 'technical,' this is 'personality.'"

"What's that tell you?"

"Well, you've done mechanical work, and don't seem to mind. You might enjoy a building trade, or specialized maintenance—at a factory or power plant, for example. You enjoy people, that's good. What about management—directing a crew?"

"I like working with people who can see what needs to be done, and do it—I'm not comfortable bossing people around."

"You might do well as an inspector—health department, construction." She tapped another area on her sheet, dropping ash which she lifted the paper to slide off. "You have a college degree—ever consider grad school?"

"No." Again he recalled Laura surprising him with her acceptance to Berkeley—maybe that whole Karmafornia disaster really was for the best—couldn't imagine being happy with her now.

"Your BA's in geography," she continued. "What appealed to you about that?"

"It's the whole picture—climate and terrain shape culture. I don't think history, agriculture, language, art, even invention make any sense otherwise. I like seeing how things relate and influence each other."

"Well, that's in essence what a good manager does—coordinates the efforts of people with specific skills to produce something none could make alone."

"But he tells 'em what to do, right?"

"I think if you saw your efforts as collaborative not a hierarchy, you'd be happy managing. How about working under deadlines—if they don't have it by such-and-so date it's worthless?"

"I've done delivery."

"We're aiming higher," she said, putting out another cigarette. She'd finished three, and he'd only been here half an hour. He made a quick calculation—six cigarettes an hour times twelve hours a day she might smoke—more than seventy? Three and half packs a day? The thought made him gag.

"Mr. Sanders?"

"I was just figuring out how much you smoke, and hoping I was wrong."

"Three packs a day, mostly here—it helps me think." She nudged the ashtray. "Anyway, where were we? Deadlines, time pressure. You know, urgent repairs—like power and phone linemen—or news services. Or sales."

"Not sales—my dad would love to have me at his realty. I couldn't stand that."

Her lighter flared, the tip of yet another cigarette crackled as she took a drag. "Let's look at specialized labor—carpentry? You'd never be out of work. And along the way you might learn enough to become a contractor—Roger Brubaker's done very well."

"What he builds has no appeal for me."

"Contracting's a huge field. What about the high end: custom homes, or historic properties? Not just anyone can do preservation—you have to be smart enough to navigate the red tape—I'm sure you'd have no problem. You might see if there's a local builder looking for help, and take it from there."

"Anna knows a few, from doing construction cleanup."

"There, you see?" She leaned forward, her tone confidential. "I won't charge you anything if I can point you a direction without making all those phone calls myself. You're sharp—you can do it. You just have to figure out which doors to knock on."

"You make it sound simple."

"Honey, if you'd seen some of the cases I get—last month I set up a woman with a job that had been listed for days in the classifieds—all she had to do was read the paper. I charged her a finder's fee. After people like that, you're a piece of cake."

"Thanks."

"If you look around you could probably find someone who needs an assistant. Won't make much money at first but it could grow into a career—learn on the job and move up…"

"I'll see what I can find." He stood extending his hand; she rose to take it. "Thank you, Ms. Abernathy."

"Nice to meet you Walter, and good luck," and as he stepped out of her office, she added, "You know, with that smile you could sell anything."

chapter 25

A Liberating No

WALT CALLED ANNA. "Drawing class starts a week from Wednesday—sign up yet?"

"No, but I have the registration form."

"Are you free Thursday night? We could see a movie, or just have coffee."

"Oh—Thursday!" she yelped—must've just noticed that was March fourth. "Walt, I'm going to disappoint you."

"It's OK. You've told me no so many times, I'm used to it by now." He thought about YES—had he played his best card, and now had nothing left?

"We can go out," she said in a tight voice. "No movie—a beer or something."

Barbara, who'd come in halfway through his phone call, stood by the fridge as he hung up. He picked up a potato that had been on the table several days, and seeing a nose in it, began to sculpt with the peeler.

She slid into a chair opposite, observing, "That girl's putting you through the wringer. Sure that's a good idea?"

"She's not an idea, she's a person." He glanced at her, then back to what he was doing.

"Walt, she's afraid of you. That can't ever work."

He dug diverging channels to define the nose. "I've backed off. Haven't stayed over since Valentine's Day, haven't pressured her at all," cleaning out and enlarging an indentation for one eye, then carving its mate.

"Interest is pressure. You asked her to marry you, didn't you?"

Was this everybody's business? "Yes I did."

"And she's stringing you along."

"I gave her till Thursday," shaving around the eye-pits to smooth them.

"Ah." She nodded, then frowned. "What good's that? Won't she just change her mind again?"

Barbara was really cued to his frustration—he felt the knot in his belly tighten. "Probably." He clenched his jaw and dug hard, and the tool glanced off the potato into his hand. If this was a knife he'd be a bloody mess, but the peeler only cut a flap of skin between two fingers.

"Anybody who has you this wound up isn't good for you—know that?"

"She *is* good for me, Barbara—I seem to be a threat though," turning the potato to attempt an ear. "She's not used to getting what she wants—I've kind of blown that apart." The earlobe was huge compared with the rest of the ear, which was too big for the head.

"Well if you have, good for you."

"Yeah. I don't feel like I've done anything wrong," shaving off the outer rim to recover proportion. "I talked to her dad."

"What's he think?"

Peeler on the table and potato in hand facing him, he marked with his thumbnail where the other ear should be, then picked up the peeler again. "He said God help me."

"That's too bad."

"Not what I was hoping to hear, but at least he listened. The narc business and bad press have him spooked."

"Where his daughter's concerned? Sure."

"I was gonna leave on New Year's and come back this week," trimming around the ear, checking to keep things as symmetrical as he could. "She convinced me that was cowardly."

"Was it?"

"Yeah. If there's gonna be a shit storm, I'd rather be someplace else."

"And that's cowardly?"

"It's not like the storm would go away just because I did. You and Stu and Romo would still be in the middle of it, and Anna too, once she was associated with me. It was just a reflex—I left a lot of places the last couple years." He used one edge of the peeler tip to outline the gentle arc of an upper lip, then moved to the lower.

"I don't want to push her," he continued. "But I keep disturbing her equilibrium," carving the face down so the lips stood out.

"What kind of 'equilibrium' is that? Look Walt, it's pretty clear. Either she doesn't mind being bounced around, or you should get out of her life."

"I know." He pinched his lips together as he shaved jaw line and chin—then he stopped, unable to see through the tears.

• • •

BARBARA COULDN'T STAND MANIPULATION —and Anna wasn't even aware of how her vacillations were twisting Walt. This drama had gone on long enough. Raking her chair back in a fury, she banged her way out, starting Plug and slamming it into gear, churning tires on the gravel. Arriving at Anna's, she slapped the door with her keys.

Anna opened, startled. "Barbara?"

"Get your coat," she ordered. "Put on your boots."

"What—where—"

"Hurry up," she snapped. Anna was taking too long fooling with her socks. "Oh for crying out loud, just *move*." The girl jumped as if she'd been goosed.

Herding her out to the car, Barbara drove tight-lipped. Anna concentrated on tying her boot laces. At home Barbara parked, snatched the keys from the ignition, and stormed around to the passenger side, flinging open the door and seizing Anna by the wrist, then propelling her toward the house.

"You cannot treat people like that," Barbara spat. "Just because he won't tell you how much he's hurting does *not* let you off the hook."

Opening the kitchen door she stepped behind Anna, gripped her shoulders, and marched her to the table. Walt sat on the far side, head down.

"Now be decent," Barbara scolded, and stepped aside, eyes ablaze.

• • •

ANNA, CONFUSED TO SUDDENLY be here, looked at Walt, then the thing by his hand—what? She picked it up—gray, damp: a head?

"Walt?"

He looked up at her—tears streaked his face.

"Oh no," her heart sinking. She'd made this joyous man so miserable—this was all wrong. She fumbled into the chair opposite and faced him, her chin on the tabletop. "Walt, I told you before. I can't marry you—that could never work."

"Is that—" He stopped to clear his throat. "Do you mean that?"

"Yes."

"A thousand noes didn't add up to YES?"

"They became a bigger NO. I—" she gulped. "You said not to apologize."

"That's right. Because you mean it."

"I mean it." She felt so much lighter saying it, getting it over with.

He smiled. "Thank you."

"Huh?"

"For being sure."

With the burden of decision lifted away, she thought she'd float. He stepped around the table, meeting her rising from her chair, and they fell into a long embrace, laughing with relief.

Barbara, her rage neutralized, declared, "I give up," and left the room.

At last Walt released Anna.

"What're you making?" she asked, nodding at his carving.

"I was just goofing around."

"How come you're so playful?"

"It's more fun than being work-ful, I guess. Speaking of which, Diane Abernathy says hello."

"Did you gossip about me?"

"Never figured out how she knows you."

"Paul and Diane Abernathy are old friends of my parents."

"Has she always smoked like that?"

"Yeah. Horrible isn't it?"

"My poor suit's exiled to the fence to air out."

"So what did she suggest?"

"She gave me a couple ideas—said I just need to get started, that it'll all flow. And since that's how my life works anyway, I believe her."

chapter 26

Punk Invasion

THREE A.M. POUNDING on the front door scared the hell out of them. Romo was dialing Lloyd's number when Walt recognized Grant and yanked him inside.

"It's just my brother," Walt told his housemate. "It's OK."

Phone in hand, Romo blinked a moment, then hung up and went back to bed.

Walt turned to the skinny young guy who stood breathless in the front hall. "You're flying high, bud."

"Hey what a great trip!" Grant exclaimed. "We drove a hundred across eastern Colorado—man, we were streakin'! In the dark!"

"Cool down, Grant—know what time it is?"

"Ah who cares—we're here."

"'We'? Somebody else outside?"

"Nah they dropped me—they got another place to crash. But we're gettin' together to catch some shows before we go back."

"Look, I have work in the—"

"A'right, a'right. Got any beer?"

"This way." Walt steered his brother into the kitchen. Handing over a bottle, he realized this was the moment Grant was likeliest to talk, so he popped another, shut the door to the rest of the house, and they sat at the table. Walt squinted at the brightness, shivering—five minutes ago he'd been asleep. "What's new, young-un?"

Grant, four-inch mohawk falling over sideways, peeled off his hoodie to reveal a snug black t-shirt with Sex Pistols printed across his chest. "The music scene's great—I got to interview Patti Smith. The papers I write for all picked it up, and I sent it to *Rolling Stone* just to see."

"Good luck with that," taking a sip, then grimacing—beer and rude awakening didn't mix. "How's your love life?"

"Huh?" As though Walt had asked if he was going to church regularly.

"You know, matters of the heart."

"Oh, um, um..." Grant trailed off, looking perplexed, unhappy. "Somebody put you up to this?"

"No, just nosy. That's a risk you take, knocking people out of bed."

"It's not that late—"

"Grant, narcs have searched this house twice since Thanksgiving—pounding on the door in the middle of the night's not cool."

"Oh shit, you been busted?"

"No. We're completely clean." Then raising his voice, making eyes at Grant, hoping he understood, "AND OF COURSE I KNOW YOU ARE," nodding intently.

"Um, sure," Grant agreed, laughing uncertainly.

Walt gestured with his eyes at the ceiling, at the speakers. Grant continued to look blank, so he scribbled a note: *We think this house is bugged.*

"Wow, so they're really after ya—"

"Not lately. We'd like to keep it that way. But I asked about your love—"

"Oh yeah: Silla was screwing some other guy and we had a big fight."

"Sorry to hear—"

"Last week I came home and they were in my bed. I mean, what was wrong with *his* bed? I told him to leave her alone, she said they weren't done yet. Can you believe that? Who cares about me? They were too busy to stop!" waving his bottle, splashing beer.

"That's bad."

"I'm gonna kill her." He snatched the towel off the fridge to mop his hand.

"Don't even say that, Grant. That's useless. Start over someplace else."

"But that house is where I'm set up—if *Rolling Stone* calls and I'm not there, nobody's gonna tell 'em where I am. I'm screwed."

"Well, it's good you came out here."

"I had to—I was goin' nuts lookin' at her—she'd be pawing him in front of me—thought it was funny."

"You should find someone more mature."

"Like Laura huh? I'd go for her."

"Your tact matches your haircut. You know what happened."

"Yeah, but she was hot."

"Maybe that's your problem: if you follow your dick around—"

"Silla and John just piss me off. Piss. Me. Off."

"If a woman can't be honest with you," Walt said, "Get out."

"Whaddya—"

"There's other ways to break up—if she stopped liking you, wouldn't you rather have her say something?"

"No. I still—"

"Go dig your grave then."

"No, she was really—I mean, before she—"

"And now it's over."

Grant deflated. "Yeah. Shit. Wha'd you do?"

"Spent two years on the road trying to clear my head."

"That work?"

"Part of the cure—more's happened here. But it was good to rely on myself: hustle up work, pick up the signals—when it's cool to stay, when it's time to go. Stuff nobody'll teach you, that you can't get through life without."

Grant swigged his beer. "I should start a band, or be a roadie. I'd love to work for Dead Kennedys, but they don't know me."

"Show 'em the Patti Smith article—everybody needs a publicist."

"I know their label—Alternative Tentacles—they put out their own records so they don't get censored."

"I'm gonna supervise you writing 'em a letter, and watch you mail it. Tell 'em to contact you here—I'm not going anywhere."

"Mmm," Grant mused. "You know, I heard Jello Biafra's from Boulder."

"So they'll notice the address. It's not like writing to Mick Jagger—they probably love to get mail."

"So, you said you work—when you around?"

"I'm training with a carpenter—just started last month. He took me on because I learned a lot being a handyman—he gives me a list and I can do most of it without bugging him."

"How much you get paid?"

"Minimum wage."

"That stinks."

"Education usually costs something," Walt shrugged. "Eventually I'll sign on for apprenticeship, and years down the line come out a journeyman carpenter, join the union, and get paid scale anyplace. And build my own house."

"Cool. That's worth doing."

"I think so."

"Mom was hoping—" Grant stopped.

"Hoping?"

"You'll come out sometime. She's worried."

"You can report back: tell her I cleaned up. That should make her happy."

"Yeah you did—what gives with that?"

"I met a woman and wanted to show her who I am."

"So you had to shave?"

"And paint my car. She just saw a bunch of hair and a lifestyle."

"Did shaving work?"

"It changed things—not the way I wanted, but it was still the right thing to do." Walt looked at him. "Ever been in jail?"

"Oh yeah, we been in the tank a few times. The guy'd go through his book like a preacher, pickin' which verse to throw at us. Vagrancy, indecent exposure. Public nuisance was their favorite—we fit their definition just by *existing*." They both laughed. "I think they hoped the drunks would beat us up, but they were cool."

Walt pushed his nearly full beer toward Grant—his brain was shutting down. "Got a sleeping bag or something?"

"Yeah, my pack's on the porch."

"Bedtime."

"Oh man, I don't know—I'm pretty wired."

"I'll put it another way—*I'm* going back to sleep. I'll show you which room you can use—we're short a housemate at the moment."

"Oh hey, if I decide to stay—"

"Talk to Romo—it's ninety a month plus utilities. Only a few rules, but they're firm."

"Float me a month?"

Walt sighed. "How much do you have?"

"Twenty-three—no, twenty-one dollars."

"Romo's not into charity, and I told you what I make. Dad might advance you a couple hundred to get set up—if he thought you were doing something worthwhile."

Grant shook his head. "He always says the same thing—'get rid of that mess on your head and get a job, then we can talk.' Could I stay rent-free if I sleep on your floor?"

"My room's small."

"I have hardly any stuff."

"Don't ask me to figure it out now—my brain's asleep and my body's about to go back and join it. Get your pack." They came down the hall quietly—not that Grant could be very quiet in combat boots—to the front door. The bell cord snagged on a safety pin in his jeans, jingling while he freed himself. They went upstairs, Grant looking around, assessing whether Walt's room really was too small for both of them.

"What time you get home?" he asked.

"Tomorrow's my drawing class—five thirty, six."

"Well, when I crash I'll be out awhile—haven't slept since Baltimore."

"When was that?"

"Sunday when we got up."

"We'll talk later. Good to see you buddy—keep the noise down."

"Yeah yeah."

Walt gave him a hug, then after Grant had awkwardly hugged him back, aimed him across the landing to Lucy's old room—he was wound up to keep chattering.

• • •

LUNA MET HER CLASS at the library and they fanned out along both sides of the creek, choosing their subjects. Besides Walt and Anna, she had two other students—a soft-faced Mexican kid probably in high school, who showed them some of his cartoons, and a thirtyish woman, the type who came to Boulder to tune her aura and pick up a man with money. She was tanned and toned in an exercise-class way, with tight-fitting clothes and big dangly earrings forever catching in her blonde-streaked hair. She chewed gum ferociously and broke pencil points with entertaining regularity, impaling every line to her pad.

Color gave Walt a toehold in his effort to translate what he saw onto a piece of paper, and Luna showed him how to layer to get intermediate shades. He still had to sketch, but adding color brought the sprig of forsythia and tuft of grass to life.

"When you're working on something close, it's important to sit still," she cautioned. "Moving your head even a few inches will change your perspective." She tapped his paper with her eraser pencil. "Why's this line here? I don't see it. Take it out." So he erased, then watched as she stood behind Anna, observing then giving advice. Anna drew better than he did, but when Luna moved on to Ramon, she was erasing too. He grinned and went back to his bright flowers.

Anna came over at the end of class, as he was gathering his materials. His pencil carton was falling apart—time to duct tape it. For now he wrapped it in his bandana.

"Wish I could draw your hair," she said, squatting while he zipped his pack.

"I'll sit for you—give it a try."

"Grandpa Francis gave me a couple lawn chairs and now it's nice enough to sit out in my backyard."

"We have another hour-plus of daylight—let's go." He stood, noticing a shadow in her eyes. Was his friendliness eroding the fragile neutrality of being fellow students? He let the motion of walking relax them before venturing conversation. "My brother showed up like the narc squad at three this morning—probably sleep till tomorrow."

"Older? Younger?"

"Turned twenty-three last month, but when he's forty, he'll probably still act fifteen. He's dedicated to being irresponsible."

"Like you?" she teased.

"I have a work ethic—he's short in that department."

"So you're not driving a bus anymore? What are you doing?"

"I'm the grunt for a solo builder—it's going pretty well. Low money, but I already knew that. More hours than I'm used to—that's the big change. He was talking about working some Saturdays too, but I don't want to turn into a drone."

"Doesn't he like time off?"

"Bill's pretty intense, not much social life—I think he'd work all the time. We've been making a laminate beam this week. It's massive, but it'll be incredibly strong, and beautiful too. Once the last layer's glued and pegged, I have to sand and polyurethane it. Quite a house—up Left Hand Canyon, with its back to a big slab of rock—great view, way up the hillside—grading that driveway must've been hairy. You'd like the place."

• • •

ALL THE TIME HE was talking animatedly, she was fading, as though he were addressing a picture of her in a room she'd vacated. The marriage issue might be resolved but nothing else was—if he ambushed her again like he had on Valentine's Day, she'd kiss him back just as hard.

In her backyard they dropped packs on the grass and sat in old metal armchairs thickened by a dozen layers of paint. Pad and pencils in hand, he aimed his gaze at a grapevine draped and twining on its support.

With his head tilted her direction, she could see multiple colors bleaching amid the dark of his hair, and applied her orange pencil then her yellow one, covering those with brown, trying to achieve gold. But drawing his hair was too much like feeling it between her fingers—

"Anna," his voice low, as though she were a frightened animal.

"Hm?" She fixed her eyes on her pad.

"We don't have to do this."

She tensed and darkened a line. "'This'?"

"Call me sometime."

She sat motionless as he packed up, waiting to look till she was sure he'd be out of sight. Then she pulled up her knees and wrapped forearms across her shins, perfectly wretched. Her brain had excellent reasons for chilling their affection—she was still nurturing that crystalline sensation she'd experienced at Joshua Tree. For now, she felt porous—it would be too easy to flow into Walt and lose herself—and he was too old for her, which was what Dad said when she told him she'd turned down Walt's offer—he couldn't hide his relief, maybe didn't think he had to. Dad must think she didn't love Walt, so now everything was cleared up: the pain like a scrape would heal, and she'd be fine. But when she told Walt no and they hugged, she was aware of his heat and longing, and wanted him as much as if she'd said yes. *Stupid girl,* she scolded herself: *He'll go back to Laura—she's worldly, like him.* Anna intended to blend quietly into the background of which she'd been such a comfortable part till he came along and jolted her into visibility. This ruckus in her heart and groin was misguided. She wasn't going to be Anna Karenina and let love swallow her life—she knew how that story turned out.

chapter 27
All Choked Up

GRANT FINALLY CAME to around noon Thursday, and found a note on top of his pack.

> *Grant—Working til 5:30 or 6—hang out. I'll fix dinner when I get home.*
>
> *Talk to Romo about renting if you're serious. Work on that letter!*
>
> *Walt*

So he was at loose ends for hours. He splashed his face, then wandered into the living room to check out their music. Mostly it was over-the-hill acts like the Grateful Dead and Bob Dylan, Joni Mitchell, Neil Young—but he found a Ramones album. The place was deserted so he cranked up the volume and turned on the kitchen speakers. Walt had left out a clipboard and paper; Grant opened the last beer and sat at the table to write.

A tapping on the door interrupted. He wasn't sure what to do, but a girl his age opened it and stepped in, looking at him as though he were the intruder.

"Anybody home?" she said.

Like he wasn't anybody. "Just me."

"Who are you?"

"Walt's brother Grant. You?"

"His friend Anna. He said you're here a few days."

"Well, I might stay, if I can hustle the money." He told her about his articles, his hopes for Dead Kennedys. "I'm writing 'em now, but it's a waste of time."

"Well, what's the worst that could happen? For them to say no?"

"I guess."

"What's the best?"

"If I could work with 'em."

"Doesn't sound like you have much to lose."

"Right." Somehow he'd got lost in shades of gray she couldn't see.

"So," she asked, "did you ever meet Walt's girlfriend Laura?"

Kind of an odd question. "Um yeah, we saw the DKs together in San Francisco. One of her housemates gave me my first punk haircut, in her kitchen in Berkeley the next morning."

"Was Walt there?"

"No, he stayed in Santa Cruz."

"Ever see them together?"

"Actually—that was weird—she was stayin' at his house, but right after we got there, she left. We'd been driving across the country, Walt was sailin', but as soon as he saw her his mood just crashed. He was in a funk till I left."

"She's beautiful, right?"

Grant squinted at Anna. "Why do you care? That's over."

"Maybe he just wishes it was." She perched on the edge of the table, rolling up her shirtsleeves. "How well do you know your brother?"

"Haven't seen him for a couple years. We argue a lot—he likes these rock'n'roll dinosaurs, and I'm into new wave. He's really gone straight—cut his hair, even said he painted his car. I haven't seen it since I got here. What's it look like now?"

"Just an ugly shade of brown."

"Brown? After all we did? You see it?"

"Yeah. I liked it. He said there was more—a buffalo on the trunk and dragons on the hood—those had faded."

"I painted the octopus scene—see that?"

"Yeah—it looked good."

"Brown," he repeated in disgust. "Why?"

She told him about Walt spending six days in jail, then Romo freaking out.

"Yeah, he said narcs have been here."

"And this house is probably bugged. Imagine you're on the radio."

Realization hit him. "Hey Anna, let's take a walk."

As they strolled, he said he had a few things on him. "I mean, it's practically nothing, but my stash might be enough to get 'em in trouble."

"Anything would. You can keep it at my house while you're around."

"You're not worried about getting busted?"

"It's Walt and Romo they're after—don't keep even a used pipe there."

"That's really creepy—like a police state or something." She steered toward her place, while he thought about narcs hounding Walt. "He didn't tell me." Weren't brothers supposed to help each other? Shouldn't he have known?

"They're positive the phone's tapped, there's probably bugs in the house—they assume they have no privacy."

"But if they know you're his girlfriend, they must be watching you too."

"Well, I'm not really..." She trailed off.

When she got uncomfortable, his conversation dried up. He wasn't used to talking to people outside the insular punk culture. At her apartment, he put his stash in a cottage cheese container in her freezer.

She gave him her phone number. "Call before you come by—I work odd hours."

"Hey thanks Anna."

"And talk to Walt. I can't be the friend he needs—maybe you can."

He left, realizing he should start checking out Boulder. At a convenience store, he made some copies of his article, found a Denver alternative weekly, then talked up the punk-looking guy at the counter who drew record store locations on a paper bag.

Grant got plenty of exercise, visiting those stores. The first one had a tiny new wave mag and a larger nightlife freebie—he started a collection. In the racks he found Patti Smith and Devo albums, but no DKs or Sex Pistols. The next place was better, and the guy working there knew some people. They talked awhile about the pitiful local scene, and Denver's which was better. Boulder was a clean-cut town like College Park, which Grant had been glad to leave. Students might not have money but their parents did. Baltimore was a real city: tough, blue-collar depressed, no middle-class family to lean on when things didn't work out. Maybe Denver was more like that.

He got home and Walt wasn't back, so he called the house where his buddies were staying. They'd gone to Denver for the evening. Without talking to him—what a pisser. If he'd crashed with them, he wouldn't be stuck here alone.

Walt got home at 6:15 saying he'd run a hand sander all day and thought his arms would drop off. Grant, reciting his record store trek, forgot to mention Anna.

"Has your diet improved at all?" Walt asked. "Want some rice stuff?"

"I'll eat anything—I don't care."

From the fridge Walt got half an onion, bell pepper, a handful of snow peas, and four spears of asparagus, and the pot of rice. While the vegetables were sautéing, he poked around in the fridge. "Coulda sworn I had one more beer."

"Oh sorry—I drank it. I'll get you a six-pack. Where's the liquor store?"

"A couple blocks away—I think they have Wisconsin beer on sale right now—it's cheap. If you hurry up you'll get back before this is ready."

Grant scrambled out, smacking himself for not realizing he'd swiped Walt's last beer. He must really want one after such a tough day. Liquor World was incredible—he'd never seen so much wine, booze, and beer in one place—the walk-in cooler was the size of most liquor stores. Customers were going right in there so he did too, looking at cases of longnecks stacked five high. He listened to a couple guys discussing the Huber—passable, they said.

Grant hoisted a case and carried it out to the register. The guy looked at his ID then charged him $10.99 plus tax.

"But it says $5.99—"

"Plus a bottle deposit—when you bring 'em back, you get your five bucks."

That was half his money, but Walt should pay him something. His arms were hurting by the time he plonked the case inside the kitchen door.

"What'd you get?" Walt asked, coming to look. "Oh, longnecks. That's cool. But I thought you didn't have much money."

"I don't," telling him about the deposit.

"Well," Walt shrugged, "it's cheap. Stick a few in the fridge and move the case to the corner." He served bowls and set them on the table.

After stowing half a dozen, Grant put out two to drink.

"Good choice," Walt said after his first swallow. "So did you complete your assignment?"

"You can read the draft of my letter."

"After dinner, if I don't fall asleep—what a day. Packed a big lunch but about three I completely ran out of gas. Guess I need more snacks. I didn't leave till quarter to six, but Bill was pissed—he wanted the first coat on the beam so it could dry overnight."

"Sounds like a ballbuster."

"Kind of—he's testing me. I see why he usually works alone."

"Anna came by."

Walt kind of gasped, Grant looking up saw his eyes bug out, one hand slapping at his chest then gesturing to his throat. Moving behind his brother, Grant put his hands together into a fist just beneath Walt's breastbone, pulling up and toward him sharply—about the only thing he remembered from school was Mr. Maggio in eighth grade PE making them all learn First Aid and CPR—and hey, it *was* useful. While Walt hunched over the table panting, Grant's chest expanded. Pride was at odds with everything in his lifestyle but it did feel good to know how to save someone from choking.

"Thanks," Walt wheezed.

"Y'all right man?'

He nodded.

Grant sat again. "What happened?"

"You said—" Walt rasped.

"Anna came by—she asked about Laura."

Walt rubbed his throat gently. "That figures."

"Hey man, what is it with you and women? You were like this with Laura too."

"Like what?"

"All depressed. She asked how you and Laura were together, I told her as soon as you saw her you crashed. Don't you remember?"

Walt explained about Laura being in prison. "She's got a parole hearing next month, and this other guy said all she thinks about is me."

"Maybe she just wants to apologize."

"If you aim at somebody and shoot him, does an apology mean anything?"

Grant didn't get it. "Why's Anna care?"

"She's insecure—she thinks because Laura's beautiful I'll go back to her."

"I would—I'd love to see her."

"If you stick around, you're welcome to—I'm told she'll be out of the slammer May first. You and Anna and Tom and Eddie can all party with her—just leave me out of it."

They finished dinner and cleared up.

"So, wanna go find some music?" Grant suggested.

"I'm taking a hot bath. My arms and shoulders are gonna kill me tomorrow. But ask Romo—maybe he'll go out."

The clubs had cover charges plus a one-drink minimum—had to come up with some bucks. Romo and Stu finally settled on a band to hear so Grant tapped on the bathroom door; after a pause, Walt invited him in. He was lying in the tub with a washcloth covering his privates. Grant leaned against the wall noticing the patch of hair on his brother's chest—had just a few sprouts himself. Walt was lean but compared to him, solid.

"I'll pay you back soon's I sell my article."

"I'll reimburse you for the bottle deposit and half the beer," Walt decided.

"Ten?"

"I sweat three hours to clear ten bucks—why should I give it to you?"

"No no, I'll pay you back—don't be such a hard-ass."

"Do you owe everybody?"

"No," Grant said indignantly, but as he made a mental tally, realized that actually, he did. "Shit. I guess."

"So why should I bankroll you?"

"Because I'm your brother and I came all the way out here. I didn't have to visit you, and listen to you moan about your girlfriends. Gimme a break."

"You know, when I'm tired I feel myself turning into Dad. It's scary."

"And it stinks."

"Take my money and get outta here."

"Where's your wallet?"

"On my dresser. If you take more than ten I'll pound you."

"You couldn't pound a banana," Grant laughed, exiting the bathroom. Liberating the twenty, he left with Romo and Stu.

● ● ●

AFTER HIS HOT BATH, Walt pulled on his jeans but left his shirt off so he could apply Tiger Balm. The whole zone between his shoulder blades, up to his skull and down to the base of his rib cage was so tight it felt taped together. Unable to reach the middle of his back where the knots started, he was relieved to hear the kitchen door bang—Barbara had come home.

"Save me," he moaned, coming into the living room extending the pungent little jar. "Can you smear this on my back please please?"

"Well, if you put it like that…"

He flattened his chest to the wall while her fingers worked in the ointment. "Ever walk on anybody?" he asked.

She laughed. "You expect me to admit that?"

"Walk on my back—I'd pay you if Grant didn't already rob me." He knew without even looking that his brother had scorned the five and singles, going for that fat twenty.

"Get a towel," she said.

He lay face down on it, she kicked off her flip-flops and carefully stepped up. He smiled as she trod her way alongside his spine, compressing him between her focused weight and the hardwood floor—of course a California girl would know how to do this.

"Arms?" he managed to say.

She stepped off his back and put one foot over his tricep, toes up by his shoulder, bearing down. As she did his other arm, he groaned, "Oh my god, and shoulders."

She laughed, and after she'd gone over everything he begged her to tread on and crush, she stepped off.

"I'm deeply in your debt, Barbara. Ask and receive."

"I'll remember that."

Rolling over, he pushed his shoulders against the floor, looking up at her. "How's it going with Lloyd?"

"Slowly. I like that. I've never been wooed before."

"One of these days he'll kiss you, and that'll be the end of wooing."

"No, we've kissed."

"And stopped there?"

"I didn't say that."

"It's none of my business lady," he said, climbing to his feet.

"Yes I know. I'll tell you when to butt out," her eyes sparkling.

He liked the way they could tease each other, intensity under their camaraderie. "Barbara, how can I miss California when you're around? It's here—it's you."

"And do you love California?" she lilted.

"Second only to my tragic sweetheart." He stretched, feeling tendons pop and sting in his upper back and shoulders.

As he headed upstairs, she called, "Sleep tight, Walt."

"Loose you mean. Thank you ma'am."

chapter 28

Constructive

WALT'S BOSS WENT easy on him the next day, giving him lightweight tasks then knocking off early. Sitting in a sunbeam on the porch they shared a cold six-pack, a bag of tortilla chips, and a jar of salsa. Bill pulled the band from his hair and shook it loose, dark and smooth. Though barely taller, he outweighed Walt by seventy-five pounds. His hands were coarse but strong, his face blunt-featured except a scar originating in his upper lip that ran ruler straight horizontally across his cheek, stopping an inch short of his ear.

Walt looked out across the canyon where above the cliffs a big bird was riding an updraft—might be a golden eagle—there were some around here. With April coming to an end, spring had crept in where the sun hit, the willows greening up, new grass pushing aside the dry yellow stalks of winter. Down on the flats between this house and Left Hand Creek, two magpies were out every day, making raucous calls which to Walt sounded like laughter—didn't hear them much after installing the last windows, and the roof going up would shut out this flawless sky. He chafed at having so little time to enjoy the view and fresh air. Usually he was so focused on what he was doing, picking up pointers and thinking about ways to simplify tasks, he really wasn't aware of his surroundings. This weekend they'd switch to daylight saving time—would Bill expect him to work that extra hour of afternoon light?

"Good goin' on that beam, Walt. I can put the other two coats on this weekend—Monday the crane's comin' and we raise the sucker."

"Anybody else helping?"

"Don't need 'em. I know the operator—he's good. It won't even wiggle."

"And you're sure he can get up this road?"

"Setup'll be tricky—have to jack up his back end to stabilize the rig."

"What happens if he drops it?" Walt had no idea how many tons that beam weighed, except it would crush whatever it landed on.

"He won't." Bill laughed, "I don't expect ya to stand under it." He popped another beer. "Surprised ya could run a sander this morning—busted yer butt yesterday."

"It's OK—I like seeing this place come together."

"Been eight weeks since ya started—ready for apprenticeship?"

"You're the expert—am I?"

"I think so. Reason I ask is, I'm workin' up prelims for the next job—a house up near Mt. Meeker. That'll take a week, and I'll need you stayin' here. The way my contracts read, the place is never vacant once there's a structure till I'm done."

"That why you're living on-site?"

"Yeah. And I don't mind—I kinda meld with it, listen to the wind go through at night, hear the animals come around. But for that week it'd be you. Up for that?"

"Will the phone be in?"

"I doubt it."

Walt thought about being here when Laura arrived—the whole show could go on without him. "Yeah, I think that's OK."

"Pretty soon I'll know the date—if you can do that, you'll really be on board."

Walt opened his second beer. It tasted so good, filtering over his exhaustion.

Bill handed him a joint. "Sinsemilla. Humboldt Heaven."

Walt held it under his nose a moment, savoring the fragrance before lighting it. They smoked half, then Walt tamped it out and offered it back.

Bill waved him off. "It's yours."

"I have no place to keep it," Walt said regretfully.

"Oh yeah, ya told me 'bout that. Why don't ya move?"

"We're sticking it out together for our lawsuit."

Bill brought over the boombox and flipped on FM radio. The signal came and went here, depending on the weather. Now it was clear, playing some Traffic.

"If I stayed up here a week," Walt said, "would it be OK to have a friend visit?"

"A girlfriend?"

"Well, maybe she'll call." In his mind he and Anna were still connected despite her withdrawal. Once Laura'd been and gone, she'd see the compass needle of his heart truing on her.

"Have a fight?"

"We don't fight, she just pulls back. What we've got's too good for her, so she keeps jumping out."

Bill laughed. His scar broke the symmetry of his face when he smiled and made him look fierce when he didn't: the kind of guy you'd instinctively leave alone in a bar.

"How'd you get that?" Walt asked, tracing his own cheek, "or should I ask?"

"It's OK. People stare and I can hear 'em thinkin' but they won't say anything." He swallowed some beer and gazed skyward. "Happened five years ago. I was workin' on a house up Sunshine Canyon, puttin' in windows. It was kinda windy so I really wanted to get 'em in—there was weather comin'. It was a big-ass window—y'know, the kind birds crash into—and I had two nails in the frame when the wind pushed it loose. My hammer came back and the claw end hit me in the face while I was hangin' onto the goddamn window with my other hand and both shoulders, tryin' to keep it from knockin' me down—if I fell with a piece of glass that size, I'd look a lot worse'n this. I dropped the hammer then I had 'a move back and kneel with it—thing musta weighed two fifty—and set it down without breakin' it. I tied a bandana around my face to catch the blood, and finished puttin' it in."

"You didn't have a helper?"

"Shoulda—a day laborer'd cost a lot less'n that window." Bill shook his head. "Helpers don't last—want to knock off when they're tired, not when the day's over."

"Like I did yesterday?"

"Well, if ya stayed to finish, what would that beam look like? Can't paint in the dark, or polyurethane either—miss spots, or it drips and runs. So you were right, even if I wasn't too happy."

"How long you been doing this?"

"My dad and I had it out when I was seventeen so I went to live with my uncle outside Nederland—place was fallin' down—an A-frame on cinder blocks. The windows cracked, the walls leaked around 'em—woulda made more sense to knock it down and start over but he was a patcher, so he put me to work patchin'. Got m' GED takin' night classes, rest of the time I was either helpin' him or hirin' myself out to hippies. Learned a lot, didn't matter if I messed up—they didn't know the difference, and on those shacks it didn't matter—I'd just keep workin', long's they could pay me. I had a waiting list." He laughed at the memory. "So your résumé looked good—ya made a living improvisin'. Learn fast that way, don't ya?'

"Enough to get by," Walt said. "I'd be tuning up somebody's car out in front of his house, and by the time I was done I'd have another job lined up. Then they'd find out I could fix the lawn mower, and I'd be in business. I'd stick around till somebody vibed me wrong or I got itchy feet, then I'd be on my way."

"Never parked anyplace?"

"Spent two winters in Chico, California, though I traveled the rest of the year—got close to going back on New Year's."

"But you're here."

"Yeah, I stuck it out this time—Anna convinced me."

"All they want is to get married," Bill said sourly.

"She turned me down, but she knows I'm hers anytime she calls."

"Hnh! When I wanna get laid, I ain't waitin' for no phone to ring."

"She's all I want."

"You can tell the difference? I'll stick mine anywhere when I'm on."

"Never tried love?"

Bill laughed a little too hard. "I got no use for that emotional BS."

"For me that's what makes sex worthwhile."

Housebound

STEFAN SCHEDULED A major floor job in early May—a strip, seal, and wax job in a bar, starting Saturday night at closing to give it maximum drying time. Anna was drafted to wet-vac and rinse while Stefan ran the buffer, with a helper doing edges and details. She got to Hole in the Wall just before two a.m., rested and ready; Stefan drove up in the floor van with a woman.

Anna introduced herself, taking the wet-vac out of the van.

"Call me Rye," the new helper said, lifting out the mop bucket and wringer and a heavy extension cord, her movements lithe and graceful. When they brought equipment indoors, Anna got a better look at her. Hair indifferently cut, but attractive because it framed such a sculpted face. She seemed planted in herself, not requiring anyone's approval. Superior. The kind of woman Anna admired from a safe distance.

"This is pretty hard work," she warned. Rye couldn't weigh more than one twenty.

"I'm strong," said the newcomer. "Don't worry about me." Not cold, not mean: hard, like Rye was a diamond and everyone around her chalk. As they assembled equipment in the back, the manager shooed out the last customers and locked up. In ten minutes, the bartender and waitresses were gone.

"I thought they were moving the tables and chairs," Anna said to Stefan. This furniture was heavy—tables with cast-iron bases, thick wood armchairs that weighed fifteen pounds apiece and didn't stack readily. Other than a small carpeted bandstand by the front wall, the whole place was the floor they'd be working on. Anna figured there were twenty-five tables and close to eighty chairs.

Stefan shrugged. "You saw everybody leave—you don't think he's moving tables, do you?" indicating the manager.

"No, but—"

"We'll do it."

He'd charge something, so he didn't mind, but Anna was glowering.

"Rye," Stefan said, "give her a hand—clear the whole floor."

"We can carry two tables at once, face to face," Rye said as Anna joined her. True to her word she was strong, and quick too—took only a couple minutes to set all the tables on the little patch of carpet.

"This ticks me off," Anna said.

"Put that energy to work," Rye scolded. "I got no use for whiners," moving fast, grabbing the top of a chair back in each hand and swinging them, following their forward arcs so they seemed to fly over, to fit in gaps between the table bases—how'd she do that? After watching her move another pair, Anna was inspired to try. Half flinging half carrying a chair, she was surprised at how little she felt its weight. The manager paused to watch them work. If the janitor had showed up when he was supposed to, he would have spent forty-five minutes at this, but by the time he'd figured the night's take and charted the work schedules for the coming week, they were done: ten minutes.

"Hey Stefan," he laughed, "are they for rent?"

Stefan grinned. "You can't afford 'em."

"It's all physics," Rye said, putting a five-gallon bucket under the spigot in the back hall mop closet, running hot water.

"That was fun," Anna said. "Half full's good. Now about a quart of stripper." Rye shut off the water and moved her bucket; Anna put the mop bucket under and turned the water back on. "Where'd you learn that?"

"Used to unload trucks—we'd have to sort stuff from one set of pallets to another. If you can get some swing into it, weight lifts itself. I could move a fifty-pound case as high as my head that way. Straight lifting woulda killed me."

"I had to learn some tricks so I could move ladders." Anna shut off the water and lifted the mop bucket out of the sink, splashing in acetic acid, setting in the wringer, and dousing the mop head.

"Ever use a buffer?" Rye asked.

"No."

"That's physics too. I'll show you, if you're interested."

"Stefan thought I could do floors—he said I have great waxing technique. But I think he's planning to run the buffer tonight."

"We shall see," Rye said. They left the buckets in the back hall while Rye dust mopped, swiveling the head to cover a wide swath quickly. Anna got the brush and dustpan—Rye was supposed to be the helper but she'd taken the lead. Stefan tossed down a rough pad, then filled the buffer tank with stripper solution, uncoiling the cord and going to plug it in. By the time he came back, Rye had attached the block, adjusted the arm to hip level, and started the machine, letting stripper pool onto the floor.

"Go ahead," he waved, leaning on the bar to watch. Anna plugged in the wet-vac and assembled the wand and hose while Rye worked her way to the back edge, the buffer kissing the baseboard. She moved smoothly, gliding in the liquid as the wax softened, graceful as a skater, the machine going wherever she sent it. Anna watched till a section was done then vacuumed, following that with the rinse mop.

"Anna," Stefan said, "put on some gloves and do the edges, and make sure you get the splatters off the baseboards." Rye was running the buffer as if she'd been doing it all her life, winning over Stefan completely—he loved competence. When they'd done about half the floor, Rye invited Anna to try the machine.

"Set the arm a little lower—I'm taller than you. Lock it in place." Anna moved the lever down to clamp the arm. "It spins clockwise. When you lift the handle it'll move to the right, lower it to go left. Just use a light touch. You should be able to control it with one finger and thumb." She demonstrated, pressing the flipper to the handle and moving the machine right then left, easing it forward then stepping back with it. She released the flipper, letting the handle rotate to Anna's hands. Anna gripped, it bucked, she let go—not the same machine Rye'd been using.

"It has a lot of torque—you can't overpower it. Go easy. Try again." This time Anna moved the handle gingerly, and it began to act the way it had for Rye. "Keep it centered on the pad if you don't want it slinging stripper around. Stop it a sec." Anna tilted it back on its wheels, pivoting to set it over the pad, then resumed buffing, Rye a step behind her encouraging.

"So where'd you learn this?" Anna ventured again when they paused to empty the wet-vac and refresh the mop bucket. "Were you in building services?"

"Something like that," her tone blunting further questions. Still, Anna would get to know her better—Stefan was sure to keep her on. Rye didn't mind trading off chores, scrubbing edges, but she was in charge and they both knew it.

Watching Anna mop down the sealer coat, Rye complimented her. "Very smooth. Didn't miss a spot anywhere."

"All right," Stefan said, "let's load everything except the mop and wax. Anna, you can finish and lock up. Here's the key—give it three coats."

"What about the tables and chairs?"

"They'll put 'em back tomorrow. I want the wax to set up as long as possible."

"What about me?" Rye asked.

"You're done for tonight. I'll give you a ride home."

"How'm I getting home?" Anna asked.

"Drop us at my car, then keep the van till tomorrow." Sending Rye out with the wet-vac, he turned to Anna. "She'll probably be our regular floor person—she seems to know a lot—but she just started—I can't leave her here by herself."

While she waxed, Anna wondered if Stefan was putting moves on Rye. She'd never seen him with any woman who wasn't gorgeous, and the way he'd watched her working wasn't just professional admiration. She dismissed the thought; he could hustle whomever he pleased.

• • •

SATURDAY WALT PACKED UP his sleeping bag, a box of food, two dozen cassettes, his drawing materials, and a couple books. This would be a solitary birthday—good for reflection. Felt like he was leaving as he drove out of town—spring, heading north—the migratory urge pulled at him, and he turned west reluctantly, up Left Hand Canyon to the construction site.

"All right, I got a list," Bill said. "Let's walk through—should have everything ya need. I'll stop by Tuesday or Wednesday to see how you're doin'." Starting upstairs, they went room by room, Walt making notes as Bill pointed out things that had to be done. "If ya wanna slack off, there's a ton of little shit. Wear the respirator and neoprene gloves when ya grout and seal—solvents make ya dopey."

"This is more than I can do in a week."

"Yeah, construction's like that—eighty percent of the work takes twenty percent of the time. It's that last twenty percent that gets ya, but that's what the customer sees. Details, man. Gotta look good—no matter how sturdy the place is, if the trim don't match at the corners they'll never stop yangin'." He grinned at Walt. "That's why I hired you—this piddly shit aggravates me, cleanup especially."

"I know a company that does construction cleanup."

"They probably cost more'n you."

"By the time you buy all the gear, might be cheaper to hire somebody."

Bill sighed. He hated to shell out. He hired an electrician and plumber because code required them—he'd do all that himself otherwise. He was already spending money on Walt—a bargain, but since he usually did everything, it rankled every time he wrote a paycheck. "Well, we gotta be done by Memorial Day weekend—that's when they're movin' in. I'll be back Sunday, then ya can have a day off if you want."

"I'll be ready—how about two?"

"Only if you're pretty far down this list."

"I figure I'll do the grouting first."

"Well, it's prepped. Be careful with fire—no smoking in the house. Wish the phone was in—think they said end of next week." They walked out onto the porch together, Bill squinting then putting on his sunglasses. He shook Walt's hand. "Hey buddy, I'm countin' on ya—be good." Getting in his truck, he rolled down the driveway, the engine coughed, he took the long sloping curve, gone.

The fridge, in the dining room for now, was on; Walt put his per-ishables in it, set his grocery box beside it, and carried his sleeping bag and pad to a corner of the big living room, out from under the beam. He piled his tapes next to Bill's boombox then looked over the list, pen in hand, prioritizing. He'd stepped outside the flow. Romo and Tom had directions to this house, but nobody else knew where he was. He'd been missing Luna's class, so he hadn't heard from Anna since that day she tried drawing his hair. At least Laura wouldn't find him. He went upstairs to grout the master bath.

chapter 30

Cat out of the Bag

UPHOLSTERY WORK WAS sparse, so Anna got drafted to help on floor jobs. Stefan invited her to have a seat in the office and sent Karen out on errands, then he settled behind the desk and looked at her.

"I know this bugs you, Anna, having to work as Rye's helper, but why should I hire somebody else while you need hours? Besides, I want you on the job with her. You know we're bonded—"

"So if something gets broken the insurance pays."

"Not just broken—if an employee steals, I'm covered, and so's the homeowner."

"Don't you trust her?"

He made a face.

"All right," she said, "so I'm keeping an eye on her."

"You made a good team at Hole in the Wall."

"I was supposed to lead but she just took over."

"Anna, if I send you both out on a job where she knows what to do and you sort of do, who do you think's going to be in charge, regardless of what I say?"

She looked at the schedule book lying open on the desk, reading it upside down—she and Rye had three jobs together this week. "I just feel like I've been demoted."

"Well you haven't. But there's no room for prima donnas here—we all have to be flexible, willing to do the work that comes up."

"I know."

"So adjust your attitude, or you're done." He stood and smiled. "Cheer up—the manager at Hole in the Wall's really happy with the floors, and it's time for another company meeting so we'll hold it there—on the house. If you and Rye want to work something out, we'll be talking about schedules."

"But you don't want her working solo?"

"Not yet."

"Something the matter?"

He just moved his head quickly, as though shaking off water—if she wanted to know she'd have to ask Rye. He left to give some estimates. While she waited for Karen to come back, she flipped through the schedule book: an upholstery job next week, some construction cleanup. The window washer was booked every day, the carpet guy was fairly busy too. Well, she didn't want to work full time—she shouldn't complain.

Karen returned and completed jobsheets for the week, giving Anna the billing information—something funny about that; Rye as lead should have gotten it.

• • •

"YOU DRIVE," RYE SAID.

"Don't know your way around Boulder?" Anna backed the van out.

"It's built up since I went to school here."

"Yeah, it keeps sprawling. If I wasn't in this business I wouldn't know where half these new subdivisions are." She drove east, through clots of traffic that eased finally. "Where you from, Rye?" she asked casually.

"Little town on the high plains—you never heard of it."

"Try me—I'm a native."

"Carling."

"Haven't been there but I know where it is."

"It was holding steady for a while, but now it's shrinking. An old friend of mine's here because he couldn't find work there. I'm crashing with him at the moment, but soon as I get paid I'm getting my own place."

Their job was to clean, wax, and buff hardwood floors in a large open living-dining room. The homeowner let them in, then left for work. Their major task was moving furniture. They carefully stacked things in the kitchen and on the deck, then rolled up the big area rug and stashed it in the hall. Rye dust mopped, Anna behind her damp mopping, then Rye made a circular pad of #2 steel wool and with a putty knife mushed paste wax into the strands. While Anna used a rolled-up piece of steel wool to clean the edges, Rye buffed, stopping to glob more wax on the pad, then they took a break out back while it set up. From here they had a good view of the mountains.

Anna pointed out a thick white cloud bank sitting behind the foothills, its upper edge smooth. "That's snow there, coming in—bet it'll hit this afternoon."

"It's too warm," Rye said.

"It can cool off fast." Anna hoped the storm wouldn't dump too much—with the trees leafed out, a heavy snowfall would break branches.

Back inside, Rye put the thick woolly buffing pad down, and after running the machine briefly, handed it off. "Get some practice," she said. "I won't be here forever." Anna kept an eye on her, but Rye just went outside and leaned on the deck rail, looking pensive. When they moved things back, Anna was glad she'd sketched out the locations of chairs and little tables—how could people even walk through a room with so much stuff in it? She left the invoice on the dining room table, then they loaded everything and drove back downtown.

"I'm meeting my friend for lunch," Rye said. "Want to join us?"

"Where?"

"Daddy's in the Alley."

"Sure, haven't been there for a while."

"Isn't it good anymore?" Rye asked.

"I'm too cheap to eat out."

Rye laughed. "Eddie's buying. I can't afford anything. But—"

"No no," Anna assured her, "I'll pay for mine."

He wasn't there yet. Rye picked a table by the window; the waitress brought water.

"Rye's an unusual name," Anna remarked.

"My last name's Reiner, so people started calling me Rye."

Curiosity overcame her reticence. "Which people?"

"Where I was."

"Want to tell me?"

"Nope."

Anna inhaled slowly, to settle the sting of rebuff. "So what brings you here?"

"I'm looking for somebody actually," gazing toward the sidewalk as if the person in question might be strolling by.

Anna's body went perfectly still, her lungs motionless—perhaps her heart had stopped too. *Laura.* What should she do? They were scheduled to work together this afternoon and tomorrow. If Anna ducked out because she couldn't deal with her, Stefan would be fed up and fire her. Should she admit she knew Walt? Pretend nothing was different? But her immobility drew Rye's attention, those keen blue eyes.

"You look like you're in shock. Why." An interrogator's statement.

Anna's face and neck went crimson. "I—I'll tell you sometime. Not now."

Rye half squinted, trying to decode her reaction.

"Hey, sorry I'm late," Eddie came in breathless, dropping into a chair with Rye to his left, Anna to his right.

"Eddie, my coworker Anna."

"I'm buying my own lunch," Anna said, "don't worry."

"Fine," he agreed. "Figure out what you're getting?"

"The cole salad," Rye said. "How about you?"

"I always get the same thing here—sesame noodles. Anna?"

"Think I'll get huevos rancheros and coffee."

"I'm drinking water," Rye said. "Coffee makes me irritable."

"Well, we should avoid that at all costs," Eddie laughed. He drew out Anna, asking about work, but she could feel Rye watching her like a bird of prey testing the wind, gauging distance, choosing her opportunity. When the waitress brought their food, a moment or two passed before Anna really looked at her plate.

"Oh what is this?" she demanded. "Does this look like huevos rancheros to you?"

Rye smirked. "What were you expecting?"

"You know, they're supposed to put the tortilla on the plate—corn not flour—they didn't even get that right—then the beans, then the fried eggs, with a little cheese on top. Why are the beans in this side dish?"

"That's what the menu said," Rye observed. "Beans optional."

"That's not huevos rancheros. What am I supposed to do, assemble it now?"

"Send it back."

"It's not cooked wrong, it's misunderstood." Anna lifted the eggs to pour the pinto beans—not even refried—underneath, but as she shifted the fork, one of the underdone yolks broke, flooding the tortilla yellow. One of these days she was going to learn not to order food she knew how to fix; nobody else could do it right. She dumped the rest of the beans on top, liquid and all—it was just a mess now—and tasted the salsa—not even spicy. She slopped that on, feeling exactly like this meal—wrong and ugly. Would've left then, put money on the table and a napkin over her plate—but she had to work with Rye in half an hour. Shaking salt into her palm and pinching it out to season the eggs, she tossed the rest over her left shoulder and dusted off her hands.

"Did you get him?" Rye asked.

"Get who?" Her stomach clenched in panic.

"The devil. Isn't that the superstition? That you're throwing salt in the devil's face?" Her voice had spines. "So'd you get him?"

"Probably not." She couldn't meet Rye's—Laura's—eyes now. While she poked through her food spearing a bean and eating it, Rye and Eddie half turned to each other, conversing as though she weren't there.

"Any luck?" he asked.

"He's gone. I can't figure it out. I called Tom but he wouldn't say anything."

"He's afraid."

"Hah!" she barked. "Afraid of what—my undershirt?" but clenched on her laugh—not really funny.

"He said he doesn't care."

"You said that. I haven't heard him say it."

"He won't—he doesn't want to talk to you."

"Too bad. I've waited a long time."

"Didn't he?"

"Don't give me that," she threatened. "I lost everything. Try it sometime."

"No thanks."

If ever Anna had wanted to disappear it was now, but Rye's attention pinioned her—she could talk to Eddie but Anna wasn't out of her thought for a second.

"He was in the news," he said quietly.

"You didn't tell me," Rye said eagerly. "When?"

"Around Christmas."

"After work this afternoon I'm going to the library."

"Still doing your research first—"

"Damn right. That's so chickenshit, trying to hide—who's he kidding?"

By the time Eddie and Rye were done, Anna had eaten half a dozen beans and three chunks of tomato—between shock and the disaster on her plate, her appetite was dead. She contributed money for her food and the tip, then followed them out. She consulted the jobsheet for the next location. It wasn't far.

"You could drive," she offered. "You know where 4th Street is."

"I don't have a driver's license," Rye said.

Well, that wasn't something you could get in prison, was it? Anna felt bad, as though her suggestion had been an insult. She drove cautiously, so rattled she wouldn't have been surprised to hit somebody on the way.

Arriving, they walked together to the house. A thirtyish guy came to the door.

"We're here to do the floors," Anna said. "For Bruce Aronson?"

"That's me. Come on in, I'll show you."

But he was pointing out areas Stefan hadn't included in his bid; once they'd toured the rooms, Anna showed him what was on her sheet.

"Oh, I said 'the floors'—I assumed that meant the whole house."

She doubted that—Stefan was thorough—but when she called the office to clarify, he was out.

"Tell you what, Mr. Aronson, I can add the bedrooms for another $18 each, as long as we don't have to move furniture."

"There isn't much."

"I know, but it takes two passes to do a room if we move the bed."

"So how much more would that cost?"

"Twice as much."

"That's outrageous," he said in disgust.

"It's twice the work," wishing Stefan were here—Aronson was getting pissed off. "But you know, we can just dust mop under the beds—it's not like the floor's getting a lot of traffic under there."

He laughed, to her relief. "That's true. All right, if you make it look good, you can leave the beds where they are. So how much more for the bedrooms?"

"Three at $18 each is $54."

"Fifty?"

"All right, fifty. Can you leave us a check?"

"No, I don't pay till a job's done. Don't worry, I know Stefan. I'll mail it."

Written on her jobsheet was Get check!! Unable to press anymore, she passed the sheet to her coworker.

"We were told to get payment today," Rye said firmly, meeting his eyes. "If you're not satisfied with the job we do, call the office— we're not some fly-by-night outfit."

Anna got out her invoice pad and wrote Stefan's bid, then the bedrooms, totaled it, and handed him the bill. Aronson looked startled, as though adding $50 wasn't supposed to increase what he owed; he opened his mouth to argue again, but Rye was standing there like a guard dog ready to take his leg off if he made the wrong move. He sighed loudly—rudely—and wrote a check for the full amount. Anna jotted *Paid* on the invoice and gave him the carbon copy.

"How long do you expect to be here?" he asked.

"Should take about three hours," Anna guessed.

"That long?" He rolled his eyes as though he could do it in half that time, then went out to his BMW and drove off. The women looked at each other and laughed. Anna was grateful for his unpleasantness deflecting Rye's attention.

They worked carefully, moving stuff onto the blankets. From under one bed they pulled a suitcase; from the next, shoes; and from the third, girly magazines.

"Bet this is his room," Rye said derisively, tossing *Playboys* on the bed.

"I don't really care," Anna shrugged. "When my brothers were in high school they bought these. It's pretty common."

"I hate this standardized male notion of beauty."

"That's not what Walt thinks," Anna said, clamping her mouth shut uselessly after the words were out.

"I guessed you knew him," Rye smiled slightly. "I saw it at Daddy's in the Alley, I just didn't want to say anything in front of Eddie."

Anna sat on the bed, dizzy—closing her eyes she saw Walt's face when he'd proposed to her—that brilliance, that love.

"So am I wasting my time?" Rye asked roughly.

"I don't know," Anna whispered. "I guess you should ask him."

"What's his phone number?"

She recited it, numb, watched her tuck the note into her jeans pocket.

"Hey," Rye said, "we've got a job here."

Anna dragged herself to standing.

While they worked, Rye—she said she wasn't Laura anymore—quizzed her—how long she'd known Walt, how close they were. "Was he in your past lives anywhere?"

"I asked him," Anna said. "He told me he was beyond that."

"Ha," Rye laughed scornfully. "Our history's in our souls—we can't just erase it."

"Even if those lines are wrong?" Anna explained about Luna and her drawing class mantra—"Erase, erase, erase."

"It's not that simple. You can't erase what happened."

"We do it all the time," Anna said. "It's called forgetting."

"No, it can slip out of memory without being gone. It has resonance still." They put things back under the beds, neatly so it was obvious they'd been moved, then smoothed the blankets. Anna arranged dining room chairs while Rye buffed out the wax in the last area.

• • •

AT THE OFFICE, RYE grabbed her pack. "See you in the morning."

"The job's at 8:45—let's meet here at 8:20," Anna said.

"What's the date today?"

"The tenth."

"Right," Rye grinned, and headed off up the street.

Anna was making dinner when it hit her—tomorrow was Walt's birthday, and Laura—Rye—was going to see him. She felt so bad she sat in her rocking chair with her eyes closed, the burn smell finally getting her attention. Eating scorched rice, she thought about how quickly she'd confessed, how easily Rye took charge—was that how she'd deal with Walt?

Wanting a strong drink and strong music, she called Burke.

"Well," he said, "Monday nights there's no live music."

"Come over with some records then, and alcohol."

"What do you want to drink?"

"Pepper vodka." Russian vodka with peppercorns in it—Cory'd kept a bottle in his freezer so it was almost viscous, cold and hot at the same time—a drink to encompass her moods.

"Not something I keep around," Burke said. "Meet me at Liquor World," so she grabbed her flannel shirt, but when she came outside snow was falling thickly. The storm had taken longer to show up than she'd predicted, only starting moments ago, but already big flakes were skewered on grass blades. The air was soft but not that cold, snow melting on the sidewalk and her skin. She went back in for her cowboy coat, then headed out again. The snow was coming down in clumps, cheering her in spite of herself. She wondered whether Walt would step out into it, or if he was so burdened with this new job he didn't have time for joy anymore. Suddenly she wanted to be with him.

Burke was at the store, dawdling among the red wines, hmm-ing and frowning like a connoisseur.

Coming up unseen, she asked, "Is that one good?"

Startled, he lost his grip on the bottle he'd been handling, catching it just in time. "Don't do that," he scolded. "This bottle costs $23.50."

They wandered aisles, she found the vodka she wanted—Stolichnaya Pertsovka.

"What's wrong with brandy?" Burke asked.

"Nothing—buy some if you want."

"I can't afford booze so I'm just advising. We can go back to your apartment. I grabbed some records—they're in my truck."

"First we're going to Walt's," she said.

But when they got there, his car was gone. Making Burke wait, she went in—hadn't been here since March fourth and didn't want to explain her presence to anybody—but Stu told her Walt was staying at his jobsite for the week. Anna copied the directions and came back out.

She told Burke, "I'll invest five bucks in your gas tank."

"What for?" He folded his arms, looking at her askance.

"All right," she said. "Here's the plan—first I'll buy you gas. Then you're driving to my apartment so I can get a couple things. Then you're giving me a ride up Left Hand Canyon—not that far, but the note says the driveway's steep."

He was shaking his head. "And then what?"

"Then you can pick me up tomorrow."

"Oh really. A taxi costs more than that, you know."

"Please Burke?"

"Leave me the vodka and I'll do it."

"I just bought this—"

"But I'm the one who's going to need it."

She sagged. "I'm really bad."

"I'll say—I thought you wanted to see me, but you just want a cheap ride."

"Let's go back to Liquor World and I'll get you a pint of brandy, all right?"

He got a sly look on his face. "I know—you don't even have to buy me liquor."

"What do you want?" Brandy was sure to be easier.

"You have to tell me why all of a sudden you want to see Walt. You have the aura of a skunk. I want a story—a true story."

So in the whirling snow on their slow drive north, she told him about Rye.

"I think that's very funny," he said, "to end up working with her—Walt will too."

"He'll be miserable because I gave her his phone number."

"I'll bet you a pint of VSOP Courvoisier that it's you he really wants, not this 'Rye.' He'll see her and come back to you."

"I'll take that bet." At least she'd get something. They shook on it, then realized he'd missed the Left Hand Canyon turnoff in the flying snow—he made a U-turn back to the junction.

"So when do I have to pick you up?" he asked.

"Seven should do it."

"I thought you said he's working—can he really take off a whole day?"

"In the morning," she said.

"What?" Both his hands came off the wheel, and when he grabbed again the pickup fishtailed. He eased off the gas to regain control, then grousing at the windshield, said, "I can't function before ten—you know that."

"I'll lose my job if you don't. I can't tick off Stefan right now."

"You. Are. Bad," Burke pronounced as he downshifted.

"If you can't do that, sit in the truck and give me a ride later tonight."

"You've lost your mind completely—I'm doing no such thing."

"By 7:30 then? Please?"

He grumbled, "You're going to owe me big time."

The landmarks on Romo's directions were invisible, but as the canyon narrowed, she was sure they'd passed the driveway. Burke found a place to pull off, waited for a Jeep to go by, then turned around, driving slowly while Anna craned her neck.

"Here, turn here." The new mailbox, too clean and smooth for snow to cling to, was her clue—they bumped over a narrow bridge, the road curving then climbing abruptly. Burke put the truck in granny gear, they slipped a few times on wet gravel negotiating the curve, then arrived at a level spot, almost colliding with Walt's car.

"Don't leave yet," she said.

"Are you kidding? After driving all the way out here, I intend to come in."

chapter 31

Happy Birthday

WALT HEARD THE truck and figured Bill was back, but out of the snowfall came Anna and Burke. He stood a moment in blank amazement, then joy and surprise bubbled up together, effervescing the heaviness of a day's work from his muscles.

"Brought you a birthday present," Anna said.

"Is it Tuesday already?" If it was, his schedule was in trouble.

"No, I'm early."

His smile was radiant. "Come in, leave boots and wet things in the entry." They kept coats on—Bill was a cheapskate—using hot water was OK, but he'd told Walt to keep the heat at fifty.

Walt stood waiting; Anna glanced from him to Burke. Walt's hands twitched at his sides, delight churning with uncertainty—she wouldn't come all this way then change her mind, would she?

"Hug him, dammit," Burke ordered.

She felt lost somewhere inside her skin, brain gone, nerves calling to emptiness, but made her legs walk and arms reach around Walt, her heart near his. He lifted her off her feet and turned stately circles one after another, her toes brushing the carpet, upcast eyes watching the beam like clock hands moving as he rotated. Her head swam, she closed her eyes, his mouth making contact became her center of gravity. He was still turning, slower now, but she couldn't tell—beyond dizzy, she was in orbit, gripping him so she didn't tumble back to Earth. When he stopped they both fell, rolling onto their backs while the carpet heaved and whirled under them, his rough thumb stroking the back of her hand.

Burke stood over them. "Show me this house."

They staggered up and Walt gave the grand tour, turning on what lights there were so they could admire the wide empty space, that massive beam at the ridge of the roof, tongue-and-groove cedar slanting away to both sides. On the second floor he showed them the master bath he'd worked on that day, sealing the grout.

"It won't be cured till late tomorrow but I've planned a nice long soak." Anna took his hand as he led them through the bedrooms, their ceilings a continuation of the main room—glass at the tops of interior walls traded views and light with the rest of the house, while windows on the perimeter looked onto the dense snowfall. "I told Bill to hire Perfectly Clean to do the windows."

"Bet the ladder work's hairy," Anna said.

"There's eye anchors in the soffits all the way around so you can rope up—we did, to put up the insulation and siding."

Looking at those long windows, she shook her head.

"Now," he said, "you have to see the rock." He led to the back and opened the door. The master bedroom ran the width of the house, a huge upright slab of sandstone forming its back wall, supporting the beam, the stone rising higher than the house on the south side, descending toward the north where windows spanned the gap between rock and ceiling, the glass cut to match the undulating sandstone that dropped to knee height at the corner.

"Won't those windows leak?" Burke asked.

"Who knows? We ran a layer of rubber at the bottom of the glass, then cooked it to the rock with a blowtorch. Isn't it amazing?"

"This room's an icebox," Anna said. "Imagine how cold it'll be in January."

"It's so beautiful." Walt didn't care that it was hugely impractical—he'd never seen such a wonderful room. Traceries of lichen put to shame the finest framed art, and no paint job could measure up to this wild stone's thousand shades. The expanse of glass gave the room a cathedral air, the end of the beam planted on the slab whose colors were evoked in the cedar ceiling. Right now the windows showed nothing but snow, falling so densely that trees ten feet from the house were hidden. Walt switched off the lights and by the whiteness they admired the pale grain in the cedar, the variegated striping of the beam, the snow-defined lip of the rock just outside. They went downstairs where the stone forming the back wall was darker where excavation had exposed it.

The tour was over, and Walt and Anna were holding hands. Burke said, "Sure I can make it up this road tomorrow?"

"Cross the bridge and honk," Anna said. "I'll be listening, and hike down."

"You better be paying attention."

Walt laughed. "I'll set my alarm."

"Let me have one drink then I'm going," Burke said, and Anna fetched the bottle she'd stuck in the freezer, Walt offering his coffee mug as a shotglass. The vodka hadn't been refrigerated long but it was cool and hot, and Burke admitted it had charm.

As his taillights disappeared into the swirl of snow, Anna followed Walt up to the master bedroom, wishing she had her sleeping bag. All she'd brought were the bottle of vodka, her diaphragm kit, and a change of underwear. In her myopic way she'd pictured this visit with Walt as an isolated event—it had nothing to do with the snowstorm, or Burke, or even spending the night—just an interlude sneaked out of the onrush of time. But now that she was here the house was real, it was cold, she was staying, and Walt was surely wondering why. *I am completely untrustworthy*, she thought, but what she said was, "I just wanted to wish you happy birthday."

• • •

HE SPREAD HIS SLEEPING bag near the center of the room, though not under that beam—he could feel its weight every time he looked at it. The owners would probably put their bed directly beneath it, but he'd have nightmares of being crushed.

"Some house, huh?" He stepped close behind her, pulling her against him.

"What a place. These windows…"

"Yeah." He rubbed his cheek against her hair and felt his stubble snag. "I should shave now, or else forget it. Want me to?"

"Yes please."

"Count lichens, or snowflakes, or heartbeats while you're waiting." In the master bath he lathered and shaved, careful not to splash outside the sink; when he came back she was pacing by the windows, swinging her arms, and as he met her with a hug he said, "Shh. Listen." They could hear only a great closed silence—no wind, no jets, no dogs, no far-off traffic—everything had stopped but snowfall. Their ears seeking some audible detail imagined the tap of snowflakes on glass; their socks brushing the carpet seemed noisy, the hiss of nylon almost a rasp as they moved his sleeping bag.

"I have a blanket in my trunk," Walt said. "Want me to get it?"

"Yeah—that rock is so cold, we might as well be outside."

"But this room's where we have to be. I have a theory."

"Which is?"

"That you're related to this sandstone, and you blush because your skin remembers that. So when the sun comes up and everything's glowing red, I want to see if you are too."

"Go get the blanket?"

Returning he wrapped her in it, and when both were down to socks she opened the edges to include him. They sank to knees then hips then stretched out, rolling across the wide carpet, trying to stay in the blanket, laughing as it either unrolled or tangled so tight they had to flop back the other way. They played a long time before settling into sex, his heart light and clean as snowflakes. When they rested he looked up—that beam, straight overhead. On his knees he carried her, blanket and all, over to his foam pad, lying down with the zipped-open sleeping bag for a cover.

• • •

SHE FLOATED, TRYING TO remember which wall she'd set her glasses next to. People took eyesight for granted. People—

"Walt?"

"Hm?"

"I met Laura."

"Mm," he said drowsily. "Did she bite?"

"Well, kind of. Stefan hired her and we've been working together."

"Is she any good?"

"She's better at floors than I am—in five minutes she was running the job."

"Sounds about right."

"She's coming to see you tomorrow."

By now he was awake, but seemed unconcerned. "How's she know where I am?"

"I told her—to get it over with."

"Get what over with? What are you expecting?"

"She takes charge—that's what she'll do with you."

"Not necessarily."

"She told her friend you're kidding yourself, hiding from her."

"That's true." He kissed her jaw. "Don't worry about it. It's out of your hands now." They drifted awhile in the stillness. Snuggling her closer he said, "So—"

"I couldn't stand that she's going to show up for your birthday but I wouldn't. That just seemed wrong."

• • •

HE LET TOMORROW GO — loving Anna was the only preparation that could make any difference.

Sometime in the night the storm ended, and looking out the north windows he saw blackness, heard the soughing of wind followed by flomping as branches shed snow. He listened awhile then stroked her awake to receive him again, and as she swam to consciousness, he attuned her to the sounds he'd been enjoying. They faded back to sleep smiling.

Hours later they opened their eyes in the chill as color woke every surface of the room. He looked from the rosy wall to the scarlet-tinged snow in the trees just beyond the window, to Anna, her face red as a blush in the early light.

"It's true," he whispered.

"What is?" she mumbled, not awake yet.

"You match the sandstone." He laughed and squeezed her.

Her heart was icing over. "Walt, I feel like I'll never be with you again."

"Then let this moment expand and fill the world." He brushed the hair off her forehead, wishing he could stall out the clock, the morning, the future. Sun rising changed the glow to lighter shades, finally glinting off the snow to fully illumine the room, the rock its true sandstone hues, every other surface borrowing its colors.

"This is my favorite birthday moment of this life—you, this room, the snow. Even the cold."

She wanted to forget everything too, but—they'd get up, Burke would come, Rye would take her place. This Walt interlude would fade. Well, at least he'd blotted out Cory. Was Harold right? Had she traded one unworkable attraction for another? Would she drag this loss to the doorstep of her next—

"Anna stop." He knew what was going through her mind and heart, so familiar because he'd done that himself. Misery weighed as much as anger or resentment—not the way to rise through circumstance. Laughter and joy: those were wings. Her eyes pooled with unshed tears. His were bright. He said, "Is snow sad because it melts?"

"Yes." She didn't even hesitate.

"If it didn't melt could the plants drink it?"

"They need it, but it's still sad."

"What if it melted on a silly person's bare skin—would that be sad?"

Despite herself she laughed. "No."

"Be that snow then—melt on me. Freeze my skin so my blood jumps." He coated her face with wet kisses then blew on them, holding her away to watch goosebumps sprout down her neck and breasts. Laughing he sat up and grabbed her foot still in its sock, bit her arch through the wool, and releasing it ran the backs of his fingers up her hamstring; she shivered.

"Roll me," tucking himself into a naked ball and rocking from elbow to elbow. She pulled the blanket around her and pushed him like a big knobby seed across the carpet, her effort warming her, the blanket sliding off. When they arrived at the rock he unfolded. "Your turn." She curled her arms around her knees and ducked her head; he rolled her around, turning her by a wall, coming to rest near the sleeping bag.

"In *Stranger in a Strange Land*," he said, "Valentine Michael Smith used to say 'I am only an egg.' Remember?"

"Yeah. That's true."

"When the shell constricts you, start chipping at it—it's time to come out." He kissed her inner thigh. "Sorry you can't use the shower. You'll just have to smell funky today."

She laughed—Rye would notice, and that was just fine.

Downstairs she opened the fridge—eggs and corn tortillas. "Got any beans?"

"A couple cans."

"A skillet?"

"Sure. The stove's not hooked up—we use a hotplate." In the mudroom by the kitchen door, plywood on sawhorses formed a makeshift table with a hotplate, toaster oven, and percolator. He had a cast-iron skillet and lid, a pan, and a few utensils.

He started coffee. She fried and mashed the beans, adding salsa, and once they were paste she pushed them to one edge of the skillet and laid in a tortilla, turning and flipping it to heat evenly.

"How about plates?" she asked.

"I've been using this pie tin."

She flopped in the tortilla and smeared it with refried beans, he spread on salsa while she fried a pair of eggs. As the whites lost their transparency, she splashed in watery coffee and set the lid on to steam them, turning off the heat, then in a moment served the eggs on top of the prepared tortilla.

"Fork or spoon?" he offered. "Choose your weapon."

"Spoon's fine."

He shaved cheese over the eggs. "The coffee's not ready."

"But the vodka is." Overnight it had achieved the proper viscosity.

"Happy birthday Walt," she tossed back a shot, fire and chill racing each other down her throat. She poured one for him.

"Thank you Anna," he toasted, taking his shot, then set down the mug so they could kiss. He leaned against the counter, the pie tin between them.

"I had the worst huevos rancheros yesterday." She described her lunch.

"You should open your own café—rainbow vegetables, piled toast, huevos perfectos." He kissed her again. "You are my huevo perfecto." As he reheated the skillet for round two, he asked, "So when's Laura gonna show?"

"We have a job this morning—I think we'll be done around one. I don't know how she plans to get out here—she doesn't have a driver's license."

"That won't stop her."

"No," she agreed.

"Well, today I'm grouting the kitchen floor. If she shows up before I'm done she'll just have to wait."

"I looked at the bathroom—you do good work."

"Thank you." As though he had to defend the house he said, "I know it's dumb to build against that rock—the windows'll probably leak, might even crack, and all this open space is ridiculous to heat—but I love it anyway. Someday I'll build a house, and draw on things about this one."

"Speaking of drawing—the last class is tomorrow."

"I know. This job swallowed up everything else. Tell Luna I'm there in spirit."

When they'd finished the second plate of huevos she looked outside, worrying. "I should walk down to the bridge. Burke'll be late—I'll have to hustle."

"Leave me a business card to give Bill—I don't want to wash these windows."

"It won't be me."

"Construction cleanup too."

She half smiled. "Don't try so hard—it's all right."

They came out into the bright morning, chucking blobs of soft wet snow at each other as they descended the driveway. Near the mailbox, they leaned against a pine tree to smooch. Burke drove up, Walt gave her one more kiss and pressed her hand.

"Thank you," he smiled.

"Happy birthday."

He winked at her and headed back to the house, ache and light spinning together in his heart till they seemed one.

chapter 32

After All This Time

STEFAN FIDGETED OUT by the floor van—Anna hadn't answered her phone. Rye was capable of doing the job alone but his bond wouldn't cover that since she was on parole.

"Sorry I'm late," Anna said as Burke drove away.

"Karen's not in yet," Stefan said. "I'll call the customer—got everything you need?" Rye had already loaded things and was seated in the van's passenger seat reading a free newspaper, but Anna had to prove she was conscious. He watched her scan the jobsheet.

"Do we have plug adapters?" She dug through the box between the seats where small things ended up. Houses often lacked three-prong outlets but all their equipment required them. She made a dash into the office for two off the back shelf, catching Stefan's nod of satisfaction. He went in to call while she and Rye drove to the job.

Rye said she'd read about Walt's stint in jail, and seemed amused—Anna reminded herself she'd just been in prison, but that air of superiority gave her a chill.

"Walt and I have formed a coalition of the spineless," she said as they emptied wet-vac and mop bucket into the toilet.

Rye snorted.

"More than other people anyway." He wasn't really spineless, he just didn't push. Maybe Rye couldn't tell the difference.

"Are you trying to keep me from seeing him?" she accused.

"I gave you his number." Anna was hiding nothing. What she and Walt felt was outside Rye's visible spectrum, that was all.

"You know I'm going to see him today."

"I figured you would."

"It's his birthday."

"I know. I was with him last night."

Rye stopped with the mop in her hand, her voice hard. "Trying to wear him out?"

Anna blushed almost purple. "No," she squeaked. "Let's just finish here." They worked in silence.

Back at the office Karen showed them the schedule—an upholstery job Friday but no more floors until that construction cleanup next week. Rye asked when she could get her paycheck, then left.

Anna walked home wishing she'd kept the vodka. She could use a drink. Sun was compacting the snow, tree limbs bowed but didn't break, hyacinths looked funny frilled in white. By her house she found a lilac bush blooming and cut one small snow-capped flower cluster, which she set in a tall glass of water on her windowsill. Moving her rocking chair close, she sat with pad and pencils, drawing, focusing on shapes then colors. When she was done an hour later, she closed her eyes and saw that big room in shades of red. Walt's theory about her blushes made her feel connected to something larger, not a child unable to control herself. Rye was there now to collect his attention like an overdue bill. Would he argue? Break down? What if—

Disgusted with herself, she stopped.

• • •

RYE TOOK A CITY bus as far north as it would go, then hitchhiked; two teenage boys in a small pickup pulled over, snow melting off a dirt bike roped upright in the truckbed.

"Where y' goin'?" one asked.

"Left Hand Canyon."

"Hop in." The kid on the passenger side scooted to the middle and she sat, pulling the door shut then relaxing against it. They looked like overgrown urchins—thin faces, bony wrists sticking out the sleeves of their jean jackets, their hair buzz cut. The one next to her had a tobacco pinch between lip and gum and an empty tuna can he spat into. This could be the outskirts of Carling not Boulder: pastures and country kids. Nothing to go back to there, but sometimes she got a twinge—in her DNA she guessed.

"This is it, thanks." They let her out, and once the string of cars passed, she walked toward the canyon, enjoying the damp scent of melting snow, every fence post hatted in white. Another warm day, this would be melted except in deep shadows. Ponderosas low on the slopes still wore snow, though higher up the wind had tossed them bare. She found the driveway and studied the footprints: a single set ran straight, two others ranged in arcs dodging each other, diverging, sliding.

From the flats the house looked like a cube with a pointed roof, simple and bold as a child's design. As she climbed, she could see the ceiling through an expanse of glass, wood slanting away to either side of the central beam that bore the roof overhang. Rounding the curve she saw the front porch with its own roof, the door just off center. A car was parked in front—a Dodge Dart, the right vintage but brown, snow receding from its hood, trunk, and roof. Well, she'd changed—why shouldn't he? A hippie-mobile might not suit him anymore. She came up on the porch and thumped the glass door, a bass note. No response. She knocked again and tried the knob—unlocked.

"Hello—Walt?"

"In here," came a muffled reply.

She stepped in, closing the door.

"Take off your boots," he said more clearly—she still couldn't see him. She lifted one foot at a time to untie and pull the laces, pried them off, then came toward the sound. Walt with his back to her was kneeling on terra cotta tiles in the kitchen, trowel in one glove and rag in the other, a tray of grout to his right. He turned, wearing a respirator—the fumes were just now hitting her.

"Shouldn't you have a window open?"

"They are," he said through the apparatus, nodding to where several double-hung windows were raised.

"Guess you need a fan."

He lifted the respirator. "Are you a fan?"

She pursed her lips. "Maybe. Hi Walt."

"Hello. I have to finish before the grout sets up—another hour maybe. There's a couple books in the corner—help yourself."

"Can't you talk?"

"Not through a respirator, no," and pulled it back over his nose and mouth, returning to his task. She walked over and nudged his books with her toe—*The Restaurant at the End of the Universe* and a book of short stories by Ray Bradbury. Still in outer space. She picked through his tapes, chose B.B. King, and looked around for his tape deck, moving back to see into the kitchen—no sign of it.

"Hey Walt, where's your boombox?"

He gestured with his head upward so she climbed the stairs, looking into the front bedrooms then opening the door to the back. What absurdity was this? Who'd want a rock for a wall? Cold, rough—she'd had enough of that thank you. In her cell, what wasn't metal or cinder block was plastic, all of it cold and ugly. And the smell. God, she'd be smelling that the rest of her life. Bleach and mold, urine, fear, sweat, menstrual blood, intestinal gas, and the greasy meat reek of whatever slop-of-the-day they were expected to eat, blended with the stench of canned vegetables. Everything was slightly damp, mold grew wherever Clorox didn't go. Athlete's foot was rampant—painting between toes with bleach was the only way to get rid of it. Of course that killed skin too, it just didn't itch quite as much as the fungus.

The fumes rose. This room with the rock didn't stink because the door'd been closed, but it was cold—like that should surprise anybody. Bringing the boombox down to the living room, she plugged it in and started the tape, pacing. She needed to calm herself—always did yoga on an empty stomach so she took off her jacket, jeans, flannel shirt, and bra, and in undies and undershirt began moving smoothly through her stretches to stay warm.

It hadn't been easy to stay fit in prison. Starchy, fatty, and sugary foods, hardly any fresh greens or fruit. She'd managed by eating very little and staying active. Even in her cell she could do yoga and isometrics, and when they needed crews for labor she volunteered, learning floor maintenance. A big black dyke asked if she liked wheat or white but she said rye, and since that fit with her last name anyhow, from then on she was Rye. She didn't feel like Laura anymore—Rye was smart, self-reliant, alert, with a caustic tongue and a glare to match. A snake didn't have to be big to be poisonous and they all knew it. She didn't mind helping people but she never forgot if anyone crossed her. She discovered the two meanest bull dykes were illiterate, and teaching them to read and write won their respect. She found a niche—helping others with their appeals—and earned the praise of the warden who wasn't sure why this middle-class white girl was in here anyway.

Thinking about Walt had kept her cool when she was ready to explode, made it easy to rebuff the predators. With no word to the contrary, she could assume he still cared; they were connected weren't they? They'd seen it, tripping in his snow-bound car on Donner Pass. He must've realized that after she killed Cob she was free for him, waiting as he'd waited for her. She'd get out and they'd be together—who else could ever understand? Eddie had faithfully answered her letters, cautiously advancing his affection. But when she showed up on his doorstep, he thought she was going to fall into his arms. Where'd he get that idea? After she torpedoed his silly notion, he was good enough to offer space till she got money ahead to move, but things chilled between them—fine with her. All she wanted was Walt: to see him, to love him, to dig back through her layers of callous and ice, find the heart he'd touched. His mind had traveled clear across the country to hers, to pledge their future.

She tuned in to her body, stretching, relaxing, extending her mind into breath and movement, a vestige of her attention on the sounds in the kitchen, noticing the solvent stench every time she was upright. She wanted Walt to watch her finish, but when she'd done all the asanas she could think of the trowel still scraped on the tiles, the rag shushing after. She went back through the poses, more of her listening now, a seed of impatience swelling and opening inside her till finally she quit, put her jeans back on against the cold, and came to the kitchen doorway. He had two rows of tiles to go, so she moved back far enough to be out of range of the stronger fumes, watching as he smeared grout into the wide gaps, worked it all the way to the subfloor, smoothed then followed with the now-gray rag, easing the grout to the contours of the tiles. When he got to the threshold, he set the trowel in the tray and moved that to a slab of cardboard on the carpet.

He stood slowly, the straps of his kneepads pulling his pant legs up in back, and surveyed his work, then dropped the rag into the tray, cleaned his gloves and soaking a fresh rag in mineral spirits, went back across the floor, stepping in the centers of tiles to the far end, wiping the surfaces; after three rows wetting another rag to continue. Finished, he took the pungent rags in the grout tray out to the gravel to clean up, then peeled off his gloves, and removed the respirator. Back indoors, he unbuckled the kneepads and dropped them in a bucket, flexed his knees, then straightened, groaning.

She stood watching.

"Hello Laura. It's been a while."

"Call me Rye."

"Rye then. Hi Rye."

"Are you Halt Walt?"

"At the moment—halt or lame. If you'll excuse me I'd like to wash my face and rinse the sweat from my hair."

"We could take a shower."

"No we couldn't—that grout's still curing."

"Take a break. Have you had lunch?"

"Not today. Is it lunchtime?"

"It's close to three. Happy birthday."

"Some of it anyway."

"Which part?"

He smiled inwardly—his face looked strange with the red indentations from the respirator, the skin it had covered white and sweaty. "Anna came up last night—she said you've been working together."

"I don't know how much longer."

"Anyway. That was the happy part."

"Getting married?" trying to keep the snide edge out of her tone.

"She turned me down."

"Because you're waiting for me."

"Not anymore—you took care of that."

"She said you've formed the 'coalition of the spineless.' What a phrase."

"It's accurate." He walked over to his food box. "I find after I work with these solvents I have to eat bread—plain bread. Want something?"

"What is there?" She opened the fridge. "Got any avocados? Fruit?"

"Dig, find, eat." He was tired. Bagel in hand, he went out on the porch where he could breathe fresh air and sit with his back to the house, legs extended. She sat a foot away, ankles crossed, peeling an orange.

"She reminds me of Stream," she said.

"Who, Anna?"

"Yeah. Innocent, clear. Easily baffled."

"Did you baffle her?"

"I thought she was going to choke when she figured out who I was."

"Well, all she knows is the damage."

She dismissed that. "C'mon Walt—three years ago?"

"I didn't trust my heart until I met her last fall. When you were done there wasn't much left of me, Laura."

"Rye."

"Whoever you are. Maybe you're not even her and we're prolonging a charade having this conversation."

"Laura's under all this—this chitin. This exoskeleton. You're the one who loved her, who can help her find her way out."

"I don't think so. If I refuse are you gonna pull your steamroller act? How much do you respect me and what I want? Are you still so greedy?" He tore the bagel into small pieces and chewed carefully as he talked.

"I need you Walt," she said quietly, pulling her orange in half. "Is that greed?"

"Depends on what it makes you do. You always trumped me."

"If I waited for you to make up your mind—"

"Remember when Cob took what he wanted? That's what you did to me."

"You were so depressed," she said. "I made you stay with me so it wouldn't get worse. It was all for you—I shouldn't have gone back to him, but I never stopped loving you."

"You loved him because you wanted someone you couldn't push around."

"He tried to pull that shit again, that day. That's why I hit him. I wasn't going back to slavery—didn't work for me."

"But for me it was OK, huh? 'Give me space so I can have the world's biggest orgasm.' 'Come here I want you.' 'He's suicidal—go talk him out of it.'"

"But I didn't—"

"Sure you did. I was such a convenience—instant sex. Just add Walt and stir." He took a slow breath. "I'm all done bein' your stir-stick, toots. Get yourself a dildo."

She slapped his face so hard his ears rang, the imprint lingering as cold lines with hot edges. He sat like a rag doll, head leaning away from her, pain and distress clamoring in his brain while his heart was saying, *See? Nothing's different.*

"Oh Walt," she whispered. "I didn't—"

Resting his hands on the porch on either side of his hips, he looked her in the face, eye to eye for the first time. "You did. You just did. It's been obvious to me for some time—can you see now?"

"We were friends," she said, as though talking to herself. "We looked after each other. Weren't we? Didn't we?"

"Memory can tie you down but it can't free you."

"I'll do anything for you. How can I prove I still love you?"

"By walking down that driveway, out of my life."

"So you can get it on with that pathetic child?" she snapped.

"Anna's brought me more joy than I thought possible."

"Men like weak women," she said acidly. "Having your authority unchallenged."

"I have no authority—you're talking to the wrong guy. You still miss Cob."

"Yes I do," she flared. "At least he was a man."

"Bitterness hasn't done you any good, Laura."

"Rye."

"Laura." He grinned, feeling the afterimage of her slap pull at his cheek. "You shouldn't assume things about me. I haven't been waiting all this time for some lame apology—I've been tuned into the cosmic laughter. While you've been putting on armor I've been taking mine off—pretty soon there'll be nothing between me and the world. We're going opposite directions—I don't see any more conjunctions here."

His detachment seemed rehearsed. Once he was in her, their love would flood back, they'd work out a reconciliation, tears and apologies, and she'd feel whole. They both would. "Would you kiss me?" She'd beg if she had to—once she'd reached him—

"Why? What would that accomplish?"

"As long as you avoid contact, you can pretend you don't care. You might be fooled but I'm not."

"Laura, you didn't return to slavery—why should I?"

"It's true then—you do want me."

"I want to wash up." He clambered to his feet, stepped over her legs and went inside, upstairs to the master bath. Ducking his head beneath the faucet, he rinsed his face then hair, using his hands as squeegees then wrapping his towel around his head—much better. He should work a couple more hours, but grouting the other bathroom would take longer; he'd do something easy. He looked at his face. The marks of the respirator were fading, and two red patches remained from her hand. When Anna was on mescaline, striking him had been part of freeing herself. Laura's slap seemed like selfishness, with a little hatred of the truth in there somewhere.

Downstairs he consulted his list, checking off *Grout Kitchen Floor. Install Sconce Lighting*—not too strenuous. All that stuff was stashed in the living room closet. He took out the boxes—six of them. This room was going to look like a restaurant; did they realize that? He went to the electric panel in the back wall where they'd roughed in the laundry room, flipped the breakers for the living room, heard the fridge kick off, and got his pair of screwdrivers and the cordless drill. He consulted the blueprint to make sure he was using the right junction boxes, distributing the sconces before coming back to the first. He worked methodically, aware of Laura standing near, watching, jittery energy seething off her. When the fixture was mounted, he put in a bulb and flipped the breaker to test—it came on. He turned the breaker off again, took the vodka out of the freezer and poured a shot into his mug, put that in Laura's hand, then began unpacking the next sconce.

Without turning around, he said, "It's pepper vodka—my birthday present."

"Anna give you this?"

"Yep. Although she's probably wishing she was having a drink right now."

She tasted it. "Interesting."

"I kinda like it," he agreed. "Not that I drink much."

"I stayed away from it, inside. I wouldn't have been able to stop. That was so bad Walt—thinking about you was all that kept me going."

"That was a one-way conversation and you know it."

"Because you were too cowardly to hold up your end."

"Yes I was cowardly—I ran for years—nobody knew where I was unless they were there too. When Eddie found me in Boulder I couldn't run anymore. Then I met Anna and I didn't want to."

"You love her," she said.

"Yes."

"But she won't marry you. What kind of future's that, Walt?"

"She's young—in a couple years she might come around—I can wait."

That killed her. This girl he claimed to love wasn't even a rival; she didn't register a blip, she was so insubstantial. How could he—

"She's not worth—"

"I'll decide how I spend my time, if you don't mind."

He finished the second sconce. When he turned she was right there, shirt open, undershirt showing, so close he could smell her hair; he pulled his hands back like a child warned not to touch, she put her hand over his and drew his palm to rest on the curve where her waist tapered to her hip. Her desire heated the air, her eyes soft now, asking, wishing.

"Can't help you, Laura," he said tightly, pulling his hand back, but hers was still holding it and they had a little tug-of-war as she moved to place it on her breast while he resisted. "Forced sex is rape," he said. "Don't do that."

"I know you want me—you'll remember when we're together."

He jerked his hand free. "If I fuck you and it does nothing for me, then will you give up and leave me alone?"

The ugliness made her hesitate, but she was sure. "Yes."

"Let's do it now, right here." He unzipped his jeans and kicked them off, stepping out of his boxers while she removed jeans, shirt, undies—left on her undershirt. She tried to kiss him but his mouth was closed and tense. His dick was limp so she stroked. Nothing happened. She crouched taking the head in her mouth, sucking gently then harder, feeling him respond, chopping at the backs of his knees so they bent. As he sank to the carpet she followed, mouth on his dick coaxing more. He lay flat, letting her do what she wanted, focusing on the moment when he'd squirt and could go back to work. She straddled him, hot inside, then wrapping her legs around his, rolled him on top.

"You said you'd fuck me," she urged.

"Yeah I did," straightening his arms, shoving at her, hating this—she still didn't get it. He flashed on giving them a sperm sample in jail, and ejaculated, pulled out despite her grappling, rocked back onto his knees and stood up. She was breathing hard—fury? the exertion of trying to make him feel something? But he didn't look at her. Upstairs, he washed off in the bathroom sink, dried himself with his wet towel, and pulled on boxers then jeans. He came down and picked up the screwdrivers that had fallen from his back pocket and started installing the third sconce. She was quiet till he'd tightened the last screw, then he heard her moving, getting dressed.

"That was dishonest," she said finally.

"That's all I had for you. That's it. Now you're free."

"Oh I'm free, am I?" she raged.

"Or not—that's up to you," moving to the next sconce.

"Is it semantics? What if I asked you to make love?"

"Then I couldn't. When you beat the L outta your lover, know what you've got?"

"What?"

"Over. The Walt and Laura Show is over. I've moved on and you should too."

He heard her pace while he twisted wires and spun on wire nuts. "Where?" she asked. "Where do I start?"

"Berkeley. Get your degree and do something with it."

"I can't go back there now."

"Why not? College population turns over every few years—it'll be like a new place. You always said they had the best combination of courses and opportunities."

"You just don't want me around."

"If I was transparent you could look inside me and not find yourself anywhere. That died three years ago." He turned to look at her. "Since you don't have a lot of patience, you'll probably get over it faster than I did."

As the sun moved toward the far ridge and he checked items off his list, he worried that she wasn't leaving. He wanted to stay neutral now, not draw the wrath he could sense percolating, but she wasn't heeding the message. He heard a truck laboring up the driveway; around the last curve came Bill.

He swung in the door, a six-pack bag in his arm.

"Didn't know when to expect you," Walt said.

"Hit a lull so I thought I'd come relieve you."

"Thanks—it's my birthday."

Bill stopped, surprised. "Shit, ya gotta tell me these things." After a moment's thought, he said, "Take off—I'm here for the night. Be back by nine in the morning." Then he noticed Laura, pacing on the balcony in front of one of the smaller bedrooms. "She your girlfriend?" Still hoping to rekindle Walt's interest, she was wearing an open flannel shirt over her form-fitting undershirt.

"My ex."

"Not the one you were tellin' me about?"

"No. Come see the kitchen floor." They walked over together, Bill turned on kitchen lights and squatted to get a close look.

"Good job buddy," he praised, straightening. "I hate grouting."

"I'll do the second bathroom tomorrow—the master bath's sealed and curing."

"So what's she doin' here?" Bill asked in a low voice. "She's hot."

"And I'm not. Came to rake over some ancient history. Shoulda left but she can't take a hint."

"You leave—she can stay if she wants."

Walt put the tools back in the bucket near the door and started a grocery list. "Laura," he raised his voice, "I'm going back to Boulder for the night, but Bill says you're welcome to stay."

Joining them, she said, "Friends call me Rye." She and Bill shook hands, assessing each other.

"Like what we've done here?" Bill asked.

"I don't think that works, having a rock as one of your walls."

"You don't like how the bedroom looks?"

"That room'll always be cold," she said.

"Maybe, but it's beautiful." His eyes warmed. "So are you— wanna stay?"

"I don't know—the friend I'm crashing with will get worried."

"Walt can call 'em, right buddy?"

"Hm?" Walt said. "Sure."

"Like sinsemilla?" Bill asked her, rocking on the balls of his feet.

She looked at Walt—he shrugged—it was up to her. He really didn't care.

"I haven't had good dope in a long long time," she said.

"This is the best, I guarantee." Bill laughed, "I must be psychic—I scored a mattress today. Hey Walt, gimme a hand bringin' it in."

"Sure—where you want it?"

"The master bedroom, where else?"

They went out to his truck, got out the stained double-bed mattress, and carried it upstairs. It smelled faintly of urine.

"We should protect the carpet," Walt suggested.

Bill sniffed. "Yeah. Go get a drop cloth." They spread the plastic near the northeast corner, then put the mattress on it. As Walt turned to go, Bill said, "Sure this is cool?"

"She can look after herself."

"Want some smoke? Take one." He gave Walt a short fat joint then got out another and closed the matchbox. "Here," Bill shoved a fifty into his hand. "Happy birthday. Next time say somethin'."

Walt grinned. "Thanks." He got serious. "Don't hurt her, OK?"

"Why would I—"

"Just don't. She needs affection and I can't give her any."

"Not that I will," Bill snorted.

"From you she won't expect it." On his way out he waved at Laura who stood to one side, wondering if staying was a good idea. She knew nothing about this guy, except with that scar on his lip he might be defensive, and mask that in roughness.

chapter 33

Closing the Door

WALT DROVE STRAIGHT to Anna's but she wasn't home. He considered leaving a note, decided not to, and drove to the natural foods store downtown. He selected some salad greens and things to go with them, a baguette, and a box of crackers. In the bulk area, he loaded up on nuts and dried fruit and chocolate chips, then got cans of beans and a carton of eggs—he'd liked Anna's huevos rancheros. More oranges, cheese, salsa, chips—starting to look like a lot. He set down his overflowing basket in the checkout line, nudging it forward with his foot as he neared the belt.

"That's a lot of food for one person." Anna stood behind him in line, grinning.

"What if it's for two?" he asked, eyes dancing. "That make more sense?"

"Which two?"

"Me and you, who else?"

"What about your job?" Her face contracted. "You didn't get fired because I was there, did you?"

"No no, Bill showed up and gave me the night off." His smile danced into her eyes. "May I spend it with you please please please?"

"What about birthday cake?"

"We'll go out for dessert. Invite Burke. Bill laid some money on me—my treat."

"Do your housemates know you're back?"

"No, and I should call Tom—he was gonna drive up tomorrow."

When he'd put his food on the belt he grabbed her basket and unloaded that too, then dropped the wood divider behind hers, grouping them together.

"Don't do that." She pulled back her groceries.

"I want to." They jockeyed, and he packed his food into a box as the clerk rang things up. She put her hand on the first item of Anna's.

"No, this is separate," Anna said.

The clerk totaled Walt's bill; he paid, then waited while she rang up hers. As Anna got out her checkbook, he handed the clerk a twenty, and over Anna's protests scooped up her bag in one hand and his box in the other, heading for his car.

"Hold on a sec," she said. "I want to use the phone."

"You have one at home."

"Just wait in the car." He loaded everything, tearing open his bag of carrots and eating one while he leaned back on the hood. The snow was almost entirely gone, traces hiding in the crooks of trees or shaded stairwells, but everything fresh because of it.

At Anna's, he piled his perishables in her fridge, the rest in the box on top.

"What do you want for dinner?" she asked.

"Salad and bread with cheese."

"We could have a glass of wine with dinner," she said, "but that's all—we're meeting Burke at the deli at 7:30."

"It's 6:45," he said. "Let's get cracking here."

She opened the wine while he tore lettuce; she helped chop vegetables, he sliced part of the baguette, and they sat facing each other.

He raised his jelly glass. "To surprises."

"Many happy returns, Walt."

"That's what today feels like—returns."

"Did—" She bit her lip—why spoil it?

"Yeah," he said, "Laura showed up. Maybe she believes me, maybe not, but I felt nothing. Guess I was afraid to find out. I'm sorry I put you through that."

"So you talked?"

"And— Yeah. All that." He smiled brightly. "That's really over."

"Where is she now?"

"Bill hustled her, so she stayed. Hope that's not a mistake—he's tough."

"If he hurts her, she'll blame you."

"Maybe," he shrugged. "But it was her choice. She may think she's getting back at me, but she's only punishing herself." He sighed. "Oh Anna, what a drain."

Done eating, they piled things in the sink and hurried downtown. Burke was sitting on a brick planter in front of the deli, twisting blades of grass together and tying others around them, forming small people. He showed them two he'd already made. Anna insisted on trying, so Walt did too. It was tricky—the knots unfolded if they were loose, but pulling hard enough to tighten them broke the grass blades. When they'd each made one, Burke carried them in.

Anna consulted with the hostess, who led them to a back room where two tables had been pushed together. There sat Romo, Stu, Tom, Barbara and Lloyd, Terry and Stefan; they moved around to make room, putting Walt at the center closest to everyone. Their waitress set a slice of raspberry-swirl cheesecake with a lit candle in front of him and the other waitri came over to sing "Happy Birthday." He grinned and blew out the little flame, then everyone ordered dessert and coffee.

Lloyd brought them up to date on the lawsuit. They'd passed the first major hurdle; the D.A. had tried to have it thrown out and the judge had overruled him. Walt studied Barbara, sitting across. She looked happy, relaxed, gorgeous. He winked at her, she winked back and said something to Lloyd. Terry was talking to Stefan; Stu and Tom were leaning back making asides; Burke was telling Romo about other things he'd used to make people figures—paper clips, resistors, twist ties—while Romo propped the grass-men against water glasses and the sugar holder. The only person at the table saying nothing, who seemed almost not to be there, was Anna. She just folded up in a group, even when she knew everyone.

"You all right?" Walt murmured, slipping his fingertips into the hair at the back of her head, rubbing gently at the tension there. "How'd all these people know to come? Did you call 'em?"

She wished she hadn't. She and Burke and Walt could've had a perfectly pleasant evening, but now she had this crowd to deal with.

"Thank you," he said. "This is a great birthday surprise."

"Hey, I got some new records," Romo said. "Everybody want to come over?" When the waitress brought the check, Stefan pulled out his credit card, Lloyd waved his and they had a little grabbing match until Lloyd prevailed. Others got out money for the tip, refusing Walt's and Anna's attempts to contribute. They all walked in a noisy group, heading for Walt's house. Partway over, he remembered the joint in his pocket—he couldn't take it in, and his car was the opposite direction at Anna's—have to smoke it now. As they passed it, Barbara, Lloyd, Romo, and Stu partook. When the roach came back, Walt swallowed it.

At the house, they pushed furniture to the walls and cranked up the volume on the records. Anna danced with Walt, then stood aside for the next song while he partnered Barbara.

"You're easy to read," Barbara laughed to Walt. "I'd say you've set your burden down."

"Seeing Laura cleared things up for me. And Anna I hope. How about you? Lloyd's looking smitten."

She smiled winsomely. "I'd say so." She glanced around as they turned. "Take her home soon, before she stops having fun."

As Romo and Lloyd debated what to play next, Walt drew Anna aside. "Anytime you're ready to go, let me know."

"But this is your party, and your house. Don't you want to stay?"

"Only if you do—this surprise is great, but my night's reserved for you."

By the end of the next record she was visibly restless. Stefan left and Terry went upstairs; Burke lingered.

"I'll walk her home—you can take off," Walt said.

Burke frowned.

"What is it?" Walt asked him.

"Nothing."

"Come on Anna," Walt said. "Let's go." She gave Burke a stricken look, but he left. Walt got his jacket and helped her into hers. On their way through the kitchen, he tapped Barbara's fingers where they rested on Lloyd's shoulder, then he and Anna were outside in the cool spring evening. The waning moon wasn't up yet and the sky, very deep blue, was fragrant and tingling. They took side streets where more stars were visible.

"I could really see tonight how mismatched we are," Anna said. "Lloyd and Barbara make a good couple, but I'm younger than your friends—I never know what to say."

"I hear shyness speaking. Explain something please."

"What?"

"I told Laura that's finished—which is one hundred percent true. And I've told you many times how much I love you, how unimportant the things are that hang you up. And neither of you believe me." He waved his arms. "Why do I have no credibility?"

"You must be wrong for us."

"Us"? She was identifying herself with Laura?

"You've made bad choices, Walt. She was too hard for you. And I'm too young."

"I didn't choose you, I found you. My heart's not running a dating service."

"When I said I couldn't marry you, I never imagined we'd still be having this conversation."

"You really don't want to see me anymore? Not at all?" He was in free fall.

"I just can't. Even Burke finally agrees with me."

"Then why did he drive you out to see me last night?"

"So I could say goodbye."

Laura's letter all over again, a boot to his midsection. He stumbled a few steps before steadying to walk. "Well, I'll get my groceries so I don't have to bother you tomorrow."

They turned at the end of her street. She said, "You and Laura are the same, Walt. You won't accept that the one you love can't return your feelings."

He said nothing till they reached her apartment, but as he was packing his food from the fridge back into his box, he paused. "Anna, promise me something?"

"Not until you say—what?"

"Don't hide from me. I live in this town, you do too. So when you see me, in the store or on the street, or in line to see a movie, please don't hide. If you want me not to speak to you I won't, but I can't pretend you're not there."

"You didn't take 'no' before—I think you still won't."

"When you're a couple years older, maybe you'll reconsider."

"If that's the only way you can let go, do it."

He carried his box to the door, put his hand on the knob. "A kiss for my birthday?" he ventured.

"I gave it to you this morning, remember?"

"Yes you did. Thank you." Out he went, and sat in Plug with his box on the seat beside him. Blown away.

• • •

COLD AND LIGHT ARRIVED together to wake him—he'd fallen asleep in the car in front of her house. If he went home to bed now he'd oversleep, or feel dead all day, or both, so he buttoned his jean jacket and walked west to the mouth of Sunshine Canyon, taking the trail up Mt. Sanitas. A few mule deer browsing on the western ridge raised their heads, ears outspread; near the bottom of the valley where a seasonal stream trickled, a badger sniffed the air, watching him before ducking into its burrow. Three small vapor clouds were moving east in an otherwise clear sky; a spindly wild plum was blooming in the crook of a broken slab of rock, two Stellar's jays traded calls from pine trees—he could see their blue bodies and black crests as they pursued each other.

He should've known early on it couldn't last—she was too shy, self-doubting, wounded—but that love had such simplicity. She'd helped him see Laura's selfishness, strengthened his heart to fend her off. All this time she'd clung to her fear as a means of keeping his attention from overwhelming her, and now that Laura had ceased to be a threat, her only refuge was the truth. So maybe he'd helped her cultivate the will to resist him. Good job Walt. Well and thoroughly done.

chapter 34

That Second Bounce

LAURA WAS SORE when the dawn chill woke her—Bill had rolled taking the blanket with him, but if she tried to get some covers back he'd probably ball her again. It had been all right at first, the sinsemilla such a great high. In the darkness he seemed to forget his scar, kissing her briefly as though knocking before coming in, then focusing on her body. He was twice her weight and didn't know not to lean on her—she kept pushing his chest away enough to breathe. The dope kept him going a long time; when he finally came, he just collapsed and she had to drag herself out from underneath.

In prison she'd dreamt about sex, missing Walt and Cob, mutual effort, pleasure. Walt had meant to do something crude and fast yesterday—she should've realized from the way he offered—but to Bill she might as well be one of those inflatable dolls. Gathering her clothes she went to the master bath to wash up, glad she'd been wearing her diaphragm. She couldn't imagine a rubber surviving all that jamming; her whole pelvis ached.

Idiot, she told herself. *Serves you right.* Walt had done nothing to dissuade her—was that revenge? Did he really not know what Bill was like? Downstairs she took his B.B. King tape. It had "The Thrill Is Gone" and "To Know You Is to Love You," flip sides of the last phase of her life. Grabbing a bag of almonds and an orange, she left.

It was early to hitch but she didn't want to be around when Bill woke up. They hadn't talked much; what was the point of him knowing her past? She could imagine him discussing her over a drink with some crude pal, describing her body, the other guy thinking he'd missed something. Reaching the road she crossed to walk facing traffic, out of the canyon. A red-tailed hawk perched on a fence post and she stopped, looking at him a long time before he finally jumped into the air and flapped upward, climbing toward the ridge where he landed in the top of a big pine. It was so fine to be out, free to walk where she wanted, to choose what she ate and where she stood. People took liberty for granted. She never would again.

At the junction she fished for a ride. An industrial truck went by, a pickup with four people in the cab. A souped-up Camaro slewed over, stopping in a spray of gravel. She opened the passenger door; a wiry guy exhaled cigarette smoke at her.

"Where y' goin'?" he asked.

"Into Boulder."

"I can drop y' at 28th and the Diagonal."

The car reeked of smoke, the guy had a nervous tic below his eye. Something about him she didn't like.

"No, I'm headed downtown. Thanks anyway." She closed the door and he peeled out. Next to stop was a rusted Chevy Nova with Pennsylvania plates; a wide guy with black hair and a thick beard threw newspapers into the back.

"Where you headed?" she asked.

"Downtown Boulder."

He was pretty big but his vibe was all right so she got in, putting on her seatbelt.

"Early to be thumbin'," he remarked, pulling onto the highway.

"I'm an early riser."

"Me too for now—I clean a bar downtown—they lemme in 6:30, gotta be done 10:30. It's a crappy job."

"Which bar?"

"Choppers." The biker bar, knife fight central. "Ever go there?"

"I don't go to bars," she said flatly.

"How bout the Bustop? Tried to get a job as a bouncer but I'm not big enough." He laughed roughly. "Not big enough, get it?" The Bustop was the strip club out at the north end of town. Years ago she'd gone to Ladies' Night with some friends, stuffing dollar bills into the men's G-strings, laughing over the role reversal as they ogled and rated the dancers. But last night had made her realize how much she wanted kindness—more than pleasure—maybe as much as freedom. Where was she going to find that now?

"Got some green?" the driver asked suddenly, rubbing two fingers against his thumb.

"Not much—why?"

"Y'know what they say—gas, grass, or ass—nobody rides free." He looked away from the road a moment to stare at her.

"I'm not going far—I'll give you two bucks."

"Two bucks ain' nothin'," he said. "I'd rather have ass."

"Not for sale."

"Didn't say I'd pay, did I?"

"Let me out then, I'll get another ride."

"Oh no, you got a ride, right here. You ride then I do."

The car was going too fast for her to jump out but he'd have to slow down once he hit town. She located the door handle, planning her move, then stilled herself.

"Ever been in prison?" she asked.

"Jail."

"No, prison. Not the same."

"Guess not—you?"

"I'm on parole."

"Wha'd you do?" his voice taking on an edge of discomfort.

"Killed a man for mistreating me."

"Oh yeah?" Not sure he believed her.

"Yeah," she said, voice like stone.

He didn't say anything for a moment, staring ahead through the windshield, then suddenly pulled over. "Get out," he ordered.

She moved away while he drove off. Well, she was about halfway to town—not such a long walk now. This particular highway fell right along the demarcation between the Rockies and the Great Plains: one could stand here and facing east see the faint swell of the Earth's curvature, the outlying mesas giving way to the huge spread of grass-lands taken over by human toil. Turning west one looked upward at foothills, timbered mountains, and beyond those—but not far—the high peaks—a landscape not cultivated so much as pried from the grip of the surrounding wildness, houses and ranches and mines in temporary truce with gravity, altitude, weather.

Walt had told her it was a field trip out here that made him choose his major. Every other science focused on some element— earth or plant life or molecular behavior or physical law—while geography sought to unify them—settle here, travel this route, use these resources—cultural distinctions grew out of interaction with terrain and climate. She'd teased him more than once about how useless his degree would be, but maybe understanding how it was all connected was as worthwhile as the details of biology—her field.

Crossing the blacktop, she walked on the east shoulder alongside a big horse pasture. She noticed two foals out playing in the early morning, and went over to the fence to watch. They were at most a month old, with short necks and bodies and ridiculously long skinny legs, and they snorted and jumped, flapping their stubby tails. One was a pinto, white patches extending into his brushy mane, the other reddish brown with a gold mane and tail. The pinto sidled her direction, got within a few yards, then reared and turned, galloping away. She laughed as they bumped each other, nipped, kicked out their knobby legs and chased each other around.

The day was warming by the time she went back up to the road to continue her walk. Then here came Walt—she recognized Plug even with that ugly paint job. She waved. He pulled over, she opened the passenger door.

"Haven't had much luck hitching this morning," she said.

"Aren't you going the wrong way?"

"Been doing that awhile now," she laughed.

"Haven't we all. Want breakfast?"

"Yes I do."

"Hop in—I'm early—we'll go to Royal Crown." Making a U-turn, he accelerated back to town.

"Why'd you pick me up?"

"I saw you waving so I stopped. After that was I supposed to just drive away?"

"Well, you could've."

"No I couldn't." After a pause he asked, "Everything OK last night?"

"I won't do that again—I'd rather be lonely by myself." But he was so sad. "I think you're the one who got hurt."

"Yeah," he exhaled.

They chose a table near the kitchen where they couldn't really see anyone and the noise from the dishwasher masked their conversation, as though they were meeting in secret.

"Doesn't she love you?" she asked once the waitress had poured coffee.

"She decided she's too young for me—guess you were right."

"She seemed naïve." She sipped. "You must've liked that."

"She was fun, and we'd do silly things together. She made me happier than I've ever been." He closed his eyes, pain coming off him in pulses.

"Did she shut you out because of me?"

"No, it was never gonna last—I was a fool to think so, to hope for that."

"So what'll you do now, Walt?"

"Work, learn. Start over—again."

The waitress set down their plates, refilled their cups, and stepped away.

"What about you, Laura? Rye? Are you Rye now?"

But did that persona belong behind bars, too harsh for the free world? Was Walt right? Was being vulnerable a better way to live? "Maybe not," twisting her mouth.

"Why not?" he laughed. "You're looking wry."

Her heart flooded warm. "Then maybe I am. I kind of like it. But if I'm not Laura, does that mean you don't know me?"

"Yeah. But I don't anyway. Remember when we were tripping on Donner Pass? I know a dragon that died, that's all. A Greek with one too many lovers."

"Would an apology mean anything?"

"No," he said. "It's a karmic debt now. Don't worry, you'll get the bill."

"Cob sure did—he paid and paid, it took him apart."

"But he didn't learn, did he?"

"He learned then forgot, or disregarded the lesson."

"Didn't learn," Walt said. "What you learn becomes part of you."

"But I didn't either I guess, chasing you when you made it clear you didn't want to be caught."

"None of us learned, Laura—Rye. I bulldozed Anna the way you did me. I wanted her so much I ignored all her signals that she couldn't handle it, told her not to believe her gut saying it wouldn't work." He spread jam on his toast. "She kept changing her mind, was the thing. She'd tell me to stay away, then the next time I'd see her, one touch and we were—" He pushed hash browns into the egg yolk and took a bite, then looked up, their eyes meeting—not surfaces this time of desire and disappointment, but the eyes of travelers who'd been some miles together.

"Maybe it'll work out," she said. "She'll hit a couple bumps then realize how kind you are, and want you back. That's what happened to me."

He half smiled at the plea behind her words. "Kindness never did it for you."

"It would now."

He shook his head. "Think I'll just roll over for you?"

"No. I think you spent too long recovering to do anything that foolish."

"That's right," he said.

"But can we close that chapter with a smile?"

"How do you mean?" He should be wary but his heart was too battered to care.

"Have a last fling, sincerely this time?"

"Come on, you're still trying to trap me."

"No, I swear. I know you're done with me, and I know why. And you're right."

"'But'—"

"'And,'" she corrected. "Instead of finishing on a sour note, let's play one more. Only one."

"Why would I do that?"

"Because you're hurting right now, because a touch and a kiss is what you need."

He could never defend himself from the truth. "It's too soon for me to have another lover," he said to the remnants of his breakfast.

"Just a touch. Then we can both walk away clean, you go your way and I go mine, like the song says." She finished her eggs and ate the orange wedge and parsley, then pushed the plate away with its heap of hash browns and second piece of toast. She reached into her backpack.

"I'll get it," he said, pulling out the fifty he still hadn't broken. "My birthday money." He checked the clock; almost eight. "Not a lotta time—c'mon."

Romo had already left for the bus lot, Terry and Stu were having breakfast, Barbara was in the bathroom. He and Rye waved on their way upstairs. His room seemed different after nights away—cramped after the big space of that house. In a few motions he and Laura stood naked, and spent a moment scanning each other for familiarity and changes. He touched the flawless swell of her hip.

"He bruised you. Look out for yourself better, Rye."

"Just another day in prison. After making the choice that put me there, my options were gone."

"Cob made you so beautiful." That still amazed him.

"He hated people saying that—he just brought what I had to the surface."

"Have you enjoyed your looks?"

"Not very much—maybe I'll get to."

"Might as well." They moved their hands on each other, remembering, and when their mouths finally met it was a discussion of their senses, documentary, an exchange of flavors and textures. He stepped his legs apart and flexed them, she arched a thigh against his hip, her labia touching his head. She winced.

"Lotion?" he suggested.

"Please." Both chuckled—sure took the shine off her image of Cob to realize he'd been as oblivious to her feelings as that neanderthal Bill. She smeared Walt's hard-on and eased him in, lifting her other leg while he laced fingers behind her waist to hold her, leaning back as counterweight. She wrapped her knees against his thighs and tucked her feet around his shins so she could raise and lower herself on him, hands on his shoulders. He stepped, and about to lose his balance, moved to the mattress where they lay down, rolling so she was on top, then he was, finding a rhythm and playing it, inside each other circling like two colors of smoke, together but distinct. Still joined though he was slipping away, her leg across his to keep him near, they smiled.

"Hello Walt, and thank you very much."

"Hi Rye, best of luck." They kissed lightly, then just lay quiet in a loose embrace. Time held them close, then gradually set them back in the world.

"I have to get to work," Walt said. "I'm supposed to be there at nine."

"It's close to nine."

"So I'll be a couple minutes late."

"Did you have a good birthday?"

He laughed. "A complete one—birth, life, death, and now rebirth. More than you can expect of a day. May the gods zap me if I complain." He dressed slowly, standing to finish.

"Mind if I take a nap before I leave?" She felt too good to move.

"That's OK, just—"

"Not to worry—when you get back I'll be gone."

He knelt to tousle her hair. "Bye toots—take care."

• • •

BY SUNDAY AFTERNOON, THE grapevine was a live wire—not only his housemates but Burke and Stefan seemed to know, and, he supposed, Anna, though how would he ever find out?

Barbara sat with him in the kitchen trying to read his grin. "So after dismissing her you brought her home to bed—how does that work?"

"If you knew how bad we felt Wednesday before I picked her up, and how whole we both felt afterwards, you'd understand."

"So what's next?"

"The future, I guess. Work and play."

"Play?" she asked playfully.

"Well sure."

"I know just the thing. I found this after the party." She poked around in the cigar box on the counter, home to random junk, and got out a hot-pink superball an inch in diameter, throwing it hard at the floor. It ricocheted to the ceiling then hit the table, back to the ceiling as Walt grabbed at it, angled off the face of the fridge, bop-bop-bopping under the table, losing momentum against the cabinet near the door. Walt leaned back in his chair and picked it up, hurling it floorward again, grinning for all he was worth as it leaped wide on that mysterious second bounce, zigzagging through the airspace, unpredictable as joy.